C000319731

Steve Radnor leaned up ▮▮▮▮ spoke in a quiet voice. He ▮▮▮ desperate than he had inferre▮

"I don't want to go to priso ▮▮▮▮▮▮▮▮ i didn't hurt anybody. I don't have a gun, even, not since the war. I don't think I'd do well in prison; I wouldn't last a day. Tell the old man, thanks for helping."

"We haven't done anything yet."

"You will, you got the lady here," said Radnor, tipping a little nod towards Stephanie. "The cats, they know. The lady will sort things out, she will, and they'll keep her safe. They know. Thanks for helping."

Stephanie Baynes wants to investigate things; mostly she wants to find sound, rational explanations for things other people think are supernatural. But a meeting with Lord Martin Latham shows her a world where her explanations mean nothing – and her safety may depend on a supernatural cat goddess.

Servants of Fey Manor

By Peter Cooper

Copyright 2021 Peter Cooper. All rights reserved

No part of this book may be reproduced, stored in a retrieval system or transmitted by any means without the written permission of the author

First published by Peter Ralph   June 2023

ISBN: 978-1-8381078-5-7

Acknowledgements

My thanks to the many people who have encouraged me in the creation of this story. To my wife Audrey who said it was one of my best (she's read some of my worst), to my son Phil for his proof-reading skills, to Sam Thompson for his editing skills, and for the LARP group who, unknown to themselves, inspired me to write a story about fey beings who have come to this world to do battle with the evil they found there – not evil witches and sorcerers, but corrupt businessmen and politicians.

Cover design by Seraphim Bryant, MA; bluefalcon1983.com

People of Fey Manor

You don't need to read the other stories in the series in order to understand this one. However, just to keep you informed as to what has happened so far, here is a short summary including spoilers.

Michael Varmeter has inherited a position in charge of Nieziemski Manor in Buckinghamshire. Along with his comfortable rooms and a huge amount of money, the estate includes around a hundred fey people (calling themselves 'The People'), hiding from human society.

Lady Venner. The People at the Manor include Lady Venner of the fey, blue-skinned Queen of the Seelie Court and her naiads and dryads who live in the lake and forests at the back of the manor.

Lady Marika of the sidhe, Queen of the Unseelie Court and her entourage of (mostly) goblins live mostly in the house itself, occupying the first and top floors. Lady Marika was recently injured in battle with the vampires of the Romanian Embassy.

Balaur. A dragon who appears as a dwarf in an ill-fitting suit, Balaur is the most powerful of the fey People. He is not aligned directly to the Seelie or the Unseelie Courts, but he oversees their activities. His main purpose is to track down fey People who are lost and offer them a chance to re-join their fey family. He found Michael and persuaded him to accept his inheritance at Nieziemski Manor.

Martin Latham. One of the characters involved in Michael's exploits was Lord Martin Latham, who has a past with the ambassador, Iliana Vaduva, at the Romanian Embassy. With Iliana dead, Martin is now free of free of their influence.

The Angel Trust is an organisation set up to investigate supernatural phenomena and financed by the Nieziemski Manor Estate.

Book 7
Conversations in the Dark

One

Stephanie Baynes would not have considered herself a serious person – not too serious, anyway. After all, she wanted to become a paranormal investigator, and you shouldn't take things too seriously for that. However, she was getting fed up with this funfair. Of course, if she'd come with her friends and with the intention of enjoying the place a bit more, she might have been in a happier mood. But she was here to *investigate*.

She'd finally found the 'attraction' she was looking for, and it seemed like someone had hidden it away on purpose. Everywhere else had queuing space, flashy lights and signage, but this place was just a little tent in sun-faded reds, yellows and oranges and a small notice board reading: 'Jing Shen, Psychic', and in small print underneath: 'for entertainment purposes only'. A second, hand-written sign advertised fortunes told and prices. There were no other customers around so she walked straight in. A man in a turban (do Chinese people wear turbans?) was seated at a small, round table, eating a sandwich. As she came in, he quickly put away his lunch, brushed himself down and turned his now-serious face towards her.

"Didn't see me coming?" she quipped.

"Ah, a sceptic," said Jing Shen in an accent that Stephanie could not completely identify. "I like a sceptic. I like the look on their faces when I tell them something I couldn't possibly know."

"Tell me something, then."

"Put your money in the box, please."

Stephanie reached into her handbag and pulled a five-pound-note out of her purse without actually taking the purse out of the handbag. She put it in the padlocked wooden slotted box at the edge of the table, watched very carefully by the psychic.

"You're a student," said Jing Shen.

"How did you know?" she asked.

"Surely you don't need to ask that question," said the psychic with a smile.

"Am I going to meet a tall, dark stranger?" she asked.

"It depends on what you mean by 'meet'."

"What do you mean?"

"You will come into contact with someone around your age. A man. Tall? Well, taller than you. Today. Within the next hour or so. Whether you 'meet' him or not will be up to you."

"Really?"

"You don't have a boyfriend, or a partner, at the moment. Perhaps you are looking for one."

"Definitely not."

The man laughed. "But these things happen even if you are not looking for them."

"Is this your psychic reading of me?"

"Of course. And you're not impressed yet."

"Keep going. So far you have made a wild guess at my status as a student, probably because of my age and clothing, and told me I may or may not meet someone. Now you should be able to work out that I don't have much money – because I am a student – so that should come into your spiel next."

"Your family doesn't come from around here. In fact, they don't even live in the Midlands. Nearer London, perhaps?"

"My accent? And the fact that I am a student?"

"Why don't you just let me tell your fortune, Miss…"

"I imagine, with your powers, you would already know my name."

"The ether does not work that way."

"Neither does a degree in psychology, does it, Mr Clements?" she said. He looked at her carefully.

"And I lied," she continued. "I'm not a student. But to be fair to you, I have recently finished a course in journalism at Stoke University, so I was a student until earlier this year."

"A journalist?" said 'Jing Shen' Clements, losing his exotic accent. "Has your newspaper given you me as an assignment? That would be scraping *below* the bottom of the barrel if you ask me."

"I don't work for a newspaper," said Stephanie. "You really aren't very good at this, are you?"

"You know my real name, and you probably also know that I am a teacher in my 'real life'," said the man. "I use my psychology skills to read people and earn a bit of extra cash during the holidays doing this. My students already know this, and so do my employers – it's not exactly scandal material. It's not even very newsworthy. Oh, and the sign outside my tent does say 'for entertainment purposes only', so you could say I am an entertainer rather than a psychic. And my stage name is Chinese for 'psychic'."

"I'd like my money back," said Stephanie.

"I've given you what you paid for," said the pseudo-psychic with a laugh. "And who knows, at a busy funfair, you probably will come across a tall, dark stranger."

"You're a fake."

"I'm an entertainer. But in the interests of being helpful, I will give you your money back." He reached down to a shelf below the table top and pulled out a key, which he used to start unlocking his cash box.

"Keep it," she said, changing her mind, and she stormed out of the tent. She was fed up. In her very short career as a paranormal investigator, she'd not met a single ghost, she had uncovered a couple of fakes, including Mr 'Jing Shen' Clements, and she had, most of all, not found a way to make money out of it. Debunking funfair psychics would hardly bring a mass of readers flocking to a blog, after all. Her family's support and financial assistance wouldn't hold out much longer. She could imagine her mother's face as she tried hard to refrain from saying, "Why can't you be like your sister Paula – she's a big lawyer earning decent money in London?"

She wandered around the fairground, unable to appreciate the joy in the shouts and squeals of the children (and possibly some of the adults) on their rides, seeing the bright colours but not responding to the excitement they were out to bring. It just seemed like one big sham. No, she didn't want to be like her lawyer sister in London. Neither did she want to work for a newspaper again – she had spent a few months on a local paper after she had finished her course, and it wasn't even remotely as glamourous as she thought it might be. Her most exciting assignment was interviewing an old lady when her cat had returned after having been missing for two weeks.

Most of the overpriced cafes and burger bars here at the funfair were quite full, but she managed to find one with a free table and ordered a coffee. She sat and nurtured her misery for a minute or two.

"Mind if I join you?" said a rich, male voice. She'd had her head down staring at her drink, so she hadn't seen him approach. She wondered if it was a tall, dark stranger. She looked up to see a man dressed in a long, dark coat, a wide brimmed cowboy hat and sunglasses. He seemed to be covering as much of his flesh as possible. But he was tall, and dark-haired if not dark-skinned, and a stranger. She looked around to see if she could see another free table to direct him to, but they all seemed to be full, so she shrugged and nodded, and he sat down opposite her with his cold drink.

"Hot day," he said.

"Even hotter if you wear a big, heavy coat," she replied, unable to stop herself being rude.

"It's not heavy. I had it made specially, so I could cover up in sunny weather. I burn easily."

She returned her focus to her coffee, feeling too hot and wishing she'd ordered a cold drink instead.

"I'm Martin," he said.

"OK," she replied, hoping he'd take the hint and leave her alone.

"What's your favourite ride? I'll join you on one."

"No thanks."

"Not into funfairs? How about a trip into Birmingham?" he said, continuing to pester her. "I could take you to meet some friends of mine. You'd like them – they're werewolves."

"Werewolves?"

"I thought that would pique your interest, Miss Baynes."

"No, thank you," she said again. Then she looked up as she realised what he had said. She remained calm, at least on the outside. "You know my name."

"I've read your paper on the Beast of Bodmin."

"You're a university professor?" she asked.

"No."

"Then how do you get to see my paper?"

"I'm Martin Latham," he replied as if that would be explanation enough. Stephanie had not actually met this man before, but she knew about him. Lord Martin Latham was a local celebrity. His family had donated generous support to her university over the years. But Stephanie still felt that this didn't give him permission to read her coursework.

"So you read my paper? Isn't that against the rules or something?"

"The best papers are shared on the Net," he explained.

Stephanie was embarrassed – someone at the university had considered her work as one of 'the best'. But how did Lord Latham know that she was the Stephanie Baynes who wrote the paper?

"Have you been stalking me?" she challenged him.

He had to think carefully about answering her. "I think I'd prefer not to call it stalking. I have been searching for you, Stephanie Baynes, but only for the best of reasons. I'd like to offer you a job."

"That's a coincidence. I've just left a job," she said. He was making her feel nervous. Would he know where she lived? Had he followed her around the funfair?

"I know. You were wasted on that newspaper. You want something more fulfilling."

"And working for you will be fulfilling?"

"Oh, yes. It will put you in touch with a world you never knew existed."

"Werewolves?"

"And more. Although the werewolves themselves might disappoint you as much as the fake fortune teller did."

Stephanie was reluctant to accept everything he was saying at face value. Everything worth having is worth working for, her mother used to say, so when some local millionaire lord turns up and offers her the job she really wanted, it's a gift, not an earned reward. So there must be something wrong, something that will end up getting her into trouble of some kind.

She looked up at him, studying what she could see of his face beneath his big extra-dark sunglasses and his turned-up collar. The small amount of face that was showing was a little pallid, but he was quite good-looking in spite of that. He looked fairly young, possibly in his twenties or thirties (like the psychic 'entertainer' had said) but it was hard to tell from here. She might be able to tell if she was able to look into his eyes. She'd heard a lot about him from chatter at the uni, how he was charming, friendly, easy to get along with, mysterious, and was rarely seen without a beautiful woman at his arm. Well, there was no such person near him right now.

She was a little nervous of him – his disposition was friendly, but he knew about her and talked about her research… and werewolves. She was aware that some time had passed without either of them saying anything.

"Why?" she asked.

"Because I investigate the unusual, and your work shows that you have dug quite deep into unusual subjects. Like the Beast of Bodmin. Why did you choose *that* as a subject?"

"I had an experience with a big cat when I was a girl."

"Really?" his voice seemed to light up. "That's brilliant. Tell me about it."

"Why?"

"You're job hunting."

"Well, yes, I suppose so," she answered cautiously.

"Do you like job hunting?"

Actually, I hate it, she thought, but she didn't want to tell him that. It didn't matter, because he read it in her face anyway.

"I'd like to save you the task of job hunting anymore," he said.

"Well, thank you," she replied, "but…" and then she ran out of words to say before she ran out of sentence.

"I imagine you'll want to be interviewed," he said. "You can't just pick up a job without an interview."

"Well, yes, I suppose so," she replied, her brain a little bit slower than her mouth. There was something about this man that exerted some kind of control over her. She wanted to refuse him, but was compelled to go along with his lead.

"Then tell me about your meeting with the Beast of Bodmin."

"No, it wasn't that," she said. "I used to live in Kent – a little village along from Gravesend. There was a big cat there, too."

"They get about a bit, cats, don't they?"

Was he making fun of her?

"Are you making fun of me?"

"No. I'm interviewing you with the intention of offering you a genuine, well-paid job as a researcher – and the job comes with accommodation. Please…" and he made a small gesture with his hand for her to continue her story.

"I came face-to-face with a big cat, something like the size of a puma, just once when I was about thirteen. I saved it."

"Was it hurt?"

"No, I stopped someone from hurting it. I like cats."

"Because they are cute and cuddly?"

"Because they are mysterious," said Stephanie. She still thought he might be making fun of her.

"There are a number of stories about strange cat-like creatures," he said. Was he just saying that because it was her subject and he wanted to engage her? "Bodmin, Kent, and I think there are some up north, too."

"The Yorkshire Moors, yes," Stephanie confirmed. She'd done some studies on those cats, too. But he would know that, of course, if he'd read her work.

"Or is it the same strange creature that travels the country?"

"Strange creature? It's a cat. I saw it. Bigger than a wild cat, smaller than a lion. It was like a puma. I think that in the early twentieth century, rich people got exotic pets, but when animal rights laws came in, people released them into the wild. But you know that, don't you, because you've read my work?"

"*Like* a puma. You didn't say it was a puma, you said *like*."

"It wasn't exactly a species of cat I recognised. I was thirteen years old at the time. It might have been a puma, or some sort of lynx."

"Or alien shape-shifters in league with the government."

Stephanie laughed, and then stopped. He was drawing her in, and she didn't want to be drawn in.

"What do you think of conspiracy theorists?" asked Martin.

"Three quarters of them are nutcases," Stephanie replied, daring an argument with this unusual young man.

"Three quarters? Then we should only have to speak to four of them, and one might talk sense."

She laughed again and he smiled at her, presumably because he had *wanted* to make her laugh and had just scored a victory. There was something about him that seemed to grab her attention. Perhaps it was that *he* was a mystery, and she loved mysteries. But she also loved the idea of a safe life, and he didn't feel safe.

"Come on, then," he said and stood up. For some reason she couldn't fathom, she got up, picked up her little, tatty handbag, and followed him.

"My mum always said I shouldn't go with strange men, and you seem pretty strange to me."

"Oh, I'm strange alright," he said, walking a little ahead of her towards the funfair car park. She followed him as if he was somehow compelling her to follow.

"Lord Martin Latham," she said out loud as she caught up with him.

"Just Martin, please," he said. "I may be strange, but I'm… safe."

"Safe?" she said. "Should I be disappointed?" she responded, shocking herself as she realised that she was flirting with him.

"Okay, I'm not safe," he said with grim honesty, "but you're safe with me. At least, you are now that I'm not being hunted anymore. Would you like to come and take a look at where you'd be working, if you decided to accept my offer?"

"Thanks." *But I haven't accepted your offer. Not yet. And what does 'not being hunted anymore' mean?*

He escorted his new companion to his Range Rover which was parked in a 'reserved' space near to the entrance of the funfair. It was a nice car, too. A flimsy thought crossed Stephanie's mind: she had just met every girl's dream – a handsome, intelligent, rich and titled gentleman (although she didn't really know about the 'gentleman' part). Martin had adjusted his collar to make sure it was as high as it could possibly be, and then he pulled his black cowboy hat as far over his face as it would go. It seemed to suit him and he wore it as if he couldn't be without it. The weather was hot and sunny, being the middle of August, and yet it was the light that seemed to bother him, not the heat.

His vehicle was roomy and comfortable, with tinted windows like enormous sunglasses. Stephanie sat back in the plush seat that seemed to envelope her and then fastened her seatbelt. Martin reversed slowly out of his parking space, and then started to drive. Stephanie could not help feeling that stepping into Martin's car was like stepping into an overcast evening. There was something different about being in there, as if the real world outside wasn't allowed in with them.

"Do you believe that there are creatures living among us who are not human?" he asked as they journeyed together.

"You mean animals?" she teased him. He seemed to intimidate her and empower her at the same time.

"No, I mean intelligent, sentient beings. Maybe some of them pass themselves off as human. But they aren't."

"Aliens?"

"Not really. I am talking about something supernatural."

"I guessed you might be, which was why I tried to cover everything else first. When you said you wanted a researcher, and you read my paper, and you've been stalking me, I sort-of worked out that you want me to research supernatural stuff, because you must know that's what interests me the most."

"I wasn't stalking you."

"Looking for me, then."

"Ghosts?" said Martin.

"Not sure," Stephanie replied. "I have been in a couple of old buildings that are supposed to be haunted, but I didn't see anything to convince me."

"Fairies?"

"No."

"What about the Fey? What people call fairies, but different."

"You're not making fun?"

"No."

"Fey?"

"Mermaids, dryads, goblins…" he said.

"There was something on the news earlier this year. It was the London floods – people said they were rescued by mermaids when they were trapped in the Underground." Did he know that her sister Paula had been in London at the time of the floods, and was that why he brought up mermaids?

"So?" he egged her on.

"My guess is they were rescued by someone, but not actual mermaids. I mean, how would mermaids get into the London Underground?"

"By helicopter?" Martin suggested.

"Ho ho," she replied flatly. "Although, I would guess that if there were intelligent aquatic creatures, we might call them mermaids."

"I've seen some."

"You're kidding."

"And you're right – they weren't actually called mermaids. And the werewolves I mentioned earlier are for real, too. Although they weren't anywhere near as interesting."

"Are you interviewing me? I mean, is this all part of the interview?" she asked.

"Yes."

"Why?"

"Because I really am looking for a researcher. But I need you to get past trying to find out whether some fortune-teller is for real or not, and work on real supernatural stuff. There's an organisation called the Angel Trust, and now that I have become a little more… free… in my work here, I want to get more involved with them. I could do with someone who has a bit of an imagination, someone who is not prepared to take something at face value, and who is prepared to argue with me."

"What are you researching?"

"I'll be looking into things that are a little unusual – the mysterious, the weird, the kind of thing you often wrote about in your research papers."

"Not all of my work would have got onto the Net. One of my tutors almost threw me out of his class."

"I'm glad he didn't. The Angel Trust works with people like you. People with imagination. They are in the middle of some very interesting projects at the moment."

"So I'll be working for this Angel Trust?"

"No, you'll be working for me. I want someone with the same kind of attitude towards science that you've got – questioning, open-minded and creative. I do get to work with the Trust sometimes. They are interesting people, you'd like them."

"Conspiracy theorists?"

"No. If anything, they are the conspiracy that the conspiracy theorists theorise about."

"What?"

"They get involved with stuff outside the mainstream news. Will you work for me?"

"Show me the job first, and I'll think about it," she replied, trying to sound as cool as possible. Actually, she was getting quite excited at the idea, and she rather wanted to say 'yes' without thinking about it any further. Job-hunting was not an exercise she enjoyed, and accepting a job with this rich oddball might be just what she needed. She wanted exactly the job he was describing. But she checked herself for a moment, and thought about it more carefully – it all seemed too good to be true. There was an old saying her father often quoted; if it seems too good to be true, it probably is. She would want to check it out properly before really committing herself.

A few minutes later, Lord Martin Latham drove the Range Rover into a gravel driveway belonging to a large house set in leafy countryside, a mile or two away from the town centre. They pulled up in front of the door and got out of the car.

The house looked like a smaller version of one of the great old country mansions in which Sherlock Holmes might have solved some murder. There were several white-painted, old-fashioned wooden windows at its front, flanking a large, oak Victorian front door with concrete steps. The building was made of a dark Yorkshire stone, each of the large blocks in the wall textured to catch the light in such a way that the grey stone looked almost colourful. Green ivy grew up to the second floor of the house, particularly at the corners of the building, framing the stonework with a softening splash of nature. With its spotless red-tiled roof and its square shape in nicely-kept gardens, it looked well looked-after. If the house had been a little larger, film companies might possibly have wanted to borrow it for historical dramas or Bronte re-makes. However, Stephanie thought, this place was still a little too big for one person. There were also too many cars parked in the driveway for one person. A nice-looking, nearly-new Skoda was settled next to where Martin had parked the Range Rover.

He led her past the front door towards the side of the building. On the opposite side of the driveway to the big house, set back behind the main building from the road, there was another, smaller building. It had possibly once been a barn, now converted into a residence with an ordinary front door, which he unlocked with a key from his pocket.

They entered a small, rectangular hallway with three doors (in addition to the one they had come in by), one on one wall and two on the other. The furthest door was next to a stairway going up. The inside of the old building looked modern and pleasantly, but not extravagantly, decorated.

They entered the room on the left, which was a fairly sizeable room with plenty of office equipment. There were two computers, both appearing to be top of the range models to Stephanie, on two of the tables in the room. There were also three wheeled office chairs in the room. There was a small window with a dying potted plant sitting on its sill. And an empty space in the corner large enough to fit her entire university apartment.

"Who else works here?"

"Nobody. Just me. At the moment," he said, sitting on one of the chairs and spinning it like a child discovering a new toy.

"Why so much equipment?"

"I was hoping to share the office with my researcher," he answered, his feet stopping the spin so he could look directly at her. "That would be you, of course, if you accept the job."

She was certainly beginning to feel that things were moving a little faster than she could cope with. There was something about Lord Martin Latham that made her feel uneasy, as if he was controlling her or manipulating her. Perhaps she should pack up and go home now?

No chance.

"And you said something about accommodation?"

"Here," he answered. "The room opposite is a lounge, currently fully furnished, with a well-equipped kitchen adjoining. There are two bedrooms and a bathroom upstairs; they are not furnished, except for one bed. I live in the main house."

"The whole house?"

"I have a bedroom for each day of the week, although I spend most of my sleeping hours in the Sunday room. I had this barn converted to accommodate a possible researcher – you, as it turns out."

"Possibly."

"You haven't said 'no' yet."

"You live alone?"

"I have guests sometimes, but yes, I live alone. And if you come and live here, I will still live alone; this part of the estate is completely separate."

"I saw another car in the driveway? The Skoda?"

"That's mine as well. If you want the job, you can use it. Call it a company car."

"A company Skoda. That's inspired."

"You can drive, can't you?"

"Yes. And I'll need to, stuck out here in the middle of nowhere."

"We're less than three miles from the town centre!" he faked a complaint, still grinning as if he had a little private joke going on in his head.

She looked at him. He seemed kind and was humorous, and in a strange way, scary. On the face of it, this really was too good to be true, or at least it felt that way at the moment – she didn't know what she was about to get involved in.

"Are you a conspiracy theorist?" she asked, just to be sure.

"No," he answered with a charming grin. "Three quarters of them are nutcases."

Stephanie sat at one of the computers for a while. She turned it on and it booted up in a matter of seconds, not like her little laptop at home. Martin told her the password and she clicked around, finding a few files on it already, including one labelled 'Angel Trust' and another, 'Niz Manor'. When she clicked on the latter, it asked her for another password. She couldn't access the Niz Manor file.

"Niz Manor?"

"That one's private for now," he said. "The other one, the Angel Trust one, I'd be happy for you to fill in the details as you discover them. I'm expecting a visitor from the Angel Trust this afternoon. Can you stay around to meet him?"

"When is he coming?"

Martin looked at his wristwatch. "Soon. In fact this could be him right... now." And he pointed out of the window. Stephanie looked out but saw nothing.

"It would've been good if he *did* turn up when I said, though, wouldn't it?" said Martin with a laugh.

Two

Stephanie and her older sister Paula had been bookworms from a young age. They both loved studying, and helped and competed with each other in their lessons. Paula was a really good-looking young woman, and people had often suggested that she become a model. She hadn't given up her studies for a career in modelling, but had become a lawyer, earning pretty decent money working for a big law firm in London. She had been in London during the floods earlier in the year, although she worked in offices that were a safe distance from the Thames when it burst its banks, or whatever happened to cause the mermaids, or whatever they were, to be 'helicoptered' in to the rescue.

Whilst Stephanie, too, loved studying, she couldn't imagine anything more boring than law as a subject, and she chose investigative reporting and research as her university subjects. She really wanted the face-to-face research rather than spending her life in front of a computer but she loved the hunt for facts and sorting truth from fabrication. She'd used the Internet a lot, and became quite good at discerning true, provable facts (which were quite rare and hard to find) from fantasy or fabrication (which was as common as air). She was particularly unhappy with conspiracy theories, and did her best to find normal, uncomplicated, *scientific* explanations for everything she found on the Internet that might come under that heading.

The paper that Martin had said he had read was a piece she'd put in for her finals. She had, in fact, been working on it for years, just for fun, long before she'd ever decided to go to university. At her home in Kent, there had been a mysterious big cat similar to its more famous Bodmin sibling, and her short contact with the animal had inspired her to look into the mysterious – not just cats, but anything mysterious. Ghosts, aliens and supernatural powers were amongst the oddities she glanced at on her computer in the privacy of her small upstairs apartment near the university.

She had discounted UFO's quickly because of the huge number of sites that were devoted to the subject, concluding that it would take hundreds of people hundreds of years to get through the information, and enough people were already ploughing through the millions of sites. Ghosts and psychics followed, as she quickly dismissed the more outrageous and the most thoroughly investigated of the mysteries, although the ghost of Pittville Circus Road, Cheltenham, fascinated her, partly because she seemed to remember that she had some distant relatives living in Cheltenham, and partly because it seemed to be the most thoroughly and scientifically investigated ghost story of them all – at least in this country. She also lingered a while on the Loch Ness monster which, she felt, might have a similar story to 'the Cat', but when she read the theories of a submarine tunnel between the Loch and the open sea, she realised that the mystery of the monster was not an easily solvable puzzle. People had, after all, been exploring Loch Ness and its mysteries for many years, and she hardly thought she could give them closure after only a few hours at a computer.

The problem was that the popular 'mystery' subjects had enormous amounts of cyberspace devoted to them, and available information included a great deal of rubbish. However, she would learn in the next few weeks that even outrageous or fantastic sources of information should not be dismissed without a second look.

And there were smaller mysteries, little individual pockets of intrigue that piqued her curiosity, like the possibility of a werewolf pack living in nearby Birmingham, or a man who claimed that the London floods were actually caused by someone who could control the weather. Martin's suggestion that creatures disguised as human but being able to swim like mermaids made Stephanie think of all the mysteries in the world that needed solving. The cat she saw when she was a child also came to mind again. Was there a link between an explainable big cat from (possibly) Bodmin and some of the more outrageous theories of psychic powers, ghosts or mermaids?

Now, in what might become her office, she bashed a few keys and looked up a few things on Martin's top-of-the-range computer. She was fascinated by the Angel Trust file, which included an interesting but short piece on werewolves, a piece on Irish travellers and the supernatural, and an empty file on the Romanian Embassy. Stephanie imagined that it had not always been empty, but was recently cleared. Her sister Paula had dated someone from the embassy last year, but it hadn't lasted. And she'd read something in the news in the last few weeks, some scandal, but she couldn't remember the details.

"So tell me about the Angel Trust?" she asked Martin, who was still looking out of the window waiting for his visitor.

"It's an organisation created some years ago by…" started Martin, then he noticed his guest arriving. "*He* might be able to tell you better than me. He works for them."

A smart black car parked in the driveway, quite close to the front door of the main house. A man stepped out of the vehicle. He was probably in his late twenties, wearing a 'men in black' suit, including sunglasses. Well, it was a hot, sunny day and at least he wasn't completely covered up like Martin had been. Martin went to the door of the annex and waved at the newcomer.

"Clif," he called. "Over this side." The newcomer joined them, stopping at the doorway of the large office in order to take in the surroundings. He looked at Stephanie carefully, as if he was trying to work out who she was. She was suspicious of him, but she didn't really know why. Perhaps it was simply that she was a little out of her comfort zone.

"Stephanie Baynes," said Martin by way of introduction.

"Clifton Chase," said the visitor, taking off his sunglasses and offering her his hand. She walked over to the doorway and shook it. He held onto it and looked her over carefully, until she began to feel uncomfortable (not for the first time today).

"Stephanie is going to work for me," said Martin, breaking the tension. Clifton Chase let her go.

"Oh? I thought she didn't look like one of your regular ladies. What kind of job? Not your housekeeper, and you already have a cleaner who comes in a couple of times a week, and that man from down the road does your gardening…" he turned to

Stephanie, "He hates gardening. So I expect you must be the researcher he was thinking about."

"Yes," said Stephanie. "I suppose I must."

"Martin has been flirting with the Angel Trust, and now all of a sudden he wants to take us a bit more seriously," said Chase with some humour. "*We* have researchers, so he wants one." Martin chuckled at the comment.

"What is the Angel Trust?" she asked, trying to take control of the conversation.

"It's an organisation set up to investigate certain…" he started, and then he turned to Martin. "What have you told her so far?"

"I was waiting for you to get here," said Martin.

Clif meandered over to one of the chairs and sat down like he owned the place.

"The Angel Trust started as an organisation that was set up to hunt… creatures, way back more than a hundred years ago."

"Creatures?"

"Specifically, vampires," said Clif. "Although, I don't believe they ever actually caught any. It was started towards the end of the nineteenth century by an ancestor of Lord Martin here, but he won't tell us any details. If he knows anything. In more recent times we investigate supernatural events, creatures, objects. For the first half of this year my boss, the warden, was looking into magically imbued artefacts, but that's been closed down now."

"Magically…" started Stephanie. "Like magic swords and stuff?"

"Not exactly – more like amulets and things that enhance a person's original abilities."

"What?" said Stephanie, still unsure as to whether this whole thing was a joke. "You mean like magic items to make you stronger or run faster?"

"More supernatural that that. More like… How much does she know?" Clif asked Martin.

"She hasn't even agreed to work for me yet," answered Martin.

Clif turned back to Stephanie. "I wouldn't say I have a right to advise you, but if you say 'yes', you are getting into a really strange world."

"I think I get that," she said. "So what do you do for the Angel Trust?"

"I poke around into other people's business. I investigate whatever the warden tells me to. I'm waiting for some news on Mbalaya, to see if it's something that might interest the Trust, but my current assignment is to get Lord Martin here to tell me what he really knows about the beginnings of the Trust. I knew he was going to recruit a researcher, but I didn't know he'd actually done it yet."

"Mbalaya?" said Stephanie.

"A country in Africa that has recently ejected archaeologist Georges Bouvon from his work there. Professor Bouvon believes in aliens, and I think he felt he'd found evidence of their existence out there. But in the absence of any real reason for travelling all that way, I'm here in Stoke-on-Trent investigating what Martin knows about the true beginnings of the Angel Trust."

"Other than one of my ancestors being a founding member of the original Angel Trust, I don't think I'll be able to tell you anything more," said Martin. "Lucky you were in the area so you got to meet Stephanie."

"There's a lot going on around here at the moment," said Clif. "We have three haunted houses, a mini-borealis at a farm nearby, and some possible creatures in the woods north of here."

"If one of your haunted houses is the one on Flint Street then don't waste your time," said Stephanie. "The noises are caused by air flow through the damaged roof and the weird lights are from the all-night supermarket behind the building, coupled with holes in the walls and distorted by the broken glass. And I might guess that your mysterious creatures in the woods are called partying students. They often talked about their parties in the woods, although I never actually went to one."

"And the mini-borealis?" asked Clif, laughing.

"Don't know that one," she admitted.

"It's a phenomenon occurring only in one location in the country – possibly the world. It's possibly supernatural in structure, and is happening right now in a mystical river just a few miles from here."

Martin laughed. "Stephanie, you know what causes rainbows?" he asked. "Water droplets reflecting sunlight?"

"Yes," Stephanie confirmed.

"Well, there's a river near here that seems to create a lot of its own mini-rainbows. It happens in hot weather when enough water has evaporated and when the sun is high enough in the sky. It is not, in any way, supernatural."

"Although it doesn't occur on any river anywhere else in the world," said Clif.

"I don't know why the Angel Trust would waste your time with it," said Martin.

"I get to see pretty rainbows," Clif shrugged. "Sometimes my investigations lead somewhere, sometimes they don't. But thanks for the heads up on Flint Street and the woods."

After a bit of chatter between the two men, Martin suggested that Stephanie should look around where she would be living if she accepted his invitation. Then he escorted Clif to his car.

She went upstairs to see the fabulous bedrooms, including a bed that looked even more comfortable than the one she had at home in Kent. She'd never really felt truly at home in her college rooms bed, so this was going to be wonderful. Then she went down to the lounge and out of the back door to the fields.

She looked out over the fields, which fell away in a gentle slope. At the edge of the grassy area a couple of hundred metres away, a dog nosed around by the distant trees. At least, it looked like a dog to start with, although it moved like a cat. But it was too big to be a cat. She shielded her eyes with her hand to take a closer look, but it was gone.

She returned to her office.

Her office, she thought. She wanted to accept Martin's job offer, but Clifton Chase and Martin had talked about supernatural objects that enhanced supernatural powers, rainbows that didn't behave like rainbows should, mermaids and werewolves. She wanted a puzzle she could solve with a scientific explanation, like a man with a degree in psychology using it to be a fake fortune teller. Actually, she wanted something a bit meatier than that. Of course, having met the good-looking Lord Martin Latham and being a bit of a romantic, perhaps she was just letting all this stretch her imagination a bit too far. All that had happened was that she had been asked to do the research she wanted by a rich young looker who wanted to pay her.

Martin came back to the office.

"How about a trial period?" she suggested, continuing the conversation that had started before Clif had turned up at their door.

"From your end, that's fine. But as far as I'm concerned, the job is yours. Anyway, what do you think of your new accommodation? Is it much bigger than where you live now?" She hoped he was joking, since not many single new graduates could afford a place this big. But then, he was rich. Maybe he really had no idea.

"It's a pokey little bedsit," she said, confirming what he must have known.

"So you'll be glad to move 'over the shop'?"

"For sure – I have to move out soon anyway, and your rooms are brilliant."

Lord Martin Latham dropped Stephanie off at her apartment, and they arranged for him to pick her up at eight o'clock the following morning. She was excited as she breezed into her tiny rooms. She looked around the dump. She would be delighted to give it up in exchange for that proper apartment next to Martin's mini-mansion. But would she give up her current lifestyle for adventuring across the countryside on a hunt for disreputable scientists or having odd people from mysterious secret societies knocking at her door?

Then she thought, what 'current lifestyle'? She had loved university life, and had made a number of friends, although few that she expected to stay in contact with now that their courses were over. Most of her friends had already left, moved on or gone home; one of them was engaged to be married. It was all over, that life, and it was time for her to move on as well. She had to find a job somewhere in the world, working for some small town's newspaper or a scientific research post ploughing through tedious manuals and pretending to understand what she was reading. She'd just had the job of a lifetime handed to her on a plate, and although she had to ask 'why me?', she also knew she wasn't going to turn it down.

Three

The following day, back at the office, Martin and Stephanie talked about yesterday. Stephanie said she definitely wanted the job, although she had loads of questions about him, the Angel Trust, and what kind of form her actual work might take.

"Well, to be honest, I'm not sure," said Martin with a laugh. "You spend a bit of time on these computers, so you can talk to a lot of people anywhere in the world from the comfort of your office. But you might also want to travel to meet some."

"Sounds fair," she said, and he could tell she wanted to ask something else.

"But?"

"Why me?"

Martin laughed. "You knew that fairground fortune teller was a fake because you don't believe in fortune tellers. You never found a ghost in that haunted house because you don't believe in ghosts. You are determined to find a sound, logical, boring explanation for everything."

"So you employed me because I'm boring?" Stephanie teased him.

"I employed you because that's a good starting place," said Martin, tapping away at the main office computer. "Just because there is some weird stuff out there doesn't mean everything is weird. You have to try to find logical reasons for things first."

"And once you have eliminated the improbable, whatever's left, no matter how impossible, must be a werewolf."

"You're a bit fixated on werewolves, aren't you? You'll be disappointed when you actually meet one."

Stephanie and Martin made arrangements to move her stuff into her new home. They chatted for a while and then she spent some time contacting her parents and her sister to tell them she was now gainfully employed. She read up on her e-mails and the news.

She read about the situation in London that had seen a number of businessmen, politicians and lawyers involved in some kind of big conspiracy, a networking group that had turned criminal. Her sister worked for a big legal company and one of her bosses had been arrested, but the company (and her job) had come out of it more or less intact. There was also something about Mbalaya, a small North African country that had ejected all foreign ambassadors from its capital.

"Mbalaya…" she said quietly.

"What about it?" asked Martin.

"Mr Chase talked about it yesterday, and now it's on the news. What else does the Angel Trust get involved in?"

"If they've been doing something supernatural, then the Trust might get involved."

"Have you been there?"

"Africa? No. I don't like flying. Or hot midday sun. It makes my skin…"

"Mmm?"

"…burn," he finished, after mulling over his possible choice of words.

They talked a bit more about the logistics of her moving in, and then she said, out of the blue, "So tell me about werewolves."

Martin glanced at her. "I thought you going to ask me about the move, or questions brought up by our little chat with Clifton Chase."

"So are you going to tell me, or not?"

"You just started two sentences with the word 'so'."

"So?"

"A few years ago there was a report about some kind of hooliganism in Birmingham city centre – kids howling like wolves and jumping from roof to roof like free runners, stuff like that – particularly during a full moon. Have you ever been into Birmingham – the city I mean?"

"No. I don't think so. I lived in Kent, so London was the big city to visit."

"Well, it's a place of contrasts. It is the second biggest city in England, but it doesn't *feel* as big as, say, Manchester. It's a scruffy old industrial town and a bright new city, both at the same time. All the buildings are different. Rooftop to rooftop isn't too easy a thing to do – not in the city centre, anyway."

"Not a great place for some free running, then."

"Not unless you are quite good at it. Anyway, John called me and asked me to look into it."

"John?" queried Stephanie. "Someone in the Angel Trust?"

"John Borland, yes – the warden. That's the Angel Trust's version of a CEO. He wondered if there was something more than human in the hooliganism."

"You are joking – the Angel Trust knew about the werewolves? And you sometimes work for them?"

"Stoke is nearer Birmingham than they are – they have their main offices in Southampton – and sometimes the Trust asks for my help. And no, I have never *worked* for them."

"So there really are such things as werewolves," said Stephanie, returning them to the present.

"Not in the sense that you would imagine. It took me three months to track them down, because they only took part in their activities for three or four days a month. You know – full moons and a couple of days either side. Basically, there were a group of young friends who all went to the same gym – they all liked the same type of gymnastics. They were like animals, leaping about the equipment and doing the most spectacular stunts you could imagine. At the height of the full moon, they got a little over-excited and went out into the streets. Or rather the rooftops."

"So they turned into werewolves."

"Not exactly. They were always werewolves. I mean, they didn't grow hair and pointy-ears or fangs or anything; they just had wolf-like habits and tendencies. They liked their steaks rare, and they were very acrobatic. But they were human, at least for the most part."

"So how did they become… like that?"

"I was dealing with the people themselves, not looking into causes. Some bad magic from their past? A curse, perhaps, or maybe they were born on a convergence of ley lines? I don't know."

"So what happened to them, to the werewolves?"

"I had a word with them, and then with the owner of the gym, and suggested that their plight would get worse if they were too public about their skills. They still have lots of fun at full moons, but they are a little more discreet about it these days."

"They still live in Birmingham?"

"A couple of them have taken up sports coaching elsewhere in the country – they felt they could never take up competitive sports directly; they thought they might not pass the medical tests; but they make good trainers and sparring partners. Most of the others work behind fast food counters or as warehouse assistants – a boring life until they meet at the gym on one weekend in four to have some fun together."

A couple of days later, the removals company (paid for by Martin) arrived in a small van with Stephanie's few possessions. What she had would hardly fill a single room here in Martin's mansion, as she'd started to call it. She had dumped her old computer when she was sorting through her things to move, and the rest of what she owned didn't amount to very much. Her parents had been good to her, in that they had paid her way through university so she didn't have a debt, but they weren't rich, and she hadn't wasted what little money she had on surplus stuff. Now, she looked at this new bedroom, empty at the moment apart from a lovely fluffy buff-coloured carpet and a queen-sized bed, and she wondered about her future. Would she be working for Martin for a long time? How much of the work would be *with* him, travelling across the land looking for answers together, and how much would be just researching stuff on a computer? For that matter, which option would she prefer?

Martin had said that he didn't like flying and hot sun, so that implied that they would stay in this country. That was good, because she was happy to be 'at home' and couldn't hold a conversation in any language but English. Also, he'd suggested that John Borland's organisation, the Angel Trust, based in Southampton, gave him *local* research jobs to do, which would probably limit her research to the general area of the Midlands.

She'd contacted her parents and told them the good news, but she had been a little vague to them about what the job entailed, mostly because she was a little unsure about it herself.

She moved the office around a little, creating 'living space' in the large room as well as 'working space'. She also cleared the clutter around the small front-facing window and moved her desk close enough so that she could see out of it. She could see the front entrance to the main house so if Clifton Chase or any other mysterious visitor called again she would be able to look out and see who it was. Martin didn't disturb her much, but he approved (and ordered and paid for) a suite of comfortable furniture for that large space in the office, and left her, mostly, to herself.

She sat in the office, 'researching'. She opened up her computer and looked up ley lines. Martin had said something about them in their various conversations over the last few days. She had an idea as to what ley lines actually were from her studies at university, and she knew, or at least she thought she had heard somewhere, that they had something to do with ancient druids and Paganism, (not to mention witchcraft), but she didn't really know much about the subject.

Ley lines, she had discovered at university, were lines of power marked by special marker sites. While they originated in ancient times, they were rediscovered in June 1921 by a Herefordshire businessman, Alfred Watkins, while looking at a map for places of interest. He noticed a pattern of lines marked by the country's high places, and wrote about them in a book entitled 'The Old Straight Track'. It seemed that he recognised a pattern in the lines, and investigated them further. Ley lines, or leys, joined a number of well-known (and lesser known) sites of ancient power. In this book, Watkins referred to sites in Britain, but in fact, there were ley lines all the way across the world, and other ancient societies as well as pagan ones understood the power of certain locations.

She also looked for cross-references in the information she had looked up on leys. The High Places, for example, were mentioned in the Christian Bible as places where people worshipped false gods, and they were condemned by the Israelite God (but not by its kings, it seemed). The Ancient Greeks also had ley lines and high places, many associated with Hermes, the messenger of the gods. In Roman times the high places may have marked the meeting points of major trade routes, as Romans often used high places, such as hilltops, to light fires to build their roads, which linked both with ley lines and routes of communication.

Ley lines were also used in conjunction with geomancy, which was the ancient art of divination using handfuls of earth, but the name geomancy also became linked with the ancient Chinese art of feng shui, by which the location and orientation of houses and tombs was determined, paying regard to the topography of the local landscape. Further exploration led to Stephanie finding references to yin and yang, fire and water, and, most specifically, the mystical location of 'special' towns and villages.

There was, of course, far too much information on the net, and Stephanie got to the point where she found herself not understanding the words in front of her. She turned off her computer. A short while later she went to bed, but, as comfortable as her new bed was, she lay awake for some time as her head buzzed with all the information she had tried to take in.

When she eventually got to sleep, she dreamed of when she was thirteen years old. She had fallen in, and out of, love with Mitchel Byron Shepherd, a hunter in his late thirties, whose main stalking grounds were, at least when young Stephanie knew him, the wilds of north Kent. His prey for that particular summer was the mysterious cat-like beast that stalked a region of Kent between Gravesend and Rochester. The young teenage Stephanie had joined him in his hunt for this beast – whether he wanted her along or not.

The creature was a myth, a local legend. Occasionally, it would appear to terrorise the local householders and farmers, or at least, that's how the *Gravesend Messenger* newspaper reported it. What actually happened was that it occasionally appeared, much to the amusement and surprise of the locals and, annoyingly, it never seemed to turn up when any of them had a camera handy. Perhaps, occasionally, somebody might get a hazy photograph of an animal that may have been nothing more than a large alley-cat, but nobody had got a clear picture or any real evidence that the creature truly existed. Byron Shepherd, a local landowner's son, had enjoyed a hunting trip in Africa with some friends from university many years earlier and, after that fortnight, fancied himself as a big game hunter, so he went about trying to track down the cat using the methods he had learned all those years ago on the one and only real hunt he'd ever been on.

He made a den up a tree on the farmland owned by his father near the town of Shorne, a small village just south of the main road between Gravesend and Charles Dickens' home town of Higham. Stephanie, who was fascinated by Shepherd and how he appeared, to her at least, to be an adventurer, watched as he made his hide with planks, dead branches and netting, which picked up falling leaves easily. It was late in the school summer holidays, and all of Stephanie's friends were away on their family vacations. Her parents, who were both teachers, had taken her away right at the beginning of the summer break, so this left her with four weeks out of six away from most of her friends. She idled the time in the fields, and spent as much time with Byron as possible.

"You're after the Cat, aren't you?" she asked him. "Can I join you?"

The local people called the beast 'the Cat', and she knew that Byron was a hunter, and nobody had ever seen the Cat close up, and she was here with him – they were going to share an adventure!

"You must be still and quiet," he looked at her and repeated, "and *quiet*, for a long time if you want to join me in the hide."

"Oh, can I?" she asked with childish enthusiasm.

"Promise," he said.

"I'll-be-still-and-quiet," she said quickly, and he helped her up into the tree. The hide was only about a metre or so off the ground, but Byron had made it so that there were good views in all directions, and yet nobody, or, in fact, no animal, could see you unless they knew exactly where to look and were standing quite close by. He had also, of course, chosen a tree that was close to where many of the Cat sightings had taken place.

Once in the tree, he settled down, with Stephanie next to him, and waited. She was remarkably quiet, asking no questions, but sitting still and alert, watching out for the mysterious beast. She faced a different direction from him, leaning her back against his shoulder so that the two of them could view the widest area, and she kept a good watch for him. He was surprised at her concentration span. He had expected her to be a pest, but she was turning out to be a help.

She had turned serious when she saw some of the equipment that he'd stowed up there in the tree. There was a small camera, some binoculars, and a gun. It was the gun that had silenced her. It was a rifle, like the hunters had in films she had seen, but with a long, small-bored barrel. She realised that he was serious about his hunt, and that adventures weren't as jolly and 'Famous Five' as she had originally thought. Perhaps he thought that the Cat was a pest to be exterminated, or a trophy to be won. Whatever he thought, the gun changed her thoughts about him, and she stopped being starry-eyed about him from that moment.

Her silly crush on him had never really been serious, anyway. She looked down at herself. She was flat-chested and straight-hipped, unlike many of her school friends. She was what her mum or some other adults might call a late developer. That didn't bother her like it might have worried some girls, as she knew that there was plenty of time for her. Apparently, her sister, now in her last year at university, was just as boy-looking as Stephanie when she was thirteen, and now she was so stunningly feminine that someone had suggested that she should give up university for a modelling career. Perhaps one day she, Stephanie, would be given the chance to be a model, too. It was every girl's fantasy. Well, nearly every girl. Stephanie wasn't all that bothered. As long as her striking blue eyes didn't change colour, that would be enough for her. She resumed her watch for the beast.

The day passed with no sightings. At home at the end of the day, Stephanie researched big cats and wondered which species they might see, should it turn up. Four more days passed, and Stephanie spent three of them in the hide with Byron, watching out for the Cat. They took breaks to eat sandwiches, and had a few short, grown-up conversations in quiet tones, where Stephanie impressed Byron with her ability to stop being a child for a while, and then they resumed their long watch. On one day Stephanie went with her family to Westgate-on-Sea for a day's outing. It was a nice enough trip and the weather was good, but she was eager to get back and re-join Byron for the vigil.

On the sixth day, they saw the Cat. It was Byron who spotted it, which disappointed Stephanie a little as she really wanted it to be her. He nudged her very lightly so as not to cause any real disturbance, and pointed. It was in front of him, and therefore behind her, so she had to twist around to see it, which she did carefully and slowly so as not to make any noise and disturb the beast. She saw the magnificent animal past Byron's head. Her body still twisted uncomfortably, she rested her chin on his shoulder, her bright eyes shining with awe at the animal she was now privileged to observe.

The big cat was not *really* big, not like a lion or a tiger. It was more puma-sized, its pointed ears tufted with fur or hair at the ends, something like a lynx, only darker in colour. Stephanie had heard that it was supposed to be a black cat, like the famous Beast of Bodmin, but this animal was more of a brown colour, like the darker lions she had seen earlier that year when she had visited Whipsnade Zoo. This cat's fur seemed to gleam in the summer sun. It was keeping close to a tree, padding around it like a pet housecat. Once or twice its eyes lit up as they caught morning sunlight through the trees. Stephanie tried not to make too much noise as she drew in her breath at the sight of the lovely feline.

Byron, however, reached for his gun.

"You're not really going to kill it?" she whispered in a half-question. He did not answer her, but put the gun sight up to his eye, and positioned the firearm comfortably in his arms so that his finger rested on the trigger. He gradually, slowly, levelled the long rifle in the direction of the animal. Stephanie decided that she couldn't let that happen.

"No!" she suddenly shouted in a loud voice, jumping about the tiny hide, knocking a branch out of place so that part of the hide wall fell to the ground. The Cat, startled, ran away out of sight.

"What the hell are you...?" he began.

"You were going to shoot her!" she shouted at him.

And that was where the 'romance' ended. She considered Byron cruel and insensitive, and she grew up a little wiser to the world around her. She also decided that staying still in a hide was not the best way to hunt for cats. She was right, of course, because nobody in the area saw the animal for the rest of the summer. Anyway, she thought, there was no point in staying in wait for an animal if you weren't going to try to catch it or kill it. What would you do when it turned up? Invite it to tea? She made up her mind that she would hunt for the creature in a different way – by going to the library.

Of course, there was not much information about north Kent's mysterious moggy in the local library, although there was something about the Beast of Bodmin, which may or may not have been a similar creature. So she decided to research on the Internet. There was sure to be a great deal more information there.

Stephanie woke up fully. The image of Byron and the hide disappeared from her mind, although the face of the cat staring at her for a second before running off back into obscurity stayed in her head. In fact, over the years, this part of the dream seemed to have come back frequently.

She showered, got dressed, went downstairs, had breakfast and made her way to her office. She had just made herself a start-of-working-day cup of coffee, when she heard a car pull up outside. She looked through the window to the front of the house to see who was there. It was a young blonde woman, very attractive and dressed fairly lightly with bare arms and legs. She was laughing and happy, although Stephanie noticed her left forearm was wrapped with what appeared to be a fresh bandage. Martin followed shortly after, covered in his customary dark clothing and wide-brimmed hat. He took her arm and led her to the taxi that had attracted Stephanie's attention.

Martin gave his guest a long, lingering kiss on the lips as she began to get into the taxi, and said something like, "See you in a couple of months," before letting her go. As he turned around, Martin looked as if he might glance in Stephanie's direction, so she pulled back away from the window. It was, after all, none of her business. Martin was her boss, that was all, and she hadn't really thought of their relationship as anything else. He was good-looking, rich and charming, but that was no reason to think there should be anything 'special' between them. However, she did feel just a little disappointed, even though she didn't really understand why.

She saw his shadow pass by the window as he made his way towards her office. He came in with a big 'Good morning' and a smile that would melt icebergs. When he got there, Stephanie was seated at her desk and her computer was on again.

"Good morning," she replied, not turning in his direction in case her cheeks were red. "You sound cheerful this morning."

"I just spent the night with Carlie, so who wouldn't be happy?" he said.

"Too much information," said Stephanie with a grimace.

"You're a researcher," laughed Martin. "There's no such thing as too much information."

Stephanie opened her mouth to say something and then she closed it again. She remembered Clifton Chase's 'one of his regulars' comments. She couldn't hear clearly from her office, but she thought Martin had said something about 'in a couple of months' to the young woman. Did he only see her once every couple of months?

"I got a message this morning, when I turned on my phone," Martin said when he realised he wasn't going to get a come-back from her. "John would like to meet you."

"John?"

"John Borland. The head of the Angel Trust. The warden."

"From Southampton?" said Stephanie.

"Yes, but he'll speak to us by computer," said Martin. "I just picked up the message a couple of minutes ago when I turned on my phone just before Carlie left."

"Carlie's your girlfriend?" said Stephanie, daring to pry. She wasn't going to ask but seeing as he mentioned it...

"Sort of," replied Martin, with a little smile. "One of them, anyway."

"One of them?" Stephanie smiled back, but tried to put some shock into her voice. "Does she know that she's only one of many?"

"They all know about all the others," said Martin, and he seemed to be enjoying her confusion. "And she's not 'only' anything. None of them are 'only'; they are all special. And I didn't use the word many – that was *your* idea."

"Sorry, didn't mean to pry."

"Are you serious? You're here to investigate. I can't imagine you haven't looked me up already, and done some serious background checking into me, my family, and who, or possibly what, I am."

Stephanie coloured up a bit. She had, indeed, looked up Lord Martin Latham, and had been surprised at how little there was about him on the net. She hadn't found a single picture of him, although there had been an old one of his father with the same name, dated sometime in the 1970's. The resemblance was remarkable – at first she thought it was him because the name was the same, but then she saw the date.

"Not extensive or serious research, no," she replied. "Actually, I couldn't find very much at all. It's quite surprising that an English Lord has such a small number of entries on the Net. You are quite the mystery man."

Martin smiled, and his eyes seemed to look into the distance for a moment. "I like that you failed to find something on me. I don't want to be an open book for all to read." But he said no more about it. He quickly fired up a computer and connected to John Borland, whose face came up on the screen.

The warden of the Angel Trust was an older man, balding with short, red-brown hair which was tufty in a way that looked as if it would be untidy if it was any longer. He wore a loose-fitting white shirt and a plain, pale green tie. He seemed to be sitting at a desk, looking directly at the camera, suggesting that either there was a camera in the screen, or he had practiced looking at the camera as if he could see his audience.

"John," said Martin as he positioned himself next to Stephanie so that they could both clearly see and be seen. Stephanie leaned in to Martin a little in order to be sure she was in the picture. She thought she could smell Carlie's perfume on him.

"Martin and Miss Baynes. May I call you Stephanie?" he said.

"Of course," she said with what she hoped looked like a polite smile.

"So what's so urgent?" asked Martin.

"First things first. Stephanie, how are you settling in to your new job?"

"Very well, thank you, Mr Borland," she responded. "I am given to understand that I am actually working for Lord Latham; is that correct?"

Borland looked puzzled for a moment, then smiled as he realised what she was actually asking. "Yes, of course; sometimes he'll do me a favour, but I'm not his boss – I don't think anyone could be – so whatever you do, you are doing it for him, not me or the Angel Trust. You are very astute, though, as I am about to ask him a favour. But right now I'd love to learn something about you. Martin is careful about who he chooses to work with. It took a month or two for him to settle with Mr Chase."

"I took to Mr Chase straight away," said Stephanie with a smile.

"Well, he thinks you're wonderful," said Borland with a big smile in his voice. "Now, Stephanie, I hear you are into cats?"

"Where did you hear that?"

"From your work in the university."

"You have access to my university studies?"

"If anything has ever been written down, we have access to it."

"'We' being the Angel Trust," she confirmed. It may have been a friendly start, but it was about to get serious very quickly.

"Well, we have, over the years, become a research facility. I am sure that Martin had that in mind when he employed you." Stephanie glanced across at Martin, who looked as if he was about to argue, then changed his mind and shrugged his shoulders. John Borland continued, "The Trust now has a warden in charge; that's me. The title Warden to the Trust is something like Managing Director or CEO would be to a business. The Angel Trust is now very much respected among both scientists and world leaders – at least, those who have heard of us.

"Anyway, about cats. Something has come up this morning that I would like you to take a look at."

"About cats?" Martin repeated with some distaste in his voice. "You mean Old Rad?"

"Yes, Martin, I'm afraid so."

"Old Rad?" asked Stephanie.

"The cat man," said Martin, as if that would explain everything. "What's he done?"

"Hopefully, nothing," said Borland. "But he may be arrested for murder soon if we don't intervene."

"Murder?" said Martin. "He wouldn't hurt a fly."

"Someone's been killed and Radnor is involved in some way. I haven't got all the information just yet, but I think it may be a good idea for you to get down there and investigate. I will arrange for you to have some credit or credibility with the investigating officer."

"Isn't that more Clif Chase's area of expertise?" suggested Martin.

"Yes, but Clif is looking into the Mbalayan situation," said Borland. "So I wondered if you would help."

Stephanie refrained from asking for more details about the 'Mbalayan situation' as it was none of her business. Not that this would stop her from looking it up later – what she had seen on the news about the African country kicking out support from its neighbours interested her. She was curious to know what it had to do with the Angel Trust.

"What can you tell us about the situation?" asked Martin, who seemed to have decided to go along with whatever it was that Borland was asking.

"A body was pulled from a river near Dennington this morning – the River Rissen. It was reported to the local police officer by Steven Radnor. The body was of a man who had been shot, but they don't know what Old Rad's part in the whole thing was. I have just picked up some e-mails from the local police to the investigating officer – they are suspicious of Old Rad's part in it all."

"May I ask a question?" said Stephanie.

"Go ahead," said Borland.

"Why is this Rad person important to you?"

"Everyone's important," replied Borland.

"So investigate a murder in Scotland, or Australia," she replied. She had a feeling that Martin was enjoying her little display of defiance here. John Borland seemed to be an important man, someone of some power if he had people who could hack into e-mails between police departments and order

43

Martin around. Perhaps her words could have been a bit more polite.

"Because we investigate the unusual, Miss Baynes," Borland answered, politely tolerating her attitude. "And Old Rad, Mr Steven Radnor, is unusual."

"In what way, sir?" she responded, putting in the 'sir' because she thought it was polite after what she thought might be taken as 'an attitude'.

"He can talk to animals; well, cats in particular," said Borland. He paused for a moment, and then continued. "When this came across my desk just a few minutes ago, I thought of you, Stephanie. I thought it was about time you met another cat-lover."

Four

Steve Radnor lived in a small village named Barnhampton near to the River Rissen, a large river, and neighbouring an extensive forest. Bordering the forest there was a great deal of farmland.

As they left the house, Stephanie noticed that Martin once again wore his wide-brimmed hat and put on sunglasses, although the day was cloudy. She wondered whether this was some kind of disguise or 'persona' he was putting on. The day was cloudy, so his dislike of sunshine was not going to be an issue, unless he was worried that the clouds would suddenly conspire against him and open to let the sunshine through. Alternatively, of course, it could just be that Martin liked to look like a mystery man.

When Martin drove Stephanie to the village, she spent some of the time with her head back in the headrest and her eyes closed, and Martin took that as a sign that she didn't want to chat, so he left her to her thoughts. She wondered about werewolves and the Angel Trust and little river rainbows and ley lines and Martin's girlfriends. She thought about what Martin had told her about the werewolves of Birmingham, who might well have been just high-spirited young athletes who went a bit wild on a full moon. She wondered what kind of research the warden of the Angel Trust did, whether it was all 'spooky' stuff or how much they got involved with politics, like that African situation that Clifton Chase was involved in. She thought about how much Borland knew about her, and wondered why she wasn't more unsettled by the fact that he knew about her studies at university. She wondered if study of the supernatural was a reasonable option for her career, and how Mr Borland or Martin had got into it in the first place. She thought about her new boss and wondered if there was something spooky about *him*.

Steve Radnor's house was at the edge of the forest, a short distance away from the village and not far from the river. It was an old stone cottage that seemed at first glance to grow out of the forest itself. It was a single-floored building covered in leaves and foliage that clung to the walls and windows, and which nobody had trimmed for some years. Stephanie imagined that the inside of the house would have carpets of uncut grass, and leafy vines for wallpaper.

There was no gate in the gateway, as if its owner had never replaced it when it had deteriorated and vanished a hundred years ago. Martin parked in the narrow driveway; there were no other vehicles there. There was a low stone wall surrounding the front half of the house and the small garden, but the back of the premises seemed to be part of the forest. A black cat with tufty fur and white markings on his face and ear-tips sat on the wall and stared at them as they parked, got out of the car and walked to the front door. He seemed to be paying particular attention to Stephanie, but he didn't move from his guard-post. There was another cat perched on the pinnacle of the shallow roof. Steve Radnor, after all, was supposed to be 'the cat man', but Stephanie hadn't had time to research anything about him on her computer before leaving, so she was going to rely on Martin for his prior information on this man. Why was he in danger of being arrested?

The door was unlocked, and Martin might have known this because he simply entered rather than knocking first. He didn't take his hat off. Stephanie followed, feeling very much like a spectator in a drama she didn't fully understand. The inside of the house looked untidy, and felt as if it would look untidy even if she had her eyes closed. The hallway was a short, wide corridor with doors to the left and right, both open onto the kitchen and lounge respectively, and a third door, closed, ahead of them. Stephanie glanced into the lounge, noticing that the floor had not been swept or vacuumed this century. The place smelled of cats. Stephanie liked cats, but the smell was still a little bit on the wrong side of being pleasant.

"Rad?" Martin said, but not loudly. "Steve? It's Martin Latham."

Steve Radnor appeared from the kitchen, dirty mug in hand. He looked like his living room – untidy, not properly looked-after and old. His hair was a silver grey, and his face wrinkled. He looked like the grooves on his face had prevented him from washing properly. He peered at Martin for a moment or two, looking him over as if he was trying to make his mind up about something.

"You haven't changed much," he said as if it was a joke. "The old man sent you?"

"We're here to help," said Martin. Stephanie could not help thinking that this man wouldn't want his help, and that Martin wasn't welcome. Perhaps they had some history.

"Do I need help?" said Radnor. Two cats appeared from wherever they were hiding in the lounge, and walked around Stephanie, looking her over and ignoring Martin.

"They like you, Miss," Radnor said to her, as if that was really important. Then he looked at Martin and didn't say anything, but his expression said 'they don't like *you* at all'.

"What happened?" asked Martin.

"Early this morning Tats came in to me. He said there was a killing. One of our kind had killed another."

"Our kind?" asked Stephanie.

"A person," said Martin. "I presume that Tats is a cat."

"You haven't met Tats, have you?" Radnor said to Martin. "He was born after you were last here. That'd be twenty years or more ago."

"Sorry I haven't visited regularly," said Martin, "I didn't really feel welcome last time."

Steve Radnor either coughed, scoffed or laughed at that point. It was hard to tell which.

"I called out the police. New guy in the village, Tom Drake. Nice lad, but he hasn't got a clue. Hah – a clue – that wasn't a *deliberate* joke. Anyway, he called in the big guns, and they came straight away. They asked how I knew the guy was dead. They found him in the river, just over there. Tats saw him being shot, but he doesn't know anyone, so he couldn't…"

Martin held up his hand. "Slower, please," he said. "You're telling me that one of your cats witnessed a murder, and told you."

"Yeah."

"I imagine the police wouldn't believe you when you told them."

47

Radnor did his cough or laugh again. Stephanie had worked out that this old man believed he could talk to cats, but what appeared to have happened was that a cat had witnessed the crime and apparently told Radnor, who told the police who had then found the body. So there *was* a body, which meant that either he really could hear cats, or that he found the body himself and was using the cats as a way of dealing with it. Stephanie would have preferred the latter argument, but she was beginning to doubt herself.

"They didn't believe me, not at first, but young Drake, the local police community officer, he felt he should take a look anyway. He went into the forest by the river path, and saw the body in the river. I said he'd been shot, and when they dragged him out of the water, they found I was right."

"Did you know the dead man?"

"Yeah, he was old Jim Carson's son, Paul. Nice guy. I think he just got engaged. Poor girl, Sally Stevens. Only turned twenty-one last month. There was a big party in the village. She was kind, said I could come along, but I know they didn't really want me there."

Radnor turned his head to look at Stephanie, who was standing a little behind Martin, near the front door, trying to follow the conversation at the same time as watching the two cats as they kept circling her.

"They think I'm a bit mad, see, 'cause I talk to cats," he raised his voice to indicate he was talking to her. The distraction stopped her train of thought, which was wandering over to how old Martin would have been twenty years ago when he was last here, although Radnor had said he hadn't changed much. Maybe the old man had got his numbers confused. She nodded, and then felt embarrassed because she didn't want him to think she actually agreed with the villagers about him being a bit mad.

"But if they thought you can't really talk to cats," said Martin, "then they would have to wonder how you knew about the body."

Stephanie bent down to stroke one of the cats, a grey one, but it jumped out of her reach and ran out of the open front door.

"They don't like being fussed," Radnor explained. "They aren't house cats, not exactly. They lives out in the forest, and stays clear of the village. Feral, they calls it, but that's an unkind word. They come and visit me, and my place will keep them from the rain and cold. Apart from that, they keeps pretty much to themselves."

"But you can talk to them," said Stephanie.

"Yeah," said the old man, looking her over carefully. "An' you're not humouring me, are you? You believe me."

Stephanie had to think about this. "I don't know," she replied at last, "I supposed I might." For some reason, saying it out loud frightened her a little.

"Heh," said Radnor in his half-cough. "Young Martin, here, he believes me. That's why he brought you here. They don't like him, the cats, but they're okay with you, so he can come in 'cause you're here."

"So the cats determine who can visit you?" enquired Stephanie.

"No, it's my house. They know me in the village; they know I don't mean no 'arm, so they're okay with me. I got a bit of a pension, enough to look after me, just about, so I live 'ere in my old family mansion, heh, like Lord Martin lives out over there, and it's all okay. I get me supplies from the village, and I don't hurt anybody. But now someone's dead and old Tats has seen it, so what can I do? I has to report it; it's the right thing to do. But nobody really believes I talk to them – the cats, I mean – so I'm going to be in trouble, aren't I? That's why the old man sent you, isn't it?"

"If they know who killed the man, there isn't a problem."

"They don't," Radnor shrugged his shoulders.

"The cats saw who did it," said Stephanie.

"Yeah."

"Then they could tell you."

"They don't know the names of people," said Radnor.

"They could describe him to you."

"No," said Radnor, frustrated and struggling to be understood. "It doesn't work like that. They don't speak in English – they don't actually *speak* at all. They, well, they sort-of *feel* things, and put their feelings into my mind. I clearly got this picture of the dead man. Tats didn't see his face; it was just a man shot dead. I didn't know it was Paul Carson until they pulled him out of the river."

"Did you get the image of the shooter?" asked Stephanie.

"No," said the old man, but his face lit up as if he'd just thought of something. He looked down at the one remaining cat, a white cat with black patches over her back. "Lady, go and get Tats for me, would you?"

The cat looked up at him for a moment, and then she scooted out of the front door, turning to run towards the forest. It was almost as if he really could talk to cats. Stephanie believed the old man and didn't believe at the same time. Martin had said his world was strange, and now Stephanie was experiencing it. Old Rad went back into the kitchen to put his drink away, and Stephanie averted her eyes because she didn't want to know what his kitchen was like. He came back out again, and ushered them out of the house.

"Tats don't come in much. Only if it's really cold, or thunder. He don't like the thunder. Not that it thunders that much these days, what with climate change and all that. And fireworks. He hates fireworks. Hides under the living room table like a kitten."

Outside, Stephanie looked towards the forest. There was something creepy about it. It was alive in a way that didn't seem ordinary. There was something in there that was looking at her, and wanted her to walk in. It wasn't threatening, though; it was as if it was saying that the answers were in there. She wondered if this area was on a convergence of ley lines. Perhaps she would have to look it up when she next had access to a computer; although there was so little reliable information about where ley lines actually were.

A few minutes later, Lady came back, jumping onto the crumbling garden wall, followed by an old-looking cat with tufts of fur missing from its back. It was hard to tell from that distance, but it looked like it had one eye closed, or possibly missing. Steve Radnor took a couple of steps towards him, and said something in a kind of baby talk. The old cat seemed to stand dead still and stare at him for a moment or two, then turned and ran back into the forest.

"Hardington," said Radnor, in a low voice. "The hunter. It was the hunter; old Tats is sure. There's only one hunter. I mean, there's loads 'a people round here that hunt, but only one to the cats, only one of them with a cabin in the woods. Jack Hardington killed Paul."

"Case solved," said Martin in a low voice.

"Yes," said Stephanie, "except that as far as I recall, evidence given by a cat is not admissible in court."

"I'm sure we can work on that," said Martin, and he turned to Steve Radnor. "Look, Rad, I'll do what I can. But don't keep going on about the cats seeing everything, because they won't believe you. We'll go into the village and have a word. Is it okay if I leave the car here?"

Steve Radnor leaned up close to Martin and spoke in a quiet voice. He seemed to be more desperate than he had inferred before now.

"I don't want to go to prison, Mr Latham. I didn't hurt anybody. I don't even have a gun, not since the war. I don't think I'd do well in prison; I wouldn't last a day. Tell the old man, thanks for helping."

"We haven't done anything yet."

"You will, you got the lady here," said Radnor, tipping a little nod towards Stephanie. "The cats, they know. The lady will sort things out, she will, and they'll keep her safe. They know. Thanks for helping."

There was something about the 'they know' that sent a shiver down Stephanie's spine. They know what? And how would a cat keep her safe?

Old Rad returned to his house and closed the door. The cat on the roof, the one called Lady, and two other cats ran round to the lounge window, which was open, and went into the house. Perhaps they knew he was stressed, and went in to try and provide some comfort. Cats were supposed to sense these things in people, or at least that was what Stephanie had heard.

"I think we should take a little walk into town," suggested Martin, and led Stephanie out of the driveway towards the village. Stephanie followed, feeling a little bewildered. She looked at the forest wall behind and to her left. Something in there was watching her, but she couldn't so much see its eyes as feel them. It felt strange, but it didn't frighten her. Perhaps it should have.

The village was a slight widening of the road, a pub, a post office and a few houses, well spread out. There was also a police station on Steve Radnor's side of the village – one of the first buildings that Stephanie and Martin came across. It was a tiny place, a small room added to the side of the post office. As they approached, Martin stopped.

"Are you okay?" he asked. Stephanie nodded, although she didn't really know how to answer truthfully. Martin looked at her for a moment as if he was trying to work something out, then he knocked on the door of the police mini-station. A young officer answered. He was skinny and fresh-faced with short cropped light brown hair. He wore a spotless uniform (Stephanie guessed that he had not personally been involved in fishing the dead body out of the river) and a peaked hat that looked as if it was a tiny bit too big for his head.

"Sir?" he said.

"I'm Lord Martin Latham. I think you might have been expecting a call from me?"

"Lord…" started the young man, and then he remembered. "Oh, right, hello, er, good afternoon, m'lord…"

"No," said Martin, holding back a laugh. "Please call me Martin, or if that feels uncomfortable, Mr Latham will be fine. We're here with permission from your superintendent, to get an update on the murder case."

"Oh, yes, oh, come in," the young man stuttered, ushering them into the station room, which was a small office with a desk, some chairs, a couple of notice boards and the essential tea-making equipment. There was also a door to the back room, which might have included a toilet. The young man sat them down on the 'guest' side of the table, and searched through his notes.

"Superintendent?" Stephanie whispered to Martin.

"This morning, John Borland said he would arrange for us to have some credibility with the local officer. That must have meant the superintendent, because John has done him some favours from time to time."

"Is there something you haven't told me?" Stephanie asked, still whispering.

"Loads of stuff," Martin whispered back.

"Here," said the young officer, holding up his file. "I thought they might have taken it."

"They?" asked Martin.

"The people from Dennington – they came this morning to take over the investigation. I'm only a CSO, see, and this is a big thing. I mean, this kind of thing doesn't happen round here."

"You're Tom Drake, aren't you?"

"Yes sir. We don't have a proper police officer, here, just a community support officer. I took on the job because I wanted to see if I could go into training for a proper job."

Stephanie was surprised at how people opened up to Martin. He had a real talent. Or possibly, he hypnotised people, she thought. If someone can talk to cats, anything is possible.

"I think a lot of CSO's think that they *are* real police officers, Tom," said Martin. "Don't put your current post down. There's nothing *only* about being a CSO. How long have you been here? In the village, I mean."

"Two years, sir, from October coming."

"So you know old Steve Radnor."

"Yes sir," Tom Drake's voice became a little guarded.

"You probably know he's not a likely suspect."

"Well, actually, they think he could be the one that did it, sir. The investigating officers, sir."

"Not the hunter, Jack Hardington?"

"No sir, we checked him out first. I mean *they* did, the investigators. He had a receipt for his bullet cartridges, and they checked out okay. His hunting rifle didn't kill Paul Carson. It was a different gun."

"He wasn't shot with a rifle?"

"No, sir, he was. I mean, it wasn't Mr Hardington's rifle that killed Paul, sir, it was a different rifle."

"So Mr Hardington only owns one rifle."

"Yes, sir. And he showed us the receipts for his cartridges as soon as we asked him. They were in his wallet, and he showed us straight away. He's a gentleman, sir, lives in Dennington and has a little hut in the forest, a sort-of hunting lodge. That's why we, I mean they, checked him out straight away. He's not the killer, sir; Steve Radnor is."

"He had all the receipts and evidence in his wallet ready to show you just in case anyone was killed and he needed evidence to save himself?" said Stephanie.

"Yes ma'am. Miss. He's an organised gentleman."

"So it wasn't Hardington's gun," said Martin. "But Steve Radnor doesn't have a gun."

"They reckon he threw it in the river. But we know he knows how to use one. He was in the war, the desert war in the Gulf."

"In the last millennium," said Martin.

"What? I mean, I beg your pardon?"

"He was in the first Gulf War in 1990."

"Yes, sir, and he came back a bit, you know, different. It affected him."

"And he has no gun, neither has he used a gun since," said Martin.

"Until today," said the young officer.

"Hunters have more than one gun, surely," said Stephanie.

"He showed them his hunting lodge in the forest. It was clean. It wasn't him, sir, miss."

"Thank you for your time," said Martin, apparently indicating that there was no more to be done here.

"Anything I can do, sir," said the officer, looking a little relieved that his grilling appeared to be over. Then he looked over to Stephanie (up to then his attention had been on Martin).

"Are you staying in the village, miss?"

"I don't know," Stephanie replied.

"If you are, I could perhaps take you for something to eat. I could drive us to this place in Dennington. It's a nice place, quiet, you know."

"Is that a chat-up line?" Stephanie said with a smile. Tom looked embarrassed.

"Oh, go with him, Stephanie. Have a good time."

"No, thanks, Martin. I want to help to find out who really killed this young man."

"So do I," said Tom. "We could compare notes. I mean, you have to eat. And if you need to stay the night somewhere, I could…"

"I beg your pardon?" said Stephanie with a cheeky smile.

"No, I mean," said Tom, getting more embarrassed, "I could find you somewhere to stay the night."

"We live near Stoke, only an hour or so away," explained Martin. "So it's no trouble to go home for the night. However, as you have been so gracious, I would be happy to treat you to a meal with us at the local pub."

Tom settled back down, Martin's remarkable powers calming him. They made arrangements to meet a short while later at the pub, and turned to walk back towards Steve Radnor's house. Just then they met a tall person in his thirties with a shock of dark hair.

"Good afternoon, Mr Hardington," Tom said.

"Hardington?" said Martin, suddenly turning on the charm and walking towards the big man with his hand-shaking arm outstretched. "The hunter. Pleased to meet you, sir."

A little bewildered, Hardington took his hand.

"Lord Martin Latham," he introduced himself. "And you are from the town, Dennington, aren't you, Mr Hardington? What brings you to this little village?"

"I'm here to see my... a friend. She's had a tragedy, and I wish to offer her some comfort. Excuse me please," he said, and he walked towards one of the larger houses near to where the forest started.

"His friend being the bereaved fiancée, Sally, I imagine," said Stephanie watching him as he walked away.

"Yes," said Tom, still standing at the door of the police office. "He's a gentleman. I said so, didn't I?"

As they watched him walk down the road, a tabby cat crossed his path. The animal hissed at him, and then ran into the nearby bushes. Stephanie watched, and thought to herself; *he's definitely guilty – the cat knows it. But how do we prove it?*

Martin led her back to Steve Radnor's house, and when he was sure they were out of earshot, he quietly said to her, "Just because a cat hissed at him, it doesn't mean he's guilty of anything. Cats hiss at me."

"I expect you're guilty of lots of things," she replied.

Back at Steve Radnor's house they walked in through the unlocked front door. He was already in the entrance hall waiting for them – he must have seen them coming. His demeanour was different. He'd been mulling over the details of what had happened, and how it affected him. He was used to his apparent ability to hear cats, but he knew that the local people would never believe him, and that meant they would conclude that there was only one way he could have known that Paul Carson was dead. He was beginning, Stephanie deduced from the expression on his face, to realise the kind of trouble he was in. There were more than ten cats all around him.

"Hello, Martin," he said. "Anything?"

"Only that they know about your war record."

"What war record? I was a soldier in the Gulf. I came back with an injured leg, no money and a head full of stress from the fighting. I never touched a gun since. I moved into the old family home, but there's never been anyone to care for it with since me mam died. That's all there is. I'm a sad old man living on me own with nothing but cats for company."

"And you reported a murder which you didn't actually see."

"Yeah. Well, what should I do? Wait a couple of days until they finally find the body and then say I didn't know? I don't do lies. You know me, Martin. You know I don't have anything to do with people. It's the cats for me. They aren't as complicated. It's easier to see things from their point of view…"

"Is that how you talk to them?" said Stephanie, still trying to get her head around his unusual ability. "You somehow see things from their point of view?"

"I s'pose. Sometimes I get down on all fours so I can understand their world better. Their world is different from ours. Harsher, but somehow… I don't know… less complicated."

"You were saying," said Stephanie, "about coming home with nothing…"

"I came home just about broke. Me mam was still alive then, but she was ill. I always thought I heard cats before, but while I was here, it was like they singled me out and shared their thoughts with me. The boss, the warden, he found out somehow, and sent Martin here to check me out. He helped me get myself together, showed me how to get me pension, which gave me enough money to keep the house going and keep me living here where there's lots of cats. I'm getting old now, I don't suppose I'll last that much longer. But for as long as I do last, I want it to be here, not in prison. I didn't kill Paul; no reason why I should."

"Is there a reason why Hardington should?" asked Stephanie. "This… Sally, did you say her name was?"

"I dunno. I can work out cats, but I don't think I'm any good at understanding people."

Martin smiled. "I remember our first meeting."

"Well you would, wouldn't you? The cats just about scratched you to bits."

"I'd like to have seen that," said Stephanie.

"Don't say that," said Martin. "At least, don't say it so they can hear you."

Five

At 5 o'clock that afternoon, Tom Drake led Martin and Stephanie to his favourite table in Mr Toad's Rest, the local pub. Stephanie wondered if the village had any connection with the Wind in the Willows. Tom was also paying her lots of special attention, which she rather liked. However, she had mixed feelings about Martin encouraging her to go along with the young police officer. He had even sat them opposite each other and had seated himself on one side like a chaperone (or a tennis umpire).

She looked around her. One or two people were giving young Tom a sideways glance. It appeared the young man who'd been accepted in this community for the past two years was not so welcome now that there had been an actual crime. Stephanie supposed that the locals probably thought that she and Martin were the investigators on the case.

The three of them chatted lightly about things while they ate, and then Martin took the conversation into more serious territory.

"You said you wanted to further your career with the police. Would you be a crime scene investigator?"

"It's a horrible job," Tom replied without specifically answering the question. "You would have to examine dead bodies. Sometimes they're mutilated, or discovered rotting weeks later, stuff like that. It would turn my stomach. Did you know the police provide a counselling service for their officers who have to handle dead bodies?"

"Not your kind of thing, then. What about detective?"

"I'd quite like the sound of that," said Tom, trying to look into his future, as well as trying to impress Stephanie after his admission that he didn't like the thought of handling dead bodies.

"So what would you say is the main thing to look for in a suspect that would tell you he was guilty?"

"A signed confession would help," Tom said, glancing towards Stephanie in an attempt to impress her with his wit. She laughed for him, although she was not sure how convincing she made it sound. In the back of her mind, she was still angry that Jack Hardington was getting away with it.

"Something at the crime scene which pointed you in the right direction?"

"I suppose. Most crimes are obvious. It's not like on the telly, where there's a weave of complicated clues and people with outrageous secrets. I mean, Paul was shot, then he fell into the river which washed away some of the forensics. But we know what kind of bullet hit him. All we have to do is find the gun that shot him, and we'll be able to arrest the old man."

"What about motive?" asked Martin.

"Well, some people think that motive is the most important thing."

"Old Steve Radnor doesn't have a motive," said Stephanie.

"He might have," Tom replied thoughtfully. He was not taking her side, but he was being careful how he disagreed with her. Perhaps she could use the fact that he liked her to work on this.

"Here's a question," said Martin. "Imagine it's yesterday. Nobody's dead. It's life as usual in the village. What's your opinion of Old Rad, Steve Radnor?"

Tom didn't have to think for long. "He's an old soldier, come back to his home village to live out the rest of his days. He's gone a bit funny in the head, possibly because of his experiences in the army. Post-Traumatic Stress Disorder, or whatever they call it. He keeps pretty much to himself, except for loads of cats – most of them wild, or feral, even – that come to him to get fed. He started thinking he can talk to them. No, I mean he started thinking that *they* can talk to *him*."

"But he's harmless enough," suggested Martin. "Yesterday, I mean, would you say he was harmless?"

"Not if he killed that man."

"Before today, I mean. Would you have said he was harmless?"

"Yes, I suppose so."

"What has changed since yesterday? What has he done or said to you that makes you think he's no longer harmless?"

"He killed an innocent man."

"No, that's not what I asked. His guilt in this case is not proven – it's not even reasonable. He has no motive and he's 'harmless'; he's basically no different from yesterday."

"He knew that Paul was dead before anybody else."

"That's not big evidence," said Stephanie.

"The investigators, they'll find the evidence. Look, I'm sorry, I realise that Mr Radnor is a friend of yours…"

"I only met him today," said Stephanie with a smile.

"But you're convinced of his innocence."

"That doesn't matter," said Martin, interrupting before Stephanie could answer. "What matters is that I am not convinced of his guilt. You can't decide someone is guilty and then look for proof."

"Actually, you can. I know the law says 'innocent until proven guilty', but most times the investigators work out who is guilty first, then they put the pieces together to prove it afterwards."

"It's basic science," interrupted Stephanie, who, for some reason, wanted to argue with Martin. He just did something to her that way. "You start with observations, followed by a hypothesis. Then you look for evidence to support your case."

"Or to deny it," said Martin. "You said that Jack Hardington's gun didn't match the bullet that killed the victim. He had a receipt for the cartridges."

"Yes."

"Where did he buy the cartridges for his gun?"

"There's a gun shop in Dennington, Marshall's. All of the people round here use it."

"Lots of people round here own guns?" asked Stephanie.

"It's a farming community," answered Tom. "They hunt, some of them go clay pigeon shooting and most of them have a rabbit problem."

Stephanie remembered from Kent that people often shot rabbits that were eating their crops. She never liked it as a child, but her father had explained extensively about them being pests to farmers. In defiance, she had once asked for a rabbit for her birthday, but she didn't get one. This was before she had saved the big cat from being shot at by Byron.

"And we are looking at the only person who doesn't have a gun as the murderer?" she said.

"He's a trained soldier," said Tom. "He's the only person in the village who would ever have had the experience of killing someone."

"And the owner of the gun shop in Dennington would know this, perhaps?" said Martin. "He would be able to provide us with the evidence we need to nail Radnor."

"Martin!" said Stephanie, but he gave her a smile and she worked out what he was saying. He was siding with Tom, while also providing the means of proving Radnor's innocence. The community support officer who wanted to be a 'real' policeman may have taken a liking to Stephanie, but it was Martin who was feeding his professional ego.

"It's after six o'clock," said Stephanie. "They aren't going to be open, surely?"

"Perhaps we could get in touch with the owner. Tom, can you get in touch with him? It is important police business. Not to mention the feather in your cap if you can provide the investigating team with the information they need to make an arrest."

"I can find out if I can contact him, yes," said Tom with a little uncertainty. He had been turned against Stephanie and been persuaded to side with Martin and he was feeling a little unsure about it. But Martin's strange persuasive manner had won him over and the idea that he could impress the local detectives did appeal to him. Stephanie wondered if Martin had used his persuasive mojo on her; perhaps he had some power like the werewolves of Birmingham or the man that could hear cats.

"I'll come with you if you like," suggested Martin. He put his hand palm down out of Tom's sight to suggest to Stephanie that it should be just the two of them and that she shouldn't come along as well.

"Fine," said Tom. "Stephanie?"

"I think I'll stay here," said Stephanie. As much as she wanted to defy Martin just for the sake of it, she didn't want to trek into Dennington to meet the gunsmith. She wanted to explore the woods and its cat population instead. "I hope you find what you are looking for." She looked at Tom, but was really talking to Martin.

Martin paid the bill and they left, and Stephanie saw them head for Tom's little office. Of course, they may not have to go to Dennington – they might do it all by computer and telephone.

She walked slowly through the village past the very small number of houses that were spaced out and separated by foliage and dry-stone walls. She walked towards the woods.

As she was leaving the village, she saw a young woman standing in the front garden of a large house near the edge of the forest. Was this the house that Hardington was headed for a few hours earlier? She was a good-looking young woman around Stephanie's age. She looked sad, almost distressed. Perhaps this was the fiancée of the murdered man. She looked mournfully in the direction of the forest. Stephanie would have to walk past her to go to the woods, but she didn't really want to. She might speak to her, but what can you say to someone who has suddenly lost the man she loves?

She started walking a little slower, but stopped in front of the young lady. Obviously, Jack Hardington was no longer here.

"Hello," Stephanie said timidly, not having prepared what to say next. The dark-haired young woman looked across at her and nodded her head slightly to acknowledge she was there. Her eyes were dark with grief.

"I'm Stephanie. I'm here to… Is there anything I can do for you?"

"I'm okay."

"I'm just going for a walk in the woods. I'm, we're here to investigate…"

"I thought you might be," the woman, Sally, interrupted. "I saw you with Tom. But you aren't police."

"We're here on behalf of Steve Radnor."

"I don't think the old man did it," said Sally. Her voice was flat and she showed no emotion, as if she had used up everything she had for the day.

"Any idea who did?"

"No."

"Jack Hardington was with you earlier. I mean, he visited you just now."

"Yes. He's been very gracious. When I got engaged to Paul, I knew he wasn't happy about it. But he was polite, and he congratulated us. Now he's said he'll be around for me. I told him it was a bit soon. I think he was unhappy, but he was a gentleman."

"You don't think..." Stephanie started, but she stopped immediately. It wasn't right for her to put that idea into the head of this young woman who had suffered in this way. "I'm going for a walk. Would you like to join me?"

"No, I don't think so. Thanks for asking. I hope you find..." and her voice trailed off.

"Yeah," said Stephanie. "Me, too."

Stephanie walked on, feeling that she had just been of no use whatsoever. The houses stopped and green fields replaced them. Only a few steps further, Stephanie heard the rushing of the river. She walked over rough and rocky ground to the edge of the water. The babbling of the river was peaceful and calming, especially in the cooler, still air of the early evening. The river wasn't that deep, and when she got to the water's edge, she could see the riverbed through clear, clean water that flowed away from the woods. The banks were high because it was summer, and the waters of winter and spring had well subsided. She walked along the river's edge until the ground became more difficult, and she was able to follow a path into the forest itself. The trees were tall and the leaves made it seem like dark was coming, although at this time in the evening there was still an hour or two of daylight left.

Through the woods, in the distance, or at least as much distance as she could see through the foliage, there was a cabin. She remembered that Tom had said Jack Hardington had a cabin here. This might be it. She wondered why a man like Hardington would have a cabin in the woods. He didn't live in the village, so perhaps this was his base when he hunted in the area. And what did he hunt that needed a cabin? It wasn't just rabbits; that was certain. Perhaps it was foxes. She thought she would go and have a closer look at it. Steve Radnor had said something earlier about a cat's point of view. How would they have seen this little hut in the forest?

The land around the 'hunting lodge' had been cleared. There was a track behind the small hut that led away, possibly towards the village. It looked, from where Stephanie was at the opposite side of the building, wide enough for a vehicle. She didn't see that there was a vehicle parked behind the bushy growth at the back of the hut. She was more interested in the building itself.

The word 'cabin' made far too grand a description for what this was. It was more the shape and size of those changing rooms you see on photographs of beach fronts – she'd never actually seen one in the flesh – a single-room box, not much bigger than the hide that she had sat in back in Kent when she was a child, looking for the mysterious big cat. It was raised on logs. There were three crooked wooden steps leading up to a door in front of her, which was closed and probably locked. It was unlikely that Hardington kept a gun there, and even more unlikely that she would be able to break in to the place. But there was something she wanted to do before she made her way back to the village. She wanted to look at the place from the point of view of a cat.

She got down onto the ground. It was a little damp, and the leaves were slippery and smelly, in spite of the dry weather of the past few weeks, but she wanted to take a look under the hut. No doubt, in the rain, various animals might shelter under there – there was enough space for something as big as a fox, and the feral cats, if they weren't able to get into Old Rad's house, might find this a fair place to hide from the weather. As she looked into the gloom, she thought she saw something that would not mean much to a cat – a metal box, long and dark military green in colour, big enough to hide a spare gun in. Perhaps the hunter did have more than one gun after all.

The sudden sound of her phone ringing made her jump. She fumbled in her pocket to answer, still almost flat on the ground. By the time she pulled the phone out of her pocket, she was covered in mud and leaf-slime and sitting upright.

"Martin?" she said.

"Stephanie," Martin said, "we've spoken to the owner of the gun shop and we have found out that our Mr Hardington has more than one gun, and that he has, in the past, bought at least two different types of cartridge. Tom is getting in touch with the investigators right now to sort it out."

Stephanie looked up at the little log cabin. The door opened, and Jack Hardington stepped out onto the top step and stood, looking at her. She froze, as if she felt all the blood in her body turn to ice. He was holding a shotgun, and it was pointed at her. She let the phone drop to the ground. She should have shouted down it, so they knew who it was who killed her, but she didn't have the presence of mind to think of anything so clever. She was about to be shot and she had no strength to do anything about it.

"It looks like our mysterious killer has another victim," said the hunter, quite calmly, as his finger tightened on the trigger.

Suddenly, something leapt from the bushy growth around some of the trees nearby. It looked like a big black panther, although Stephanie was far too confused to be sure. It hit Jack Hardington hard in the side, sending him flying down from the top step of his little hut. There was a sickening crunch as his head hit an uneven root sticking out from the ground at the foot of the steps. His shotgun fell a metre or so from his body and lay still.

Stephanie saw the big, black cat. It looked huge at first, but it was smaller when she saw it leap against the tall, well-built hunter. It was bigger than a house cat, possibly the size of a lynx or a puma. As Hardington fell, it turned to look at her, and then she didn't see it any more. All she saw was the body of Jack Hardington lying still on the ground, his lifeless eyes staring in her direction, blood pooling out of an ugly wound in his head. Part of the jagged tree stump he had fallen against was embedded in his skull. But there was no big cat. It might never have been there in the first place.

She began to come back to her senses, and strained to move a little. She felt dizzy, nauseous, and struggled to take her eyes from the gruesome sight. Had she somehow caused this to happen? Or was something outside her own abilities helping her somehow? She scrabbled around for the phone. She found it, and brought it up to her ears.

"Stephanie? Stephanie, what's happening? Are you there?"

She said something into the phone, but she struggled to make coherent words. There was a dead man in front of her, and the sight of him was addling her brain. However, she couldn't look away from it.

"Hardington's hut," she managed to blurt out eventually.

"You're in the forest?" said Martin, sounding horrified. "Get out, fast. Hardington could be there."

"He's dead," she told him, her speech getting back under her control.

"We're coming there. We'll be there in a few minutes. Don't hang up."

She held the phone to her ear, and heard Martin saying things to her, although her dazed mind didn't fully understand his words. She heard the engine of a vehicle start up through her phone, as if he had managed to get to his car and race to her aid. He was too late. She felt numb in her head even as the feeling was starting to come back into her body. She thought she might try standing up. Her throat was filled with the taste of vomit and her insides were boiling hot. She sat up properly, and tried to get herself to breathe deeply. She realised that she was still staring into Hardington's dead eyes. She wanted to turn away from the body, but she was afraid that if she did it would somehow come back to life again and attack her.

Tom knew where the cabin was, so they didn't have to search, but they'd gone to Dennington to find the owner of the gun shop, so they had to drive all the way back from the town. It was only a few miles, but along country roads it was still nearly twenty minutes before they got there. To Stephanie, it felt like hours. Tom grabbed a picnic blanket from the back of his car and wrapped it around her. He helped her up, but Martin became suddenly very protective and took over from him, almost pushing the poor young officer out of the way to take control of the situation.

A few moments later, two more police cars turned up. Martin became quite angry at the policemen when they tried to question Stephanie. He gave his details to them and told them he was going to take her home immediately and they could contact her when she recovered. Tom drove them back to Martin's car and she remembered vaguely telling him something about the box under Hardington's cabin. Then Martin drove her home, talking to her all the way. He didn't say anything in particular, he just talked. She heard him, and was comforted, but didn't remember

Six

Clifton Chase came to visit Stephanie over the next few days. After a day or two and a couple of visits from Clifton, Stephanie had begun to return to her habit of actually sleeping all night. Her dreams of Jack Hardington impaled on the tree stump faded to a vague horror. The vision of those cat's eyes looking at her, however, didn't go away so easily.

She and Clif talked a lot, and Stephanie knew that he was visiting because of her experience in the woods. Perhaps Martin had asked him to visit, or maybe John Borland had sent him to find out what 'really' happened. But he didn't ask searching questions, he was just there for her. They sat and chatted in her office at first, but over the next few days she invited him into her lounge.

She talked a lot, and Clif had listened to her a lot. Martin occasionally came in to join them both for a cup of coffee. Stephanie had talked about what happened, of how Jack Hardington had pointed the gun at her, how he must have slipped on a step that might have been damp or slimy from wet leaves (in spite of the dry summer they were having), and she tried to describe her fears. Martin had stayed with her for the police interviews, and had informed her that the authorities had not needed her to be present at any inquest, as the police were happy that they had all the information they needed. She wondered if John Borland's influence might have been in action here, and she appreciated that she was being looked after by what might be some very important people.

Once or twice she had nightmares about what happened, and it was Clif rather than Martin who was the most emotional support for her. After talking out the events of the past couple of days, she started talking about other things, about her family in Kent, even a little about why she got into research. Then Clif felt could do more than just listen.

anything he said. She couldn't get the image of the dead man from her mind.

When they got back to his manor house, he walked with her to her apartment, and she nodded when he asked if she would be alright. She didn't undress for bed, but lay down on the bed and slept straight away, fully clothed. She woke up in the middle of the night, however, and she found the smell of the rotting forest leaves on her shoes and clothes made her feel ill. She threw them off, washed and changed into a nightdress, but she couldn't get back to sleep again.

As the sky began to grow light, she got up and made herself some breakfast. A few hours later, Martin and one of the police officers from last night came to visit.

Martin introduced the officer and told her, "It looks like you discovered Jack Hardington's secret, Stephanie, and he would have killed you if he'd not slipped on his step and fallen. I'm afraid he hit his head and died."

"We want to know if you saw what happened," the police officer said.

"I saw him open his door, and point the gun at me," she said. "I was looking under his cabin and saw where he stashed hi' other gun – the one he used to kill Paul Carson. I'm not sure wh' happened next."

"We know he killed Mr Carson," said the officer.

"So Old... Mr Radnor isn't a suspect anymore," she sa'

"No," confirmed Martin, "and the people in the village contrite for suspecting him, and saying they knew Hardington all along. I don't think Old Rad will have t' own drinks for a while."

"Jack Hardington wanted the girl, didn't he?" said
"So he killed Carson after they got engaged."

"Something like that," said the officer.

"What about the cat?" asked Stephanie.

"What cat?" said Martin.

"Sorry," said Stephanie, "I'm tired. I didn't ç' night. I must have dreamed something."

And she didn't mention the cat again.

At least, not yet.

Six

Clifton Chase came to visit Stephanie over the next few days. After a day or two and a couple of visits from Clifton, Stephanie had begun to return to her habit of actually sleeping all night. Her dreams of Jack Hardington impaled on the tree stump faded to a vague horror. The vision of those cat's eyes looking at her, however, didn't go away so easily.

She and Clif talked a lot, and Stephanie knew that he was visiting because of her experience in the woods. Perhaps Martin had asked him to visit, or maybe John Borland had sent him to find out what 'really' happened. But he didn't ask searching questions, he was just there for her. They sat and chatted in her office at first, but over the next few days she invited him into her lounge.

She talked a lot, and Clif had listened to her a lot. Martin occasionally came in to join them both for a cup of coffee. Stephanie had talked about what happened, of how Jack Hardington had pointed the gun at her, how he must have slipped on a step that might have been damp or slimy from wet leaves (in spite of the dry summer they were having), and she tried to describe her fears. Martin had stayed with her for the police interviews, and had informed her that the authorities had not needed her to be present at any inquest, as the police were happy that they had all the information they needed. She wondered if John Borland's influence might have been in action here, and she appreciated that she was being looked after by what might be some very important people.

Once or twice she had nightmares about what happened, and it was Clif rather than Martin who was the most emotional support for her. After talking out the events of the past couple of days, she started talking about other things, about her family in Kent, even a little about why she got into research. Then Clif felt he could do more than just listen.

anything he said. She couldn't get the image of the dead man from her mind.

When they got back to his manor house, he walked with her to her apartment, and she nodded when he asked if she would be alright. She didn't undress for bed, but lay down on the bed and slept straight away, fully clothed. She woke up in the middle of the night, however, and she found the smell of the rotting forest leaves on her shoes and clothes made her feel ill. She threw them off, washed and changed into a nightdress, but she couldn't get back to sleep again.

As the sky began to grow light, she got up and made herself some breakfast. A few hours later, Martin and one of the police officers from last night came to visit.

Martin introduced the officer and told her, "It looks like you discovered Jack Hardington's secret, Stephanie, and he would have killed you if he'd not slipped on his step and fallen. I'm afraid he hit his head and died."

"We want to know if you saw what happened," the police officer said.

"I saw him open his door, and point the gun at me," she said. "I was looking under his cabin and saw where he stashed his other gun – the one he used to kill Paul Carson. I'm not sure what happened next."

"We know he killed Mr Carson," said the officer.

"So Old... Mr Radnor isn't a suspect anymore," she said.

"No," confirmed Martin, "and the people in the village are all contrite for suspecting him, and saying they knew it was Hardington all along. I don't think Old Rad will have to buy his own drinks for a while."

"Jack Hardington wanted the girl, didn't he?" said Stephanie. "So he killed Carson after they got engaged."

"Something like that," said the officer.

"What about the cat?" asked Stephanie.

"What cat?" said Martin.

"Sorry," said Stephanie, "I'm tired. I didn't get much sleep last night. I must have dreamed something."

And she didn't mention the cat again.

At least, not yet.

"Clifton Chase," she said to him, mulling over his name late one night. He'd been staying overnight in a local pub rather than in Martin's 'one bedroom for every day of the week'. He never visited her without calling first. They talked into the night, and he shared Martin's habit of not bothering to turn the lights on. "You dress like a secret agent, and you have a name like a secret agent."

"It does sound a bit cloak-and-dagger, doesn't it?" he said with a smile. She was curled up on her sofa nursing a cup of hot chocolate, which Martin had made, feet tucked into her legs, like she used to when she was a teenager at home. "Martin tells me you know about his girlfriends."

"I know that he has visitors for the night," said Stephanie, "and he says that they know about each other, and they aren't jealous. Every man's dream, I should imagine."

"I think his young ladies think he is every *woman's* dream," said Clif with a grin.

"He must be good."

Clifton laughed. "The thing is, if you were one of those ladies, you wouldn't have ever met Steven Radnor. As far as I know, Martin doesn't discuss his Trust projects, or anything else he does, with most people. And you and I might not have met, so that would have been my loss."

Stephanie felt she might be blushing. What was he saying?

"So what do you do for the Angel Trust?" she asked, trying to keep control of the conversation. "Are you full-time with them, or do you do it as a casual favour like Martin?"

"I am full-time. In fact, sometimes it feels like I am working for them 25 hours a day, 8 days a week. But I love it. Before that I was a private investigator, and I stumbled across something spicy a few years ago that could have got me into a lot of trouble. John Borland sent someone to help me out. I was curious about what he was about, so we had a long talk about the Angel Trust and I joined up. Or he recruited me, or something. Much later, we tracked down Martin when we found he had a family connection to the founding of the Angel Trust. He says he doesn't really know much about that, but I think he's lying."

"He's keeping secrets from you," Stephanie said. "Anyway, what about this something spicy you stumbled on, back before you knew about the Trust? Can you tell me about that, or is that going to be a 'men in black' secret, too?"

Clif laughed. Over the past couple of days, he had been patient with her, standing by her when she cried, being quiet with her when she didn't want to say anything. Now he was relaxed, and it was her turn to listen to him.

"No, I think I would be allowed to tell you – although, I should swear you to secrecy."

Was he being serious?

"Ladies shouldn't swear," she responded. She liked him smiling and chatty like this.

He laughed, and then explained, "Someone on a housing estate in Bedfordshire got bored and started messing with things he shouldn't," said Clif. "He started breeding creatures that weren't, you know, normal. Monsters."

"Monsters? Seriously?"

"That's what people were saying. I didn't really believe in all that stuff, but people seemed serious when they talked about it, and they were scared. I wasn't involved with the Trust at the time, but I was an investigator, so naturally I was curious. I crept onto this estate to investigate; there were some garages out on the edges, near the farmland. The man who was in charge of these *experiments* spotted me, and set his dogs on me. But these were nasty beasts, not like ordinary dogs. It was almost like they had successfully cross-bred dogs with something else and these things were the result of their experiments. I was on the run from big, nasty, fast beasts with bony spikes coming out of their flesh. They were big and vicious, and they weren't going to stop until I was dead. Then this little bloke, like a dwarf, pulled up in his Bentley and got me to leap in, while he went out to scare off the dogs. I just had my head down, scared out of my life, and he dealt with the creatures. I didn't see what happened, what he did, but a little while later, they were gone, I was recruited to the Angel Trust and nobody heard about the 'monster experiment' again."

"You're teasing me."

"Well..." said Clif with a smile that revealed nothing. "I promise you that my story includes the truth."

"Includes," said Stephanie, "along with a lot of not-quite-truths, I imagine. I mean, how can a dwarf scare off dogs that would have killed you? Unless he was someone from The Lord of the Rings? Did he have a big axe?"

"He was a little man in a suit."

"Really?" said Stephanie, and, somehow, Clif didn't look like he was lying.

"Yes, I've had dealings with him since. He's a lawyer for the Niz Manor Estate."

"Niz Manor?" said Stephanie.

"Martin's told you about Nieziemski Manor, surely."

"Not exactly. There's a 'Niz manor' file on my computer, but it's password protected."

"Niz is my word. Martin nicked it. The real name is Nieziemski. Martin contacted them last year, shortly after the new guy took over there."

"And what do they do?"

"It's complicated – I've seen the place from a distance, but I haven't had the chance to get close to it yet. Perhaps we should ask Martin to get you an introduction."

"And what did you do when you worked with this monster-dog-fighting lawyer?"

"When I said 'had dealings with him', I mean when some of the things I've investigated for the Angel Trust went a bit weird, he was brought in to sort them out. I haven't really worked directly with him at all."

"A bit weird?"

"There was a factory where someone they couldn't identify kept fixing things."

"Fixing?"

"When something went wrong, the manager called in a friend. The workers in the factory described him as looking like a little elf or a goblin. Someone who worked there called us in and I tried to talk to the owner, but he wasn't interested. He said if he told us the truth, they'd 'take him away'. Basically, he seemed to be using an illegal worker and paying him nearly nothing to fix complex problems. When I reported back to my boss, the dwarf guy came in and visited the factory, then said everything was fine. It was just a goblin who enjoyed that kind of work."

"A goblin?"

"I thought that was a figure of speech at first, but it turns out there are real goblins."

"Of course there are," said Stephanie. She was beginning to feel that it wouldn't be long before either Martin or Clif introduced her to a unicorn.

"Then there was a rich bloke who owned a small island in the Mediterranean. Callister Andino. He made his money in energy so, like lots of people in energy, he was looking for new resources. There was an odd meeting in London about the energy crisis, and the Trust sent me to report on it because they thought some new energy ideas might have had links with the supernatural. Andino was there, and so were other people from around the world."

"Supernatural energy?" said Stephanie, and she must have sounded as if she didn't really believe what he was saying.

"Do you want to hear my story or not?"

"Sorry. Carry on."

"That was where I first saw the president of Mbalaya. There was a big discussion on how dangerous it was to experiment with untried new forms of energy, but he was in charge of a poor country, and European countries had too many laws and restrictions, so he felt it was a chance for Mbalaya to take the lead in future energy supplies. I've been trying to follow the president's progress since then. He seems to have made friends with some creatures who want to use his resources to develop new energy sources."

"Creatures? More monsters?"

"They seem to be intelligent beings, not like animals. He calls them robed monks."

"Some kind of religious order?"

"Whoever they are, they try to persuade people like the president of Mbalaya and rich energy tycoons like Callister Andino to play with dangerous power sources."

"Nuclear power is dangerous," she pointed out. "Anything that produces a huge amount of energy is going to be, by its nature."

He shrugged his shoulders, obviously deciding that he'd said enough for now. "So what really happened with you and Hardington?"

"There was a big cat," said Stephanie. It was the first time she'd told anybody. "It came out of nowhere, barged into Hardington and made him fall over. He hit his head and died."

"Cat?"

"Not a house cat. A big, puma-sized..."

"Like the one from when you were a kid."

"It's the truth!" she protested.

"I believe you," he replied.

"No, really. But after Hardington fell, he – the cat – wasn't there anymore. It's as if it wasn't really there in the first place."

"I believe you."

"And..."

"I... believe... you."

"Really?" said Stephanie, who had been afraid he would think she'd been seeing things.

"I've seen stranger things," said Clif.

"Like men dressed as monks persuading people to use untested supernatural power," grinned Stephanie.

They sat in the quiet for a while as the sky darkened outside and the room became dark and shadowy. Martin hadn't disturbed them while they had their chats together. Her inquiries had revealed that the Angel Trust did indeed investigate the supernatural, so what Clif had said about people who wanted to breed monsters was not completely outrageous. What was outrageous, however, was the idea that they might have succeeded. Stephanie remembered that, not too many days ago, Martin had said, 'Welcome to my world'. She now wondered what he really meant, and wondered if she really wanted to be a part of it after all.

"Will you go to Africa, now that they've kicked out all of the diplomats?" asked Stephanie after a while.

"I don't know. I'll probably work in London on the Mbalaya crisis. As well as the diplomats, they've also kicked out missionaries who were running food banks for their poor, and all official charity workers, businessmen, even the archaeologist who was working there. People who were a little slow to move were treated to a display of military force. Our country believed at first it was a big move by fundamentalist Islamic forces, but our political friendship with some of our Muslim neighbours revealed that they'd been kicked out, too. It's all to do with these robed monks."

"And the Angel Trust's part in this?"

"The French archaeologist, Georges Bouvon, had some interesting research there which we thought we might take a look at. Unfortunately, he has now retired to his home in France, so we never got a look at it."

"So the Trust is no longer interested in this political crisis?"

"Actually, we are. Apart from Professor Bouvon's research, the country of Mbalaya houses the largest and most powerful convergence of ley lines in the world, or at least the largest outside of Britain. We think that these robed creatures might be messing with Mbalayan politics because they want access to this supernatural resource."

Stephanie sat up in her seat. The Angel Trust was interested in the supernatural, and coincidentally (was it coincidentally?) Stephanie had been looking into ley lines, too.

"We think something is going to happen soon, and when it does, I might have to fly out to Mbalaya and try to get involved. My bags are already packed and ready at home."

"Won't that be dangerous, if they have already kicked out all westerners?"

"I don't know if you have worked it out, yet, Stephanie dear, but there is a certain amount of danger attached to working for the Trust."

"It's a good thing I only work for Martin, then," said Stephanie, and Clif gave her a long, hard look, but didn't reply. It was getting late, and it was time for him to leave. He was intending to drive back to London that night. She walked him to his car, and they met Martin, who was taking a walk in the dark of the evening.

"I think you should take Stephanie to visit that manor house in Buckinghamshire," said Clif to Martin after they had exchanged polite greetings.

"Have you…?" Martin started to ask.

"No, it's not my place. But I think I might be off to Mbalaya soon, and I think Stephanie's had an experience that needs to be explained."

"Experience?" asked Martin.

"I haven't told Martin yet," said Stephanie.

"But he must have guessed, which is why he asked me to keep an eye on you," said Clif.

"Something happened at Barnhampton? In the woods?" asked Martin.

"I thought I saw a big cat," she said.

"Like when you were a child?"

"Yes. Except this one was black. And it killed Jack Hardington."

"Ah," said Martin, as if putting pieces of a puzzle together.

"Niz Manor," said Clif, getting into his car.

"I don't think they like me there at the moment," said Martin. "Not after the embassy thing."

"You weren't involved at the embassy?" said Clif.

"Well, no, but..."

"Then why wouldn't they like you? Anyway, I thought you hid out there once." And he drove away.

"Hid?" said Stephanie, watching Clif's car until it was out of sight. "Who were you hiding from?"

"I'll get in touch with them tomorrow," Martin said, ignoring her question. "I suppose it's reasonable for you to know something about *them*."

"Nieziemski Manor?" asked Stephanie. "Like the file on your computer?"

"Yes, the file is all about them. I keep it encrypted because if anyone read that file and thought I believed it they'd have me locked up."

Stephanie slept through the night this time, but when she woke up, quite early the following morning, her head was buzzing with what Clif had told her. In fact, it was buzzing even more with what he'd *not* told her. She couldn't remember any details, but she thought she'd dreamed of the heroic Martin Latham fighting off a couple of demon-dogs to save someone – Martin Latham, not a dwarf in a suit.

She got up, and the memory of the dreams faded over her morning coffee. All except for one image, which would not leave her mind – that of a puma-sized cat, looking directly at her. But this time it was as if it was asking for her help.

Once she got to her office, she looked up some of the names Clif had told her about on the Internet.

Callister Andino was a rich and flamboyant Greek businessman who was beginning to lose his fortune. He had owned a tiny island off the coast of Greece. However, some kind of strange storm had destroyed it only a few weeks ago. Nobody had been hurt in the incident, but details of what had actually happened were vague. The island simply wasn't there anymore.

Georges Ernest Bouvon, the renowned professor of archaeology, lived in France. The word 'renowned' might have been a little out of date, though, because the archaeologist had recently claimed to have evidence that aliens may have visited the planet. In following up her investigations, she found a number of websites that spoke of aliens visiting the Earth in its dim and distant past, but none written by the professor. There were theories linking U.F.O.'s to dark energy, but a lot of them stretched the imagination beyond most science fiction stories. Ley lines got a mention, too, with theories that the network of mystical lines across the planet was a source of 'dark energy', which may have provided the means of transport for aliens who lived too far away to get to Earth by conventional means? Stephanie was beginning to see Professor Bouvon as a bit of a nutcase, the kind of person who believed in supernatural powers and intelligent life from outer space affecting the nature of universal matter. The only thing wrong with Stephanie's perception, other than that she now believed in someone who could talk to cats and a secret organisation that was in with world leaders and police inspectors and investigated the supernatural, was that the professor had been well respected by his peers, and moved in social circles that represented good common sense and sound practical philosophies. Until now.

That, of course, was where the best research would be done. She needed to find someone who was a respectable, sensible scientist of good repute who had explored these theories of aliens and earth energy. She spoke to Martin about her thoughts.

"It seems that this Georges Bouvon is just the man you want," he said.

"What I really wanted was someone sensible," she said.

"That's the point," Martin argued. "This man has the perfect pedigree. He has won all the top awards in his profession, he's a respected archaeologist, he's lectured at most of the top universities in Europe, and then, suddenly, a couple of years ago, he comes up with this ridiculous idea – aliens might have visited the Earth in the past few thousand years. Lots of people no longer take him seriously, but he's got such a good reputation that some people still listen to him. He is the respectable face of Ufology."

"I swore I would never get into U.F.O. studies. They are a minefield of wasted time."

"But now you are being paid by me, so it's not wasting your time."

"No, it's wasting *your* money."

"You said that Clif told you that the Angel Trust was interested in contacting Professor Bouvon. If that's the case, it almost certainly won't be a waste of time. How do you fancy an all-expenses-paid trip to France?"

"I would be happy to e-mail him," said Stephanie, "or I could give him a call on the telephone."

"I'm sure his office would be on e-mail, but he is in his sixties, recently retired after being thrown out of Mbalaya. He might not even visit his office anymore. And if he is a traditional archaeologist, he would be into old things, not these new-fangled e-mails. Take the trip."

"Old things? That is about the worst possible argument you've ever given me."

"Ever?" he answered with a laugh. "We have only known each other for a couple of weeks."

"I can't wait for the next few arguments, then," she said with a resigned laugh. "Very well, France it is."

"But first, I promised Clif I would get you to pay a visit to Nieziemski Manor. They might be able to help you with your cat problem."

"I don't have a cat problem."

"No, of course not. But they might be able to explain the black cat you say came to your aid in Barnhampton. And they will certainly be able to show you something of the world that the Angel Trust moves in. And that *I* move in, when I get the chance."

Martin suggested that she should pack some luggage to spend a night or two away. The helicopter company that would take her to France was in Amersham, not far from Nieziemski Manor, so she could fly on from there. In fact, he let her drive to Buckinghamshire in the company Skoda and he would make his own way home after he left her there. She almost asked him to stay with her, but she thought he was probably going to go off to spend some time with another of his girlfriends somewhere else in the country.

It was an easy journey of mostly motorways, except the last few miles, which were slower country roads. On the way Martin tried to tell Stephanie something about why Nieziemski Manor was so important to her introduction to this world. He called it an introduction. She had been with him for more than two weeks now, seen one of his many girlfriends, found out about the Angel Trust, met a man who could actually speak to cats and seen an apparition of a big cat – and he called it an introduction!

"You remember on the day I met you we talked about some strange creatures," said Martin when they had only a few miles to go. "We talked about mermaids."

"Mermaids rescuing people in the London floods, yes," said Stephanie.

"Well, they aren't called mermaids. Don't call them mermaids when you meet them."

"When I meet them?"

"I'm not saying you will meet them. When I stayed there, they didn't come out at all."

"Stayed…" Stephanie was trying to work out what he was trying to say.

"They live at the manor," he said. "And there are other People there, too. Queens of the fey."

Stephanie laughed, wondering if he was having a big joke at her expense. "And goblins and elves, no doubt. Is that what Clif was on about when he said he was rescued by a dwarf?"

"Goblins, lots of goblins, but no elves as far as I know. Although there were elves at the battle of the embassy. Clif was rescued by a dwarf? He never told me that."

"He said a dwarf in a suit came to his rescue."

"Balaur," said Martin.

"Ba-what?"

"Balaur. The dwarf. He's the manor's… solicitor."

"Oh, right," said Stephanie. "That explains everything. He probably slapped the devil-dogs with a cease-and-desist order."

Nieziemski Manor was much bigger than where Martin lived. Martin may have had a bedroom for every day of the week, a converted barn for an annex and a big field as his back garden, but this Buckinghamshire manor house was three storeys high, at least four times bigger than Martin's and had several out-buildings and a whole village under its protection. Martin's house and grounds would probably fit onto its huge, well-kept front lawn several times over.

The main house was rectangular in shape with a double-doored entrance at the middle of its wider aspect. Stephanie parked her Skoda on the large driveway. Around the front lawn and main building was a less well-kept wilderness of plants and bushes, growing into a proper forest behind and to the west of the main building. Also, on the right-hand side of the house from where she faced it, there was a large lake, surrounded by trees and bushes, possibly the straggling remains of the forest that seemed to stretch for many acres behind the main building.

A young woman came out of the house to greet them. She had short, dark hair and was dressed casually. Martin got out of the car and greeted her warmly.

"Lucy, my gorgeous little woman," he said. "Will you marry me?"

"Never in a million years," said the girl with a child-like laugh. Lucy then looked at Stephanie as she opened the door to get out. "You're two-timing me and proposing at the same time!" she giggled. "Never trust a v…"

"This is Stephanie Baynes," Martin interrupted her. "When Michael got you for a PA, I got jealous, so I hired Stephanie."

"She's the girl you spoke about when you contacted us earlier," said Lucy. She then turned her attention to Stephanie herself. "I'm Lucy Waterhouse. Pleased to meet you."

Stephanie was going to say something like 'you don't look like a goblin', but decided she wouldn't begin their relationship by being rude. Lucy showed her into the main entrance of the house, which was a huge hall with an enormous staircase leading up to both floors above. At the back of the great hall there was a nearly-life-sized wooden carving of a woodland nymph in long robes. Apart from that and an oval table and some tall-backed chairs, the hall was bare and open. Lucy led her through to a guest room while Martin knocked on the office door to the right of the entrance hall.

"I gather Martin's not staying this time," said Lucy.

"No, it's just me. Thanks for putting me up."

"No, it's great," said Lucy. "I mean, it'll be good to have another girl to talk to. I mean I chat to Jada and the others sometimes, but they're… Baynes. You're Stephanie Baynes."

"Yes," said Stephanie, cautiously.

"You look like her. Your sister, I mean. You do have a sister? Paula?"

"Yes, in London. She hasn't ever been here, has she?"

"Here? Oh, no, she doesn't know anything about us. I mean, she knows about me, because we were at college together. We were best friends for a while."

Stephanie decided not to tell this excitable young woman that Paula hadn't mentioned her before. But then, she'd never said much about when she was at college – but she did spend a couple of years of her studies at Amersham, so they might have met then.

"How much do you know about us?" asked Lucy.

"Nothing, I think," said Stephanie.

"But you've had some… experiences… and you want some kind of explanation."

"Martin told me that there are such things as mermaids. But not to call them mermaids."

"We've come to call them naiads. But they might be called selkies or kelpies in some parts of the country."

"Naiads. As in Greek mythology."

"It's a nice day. When you've settled in you might get a chance to meet them."

Lucy left Stephanie to unpack her bag in this new, luxurious room. She heard Lucy call to someone called 'Chocolate' or something similar as she returned to the main hall. Stephanie didn't take long to unpack and then she returned to the others. Martin was in the main hall with Lucy and another man of roughly their age who they introduced as Michael Varmeter, the lord of the manor.

Michael was a pleasant man, not as dark, mysterious or, for that matter, as handsome as Martin, but he wanted to look after Stephanie properly.

"We'll give you something to eat at Zana's, then Lucy's offered to show you around. She'll take you into the back garden to meet Lady Venner, and we've arranged for you to meet Lady Marika this afternoon. She may be able to help you understand what's happened to you. I've organised for Din Mawr to take Martin to the station in Amersham."

"Not before we've eaten, I hope," said Martin. "Zana's serves the best food this side of Bucharest."

"No, we'll let you eat with us first," laughed Michael.

"And then you'll be leaving me all alone here," Stephanie said to Martin.

"Believe me," said Michael. "Nobody's ever alone here."

As they ate at the local pub (which was called the Unicorn, not Zana's, unless that was one of its nicknames), Stephanie understood why Martin had said the food was so great. Michael made a joke about not eating here too often to avoid getting fat, and Lucy looked as if she could eat the world and still remain as small and slight as she was now.

They talked about her trip to France on the following day. Neither Michael nor Lucy seemed to question why Martin wasn't going to France with her – they probably already knew he had some kind of aversion to flying and didn't like sunny weather.

Afterward, Martin said his goodbyes and left them. Lucy took Stephanie by the arm and led her to the back of the house with considerable excitement and enthusiasm. Stephanie imagined that this young woman couldn't do anything without getting excited about it.

The back garden was not a garden – it was acres and acres of woodland, and it felt like walking into an enchanted forest. It was warm and pleasant, shaded but bright, full of colour and beauty. Flower seeds seemed to float in the air like living beings, so Stephanie understood why someone walking out here might believe in fairies.

Lucy led them past the huge lake well into the forest, from where Stephanie could no longer see the house. Ahead of them were three people, a tall, robed woman flanked by men who might have been her bodyguard. The woman looked a little like the wood carving in the great hall. She wore a hood to cover her head. She stopped walking towards them and signalled to her two companions, who disappeared into the woods. Then she continued forwards to meet Stephanie.

"This is Lady Venner," said Lucy.

"You are Stephanie Baynes," said the Lady. Stephanie wondered if she actually lived out here in the trees. Perhaps there was a lodge around here for her somewhere.

Then, when she took her hood off, it was as if Stephanie's eyes were suddenly opened to a new world. She was a truly beautiful person, with blue skin, elf-like ears and the most amazing deep eyes, which seemed full of compassion for Stephanie. Lady Venner was a real, live fey queen, and all the stories Stephanie had ever heard when she was a child seemed to be coming to life in this one lovely, majestic being. Stephanie was awestruck and frightened.

Lucy showed her how to greet the Lady with both hands holding hers, and the touch of the fey creature made her feel like she had stopped living in the real world and had walked into a fairy story. Or had she walked into a new real world from something much more mundane? Her terror at the realisation of the new world she was encountering went away, and she felt calm in the presence of this beautiful creature.

"I imagine meeting the People is a shock to the system," said the fey queen.

"I wonder how Lucy here deals with it," said Stephanie. Lucy giggled.

"Lucy has known us since she was a baby," replied Venner. "But you have only just met with this world, and it disturbs you, doesn't it?"

"I think 'disturb' is too light a word," said Stephanie.

"We are hiding here," said the fey queen. "Your world would be frightened of us if they knew about us. There are a few of us, and we're trying to help where we can. We're on your side."

"Thank you," said Stephanie. "I want to know about... I had a strange experience with a cat." She felt clumsy in front of this elegant fey woman.

"My sister, Lady Marika, may be able to help you understand just what it was you met," said Venner. "I think Lucy felt it was best for you to meet me first because I am more... calming than she is."

After far too short a time, Lady Venner dismissed them and they walked by the lake to return to the front of the house. They caught a brief glimpse of a female form swimming in the lake, possibly one of the naiads Lucy had told her about, but it didn't come up to say 'hello'. From what Stephanie saw, she thought that the creature was swimming naked, which made her blush and respect the lady's privacy.

They returned to the main house by the front door and, in the main hall, another fey queen was waiting for them. This one did not have blue skin, but looked more human. She was tall and regal, wearing layers of gauzy clothes. She was fairly pale-skinned with white hair. She had a small eye-patch over her left eye, and there was a scar that started above it and ran down her cheek to her mouth, giving her an ugly half-smile. To Stephanie she looked a little scary. Lucy bowed to her.

"This is Lady Marika, Queen of the Sidhe," said Lucy. Stephanie held her hands out the way Lucy had taught her the fey greeting, but Lady Marika did not respond. When she spoke, however, her words were gentle.

"Tell me about why you are here?" said the sidhe queen.

"I'm here because Martin Latham thinks I need to know things about you," Stephanie replied.

"Martin Latham?" said Marika with some sourness in her voice. "I would counsel you to have nothing to do with him, but it is too late for that. You've had an experience of some kind which needs an interpretation, am I right?"

"Yes, I suppose so," said Stephanie, feeling quite intimidated by this creature. "I was in danger recently, and was saved by the apparition of a cat. A big cat, like a panther."

Marika looked long and hard at her with her one eye, and it felt like she was looking right into her soul.

"No. Before that."

"I was a child," Stephanie said, puzzled that the sidhe queen should know something about her that she hadn't mentioned.

"A creature needed your help, and you saved it."

"I stopped someone shooting a puma, or a lynx or…"

"It was not a puma, nor a lynx," said Marika. "It was something that may not have a name in your language. Possibly it was a cait sidhe, a long way from its Scottish home. It might even have been the Bast, from further away than Scotland."

Stephanie had a vague recollection of cait sidhe from her studies at university, but she had quickly dismissed them as she was trying to find a more scientifically acceptable explanation for the cat she had seen. The word Bast was more Egyptian than Scottish, though, if she remembered her classical mythology studies correctly.

"One of your People?" Stephanie dared to ask.

"One of our legends," said Marika. "Even if it did not need saving, your actions may have tied it to you, making it your servant when you needed it."

"Wow," said Lucy, interrupting the flow between Lady Marika and Stephanie. Then she covered her mouth with her hand and said, "Sorry."

"Why is it here?" said Lady Marika, as if talking to herself.

"There have been sightings…" Stephanie started, getting into her 'I'm going to present my thesis' mode. Lady Marika put up her hand to stop her.

"No. I must think," said the Lady. "You will be staying the night?"

"Yes."

"I will see you tomorrow before you leave." Then her voice softened. "You will have trouble sleeping because of your excitement at discovering our world, but you will need your energy over the next few days, so sleep if you can. I do not like Lord Martin Latham, but he will need you, so I withdraw my earlier counsel."

Then she turned and walked upstairs without any further fuss, leaving Stephanie open-mouthed at the foot of the stairs. Lucy suggested that she should get an early night.

Lady Marika was right in that Stephanie was far too excited to sleep that night. The bed was comfortable, there was an air of relaxation around the manor and grounds, but Stephanie's mind wouldn't stop working as she tried to assimilate what she had seen. It was well past midnight when she finally dozed off and she woke up in the early hours of the morning after far too short a sleep. She got up and stepped outside her room. Along the corridor was a door, but she thought it probably led to the lake, so she made her way to the main hall where the statue of the Lady was, and out through the front door, which wasn't locked. She hesitated to go around to the lake to the back of the house because she felt it belonged to *them*.

However, they must have been watching her, because before long Lady Venner came through from the woods to greet her. She was dressed in a pale brown robe with its hood down so that Stephanie could see her face.

"I didn't know there was a world like this," she said as Lady Venner drew near. "It's so beautiful."

"Thank you," said the fey queen. "We love your world, too."

"May I ask…" Stephanie started.

"Yes."

"Why are you here?"

Lady Venner thought carefully before answering. "Every time you ask that question you will get a different answer. But for now, I will say what I said yesterday – we are here to try and help, where we can."

"How many people know about you?"

"Not many."

"I promise I will keep your secret."

"I know. Thank you."

"When you are here next to me, I feel safe and reassured. But when I think about your People hiding here in our world, it… it frightens me."

"Can you work out why?" Lady Venner asked.

"I think it's because, although I've always liked mysteries, I always wanted them to be solvable. You were never... *real* to me, just a fantasy. Maybe I always wanted something with a rational explanation."

"There *is* a rational explanation – just not one within your experience."

"I think you have offered me a whole new definition of the word 'rational'," said Stephanie. The blue-skinned fey laughed, and it affected Stephanie with a kind of emotional reassurance.

"Something is moving in the world," said Lady Venner. "In *your* world, I mean. It is something that doesn't come from us, but it is... *like* us. And not like us. We are People of peace, and this thing you will meet is not a thing of peace. You will need our help to deal with it. And it will need your help."

"I'm afraid I don't understand."

"Perhaps it will become clearer when you meet my sister again. She is awake now, and I can hear her thoughts. She is struggling with something... with what has touched your life."

Stephanie wanted to ask more, but she was afraid. She was afraid that these new 'friends' of hers were not really friends at all, but were the cause of some of the problems she seemed to be involved in investigating at the moment.

"You want to ask me something?" said Lady Venner after some time had passed in silence.

"In my investigations, something came up recently that's been preying on me," she said, aware that the creature she was speaking to, as gentle as she appeared, was a being of great power, and not one that she could challenge. "A friend told me about some... strange robed creatures, trying to get people to do things that might be dangerous. Destructive." She explained what she had heard about the situation in Mbalaya, and the destruction of the island in Greece.

Lady Venner mulled it over for a moment, then said, "I don't know of such creatures. You want to ask if they are of my People, if they are fey. They are not. They aren't goblins, either, I think. I do not believe they are part of... *us*... at all, although they may have found their way into your world the same way we did. We should have been aware of their existence, but if they think we are capable of defeating them, they may be deliberately hiding their existence from us."

Stephanie said nothing else, and stood by the lake looking out over the calm, still water. Lady Venner stood by her side for a while, and then, as the morning light became stronger, she wasn't there anymore. No naiad forms disturbed the water's surface, and Stephanie somehow felt rested even though she hadn't slept very much.

After breakfast with Lucy in the Unicorn, Stephanie packed her things and waited at the front of the house for the helicopter to pick her up and take her to France. While she was there, Lady Marika came to visit her again.

"You are blessed, Stephanie Baynes," said Marika. "Blessed by your actions. You showed compassion to the Bast, who was here in physical form. The Bast comes from Egypt, or at least an African country near Egypt. Its essence is still there. Somehow its spirit has been separated from its true nature and has attached itself to you. How it got over into this country I do not know for certain, but I believe there are waypoints across the world which would aid its travel. I think it needs to get back to Africa, to reunite with its physical form. It has connected itself to you because you can help."

"I've never been to Africa, and I have no specific plans to go there at the moment."

"When did you decide on your chosen career to be a researcher?"

"After I first saw the cat," Stephanie answered, and she realised what the Lady was getting at. "I suppose, in the long run, it could mean travelling the world."

"The Bast has a purpose, although I am not yet sure what that purpose might be. It has bonded itself to you, so you need not be afraid when things get... hard. I hope you find that my words are helpful."

"Africa," said Stephanie. "Something's going on over there at the moment. Clifton Chase might be investigating it for the Angel Trust."

"Chase?" said Marika. "I know of him, but I don't think I've met him. He may need you there."

"Need me? What will I be able to do?"

"I don't know, not for sure. But perhaps you can bring the Bast's spirit back to where its being is trapped. When it and its body are reunited it will have the power to do what it needs to do. Travel well."

Lady Marika turned and disappeared into the house as the helicopter arrived, leaving Stephanie with more questions than answers.

Seven

Professor Bouvon lived near Cholet, in the north-west of France. The helicopter pilot who was to take her there was John-James Clipper. He was in his mid-twenties, only two or three years older than Stephanie herself. He grinned at her with a mouth full of shiny white teeth and a twinkle in his eye. He was a charmer, at least in his own opinion, and he let her know that she was a VIP customer because of her connection to the manor, and that he was delighted to have her on this flight. He paid her special attention and stared at her a lot, especially when he thought she wasn't aware that he was looking.

Stephanie had flown in an aeroplane before, mostly on holidays with her parents to their favourite holiday destination in Spain, but this was a very different mode of transport. The journey was smooth and John-James flirted with her a bit, which she quite enjoyed. He informed her that they would have to re-fuel in Le Havre, where they would go through customs, before flying on to Cholet.

The whole journey only took a little over four hours. They flew over some very beautiful English countryside, the sun-splashed sea of the English Channel and had a break in Le Havre that didn't hold them up for very long. Then they continued with a further flight over some impressive vineyards and John-James commented on them sharing a bottle together. They finally landed at the small airfield near Cholet from where Lucy Waterhouse, acting for Martin, had arranged a taxi to take her to the Bouvon estate outside the town, which was less than twenty minutes away.

Georges Bouvon lived in a large farmhouse-style home on a farming estate, which seemed typical for this part of France. Although not a farmer himself, he rented out his extensive land to the local people, which made him a little extra money with their sheep farming and huge fields of vegetables. The house itself was off the main road by a mile or so and was a warm and welcoming place. Madame Bouvon met her at the garden gate and led her into the house to meet the archaeologist.

"Miss Baynes," the archaeologist greeted her in the lounge. He had a rich, deep, old-fashioned voice. Stephanie was pleased that he spoke excellent English with a glorious French accent, because her French was far from adequate. "Thank you so much for making the journey across the Channel just to hear an old man's theories."

"I believe your theories are well thought-of and worth listening to," she replied, but he laughed.

"No, I'm afraid not. Perhaps people thought I was once worth listening to. I had the ear of many scholars across the world. Unfortunately, my ideas have recently upset those very same scholars. I had the chance to stay in favour with them, but only if I agreed to drop my wild fantasies and follow the conventions that had kept me fixed in my views up to now. I might have done it, too, once, but as I was nearing retirement, I felt that I had very little left to lose other than my integrity. For that reason I will not stop saying what I believe to be the truth."

"So what is this theory of yours that your peers don't seem to like?"

Georges Bouvon, a well-built old man with a shock of white hair crowning his head, sat back in his armchair and smiled at her. She had asked a question that he loved to answer. His wife had prepared a massive afternoon 'snack' with the most beautiful fruity wine that Stephanie had ever tasted (although she was hardly a wine expert). Mme Bouvon shook her head and left them to it. Then Stephanie sat comfortably and listened.

"About three years ago I was invited by an old friend and colleague to South America, where he was puzzled by some of the symbols which he'd seen in what he thought were old Aztec tombs. Firstly, they didn't match any Aztec symbols he'd seen before, but more importantly, he did remember seeing such markings in a book I wrote a few years ago. However, he knew me quite well, and was aware that I'd never been to South America before, so he was keen to find out how they got there.

"I must tell you that it fascinated me. In the work that we do, we often find a little information which is, well, out of place in the common discoveries which we would expect to find. Not only that, but earlier that same year, I had seen those same symbols myself. The first time I came across them was a small dig in Texas, but I'd just seen them in Greenland. It was an interesting anomaly – three very different cultures sporting a unique and unusual symbol."

The old archaeologist fiddled inside his jacket pockets for a moment or two, pulling out three or four pieces of paper. He sorted through them until he found the one he was looking for, stuffing the others, including a receipt and a sweet wrapper, back in his pocket. He opened up the one piece of crumpled paper he had retained. On it there was a simple diagram consisting of two lines in the approximate shape of semi-circles arcing alongside each other until they finally met at a point, like a simple diagram of a bird-beak, or an animal claw. He held it out for Stephanie to look at, tapping it to indicate that this was the symbol he and his colleague had found.

"My first thought was that somebody was playing practical jokes, but the artwork was buried quite deep, and all tests seemed to prove them to be authentic. They dated back around six thousand years. So we both went about searching for other occurrences of this symbol. You must understand that it is a fairly simplistic symbol, so easily dismissed as, perhaps, a badly-drawn arrowhead from ancient times. But across the world there were more than twenty different cultures in as many countries, all with the same symbol. What we found next was unusual, unbelievable, even. If you drew the locations of all the symbols from different archaeological digs on a map of the world, and tried to connect them, you got the shape of that symbol made up of twenty or so map references across the world. There was one place that nobody had looked, where there had been no archaeological dig. That place was where the two arcs converged – if you like, where the talon comes to a point."

"And where was that?" Stephanie asked unnecessarily, knowing that Professor Bouvon was about to answer.

"It was in the southern Sahara Desert, in a small African country called Mbalaya. I got permission to go out and start a dig there."

"How accurate was your estimate of the location of the actual tip of the talon, so to speak?" asked Stephanie. She was fairly sure she could tell him where his target should have been – it was going to be at the convergence of ley lines.

"The various different digs had symbols of different sizes, but they were all geometrically the same – a remarkable enough phenomenon as it is. We only had to transpose the dimensions onto a map and we felt we could accurately calculate the location – the pot of gold at the end of the rainbow, in a manner of speaking. We also did some geo-physical scans, until we found some strange structural evidence under a part of the desert near a little town – a village, really – called Hemmin."

"How far did you get before the government changed its mind and threw you out?"

"Ah, you know about that?"

"I know that there is some sort of political situation going on there, yes."

Georges Bouvon's shoulders sagged a little, and his face fell. "We were progressing well; we even discovered some seriously advanced metal and stone structures buried deep under the ground about a mile from the village. Then the government asked us to leave. They gave us twenty-four hours to get out, to pack up and go home. There were no explanations – just get out."

"And that was all?"

"No. Something's going on in that country, and it has something to do with Hemmin. Shortly after we left, the people of Hemmin were ordered by their government to leave – to leave their homes, and relocate."

"Only Hemmin? Just the one village?"

"Yes, as far as I know. I've been trying to follow the politics of it all since we were asked to leave. The country, which was once comfortably allied with our own, and with Britain, I think, has suddenly cut off all communications with all of its associates in a strange attempt to become completely independent. This is a country of extreme hardship and poverty, which has been relying on humanitarian aid for several years. There has been no sign of improvement in Mbalaya's fortunes, and without the support of other countries things can only get worse for them. I did think, for a while, that we were moved on because we were getting close to something."

"Close to what, exactly?"

"Exactly? I don't know. It is all too easy to assign outrageous explanations to this talon symbol. For example, the only way that it could be drawn on the world map would be if the people who designed it could fly. The structures that the symbol has been found on across the world are estimated to be around six thousand years old. Who could fly six thousand years ago?"

"Is that why you believe in UFO's?"

"I'm not sure that I do. I just want to find an explanation that links these archaeological finds together. We have found something that we do not understand, that tells us either that early man was more advanced than we first thought, or that some outside influence guided our steps in our early development. You see, a great big arrow painted on the face of the planet suggests that whoever put it there wanted it to be noticed."

Stephanie was fascinated. She wanted to continue listening to the archaeologist's amazing and carefully thought-out hypothesis.

"After we started packing up our gear and made to leave the area, I went to the capital of the country to try to argue my case. We might have been close to the biggest find in the history of archaeology. I was shocked at what I found there. Some creatures had managed to charm their way into the president's good books and were controlling the country – apparently with his permission."

"Creatures?" said Stephanie. She'd had this conversation before, with Clifton Chase, but she didn't want to pre-empt what Professor Bouvon was going to say.

"They might have been human," said the Frenchman. "They were short, and wore robes like monks, so fully wrapped up they might have passed for people. They mostly stayed out of the way for the short time I was there at the palace, but I caught a glimpse of one. He looked like something out of a science fiction film. A little grey man."

It was getting very late before another taxi returned Stephanie to the airfield, where the pilot, John-James Clipper, was waiting as agreed. When he saw her, he stood up straight, and then offered her a low, mock bow.

"Hello again, my beautiful lady," he said, his teeth still showing white even in the night's darkness. "It's just the two of us for the journey back. Would you like to join me up front for a cosy evening for two across the Atlantic?"

She smiled a tired smile back at him, but decided not to answer with a rude rebuff for all that she wanted to. He was not being unpleasant, after all.

"Sorry, I won't be great company for you tonight. I have a lot to think about. If it's alright with you, I'll just sit on my own in the back."

He nodded, but looked at her for a moment. He became serious. "It does that, doesn't it?"

"What does what?" she responded.

"Working for the manor. There's always lots to… think about."

"I'm working for Lord Martin Latham, not the manor."

"Same thing," he said, with a shrug of his shoulders.

On the return journey, as the night rolled around them, Stephanie was surprised to find herself thinking less about all that Professor Bouvon had told her and more about Martin Latham and his involvement. Why had he sent her to France? Why didn't he go with her? How much did he, or the Angel Trust, already know about what Georges Bouvon had said? In fact, she wondered what Martin knew about this whole affair that he had not, as yet, told her. And the little grey men – were they the 'goblins' that Martin had spoken about, but she had not seen at Nieziemski Manor?

When the helicopter landed at Le Havre the sky was still dark and there wasn't much activity there. It took John-James a while to get someone to organise the refuelling of the helicopter. Stephanie tried to have a snooze while they waited, but she was not able to achieve restful sleep. With everything she had discovered over the last couple of days, she wondered if she would ever sleep properly again. Professor Bouvon believed in the possible existence of aliens, but the real aliens were fey beings posing as human and living among us. Were they out there in Mbalaya, too? Would they have placed the talon symbols there six thousand years ago, and if so, for what purpose? Perhaps she could ask them when she got back to Buckinghamshire to pick up her car.

It was full daylight when they finally got to Nieziemski Manor. John-James left the helicopter on the enormous front lawn and said his goodbyes to Stephanie, telling her he was going for breakfast at Zana's. Lucy, having seen the helicopter arrive, came out of the manor house to greet her.

"Hi. Do you need anything before you go?" she asked.

"Coffee?" suggested Stephanie, and Lucy led her through to the office where the coffee was already made and ready for her.

"How did your trip go?"

"More questions than answers," said Stephanie.

"That's about right," laughed Lucy.

"Martin said you have goblins here at the manor," said Stephanie. She thought that might be the oddest sentence she had ever spoken.

"Yes. You'll be going home soon, so you probably won't get a chance to meet one."

"Are they like little grey men?"

"More like little green men. But their flesh colours vary."

"And they wear robes like monks?"

"No, not that I've ever seen," said Lucy.

"It's all about this country in Africa," Stephanie was trying to focus her thoughts. "Mbalaya. I wondered if your People are doing something out there?"

"Doing something?"

"Where else in the world are there fey People?"

"The People here communicate with each other in this country, but they don't have a strong contact with their kind in other countries. I suppose I could ask Feen in Ogonshead if she knows anything."

"Feen?"

"Lady Marika's daughter. She's… well, it's complicated."

"It's always complicated," laughed Stephanie, taking another sip of her coffee. "Lady Marika said that my… *Bast*… protector might want to get back to Africa. And something is going on in Mbalaya. Africa."

"Are you planning a trip out there?"

"The word 'planning' hasn't been in my vocabulary since I started working for Martin Latham," said Stephanie.

Refreshed by the coffee and Lucy Waterhouse's company, she started her drive home, first calling Martin and telling him that she would rather have some time to digest what she had discovered than debriefing him as soon as she got back. He made a suggestive joke about debriefing, which made her think he must have spent some time with John-James Clipper, but agreed they wouldn't meet until tomorrow.

On the way back she began to feel a little tired, so she turned the car radio on in order to keep her going for the remaining few miles of the journey. Mbalaya was in the news again. Apparently, there had been a bad storm that had destroyed a village in the south of the country. Her tired mind didn't take it all in, and she switched channels so that she could listen to some loud music to keep her awake.

She went to bed as soon as she got in, shortly after midday.

Eight

Stephanie was restless. She slept, and she dreamed about a storm that suddenly appeared to destroy a town, and then disappeared again. She dreamed about a little kitten that became a big cat. She ran about the moors at Bodmin, trying to stop a man with a gun from hunting cats. Then the gun pointed at her, and there was the sound of shooting or someone knocking at her door. She lay in bed while her mind told her she was waking up, but the sound of shooting or knocking was still there. It was knocking, definitely knocking, and it was on the door of her office downstairs.

She woke herself up, got out of bed and wrapped herself in a dressing gown. Despite her decaffeinated state, she was more or less properly awake by the time that she had done this, and so she had the wit to check herself in the mirror before going downstairs to answer the door. Martin knocked, quite urgently, one more time before she let him in.

"Whoa," he said, looking her over with *that* smile, "I didn't mean to knock you up when you didn't have any clothes on."

"Don't," she said.

"Sorry, I didn't mean to get you up early," he corrected himself, sounding only slightly contrite, and then he took a look at his watch. "No, wait a minute, it isn't early. But I really am sorry to disturb you. I just had a call from John Borland – he wants to speak to us urgently. I'll make you a coffee while you get dressed."

Stephanie forgave him instantly and agreed. When she came back just a few minutes later, combing her hair on the way down the stairs, her hot coffee was at her desk and the computer with the largest screen was connected to John Borland in London.

"Good morning Miss Baynes," said John.

"Hello Mr Borland. Something urgent, Martin says," she said.

"Yes, I am afraid so. I sent Clifton Chase out to Mbalaya just before we heard the news yesterday about the storm that destroyed that village. We sent a photographer in from Mali nearby to take a look at the mess. He flew across the border in a helicopter, took some footage and had to get out quick when the Mbalayan air force was mobilised. They threatened to shoot him down. He then sent me this footage."

John Borland's face disappeared from the screen and was replaced by some shaky camera footage of a ruined town. Brick, wood and wattle-and-daub style buildings were devastated and their remains scattered across the landscape. It seemed there had never been a quality road going into the town, but whatever passed for a highway was ruined. Ridges and a dirt track were ploughed away almost as if they had never been there, and it was hard to identify the shape of the buildings that used to be in place. There was a little background noise on the video, but most of it was the cameraman or the helicopter pilot swearing in their shock at what they saw.

Stephanie was wide-eyed and amazed at the sight.

"Hemmin," she said. "It's Hemmin."

"It's what?" whispered Martin to her as they continued to watch the destruction.

"Professor Bouvon's town," she whispered back. "They are destroying – have destroyed a town on the biggest convergence of ley lines in Africa." She didn't actually know that for a fact, but it wasn't difficult to put the pieces together and come to that conclusion.

"That's right," said Borland, who had heard the quiet exchange between her and Martin. "I've been looking into Hemmin to see what I could find."

Someone on the video shouted that they thought Mbalayan aircraft were on the way, and they had to go. The camera shook, the scenery started moving out of the way as the helicopter turned, and then the video feed stopped.

"We are aware that people from the West living and working in Mbalaya had been ejected," Borland continued, "so I sent Mr Chase in to find out if this was the reason why – some experimental weapon, perhaps."

"Professor Bouvon told me that the indigenous population of the town were evacuated, too," Stephanie said. "The Mbalayan authorities knew this was going to happen."

"There is a further problem," said Borland. "Clifton was trying to get close to the president, but he was prevented by what he called strange creatures."

"Little grey men," said Stephanie. "That's what Professor Bouvon called them."

"Clifton called them something similar, just before his phone line crashed. Electronic communication into and out of the area has been disrupted. You can't speak to people in the country by telephone or computer."

"That's a pretty wide area to block," said Martin. "There's a powerful thing going on here. How are you going to track down Clif in all this?"

"I'm going to ask you to go in and investigate," said Borland.

Martin went quiet, and his normally pale face seemed to go even paler.

"Me?" he said.

"Us?" said Stephanie at the same time.

"Not both of us," said Martin. "It's too dangerous."

"So are you offering to go in alone?" said Borland. Martin stared at him for a moment. Stephanie knew that Martin's skin was sensitive, and he always protected himself against the sun, so a desert land was not going to be his first choice of destination. But was there more to it than that?

"So you *do* mean both of us?" Martin said, eventually.

"I will give you some time to think about it, and you know I don't want to put anyone in a dangerous situation, but my only operative, at least the only man I would give this kind of mission to, is missing. The best people to track him down are you two."

"I'm not the right person for any job that involves bright sunlight or going overseas," said Martin.

"I'm a computer person," said Stephanie. "If computers are down over there what use will I be?"

Martin nodded. "What have we got on Mbalaya and its current situation?"

"After the storm was reported yesterday morning, I looked up some details about it. The country of Mbalaya has been around for hundreds of years. It is a fairly small country, and its capital is currently called Veritas City after its president, Mikal Veritas. It has been invaded a few times, but, being in the Sahara Desert and not benefitting from any oil deposits or diamond mines, it hasn't really been a serious military objective. In 1765, the town of Hemmin was founded by Matthias Hemmin under rather strange circumstances. He was a well-respected man of some reputation – some kind of witch doctor. Matthias claimed (or possibly stole) something from the capital city and buried it in Hemmin around the time of its founding. That information was quite difficult to find, and it is likely that the people who live, or rather used to live, in that town didn't know it was there. Perhaps your Professor Bouvon was close to discovering it when he was stopped by the government there.

"Today, the president of the country is, as I have already said, Mikal Veritas, and he has been, in the past, quite co-operative with the West. He was educated at Oxford. Until a few weeks ago, Mbalaya's relationship with Europe was good. Clifton was tasked with finding out why that changed, and if there was some kind of influence in the city outside of the normal."

"Supernatural," said Stephanie.

"Okay," said Martin, "I'll go, but I can't force Stephanie to go with me."

"I volunteer, then," said Stephanie. It seemed that Lady Marika's words to her about going to Africa were coming true. "But on full pay, of course."

John Borland laughed at her pay quip and thanked them and sent them some further details. Martin, who was normally bright and confident, looked nervous and unsure.

"So tell me about why you don't want to leave the country," said Stephanie after John Borland had signed off.

"I don't mind leaving the country; it's just that I don't like leaving by plane," Martin answered, "or by boat."

"How about teleportation?" she joked, but he remained serious.

"I could probably manage that – but it is seriously difficult for me to travel overseas by conventional means."

"Seriously," Stephanie picked up the word.

Martin pulled up a second chair and sat down by Stephanie, who turned her swivel chair to face him. He checked to make sure Borland was definitely offline and that the camera and sound were turned off. He looked very serious indeed, and Stephanie realised that he usually wasn't. In fact, this might have been the first time he looked quite like that to her.

"I have Tepes Syndrome," he said.

"Tepesh," she repeated. The word rang a bell, but she did not feel she could turn to her computer to look it up because he was sitting right there, in her face, ready to explain.

"Yes," said Martin. "It causes me a few problems. Particularly with regard to travelling. I mean, it does me some good as well – I don't normally get ill. I never get a cold. I look young, but I'm quite old. I am also quite sensitive to sunlight."

"Look young?"

"I'm quite a bit older than I look. Every ten years or so my family change the records on computers everywhere to give me a new birthday in line with how old I look. The reason I said I couldn't tell Clifton Chase about my ancestors starting the Angel Trust was because they didn't. I did it."

"Mr Borland said the Angel Trust was formed in the nineteenth century," said Stephanie.

"That's right."

"So how old are you?"

"More than a hundred years old."

"Tepes," she said out loud. Having met the blue-skinned Lady Venner and the fortune-telling Lady Marika, Stephanie should not have been over-shocked by the possibility of Martin not being entirely human. However, a feeling of dread was building up in her.

"Every few weeks, I need to replenish my strength. I need to consume human blood. The young ladies who visit provide what I need."

"You're a vampire."

"I don't like to call it that, Stephanie; it gives the wrong impression. It's not like the fiction you read. I don't kill people and suck all the blood out of them; I'm not…" Martin ran out of words.

"Your ladies, the girls that come and visit, and go away with a bandage around their wrists – that was you *drinking their blood*," Stephanie said, and she felt a little sick inside.

"The ladies come and visit, and we have a fabulous night together; I'm sure you don't want to know the details; but part of it is that I drink some of their blood. It gives them a high, and it keeps me going for a few weeks. It also passes some of my antibodies on to them. They stay healthy, recover from colds and stuff quicker, that sort of thing. I don't do them any harm."

Stephanie stood up from her seat, walked over to the sofa and sat in it heavily. She stared into space for a while. Martin looked like he wanted to go over to her and put his arm around her, but he must have decided that wasn't the best course of action, given the circumstances. He stayed in his seat, and looked at her until she invited him to say or do something.

"I should have known," she said in a weak voice. "Werewolves, fey queens, goblins, naiads; there had to be vampires."

"I'm human," said Martin, "but with a condition. It's Tepes Syndrome, not vampirism – I mean, it is vampirism, but not like the fantasy books tell you – it's a medical condition. I was born on December 21st, 1843. My mother died in childbirth, and I was brought up by a community of... of like-minded people. My condition became apparent when I was fifteen – I didn't stop looking like a teenager for more than twenty years. I came across to England towards the end of the nineteenth century. I was horribly sick all through the crossing from France, and on the very few occasions I have travelled by sea since then I've been ill. I've never made a long flight in an aircraft. I need your support for this one, Stephanie."

Stephanie said nothing for a while, trying to take it in. She gathered all of the information from the last weeks together, the stuff she'd researched, the people she'd met, her experiences, particularly the 'ghost cat' that had appeared to save her from being shot. They were all, possibly, supernatural experiences. Somehow, Martin being a vampire seemed to fit into the weirdness of it all and didn't seem as impossible to her as much as she thought it should. It still frightened her, however, and she was glad she'd not yet had breakfast as she thought she would probably bring it up right now.

"I'd like to give you my support," she said, and her voice sounded like a child whispering in a storm. "But I don't know how…"

"I'll make arrangements," he said immediately, looking relieved that she had said 'yes' and ignoring the fact that she'd said 'but'. "Look, Stephanie, I know this is hard on you, but I *really* don't travel well. I'm going to need your support all the way."

"And will you… will you need my blood?" she asked, and suddenly the terror she had been trying to avoid up to now started to become real.

"No. I eat and drink like anybody else, and I only need blood every couple of months or so. And, as you already know…"

"Carlie," Stephanie answered. She took a deep breath. She wanted to say 'no', and walk away from this whole world that Martin had introduced her to. But she knew that she couldn't. Clifton Chase had visited her when she needed someone after the Hardington incident, and now he needed them – or her. And Lady Marika had said she would go to Africa.

"What do you need me to do?" she asked him at last. The dizzy sickness she felt inside was beginning to subside, at least a little, and she was beginning to feel more stable. Martin looked at her with what seemed to be relief as well as something that looked like a childish need.

"I'll do all the political stuff, talk to officials and try to charm my way into the country," said Martin. "I'll try to get a meeting with the president. Your job will be to keep me sane, or sedated, on the flight. It will probably be more than 7 hours, and I would struggle to stay sane on a twenty-minute flight. I'll take sedatives, but I'm pretty much resistant to medication. People who research my condition – and there aren't many of them – say it's about needing to be part of the land, so being in the air affects me. I don't know – hold my hand, comfort me, talk to me…"

"For seven hours?"

"I'll sleep for as much of the journey as I can. As I said, I am fairly resilient to tranquilisers, so I'll take something rhino-strength and hope it lasts."

At Birmingham International Airport, there was very little traffic for Mbalaya. They were still accepting flights into the country, for it hadn't quite cut itself off completely from the outside world. Not everyone who had been asked to leave the city had left; there were still a few who had to stay because of unfinished business. The Angel Trust had a lot of money and good contacts, so they were able to get the shortest flight there and they would be the only people in the first-class cabin.

Martin asked Stephanie to drive them there. He was twitchy and nervous as they approached the airport, and this, in turn, made Stephanie feel nervous, too. He had been the strength of their partnership up to now, and Stephanie realised that their roles would soon be reversed and she prayed that she would be up to the task.

The waiting time at the airport was soon over and they were escorted onto the plane. Martin seemed pale, but resigned. Actually, when Stephanie looked at him closely, she realised that he was always this pale, but she spoke to him mostly in shaded places; darkened rooms, or his car, which had windows that were as dark as they could legally be. Outside, he had always covered himself up.

He declared his medication at customs, which was cleared. Once they were on board and settled, he took out the tablet which was supposed to help him on the journey. He held it out in a clammy hand.

"This is one of the calmest direct flights possible," he told her. "John did us well in arranging it. If it's a smooth flight, and the weather forecast suggests it will be, then this tablet will knock me out and I will be well rested by the time we get there."

"Is it safe?"

"The tablet? No, it would more than likely kill most people. I can only take one for the journey, and my metabolism will beat it in a few hours. That's where you'll come in." He took a look at her looking at the tablet with fear in her eyes, and smiled at her. "It *won't* kill me. I have to have it this strong or it won't work at all."

He put it in his mouth and swallowed it dry.

"Get some rest yourself. I'll need you in four or five hours."

The plane took off just a few minutes later, filling Stephanie with a fatalistic dread that it was too late to change her mind now. Martin began to doze off before the plane had left the runway. She looked at him as he slept. He looked lifeless, and she was not even sure if he was breathing. He was pale and sweaty, but, in a strange way, peaceful. She *hoped* he was only sleeping. Every now and then she detected the movement of his chest. It was sleep, she assured herself, not a coma or anything she wouldn't be able to deal with. She closed her eyes, but didn't quite get to sleep herself.

The flight was smooth, and it was getting on for six hours before Martin woke up. When he did, however, he was immediately agitated. She tried to speak calmly to him.

"It's alright; we are well on the way. It will be late afternoon when we get there, in just an hour or so."

"An hour? More than an hour?" He looked her in the eyes, as if he was panicked and trying to control it. He didn't take his eyes off her face. He took a deep breath. "Tell me about your research, Stephanie, talk about the big cat you saved. What about your family? How do they feel about you working for a millionaire nutcase? Have you even told them about me?"

Stephanie held Martin's hand. The palm was clammy, and his grip was weak. She talked about her home in Kent and the big cat, and about how her family had said she did the right thing when she scared the cat away to stop Byron shooting it. She told him that they said Byron should have tried to shoot it with a camera instead of a gun. She didn't know what happened to Byron after that day and, for that matter, she didn't care.

She talked to Martin about her family, particularly about her sister, who was the more attractive of the two and had turned down a chance for a career in modelling to take up law. Martin laughed a croaky laugh and disagreed that anyone could be more beautiful than Stephanie right now, and that anyway, real beauty was about accompanying someone who needed her for the flight, even though she was afraid of him because of his condition. He looked into her eyes for the whole time, as if he was trying to make her the only thing in his life right now, blotting out the fact that they were on a plane.

"Everyone said my sister could be a model. She was gorgeous and there I was, a flat-chested, straight-hipped stick of a girl, even at thirteen. I was sixteen before I shaped up a bit, and never got to be as beautiful as her."

"But she's not a model."

"No, she's not," Stephanie said. "She's a lawyer. And every time she sees me she tells me how grateful she is that she never went down that path."

"I would very much like to meet her some time."

"No," she said sharply. "I would never let you get anywhere near her." She laughed, but he could not, for his throat was dry. A hostess had left them some juice to drink, which seemed to help a little. He clutched her arm with his hand in a grip that would have been painful if it could have been stronger, and she dribbled a little juice into his mouth.

She felt that her fear of him because he was a vam… because he had Tepes Syndrome, was diminished because she now saw him as a weak and needy man, but she didn't say as much. She spoke softly and quietly, trying to draw out whatever she was talking about because one hour of this was going to be a very long time. When they were at home in the dark in her office they could talk for hours, but right now it was hard work.

She stopped for a moment. He continued to look at her as if he was trying to blot out everything else.

"Go on," he said, and his voice seemed a little croaky.

She laughed. "You know, I think I have run out of things to say."

"What you said about your sister being beautiful…"

"I wish I hadn't told you now."

"No, what I am saying is…" He rested his head back in to the reclined chair again as if he didn't have the strength to hold it up. "You are beautiful, Stephanie. If your sister is anything like you, it's not surprising people thought she could be a model. You keep putting yourself down, but really…" he closed his eyes for a minute or so, but it must have made him focus on the flight and he opened them again, in panic. He concentrated on her, looking at her face, her eyes in particular.

She smiled back at him, trying to think of some way she could distract him with another story, but she couldn't think of anything.

"I have told you my big secret, and I didn't tell you before because I was afraid to. Now I must ask you to tell me something you have kept a secret from me."

"I've just told you my whole life story."

"When Hardington held that gun at you, you said he slipped and fell and died. Since then you have said a big cat of some kind rescued you. What did the People at Niz Manor tell you about it?"

"Why do you call it Niz Manor?"

"I can't say Nieziemski."

"You just did."

"My secret's out," he laughed, briefly, then looked exhausted again. "My other secret, I mean. But you're avoiding my question."

"Lady Marika asked about the cat I saw before, when I was young. I thought the cat that saved me from Hardington was different from the one in Kent, but... it's given me dreams."

"Nightmares?"

"Not really. Sometimes they are just confusing thoughts, sometimes they are even comforting, in a way. But I don't know what they mean. Lady Marika said the creature was a Bast. Actually, she said it was *the* Bast."

"Lady Marika doesn't like me," breathed Martin. "She has a scar and an eye missing, doesn't she?"

"Yes."

"A vampire did that. Just a few weeks ago."

"Are there a lot of vampires in Britain?"

"Not any more. Thanks to Lady Marika and her People," said Martin, then he changed the subject. "What's a Bast? *The* Bast?"

"I looked it up since – Bast, or Bastet, was the name the Egyptians gave their goddess of cats."

"Egyptians worship cats, don't they? Or they used to."

"I'm still working on that. But yes, the Bast is one of *those* cats. I have some kind of supernatural being that is protecting me. That's what Lady Marika said."

"You saved the Cat, and the Cat saved you," he whispered. She tried to think of a response to that, but the pilot announced that they were approaching their destination and that they should sit in their seats and put their belts on.

Nine

The plane landed at the little airport that served the capital city of this desert country. They were met by one of those stairways on wheels, because there were no more sophisticated facilities there. The doors to the aircraft were opened and a wall of heat met them at the stairway. It took Stephanie's breath away for a moment, and she realised what that might mean for Martin, the darkness-loving vampire. He would have to step out in desert-hot daylight and walk to the terminal. He covered himself in clothes (and his hat), put on his sunglasses and got unsteadily to his feet. His demeanour changed then, however, because they were on land. He looked stronger almost instantly. He led her down the stairs, back in control again. On the cracked tarmac where the plane was parked, he turned to her and said, "Thanks."

Stephanie, who had put on her own sunglasses and was wearing much lighter clothes in contrast with her boss, looked around her. There were a small number of light aircraft on the single-runway airfield and they all looked old and uncared-for. Some of them were probably no longer safe to be in the skies. *I bet Mbalayan planes have outside toilets*, Stephanie thought to herself. Less than twenty passengers, including the two of them, walked to passport control. The remaining passengers were encouraged to stay on the plane as it got ready to continue its flight to South Africa. Some of the passengers who had alighted here would be turned away.

It was a depressing place, with an old 1960's square brick building in front of them, where they were being ushered by airport officials. In fact, all of the buildings within sight seemed to have been built in the 1960's or before, as if very little maintenance had been done on them since then. Stephanie got the impression that she and Martin were being watched.

A large, black, bald bodyguard of a man met them as they walked through customs. He wore light khaki trousers which did not quite match the shade of his shirt, and the bulge under his jacket indicated that he was armed.

"Mister Latham?" he asked.

"*Lord* Latham," Martin answered, standing tall and stronger than he had been just a few minutes ago. "I am here for an audience with the president."

"The president is very busy, but thanks you for your time. You will be entertained in the VIP lounge here at the airport while your plane is being attended, and then you will board the aircraft and leave."

"And you are?" Martin asked. He put on his most official (and officious) voice. He would not be dismissed so easily. The big man paused, opened his mouth, and then closed it again. His problems had started when Martin had told him he was to be addressed as 'Lord Latham'. Then this lord had asked for his name. He had never been important enough to give his name before.

"Komolo," he answered, after giving himself a moment to think. "Ben Komolo."

"Mr Komolo," said Martin with a broad, pseudo-friendly smile. He had caught the man off-guard and was going to milk it. "I am not here to see you. Neither am I one for being entertained as a VIP while your country suffers. I am here to see your president. Are you the chauffeur who will take me to him?"

"No, sir, I am…" Komolo started, but Martin interrupted.

"Then find him for me, will you? I am sure my government has already contacted President Veritas, and I expect he will be waiting for me. Make whatever calls you have to, if you can find a telephone that works, and get me my chauffeur, or whatever means of transport your president can supply. But *do not come back to me and tell me you cannot do it.*"

Stephanie wondered whether this was a vampiric trait or whether Martin was just very good at this sort of stuff, but Ben Komolo was not equipped to deal with this attitude. In less than half an hour, he found them a driver and they were being driven to the palace in a big, black limousine. Apparently, landlines could work even though radio waves failed, so there was still limited communication to the president's palace. Stephanie was impressed with how quickly Martin had recovered both his strength and his wits now that they were on land again.

The palace itself was a large building with hundreds of small windows in four rows up its high walls, flanked by trees and high garden walls. It looked like the building had been extended in recent years, so that the square block shape of the original building had further built-on blocks each with the same kind of windows. If it wasn't for the fact that it had recently been whitewashed, it would have looked a little like a prison. The non-symmetrical building was based approximately in the centre of its own grounds, fronted by a large concrete courtyard that seemed to be used mainly as a car park. The main entrance, where the limousine stopped to dump its passengers, was the only one of four entranceways that was actually in use. It seemed to Stephanie that the other three access points were either heavily guarded or blocked. Having dropped them off, their driver drove his car out of the courtyard and back towards the airport.

Stephanie and Martin walked with some confidence up to the first set of guards by the main entrance. Rather, Martin walked with confidence and Stephanie followed a step or two behind with what little confidence she could muster. Now that her job of looking after Martin was over, the nerves were beginning to work their way back in. The guards were adjusting their rifles in a way that suggested not only that they had noticed them, but also that they weren't sure whose side they were on. Martin introduced himself as the British envoy on an urgent mission to see President Veritas, who would be expecting him, and he certainly didn't want to keep the president waiting.

One of the guards made a quick internal telephone call and ushered them into the main building, where they were taken to a small, air-conditioned reception lounge. Stephanie realised how hot she had become in this late afternoon sun, and she was relieved at how the air conditioning began to cool her down a little. It was not long before an official met them. He was dressed in the finery of the palace, tan brown but with trims of bright colours.

"Wait here," he said in thickly accented English. There was the sound of voices from the door he had just come through. Another voice called to him.

"The president will not see them in that room. Bring them to the main hall."

They were led through the door to the great hall, which was huge, with a decorated tiled floor and luxurious wall-coverings. It was rectangular in shape, and Stephanie felt that it was at least big enough to fit her parents' house and grounds in. Even in this poor country the leadership was rich enough for this extravagant show of opulence. Around the outside of the room there were expensive-looking chairs, and at one end of the room there was an unusual-looking ornament that seemed out of place. It looked like a full scale model of the above-ground portion of a well, sitting on the floor, but with no shaft. It was guarded by an ugly statue with arms and legs like a man. It had a head, but no face. It was basic and crudely carved, as if the artist had only just begun his work, or had given up on it as a bad job. It towered over the well like a giant, lifeless sentry, and the hairs on the back of Stephanie's neck stood on end when she looked at it.

She looked up at the balcony that overlooked all four walls of the hall. She saw what appeared to be a robed monk, one of those little grey men that Professor Bouvon had spoken about. It appeared at first to be the size of a child, or a very short man, watching over the proceedings as if he – or it – was making sure that his instructions were being carried out. Behind the little monk there was a very tall, stout guard dressed in ceremonial colours and carrying a state-of-the-art rifle. The short, cowled figure turned to the guard and whispered something, and the big man disappeared through one of the many doors that led from the balcony.

Standing near the door, and flanked by two guards, was President Mikal Veritas. Stephanie recognised him from the various photographs she had recently seen, although he was not in ceremonial clothing. He wore khaki trousers and an open-necked pale shirt.

"Lord Martin Latham," said Martin, offering his hand to the president and bristling with charm. "I am here on behalf of the British government, bringing our goodwill and concerns about your recent disaster." The guards tensed up as if they were expecting Martin to attack their leader, but the president stepped forward and took his hand with a polite smile.

"And we appreciate your personal attention," Veritas replied, well-versed in the art of politics. He spoke loudly and clearly enough to be heard, not only by Martin, but also by the guards who were standing just a few steps behind him. Stephanie wondered if they were guarding him or holding him prisoner. "Although, you would know that we have had many calls of condolences already, including a personal telephone call from your prime minister. I wonder what you have to add to his comments."

Then he spoke in a quieter voice, "Not to mention a visit from a Mr Clifton Chase of the Angel Trust yesterday. Perhaps that is the real reason you are here."

"We wanted to put in a personal appearance," Martin replied aloud, but nodded at the president's comment. "With the goodwill that exists between our countries, it seemed the most appropriate thing to do."

Veritas turned around to the guards who were watching them. "I think we do not have to worry about these guests," he said to them, and they were dismissed, allowing the president to talk more openly.

"The meeting room you were led to may be bugged," he said.

"Not in charge of your own kingdom?" said Martin quietly. "Is there some way my government can intervene on your behalf?"

"I would prefer that we had no further visits from your people," said Veritas. "I would not like to put my guests in danger. Mr Chase was here, and he left. Like you, his life was in danger. Unlike you, he escaped." Stephanie felt a cold feeling shiver through her, despite the heat outside. "I am on your side, sir, miss," he continued, "but I do not think you can help me rid myself of the burden I have brought down on my country."

"I have to try, anyway," said Martin.

"No, you don't," said Veritas. "You have to run. I will escort you to a side exit, which I know is being watched by the resistance. Perhaps they will be able to help you. It is your best option."

"Resistance?" said Stephanie.

"A few months ago, I met with some new people – they promised to make Mbalaya the richest country in the world. Now I am not a stupid man, but there was something, I don't know, *supernatural*, about their promise, something that convinced me. They wanted an experimental area to work on, and asked for Hemmin. I instructed my people to evacuate the town and gave my elite regiment, the Balayan Guard, over to them to control."

"Them?" said Martin.

"They are watching us from the balcony. They look like monks, but they don't *feel* human. They talk to each other with a look, as if they're telepathic, but give orders to the Guard in Mbalayan."

"If they aren't human, then what are they?" said Martin. Stephanie remained silent. It was a strange question to ask in the real world, but Stephanie was beginning to get used to the rather different world that Martin seemed to live and move in.

"I don't know. I have never seen much more than a face under those robes and it was pale grey with large, black eyes. I have never been religious, and I never really believed in the supernatural before then, but they have changed my mind. In the beginning, they seemed to respect my rule, but now they have taken over, and give me orders as if I was their servant. And from that entire desert out there, they chose an occupied town for their unholy experiment."

"Hemmin is situated on a convergence of ley lines," Stephanie said, finding her voice at last.

"That may be true, miss, but I think they wanted to destroy the town because there was something there that they wanted to bury."

"Like what?" asked Martin. Stephanie feared she might know what they tried to destroy, and she desperately hoped they didn't succeed.

"I don't know, but a number of residents of the town, evacuees, have formed a kind of resistance movement which protests against my leadership and, in particular, the rule of these creatures. The Guard have been given instructions to shoot on sight any members of the group, or anyone protesting near to the palace. Mr Chase asked questions about Hemmin and I think they – the creatures – considered him one of them – an enemy."

"Perhaps the people of the resistance know something."

"Perhaps, but I am unable to find out. I have tried to argue with the monks until I feel my own life is in danger. They watch everything, and they no longer tolerate my interference. I feel I'm now confined to this palace. It may be luxury, but it is still my prison. I am hardly even allowed out, and when I try to communicate with our people through our national television channel, they watch me carefully. I wish I could change things. Sometime soon I need to speak to the people, to tell them…" he realised his voice was getting louder, so he quietened to almost a whisper. "To tell them I am sorry."

"Communications are hard, though," said Martin. "Radio messages and telephone networks don't seem to work in this country."

"Our television network is cabled to homes in and around the city. Wired communications work where radio waves do not. Perhaps we can get a call for help out and anyone who hears it might then, in turn, get it out of the country. I take it that Mr Chase has failed to do this."

"I'm afraid so."

"I don't know what happened to him after he left the palace yesterday. I hope he is still alive. And if I keep you here much longer, you will not even get as far as leaving this building. They are watching us carefully. We must move now."

The president led them out of the great hall towards a side exit. A guard met them and fell in line to escort them, perhaps to make sure they left the building. Stephanie hoped that it wasn't to make sure they didn't.

"I will escort them from here," the president told his guard, who paused, unwilling to relinquish his duty so easily. "Britain is hardly an enemy of the State, Mbeki," he said sharply, and the man nodded, left them and returned to the main hall. The president walked them out of the building to the car park and pointed to a small side-gate a few metres from the main gates.

"I can take you no further, Lord Latham. If you get out of the country, tell them I have acted with my country's best interest at heart. Please tell your people that. Now, go quickly. Run away from any vehicle that comes from this palace." Then he turned and returned to the building. Stephanie watched him, and it seemed to her that the palace looked bleaker than it had when she first saw it.

They walked quickly away from the side gate, looking for a taxi or a way back to the airport. As they moved further away, Martin started slowing them down a little. Behind them, Stephanie was aware that the main palace double gates were opening.

Suddenly, an old car, a black Ford Escort of at least thirty years old, pulled up beside them from a side street where it had been parked, seemingly unnoticed. Its engine was revving up furiously. The driver was a man, but it was a woman who unwound the window and called to them from a passenger seat.

"Get in! Quickly! Your life is in danger!"

Without looking back toward the palace, Martin immediately opened the back door of the car and grabbed Stephanie by the arm, bundling her in. He then jumped in behind her. Martin was not a small man, and Stephanie had not landed in the car in the best position, so they were crushed in the back seat. As soon as they were both in, but before the door was properly closed behind them, the driver, a frail-looking Mbalayan man in his seventies, put his foot down and made the vehicle's tyres screech as he pulled away with as much haste as possible.

Stephanie was thrown against Martin as the car suddenly accelerated. She recovered herself quickly and managed to take a glimpse out of the car's dirty back window to see two armed soldiers training their guns on the vehicle. Staring frozen, she saw tiny puffs of smoke burst from the weapons, and heard a series of staggering bangs echoing towards them.

"Keep your head down, please, miss," said the elderly driver with a thick Mbalayan accent. Stephanie ducked down on the back seat and snuggled tightly against Martin, who put an arm around her. The car turned sharply into a wide road that led away from the palace, and then swerved again to avoid a dog that found itself in the direct path of the little vehicle. Stephanie's stomach turned at the lurching of the car, and she felt sick, as much from fear as from the motion of their speeding transport.

"They'll have a vehicle much faster than ours and they'll be after us in no time," the woman explained as the car turned sharply, its wheels almost leaving the road. The car swerved and turned a few more times, and the streets seemed to grow narrow, with high buildings flanking them.

Stephanie heard the vehicle's tyres squeal as they strained against the road, and almost felt the scraping of the bodywork against a wall as the driver misjudged a tight alleyway. She had her eyes tightly shut, but she still had an image of sparks flying as they rocketed through the dangerous terrain. She heard the sound of sirens somewhere behind them.

Surely, she reasoned, they wouldn't have gunned down British nationals (or whatever Martin was) on the steps of the palace itself? They were not a danger to anyone here in this country (unless Martin had developed a taste for the blood of an African president). Perhaps, in fact, the Guard were sent out only to ensure that this little old lady and her chauffeur didn't make contact. Well, they were too late for that!

The car screeched and scraped through more narrow roads that may not have been designed to take vehicles. Perhaps the car that was after them was wider, and would get stuck in some of these little alleys. She hoped so – this old banger should never have been rescued from the crusher. She was amazed that nothing had fallen off this machine yet. Of course, she couldn't tell from her position huddled in the back seat whether the car was still intact. It was making some pretty frightening engine-sounds and it was certainly labouring under the strain of the chase.

Stephanie wondered for a moment whether they were being rescued or kidnapped. The two old people in the front seats didn't look dangerous; neither did they seem to be brandishing weapons – they didn't appear to be highly-trained terrorists or activists. They were both old, probably in their seventies. Stephanie opened one eye to take a glance at the driver. He was sweating and fighting with the steering wheel as they zigzagged through the city, his gritted white teeth showing clearly in his black face as they struggled to keep control of the car. The old woman kept glancing back at them as they huddled in the back seat, and out of the back window to check and see if they were still being followed.

Somehow the vehicle, or vehicles, following them had a reasonable idea where they were going. Perhaps it was the scrape marks they had made on so many walls. Anyway, in spite of a decent head start, the clapped-out old Ford was not taking them to safety. Eventually, after just a few minutes of hectic swerving through narrow streets (although it seemed longer to Stephanie), smoke started to billow from the engine. The car came to a halt alongside a tin-hut-style shed.

"Quick, they'll be here soon," the old lady said as she nimbly got out of the car. Stephanie was creaky and stiff as she was dragged from her crouching position by Martin, and she was shaky on her legs as she followed the old man and his lady accomplice through the shed and out the other side. The tin shell of the structure was hollow, like the empty remains of an ancient World War Two bomb shelter. Then they ran across a small open courtyard and entered a large old brick building using a small hidden door through which they had to duck. Stephanie's circulation started to return and she began to recover from the drive, if not from the fear of the chase. They climbed an old, dusty set of stairs inside the solid building. Their rescuers, or escorts, or whatever they were, seemed quite nimble. They led their two guests to a hiding place at the top of the stairs. The building was tall and empty inside, a strong brick structure that might have been a factory in its recent past, but which was now deserted apart from these four new occupants. They hid by a window between planks and sheets of dry, rotten wood. From the small pane they could look down and see the smoking vehicle that they had abandoned only a few minutes ago, a couple of hundred metres away.

Two state police cars drew up beside the abandoned Ford, and four armed Balayan Guardsmen got out. They stood around the old vehicle, looking into its filthy windows, and scanning the immediate area for signs of the fugitives. There were at least eight directions in which their prey could have run, and the guards seemed reluctant to split up.

Stephanie and Martin and their two new companions huddled together in silence, waiting for the searchers to move on. Stephanie wanted to ask for an explanation, but she was afraid that, even this distance away, their pursuers would hear. Down below them, the Mbalayan soldiers seemed to be discussing what they would do next. Two of them stayed by the abandoned

Ford, and a couple more got into their vehicles and drove away. The others fanned out to search.

"They've gone back to the palace to fetch reinforcements," whispered the old woman.

"Or advice," suggested Martin. "The absence of radio communications has worked in our favour this time."

"So it will take them time to organise and coordinate their search," said the woman. "We stand a good chance of getting away in these streets."

"Who were they?" whispered Martin to their rescuers when he was sure that their pursuers were out of sight.

"They are the Balayan Guard," said the woman. "The name goes back to the founding of the country. They were the elite of our army, a force to be proud of. But the new, resurrected version is just a group of thugs, hunting down anyone who opposes our president's authority. In fact, we believe that the Guard has been gifted to our strange, robed 'guests' to use as they wish."

"And they want us dead?"

"Probably. They will believe you are spies."

"We just came here to help," said Martin. "And to find out what happened to the town of Hemmin. And to our friend."

"The man who visited yesterday?"

"Yes."

"He got away."

"You helped him?" asked Martin.

"Yes."

"And you," said Martin. "Who are you?"

"My name is Rana Steelback," she said. "I used to live in Hemmin."

Ten

Rana Steelback sat on a little hillock in the darkness, looking out towards the lights of the capital city of her country. Martin stood next to her, trying to contact John Borland on his satellite phone. It was a high-end device, not reliant on local networks or cell sites for coverage, and yet it still had no signal. The Saharan night was very cold and dark. Martin seemed at home in the dark and not affected at all by the cold, but Stephanie found herself shivering. She didn't know that the Sahara Desert could get this cold.

For some reason, Martin had trusted Rana and her companion, Harry. They'd managed to get them out of the city, which was largely protected by a wall, a throwback to when the city (then a town) was ravaged by attacks from various enemies during the Middle Ages. Mbalaya's capital, rebuilt, strengthened and now called Veritas City had, in different ages in the past, been Christian, Muslim and Pagan, all dependent upon who had conquered it. Getting over the wall might have been a problem then, but now there were so many gaps in the security surrounding the city that they found it quite easy to sneak through. Then they had kept close to the low, bushy tamarisk shrubs and crept away from the city until, finally, night fell and they felt a little safer. Harry had sneaked off to find them some transport, and Martin had lent Stephanie his jacket to protect her from some of the chill of night. And all this time, Rana had told them nothing.

Now they had eaten something that Stephanie had been afraid to ask about, possibly barbecued lizard, and they were five miles from the city with no lights or sound to suggest that anybody was close enough to know they were there. Now it was time to ask questions.

"So what happened to Hemmin?" she asked. "Was it some kind of experimental weapon?"

"It was an experiment of some kind," said the old lady in a sad, tired voice. "A week or two back we were all ordered to get out of town. We were all to be re-housed nearby. Some of us were even offered apartments in the city. None of us wanted to go. Perhaps the places they were going to send us were more luxurious, but we were all simple people. You can't farm land in the middle of a city, and most of us are too old to learn a new trade, or how to use modern technology. We were used to just walking down the street to spend time with our friends. We didn't pack up or make preparations, we just stayed in our homes. So a couple of days later, the army came and moved us by force. Some of us were beaten for putting up a fight; some were picked up and dumped in trucks. Nobody was allowed their belongings; we all were just taken away with the clothes we were wearing.

"Those of us who were left approached the soldiers and agreed to pack up and leave if they gave us just one more day. They only gave us until nightfall. So we packed up whatever we could take and ran. We scattered across the countryside. We hid in the sand and in the bush, what there is of it, and in nearby towns and villages, so that the soldiers couldn't find us."

Rana stopped for a breather. She told her story clearly, as if she had rehearsed it over and over in her head in the hope that people from outside like Martin and Stephanie would be able to hear it. Her eyes were far away, as if she was reliving the last few days.

"Did you think your lives were in danger?" Stephanie asked.

"We didn't know what to think. Those of us that could tried to sneak back to Hajar Tel. That's a small rocky hill that overlooks the town, a bit like this one looks over Veritas City. We were afraid that the soldiers might be using it as an observation post, but there was nobody, absolutely nobody anywhere near the hill or the town. There were eighteen of us, just eighteen that didn't get taken away by soldiers, and we all saw what happened."

She went quiet, and she stared into her memories of that night. Her eyes widened as she recalled what she saw. Stephanie wanted to prompt her to describe what happened next, but she knew the old woman would start again when she was ready.

"It was like a storm," she eventually continued. "There were flashes of lightning, a thick layer of something like cloud, and high winds smashing at the walls of our houses. They were all flattened – mud, stick and stone thrown about the landscape. And, the oddest thing was that, while we saw everything from up on that hill, we felt nothing. Not even the rush of air. The storm only affected the town itself, and didn't reach as far as us, only half a mile away. It was as if it was the target for some evil gods who were raining their shots down on our home."

"And you were moved out before it happened," said Martin, who had been listening silently. "That means someone knew it was going to happen."

"Or *made* it happen," Rana concluded. They were interrupted by the sound of a vehicle's engine approaching. Someone was driving without headlights, so that he would not be seen in this near-pitch-black night.

"That'll be Harry," Rana said.

The vehicle this time was an old jeep, possibly a relic from World War Two, and it stopped nearby. Someone got out of the passenger side and made his way towards them. He was quite close before they recognised Clifton Chase.

"Well, it's good to see you, Martin," he said with a smile, obviously knowing that John Borland had sent him out to try to track down his missing agent. Then he noticed Stephanie. "You brought her with you?" he sounded shocked.

"You helped me when I needed it," Stephanie said. "I had to try and do the same." Clif's attitude changed instantly and he stepped forward and gave her a big hug. She reciprocated, and found that she enjoyed it rather more than she thought she should. Perhaps it was just the relief of seeing him alive and well.

"I wouldn't have been able to make the flight without her," Martin said by way of an explanation.

"Okay," said Clif with some caution. He didn't seem to know about Martin's condition.

"I take it Rana and Harry rescued you the same way they did for us?" said Stephanie.

"Yes. Did they tell you about what happened to their home?"

"Yes."

Rana interrupted the reunion. "We'll take you to the Mali border, of course. But we'd like you to see Hemmin first."

"We'd very much like to see the ruins of the town," Martin replied. Stephanie was thinking more along the lines of 'get us out of here by the shortest possible route', but Martin was the boss and it was likely she wouldn't have been able to change his mind.

Harry turned the vehicle around and tried to find the road in the dark. Rana joined the three visitors as they started their journey rather faster than Stephanie felt was safe. The thought of being driven in the dark by an old man in an even older vehicle made her want to go back to the city and turn herself in. There was a very thin crescent moon up in the sky, but it gave off nowhere near enough light and old Harry seemed to be driving by faith more than by sight. The main road to Hemmin was not a great road anyway, and Stephanie felt every muscle tense up as she gripped the seat with one hand and Clif's hand with the other.

When they were several more miles from the capital, Harry put the jeep's lights on and the journey was slightly less unnerving. After three hours, they stopped to meet with Rana's friends, presumably more of the displaced townspeople, for breakfast in the early hours of the morning. Clifton pulled out his satellite phone, but it was still not sending or receiving.

The Hemmin camp consisted of a small number of tents and makeshift houses, six or seven cars and trucks, some clothes on a line and a small number of pots and pans that the eighteen of them had been sharing between them. Most of the members of the camp were older people, although there was a middle-aged couple and their teenage boy among them, too. Stephanie wondered how they had managed to escape from the soldiers. The young lad was thin and wiry, and in his eyes there was something that suggested that he had grown up before his time. Stephanie looked at him as he moved about the camp being helpful to the oldest members of the party, and she realised that if he had witnessed the destruction of his home town, it was no surprise that he was no longer childlike in his manner.

The people were warm and friendly, and shared their food gladly. Stephanie felt a little guilty about eating from what little they had, but she knew that she was among people whose culture it was to share, and it was probably an insult to refuse the offered food. She pondered as she ate the stale bread and stringy meat how, the richer people get, the harder it is to give anything away.

She chatted to members of this lost and lonely group of families. The one youngest adult, a middle-aged man, was cut and bruised where he had attempted to defend his home against the attacking armed men. She looked at him in the firelight.

"Does it hurt?"

"Not really," he answered, his fingers lightly touching the nastiest-looking bruise on his face. "He didn't mean it, you know."

"What?"

"The soldier. The man who did this – I could see on his face; he didn't want to throw us out of our homes. Sometimes you've just got to follow orders, you know."

"If it was you, if you were the soldier…" Stephanie started.

"No," the man interrupted sharply. "No, I wouldn't do this to my own countryman. But I'm just a farmer. I suppose I'm not even that anymore."

"I'm sorry," said Stephanie. "That was unkind of me."

"Thank you for coming," the man said. "Thank you for trying, for trying to help strangers."

Stephanie heard clearly in her head what Lady Venner had said to her when she'd asked why the Fey People were here – she had said, "We're here to help." If People from another world want to help us, how could we not help our own?

"Were you there when…" Stephanie started, but got a little tongue-tied. "Did you see it happen?"

"Yes, I left the town with my family. That's my truck over there – I drove Rana and the others back to see what they did to the town. We saw the storm. It was like somebody opened the gates of hell and let it loose on my home, and then it was over in hardly any time at all. Everything that was ours… was gone."

Stephanie put her hand on his shoulder and he nodded his appreciation, and then returned to look after a couple of old ladies.

Stephanie got a few words with Clif, who'd been moving among the people, trying to help where he could.

"Did you know Martin's a vampire?" she whispered so that only he could hear her. The people who had rescued them didn't need more grief.

Clif stared at her for a moment, then took in a big breath and smiled. "No," he said. "But it makes sense. He really didn't like the Romanian Embassy. He was on the run from them. And when we asked him about the beginnings of the Angel Trust, about his ancestors who founded the organisation, he said he didn't know anything, but I felt that wasn't true. It was him. It wasn't his ancestors – he did it himself. Vampires can't breed, not anymore, so he must be a couple of hundred years old. At least."

"They can't?"

"His girlfriends. They must provide him with the blood he needs…" Clif's voice faded to silence.

"Is cattle an appropriate term?" said Stephanie, and her laughter was slightly hysterical.

"You knew this," said Clif thoughtfully, "and you came with him anyway."

"He needed me," she said.

"You're amazing."

"Right now, I'm feeling a few inches short of useless."

But I'm not, she thought. *Lady Marika knew something. She knew I'd end up here. And she told me not to be afraid when things got hard. Were those her exact words?* Stephanie wasn't so sure now that they were so far away from civilisation, from home, and from safety.

"Did you get into the palace?" she asked him. "Did you see the robed monks – the 'little grey men'?"

"Yes."

"Are they goblins?" she asked, and wondered if she would ever have asked a question like that before she met Martin.

"No, goblins are a bit more like little green men," Clifton laughed. "And they have big noses. They're known for their noses. These creatures didn't seem to have noses at all. Anyway, goblins are on our side."

"I didn't see any goblins when I went to the manor."

"Really? I thought there were more goblins than any other species there. I've never been on a proper visit there. You're privileged."

It felt surreal, talking about goblins and listening to these misplaced people in the heavy darkness of Saharan Africa. It was almost as if this was all a dream. She wished it was. She listened to more of their stories.

These people had all seen the weird storm that had devastated their homes, and all told the same story as Rana had told them, in their own words. The man she had spoken to had mentioned that the soldiers who had come to take them from their homes were only doing a job, and were determined not to hurt anybody, but they were also afraid, and couldn't disobey orders. When this group had run into the desert, none of the soldiers had wanted to follow them. They just wanted to get away from Hemmin as quickly as possible.

Stephanie tried to empathise with their feelings of loss and bewilderment, and understood their distrust of the current government and the strange beings that were exerting their influence over the current leaders. However, she wasn't sure that the Balayan Guard would really have killed them on the steps of their own presidential palace, and probably only chased them because Rana had 'rescued' them. Nevertheless, they did have a case against their leaders, and Stephanie felt that the best course of action would be to get back to civilisation to report of what had happened, and find a way to help these people reclaim their home – or at least, build a new one.

On the flat ground a few metres away from the cooking fire where people gathered to eat, an old man, possibly the oldest of them all, sat cross-legged, facing away from the group, looking southwards towards where the town of Hemmin once stood, twenty or so miles away. He was almost bald, with just a few strands of white hair still barely clinging to his head, which seemed disproportionately large in comparison to the rest of his body. He wore loose-fitting trousers, but nothing else, apparently impervious to the cold of the night. Stephanie took a step or two towards him, but was intercepted by Rana.

"Don't disturb him. He's meditating."

"Who is he?"

"He is Elijah Akar," Rana replied in a whisper. "He's our, I'm not sure how you would say it – if we were religious, he would be our priest. If we were superstitious, he would be our witch doctor.

I suppose witch doctor is the nearest description I can give you. Some of us believe that he is descended from the man who founded our town two hundred and fifty years ago."

"Matthias Hemmin," said Stephanie.

"That's right," said Rana, surprised and pleased that Stephanie knew. "Elijah is related to Hemmin on his great-grandmother's side, I believe."

The old man came to his senses, his eyes seeming to refocus on the here and now, and he looked up at Stephanie and gave her a toothy smile.

"Something was put there," he said, and his voice was croaky. Stephanie did not know what he was talking about.

"Where?"

"In Matthias Hemmin's town."

"What was put there?"

"Something of great value. Something of great power. It was put there for its protection. Nobody was able to get to it, to do it any harm for two hundred and fifty years. It was hidden under the ground."

"What was put there?" Stephanie asked again, but the old man, like so many soothsayers, witch doctors and mystics (and for that matter, sidhe queens), would only say as much as he wanted to say. It was this thing that they had, thought Stephanie, that made them want to appear mystical, to keep people who paid them respect on their toes. And the question wasn't what, but where – and possibly when.

"Two hundred and fifty years," said Elijah, "to the day."

Stephanie said nothing. If what the old man said was true, it would certainly add to the mystique of the Hemmin incident, as well as adding to the mystique of this old witch doctor. It might just be something to say to keep his followers in awe of him, but either way, it might be something worth investigating. They were about to visit the ruins of the old town. How would they be able to take a look *under* it?

"Have you eaten enough?" asked Rana, interrupting her thoughts. "Would you like some more, or to rest a while before we go on?"

"I'm fine, thanks. You've looked after me well, but I would like to go on, if you don't mind – as soon as possible." She was no longer hungry, but the thought of being at home, or possibly eating a huge meal at Mr Toad's Rest in Barnhampton or Zana's near 'Niz' Manor, really appealed to her right now.

They got into the jeep to continue their journey. Harry drove and Clifton, Rana, Martin and Stephanie were passengers. None of the others seemed to want to see their devastated home town again. As their journey began, Stephanie looked back and saw the old man, the witch doctor, standing up now. He was looking at her – directly at her, as if she had something still to offer this mission. He'd told her something in his cryptic words that was a clue, and she'd missed it.

It seemed like no time at all had passed, but they were there. Stephanie must have dozed off for a few minutes. There was a glow on the horizon, and warmth was already beginning to flood the land. They stopped on the hill that Rana had described almost as if they were afraid to go right down to the town itself. There were wiry trees and bushes among the rocks where they hid the jeep. They quickly found a good vantage point from which to look over the remains of Hemmin.

The light of day came very quickly. Stephanie had heard somewhere that sudden daylight happened like this near the equator. The land in front and below them began to light up, and their eyes quickly adjusted. They saw the mess that was once the town of Hemmin. Buildings of various strength and structures, from little twig outhouses to hard stone and mud walls, were all smashed up together as if an earthquake had hit the town at the same time as a hurricane had been passing through. The town was just about as flat as the rest of the ground.

Rana, standing by them, covered her mouth with her hand at the sight of what was once her home.

"This town is… was on ley lines," said Stephanie.

"Ley lines," said Rana in a shaky voice. "Elijah used to talk about them. But he didn't say anything about them in the town. He used to say 'nearby'."

"He said that something had been put here," said Stephanie. "It might have been hidden here by Matthias Hemmin when it was first built. I would like to find out what it was."

"Like a magic amulet or something?" said Martin, stepping up beside them. Now that daylight was here, he had covered up and put his hat back on.

"Or a lamp that makes a djinn appear when you rub it?" said Clif, who was standing behind them.

"What else do we know about Matthias Hemmin?" asked Stephanie suddenly, ignoring the men. She had worked out what Elijah was trying to tell her. "He was a religious leader, a bit like Elijah. He founded the town."

"Yes," said Rana.

"Where was the original town?"

"Original?" said Rana.

"Elijah said 'in Matthias Hemmin's town'. He didn't refer to it as his home. So if the town's specific location has changed over the years, where was it two hundred and fifty years ago?" asked Stephanie.

Rana pointed out past her home town towards where Georges Bouvon's archaeological dig had been a few weeks back.

"Over there. The town moved to a better trading position over the years to be a little nearer the road to Mali."

"If anything had been hidden, it would be there," said Stephanie, and she climbed down from Stone Hill to the desert floor. The ground was mostly hard, with tufts of brown, dry grass and some patches of soft sand. If they had been a farming people, as Rana had said, then they would have had a hard life. Growing things in this country would have been difficult, to say the least. She broke into a run towards Bouvon's dig. She was vaguely aware that the others were following her.

It was a little over a mile to the dig, but the air was heating up and Stephanie had not slept for more than a few minutes in the last day or so. She was as tired as if she'd run a marathon by the time they arrived. Somehow, the isolated 'storm from hell' had reached out and hit the remains of Bouvon's archaeological site as well, and it, too, had been flattened.

She stood to regain her breath, doubled over, hands on her thighs, breathing heavily. The others caught up with her, Rana trailing behind, aided by Harry.

"What was hidden here?" Stephanie asked nobody in particular.

"It was something the Hemmin family and his descendants after them guarded for generations," said Rana, coming up behind them.

"Go on," said Clif.

"I don't know what it is," said Rana. "I'm not even sure Elijah knows what it is."

"Was there a crypt below the original town?" asked Stephanie.

"It wasn't a crypt," said Rana.

"Then what was it?"

"I never saw it," said Rana, "but it was supposed to be the salvation of our land when the Enemy came."

"Enemy?" asked Martin. "Enemy soldiers? Were you expecting an invasion?"

"Mbalaya has been invaded several times in its history," Stephanie said, recalling her research on the country. "I never read that anyone in particular from Hemmin ever came up to fight on the country's behalf. Not for the last two hundred and fifty years."

"So where," asked Clif, convinced that they would not get a clear description of whatever was supposed to be hidden below the town, "was the entrance to this 'not a crypt', to whatever the guardians were supposed to be guarding?"

"Somewhere right here, more or less, I think," said Rana. "This may seem stupid, but I didn't connect the destruction of the town with whatever Elijah and his family were looking after. I mean, nobody outside the town would know about it."

They all looked around, examining the area for signs of an entrance of some kind. If the purpose of the attack on Hemmin was to hide the entrance, it looked like it had worked.

"How many people have searched the ruins since the, er, incident?" asked Stephanie.

"None," said Rana. "They are all afraid, and the soldiers have driven them away."

"Luckily, no soldiers have driven us away," said Clif. He was active and animated; perhaps he'd had more sleep than the rest of them over the last thirty-six hours. Stephanie was exhausted, and Martin was suffering from the effects of the growing sunlight. He was sheltering in the shade of what little structure of the dig still remained upright, looking around to see if he could see something that the others could not. Clif paid less attention to the ruins and more to the local hillocks and dunes, just in case the Balayan Guard might be hiding there.

"I've got something!" said Martin. He had found a fallen slab, which appeared to cover a hole in the ground. Far from destroying whatever the Hemmin family had hidden, the storm had revealed it, after all. The slab that had fallen on it was huge, but cracked and broken in several places. He tried to move it, but with no success. The others gathered round to help. They could not lift it, but the five of them, working together, rocked it back and forward until they managed to slide it slightly to the side. They revealed the hole in the ground that Georges Bouvon had not quite found, and, possibly, that the grey robed monks who had taken over the palace had wanted to hide forever.

Stephanie looked down into the dark, and was filled with an unreasonable fear. This was shaping up like some sort of horror story, and here she was, the helpless little girl (for that was how she felt) who could have, if she'd had any sense, stayed at home when they had all suggested coming here to Africa. But no, she'd decided to come with them. And now this dark tomb beckoned. And, in spite of her fears, she knew that she should lead the way.

"Do you think it's big enough to get in?" asked Clif. Stephanie thought; please don't say that because I am the slimmest, I should go first.

Nobody said it.

"I should go," she heard herself say, although she had no idea what made her say it. She found it easy to go in, feet first, finding purchase as she went. One of Rana's friends had lent her a torch, but the light from it was weak. Martin eagerly followed her to get out of the sun, and the others followed more cautiously.

The tunnel that had been under the concrete and stone structure for the last two hundred and fifty years was short, with wide steps leading down into some sort of hall. The light from Stephanie's torch seemed to be soaked up by the cold walls, which reflected it back at them with an eerie glow. The group moved slowly, but it didn't take long for their eyes to become accustomed to the gloom.

The short stone stairway led to a large hall. It was hexagonal in shape, with various symbols like ancient runes carved into each of its six walls at roughly waist height. The symbols were cracked and faded, caked with dirt and dust. In the centre of the room there was the thing that they were looking for.

It was not an amulet or a magic lamp. It was not a mummified person, a creature or a solid object. It was not something in a box or on a table – it was not 'contained' at all. It was not something made of darkness; neither was it something made of light. In fact, it was best described by saying what it wasn't, rather than what it was.

It seemed to be like some kind of distortion in the air. It was clearly there, and as they looked at it, it seemed to light up. Hard as it was to describe, it was definitely there. Stephanie took a step towards it. It was like looking into something, and seeing something else, like looking at clouds. What Stephanie could see was a shape forming inside the shape. She was quite sure that the others couldn't see what she could see from where she was standing. Here, held in place by what could well be the convergence of ley lines, something was taking on an almost physical form. And the physical form that only she could see was that of a puma-sized cat.

Thoughts came into her head, as if this creature in the formless void was trying to explain itself. Was this the same creature that she had seen in Kent when she was a child? Did some form of this being save her in the woods near Dennington? Now here it was, hidden away by an African witch doctor, trapped in the storm caused by the robed monks, wanting to be released. She took another step forward, and reached out to touch it.

"Stephanie," Martin called out sharply by way of a warning, but she could hardly hear him. Her ears were filled with the sound of roaring like a waterfall, blocking out the shouts of her friends. She was *this close* to making contact, real contact, with the Bast.

"Don't!" called Clif, louder, as her fingers made contact with the energy cloud. But it was too late. As she touched the centre of the disturbance, there was a silent noise like thunder that none of them heard, but all of them felt. As the energy earthed itself through Stephanie, she was flung across the room into one of the walls by the entrance, and all the breath was driven from her lungs as she fell, senseless, to the floor.

Eleven

Nothing was happening. Stephanie felt as if she was asleep. She remembered something that felt like an electric shock and an impact, but she felt no pain. She was drifting, as if in a dream, and she was searching for the pieces of the puzzle to fit together. What had she reached out and touched? Was it the Bast, the thing at the tip of the claw, the sharp point of the talon on Professor Georges Bouvon's map?

Stephanie started to feel pain again. She took in a breath, and her back hurt where it had hit the wall. The ideas that had invaded her mind were fading like a dream in daylight, and she was brought back into the real world with a strange feeling that she should have remembered something. There had been a sensation of floating through space, memories that were not her own, of battles fought against monstrous foes, of being hidden away here for hundreds of years. But all of it could have been the product of her imagination.

Clif and Martin were both bending over her. Clif offered her some water from his flask.

"What just happened?" he asked.

"I don't know. There was something there. Did you see it? In the centre of the room."

"Yes," confirmed Martin. "We saw it. But it isn't there now."

Martin turned to look at Rana Steelback, who seemed quite shocked by everything she had seen and looked a little shaky.

"Is this what the Hemmin family have been harbouring for the last two hundred and fifty years?" he asked her.

"Yes," Stephanie answered for her. Her strength was beginning to come back, but she was still shaking.

"How did it live that long?" asked Clif.

"Was it even alive in the first place?" asked Martin.

As Stephanie regained her strength and composure, they helped her up the steps, along the corridor and through the hole in the ground back into the sunlight. It was late morning now and Martin must have been made quite uncomfortable by the blazing sun. As they stepped out into the light, they discovered that they were surrounded by soldiers. They were armed, of course, and pointing their weapons at the trespassers.

Stephanie felt faint. She ached, she was exhausted, and she was surrounded by armed soldiers. She could have collapsed on the floor in tears, but instead she felt angry.

A soldier came to her and led her by the arm towards a transport vehicle. She pulled her arm free. Another soldier knocked Martin's hat off. She marched over to pick it up for him, and heard the sound of a number of guns clicking as the soldiers prepared them to shoot her. She looked up from her crouched position on the ground, and her eyes met what she guessed was the commander of the troop, from his bearing and the shiny pips on his jacket.

"He needs it," she said. The captain nodded, and Stephanie put the hat back on Martin's head.

"You're incredible," Martin whispered to her.

"Shut up," said the captain. He walked up to Clif, whom he perceived was the leader of the fugitives. "I had orders to shoot you, but the president himself intervened on your behalf. You are to come to the capital with us. There you will answer our questions."

"The young lady, Stephanie," Clif said to the captain. "She's not with us. She came along by accident. She's a civilian and has nothing to do with any of this."

"What did you find down there?" said the captain.

"Nothing," said Clif. "Just an empty chamber."

"Gallo," the soldier shouted to one of his subordinates, and gave an order in Arabic, indicating the hole in the ground. A young soldier went into the hole, pausing as his nerves grabbed him for a moment. A short while later he returned, confirming that there was nothing in there.

The five prisoners were loaded on board a covered troop transporter where they were guarded by six soldiers. Stephanie looked around her. There were four other vehicles, each manned by more soldiers. It seemed that the president, or the grey robed monks, or whoever was in charge of the Balayan Guard these days, had sent half the army to take them prisoner. She was scared now. In fact, she was becoming so terrified that she could hardly think, and she struggled to keep herself from screaming hysterically.

Where is the Bast now? she found herself thinking. She didn't know what the creature was, or where it had gone to, but she was fairly sure that it was still alive, or at least still in existence. Was it some kind of weapon that could be used against the grey monks? Could it think? More importantly, could it travel? Was there a way it would know where they were and what was happening to them? It had found her near her home in Kent, and again in the woods near Dennington – surely it would find her here in Africa.

The convoy of military vehicles moved off onto the desert roads towards the city. Stephanie was beginning to resign herself to what was going on, and the panic was beginning to subside. A flap on the covering of the vehicle was loose, and she was able to see the dull yellow land passing by as the truck headed back towards the city at some speed. She thought she saw something shadowing them, matching the speed of the convoy. It looked almost like a big cat, like the puma-sized creature that rescued her back in England. When she tried to concentrate on it, she didn't see it any more. Perhaps it was never there in the first place; maybe it was some sort of mirage that Stephanie's mind had interpreted as a cat, but she felt some kind of relief that, possibly, *something* was there. That little thread of hope allowed some small comfort to creep its way past her fears.

The roads were not smooth and the truck was not luxurious, so the journey back to the capital was extremely uncomfortable. Stephanie leaned on Clifton's shoulder and her head began to nod a little as she dozed, but every now and then a bump in the road brought her back to sudden wakefulness. The journey was more than two hours long and, while the vehicle's covering kept out the sun, it didn't protect them from the heat. Stephanie glanced at Martin sitting opposite her, wondering if the temperature was as bad as the sunlight for him. He was sitting upright, his hands on his knees, eyes closed but not asleep. His face was calm, as if he was meditating. *I wish I could do that*, she thought.

The soldier sitting next to Martin was staring at her chest. She might have felt uncomfortable about it back home or in more familiar surroundings, but here it was just another part of this dreadful journey. She could hardly be looking her most beautiful right now. She could feel the sweat trickling down her back and was aware of damp patches on her clothes. Her trousers clung to her legs as if they were too small. She closed her eyes again and rested her head against Clif's shoulder. Her posture was wrong and it made her neck ache, so she opened her eyes again, straightened up and tried to sit in a more comfortable position. The soldier was still staring at her body.

She tried looking back at him. Then she looked harder as if she was studying him. He became uncomfortable, and looked away. She smiled to herself for the mini-victory. Then the vehicle went over a particularly large bump in the road, and the jerky movement made even Martin open his eyes.

Finally they arrived at the capital, where the roads were slightly better constructed, and the truck made its way to some barracks that appeared to be built on to the back of the palace. Yesterday, she had only seen the front and one side of the huge building. The main barracks for the Balayan Guard had been out of sight, but the built-on soldiers' quarters also housed cells. The soldiers guided them off of the transport and down steep and broken steps to a row of cells below ground level. Each of them was put in a different cell, alone.

Stephanie's cell was empty except for a bucket and a blanket. There was no mattress or bed to lie on, so she sat on the floor with her back against the wall. The crashing sound of the cell doors closing echoed in her mind long after the guards that put her there had gone. She had been given nothing to drink on the journey, and there was nothing to drink here in the prison. She wondered how Rana Steelback was coping with this treatment, but she thought that the old lady was probably quite a lot tougher than *she* felt right now.

She did not like the look or the smell of the blanket, and she wondered how she would deal with the cold night when it came.

She wanted to shout out to her friends in the accompanying cells, but she had no voice because of her thirst, and she didn't know if they were close enough to hear her anyway. There was a small window high in the cell wall, but other than that, there was no light. She didn't want to spend the night there. She looked around at the markings on the dirty cell walls. Was that dark mark on the wall near her head blood?

The soldiers had taken her watch, so she had no idea what the time was. It felt as if she'd already been in there for days when they came to get her, although it was only an hour or two later. A tall, armed guard who didn't speak opened her cell door and beckoned her out of her little box. She got to her feet slowly, aware of how much she ached. She tried to cough, but her throat hurt. The soldier led her up the steps to ground level, and into a back room situated in the main part of the palace.

The room was a little bigger than her living room had been at her childhood home in Kent. It was fairly sparsely decorated, with a small wicker mat covering some of the stone floor. There was a cupboard unit along one wall of the room, on which rested a small television. In the centre of the room there was a bare table with two chairs. Seated on one chair was the captain who had led the team that caught her. The other chair, opposite, was empty. He beckoned her to sit down.

"I am sorry you have been through this," the captain said. His voice was deep, and although he seemed quite capable of shouting, his tone was gentle. "I am Captain Jamal Kenta. You are Miss Stephanie Baynes?"

Stephanie opened her mouth to speak, but couldn't do much more than croak. She nodded instead.

"Water for the lady!" the captain called to his guard, who went off to get her something to drink. When it was just the two of them, the captain said quietly, "Miss Baynes, I do not wish to be your enemy. I dislike what is happening in my country, but I must follow orders. After the president met with you and your colleague yesterday, he seemed quite distraught. He is becoming more and more afraid of these strange visitors of ours. They seem to have more control over our orders than he does."

The tall soldier came back with a bowl, a large jug of water and a metal cup. He poured water in the bowl as well as the cup. It looked clean to Stephanie, and she even thought she could smell how fresh it was from where she was sitting. Jamal Kenta nodded his thanks to the soldier and beckoned her to drink.

"You may wash as well if you like," he said.

She drank, and coughed for drinking too fast, then drank some more. She splashed water from the bowl over her face, and then she poured herself some more from the jug, this time drinking a little more slowly. The water hurt a little as it went down her throat, but it still felt like the most beautiful drink she'd ever tasted. Captain Kenta watched as she drank, and waited until she was ready before speaking again.

"What did you find at the village?" he asked.

"Nothing."

"Please. Let us not be like this. I want to know what these creatures, these monks are afraid of that they would destroy a whole village to be rid of it."

Stephanie thought carefully about how she could word her answer so that she did not tell a lie.

"There was something there once, but whatever it was, it is gone now."

"I did not believe in magic, Miss Baynes, not until I saw the destruction of that town, and the way these creatures seem to control things. But now I find I must ask you: was this 'something' magic?"

"If the monks who are trying to control your country are bad magic," she replied carefully, "then I think whatever was underneath the old town of Hemmin was supposed to be good magic. But I don't know, not for sure."

"It is no longer there?"

"I'm afraid not."

He looked at her carefully, trying to work out whether she was lying. "When we were driving back from the town to here, I felt the hairs on the back of my head stand on end. It was as if something was travelling with us. Do you know what I mean?" The captain spoke carefully and gently, as if he was trying so hard to convince her that he was on her side.

"No, I don't," she replied.

"Miss Baynes," he said, his voice becoming a little more insistent.

"Are you saying it is possible that whatever was there may have returned to the city with us?" Stephanie asked.

"I am asking you."

"I don't know. Up to a few weeks ago I was an ordinary English girl leading an ordinary life and the whole idea of magic never occurred to me except in stories. But now... I've seen things. I can't tell you for sure but yes, I think it's possible," she replied. She continued to sip her water, and then she poured herself some more. There was not much left. "Why do you think I should know?"

"Because I understand why the old couple were there – it was their home. I know about the young man who came the day before yesterday – he is, most likely a spy for the British government. And the English Lord, the strange man – he is another British representative. But you, you I don't understand. Why are you here with them? What is so special about you that you should be here?"

"I don't know. I think I'm here by accident."

Captain Kenta laughed, but it was not a harsh laugh. "I don't think anybody is here by accident."

"No, you're right. I am here because of whatever was below Professor Bouvon's dig – what I called the old village. But I don't know why," she replied, and if she wasn't too dry, she might have started crying. She remembered the words Lady Marika spoke to her when she visited Nieziemski Manor. Somehow, she was the only person who could have released whatever was sleeping beneath the old village. "I mean, I don't know why it's me. And I wish it wasn't. But I'm... connected to it."

There was a knock on the door. Another soldier put his head around the door.

"It is about to start," the newcomer said. Kenta signalled to the tall soldier, who crossed the room to turn on the television. The picture was of a poor quality, but they could see well enough after the machine had warmed up a little.

"President Veritas is making a speech to the nation. The people have heard about the destruction of Hemmin, and the president's robed 'guests' have asked, or instructed, him to make an address to the nation."

"To make excuses for them?" said Stephanie.

"He is our president," said the captain, his voice steely now as if he would not accept any criticism of his leader, even now after all that had happened. The president's speech was about to start, and the captain stood to attention as if the man had just walked into the room. Stephanie did not know what she should do, but she didn't have the energy to stand, so she stayed where she was.

President Mikal Veritas' face filled the small screen. He wore a uniform decorated with military honours – although whether that was for show or he had earned them, Stephanie did not know.

"People of Mbalaya," he said to the camera, which was closed in on his face. "My people, I know you are concerned about recent events, and I have come to you now to explain everything to you, and to call upon you to keep on putting your trust in your country and its president."

The president's eyes flicked briefly to one side, as if he was signalling something to the cameraman. Stephanie sat up in her chair, paying close attention. The president must have briefed the cameraman beforehand, because a few seconds after his eye-movement the camera seemed to draw back, showing more of the president's body, and, more particularly, his surroundings.

"You know that we have suffered terrible droughts over the last few years, and, while we have been grateful for the aid we have received through the kindness of our neighbouring countries, it has not been enough to help us to stand on our own feet. I felt the distress of my people, and I wanted to do something to help us stand tall in the community of countries that make up our part of Africa."

The camera was pulling back further, but very slowly, as if the cameraman did not want people to notice what he was doing – or rather, he did not want those robed things to know what he was doing.

"In my desire to be the best leader I could be, the leader this country deserves, I made new allegiances; allegiances which

140

promised to make our land rich again, which would enable us to hold our heads high in the world."

The president was standing a distance away from the camera, in the grand hall of his palace. Stephanie recognised it from the very short while she had spent there yesterday. As the camera panned back further, it was clear he was being flanked by two soldiers of the Balayan Guard, who were decorated almost as richly as he was. Facing the president, there were also two other creatures, little grey men, who were shorter than the average human, who were wearing long hooded robes that covered every part of their bodies, hiding their faces and hands. They stood still, watching the president carefully, but not watching the television screens or they would have seen that they were now being shown on television. The president had paused in his speech, and the camera focus had stopped moving. Mikal Veritas' expression was one of pain and sorrow for the suffering of his people and the plight of his country – not just the poverty caused by the crop failure of the recent past, but also for the problems he himself had caused by making the allegiances that he had been talking about.

He bowed his head for a moment, and it seemed to Stephanie that the creatures watching him, trying to control him, became uneasy. Perhaps that was just her imagination.

"Sometimes," the president continued, and he started to talk faster so that he could get every word in before it was too late, "we make bad choices in our desire to do good things. That is what I have done. The people who now rule over me and the palace are responsible for the destruction of the town of Hemmin, and these people rule over the Balayan Guard as if it were their own private police force. As your president, I call upon you to rebel against this attempted invasion. Soldiers of the Balayan Guard, I call on you to serve your president, your country, and not these aliens among us."

He had run out of time. The robed monks who were watching him both raised their arms towards him, and something like a bolt of lightning flew from them and struck the president down. The president died while being watched by the people, and most especially, the soldiers, of his country, so his murder was witnessed by hundreds of thousands of people. The camera kept rolling, although it appeared from the shaky movement that its operator had fled. The nearest Balayan Guard soldier had heard the president's last instruction and then witnessed his leader's death at the hands of this cowled monster that had been ordering him about for the last couple of months. He un-holstered his pistol and shot five bullets into the nearest monk-like thing.

The creature remained standing, apparently unhurt by this attack, although his cloak moved at the impact of the bullets. His raised arm pointed towards the shooter. Someone shouted a warning, but the guardsman, too, fell dead at the curse that shot from the creature's hidden fingers. The robed monks moved out of camera range. The other guardsman stood between the bodies of his president and his colleague, and bent down to examine them both. Then he looked up at the camera, which was now pointing at him. His face was angry and his eyes seemed to be holding back tears.

"People of Mbalaya, we must fight together to drive these creatures from our land."

Captain Jamal Kenta, who had been as still as a statue throughout the horror he had witnessed, suddenly came to life. He shouted orders out of the door at his sub-commander.

"Free the prisoners and bring them to me. Then get every available man to the palace. We must find a way to remove these beings from here."

Twelve

Stephanie was led back out toward the prison block, but she was not returned to the cells. The soldiers that escorted her were now her protectors, not her captors. Her friends were released and brought up into the area at the back of the palace, where they met with Captain Kenta.

"We are sorry for the way you have been treated," he said to them.

"I think we could all do with a shower and some food and drink," said Clifton. "Perhaps we could sit down, inside the palace itself?" Stephanie was surprised at how calm he seemed after being treated in such a way.

"The palace has not yet been secured from our enemies," Kenta said, and then he called to a soldier who was running nearby to join his comrades. "How many of those creatures are holding it?"

"Four," said the soldier, a little embarrassed, neglecting to mention that the four were much smaller than them, and seemed to be unarmed. At least, they had no visible weaponry. "Our bullets don't seem to hurt them."

Stephanie hugged Rana and Harry, and held on to Martin's hand in something that was better than a handshake. She then hugged Clifton Chase as if she would never let go.

"Are you okay? What's happened?" said Clif.

"The president's dead," said Stephanie. "The monk-creatures killed him. They've become the enemy, and…" Then Stephanie stopped. She broke free of Clifton and looked around the corner towards the front of the palace.

"Stephanie," said Clifton, reaching out to pull her back. "It's dangerous."

"What do you see?" asked Martin. Stephanie looked up to the lower roof that skirted the outside of the great building. Martin tried to look in the same direction to see if he could make out what she had spotted, but he recoiled and shielded his eyes from the sun. He stepped into the shadows and tried to see from there. Stephanie saw a movement on the roof. At first, it looked like one of the soldiers trying to get a vantage point in an attempt to take back the palace. As her eyes focussed, she could make out the shape of a big cat, like a puma or lynx. Her heart leapt and she wanted to laugh out loud, but she just turned to Martin.

"Can you see it?" she said.

"I think so. It's your cat, isn't it?"

"She brought a cat?" said Clifton.

"Not exactly," said Stephanie. "*It* brought *me*, I think. I freed it when I touched it in the underground place at Hemmin. It's called the Bast."

"What?" said Clifton and Martin, both at the same time.

"Don't ask me," Stephanie replied, a tear making its way down her face. "I have no idea what I am talking about. But I need to get it around the front of the palace."

"I cannot let you go that way," said Jamal Kenta. "It's too dangerous."

"That," said Stephanie in the strongest voice that her weak will could muster, pointing to the roof where everyone could now see the beast, "is the only thing that can deal with your enemies. It needs to get into the palace."

After a moment of hesitation, Kenta nodded. He beckoned for her to follow him and they went further back behind the building. He had told her earlier that he did not believe in magic, but now he had to rely on what appeared to be a mythical creature to save his people.

Two soldiers guarded a back entrance, rather nervously. Jamal greeted them and indicated that they wanted to get past. He led Stephanie into the building, and Clifton and Martin followed very close behind. They passed through four different rooms and a corridor and climbed a set of stairs to get, finally, to the balcony that surrounded the great hall. They crouched down low to stay out of sight. The four robed monks were on the lower floor, watching the entrance to the front of the building. There were several dead bodies of soldiers on the floor around the creatures, including the president himself. Once or twice a soldier would shoot into the room, but that did no harm to the robed men.

They stood in a diamond formation, guarding the well and its ugly statue.

Stephanie looked through the handrails of the balcony. Something was happening in the well. It looked like it was filled with water, although it was inside the building. A closer inspection showed her that it was not water in the well, but some sort of mist or energy, moving and writhing as if it was coming to life. Was it somehow tapping into the ley lines that ran under the country, and drawing power from them?

Around the top of the room there were skylights, through which they could see the cat-like beast stalking. It seemed to prowl backwards and forwards on the roof of the palace, as if it couldn't find a way in.

"There!" Stephanie said to Jamal. "Can you shoot at that skylight?" The soldier pulled out his pistol and shot twice at the glass. The Bast jumped onto the window and cracks appeared where its taloned feet made contact. There was the sound of breaking glass as the windows of the skylights shattered. At the same moment two of the monks turned to see the four of them on the balcony. They raised their arms towards them.

The cat-beast leapt through the damaged window, smashing it more completely as it broke in. It landed on top of one of the monks, who seemed to melt into nothing but the clothes it had been wearing. The Bast, the Egyptian goddess who protected Pharaohs from supernatural evil, the creature that Stephanie had somehow released, turned to the next monk. A bolt of energy seemed to emit from the robed creature's outstretched arm and envelop the great cat, which now seemed bigger than a puma. Its ebony muscles glistened in the artificial lighting of the great hall. The cat stalked towards the second figure, who, like the first, melted into its clothes and vanished.

The giant feline turned to the final two monks, who backed towards the well. When they were close to it, they, too, vanished, leaving only rags. The well, however, came to life, arcing with energy. The power seemed to cloak the statue like a translucent shroud, and the stone monstrosity came to life. It creaked as it stretched out its arms, and made a loud cracking sound as its feet left the floor with a shower of dust and stones. It moved so that it stood between the cat and the well.

The cat, now appearing bigger than a tiger, its black coat glistening, leapt up at the giant stone statue, in much the same way that the smaller cat had leapt at Jack Hardington in another world far away. The stone statue was caught off-guard and fell back at the impact of this huge and very solid feline, and its newly-animated feet did not move quickly enough to retain its balance. It fell into the well.

Martin worked out what was going to happen next. He grabbed hold of Stephanie and pulled at her, shouting to the others to get back. There was a kind of explosion of light and dark matter and a pillar of energy exploded upwards through the glass of the skylights in the roof. Stephanie did not see what happened next, as Martin was pulling her away from danger, but when she next looked over the balcony, everything was gone.

There was no well any more, just a charred area in the floor of the grand chamber of the palace, covered in the debris of burned stone. The statue was gone, as was the cat. Sunlight was streaming through the gaping hole where the palace roof had been, and what looked like curtains of rain were sheeting through despite the cloudless sky. Stephanie stared into the rubble.

A moment later they were startled by an electronic beeping. It was a moment before any of them recognised the sound.

"My phone!" said Clif. "It hasn't worked since I got here."

Clifton spoke briefly to John Borland and asked for him to get in touch with the British authorities to tell them that Mbalaya would now be open for offers of help. Stephanie wandered away from him, and found a stairway down to the hall floor. Martin and Jamal followed her.

She stood in the hall near the charred and shattered floor, watching the last of the brief, strange rain splatter down. She surveyed the area, feeling a certain sense of loss at the departure of the Bast. She was tired and tearful, and not thinking straight.

"Time to go home," said Martin softly, standing behind her.

She nodded.

"I don't intend to return by plane," Martin continued. "I thought I might get a lift across land to the nearest railway station and return to England via the Channel Tunnel. Or I could persuade the people here to lend us a car with darkened windows. They probably have something for presidential parades. Will you accompany me?"

"You're the boss," she said.

"Yes, but I thought you might want to fly back with Clif. You seem to have become close."

"What?" she said, not having worked out exactly what he meant.

"When we got out of our cells, you gave him a hug – a great big warm sexy body-hug. I got a handshake."

It took Stephanie most of a minute to pull her head out of the present and parse Martin's words. Clifton had talked to her, or more to the point, listened to her when she had to unwind after being held at gunpoint and then witnessing the death of Jack Hardington. He had been the reason that Martin and she were sent out to Mbalaya. He was the chief investigator for the Angel Trust. The attention had all been on him. Stephanie and Clifton had become friends.

"It's not like that," she said. "We're friends. And he's a *person*: you're a vampire." She regretted saying that the moment it came out.

"I'm a person," he started to say, but she interrupted him.

"No, I didn't mean it like that. Don't make me say things when I'm tired and scared, I'll get it wrong. I mean, I don't know how close you can get to a vampire. I'm…"

"You're?"

She took a big breath. "I'm afraid of you."

Martin didn't answer straight away, although he opened his mouth a couple of times as if he was about to say something. He took a step closer to Stephanie and held out his arm for her to take, and possibly allow him to get close. She didn't take it, but wrapped her arms around herself.

"I haven't been scary, especially not on this trip," he said eventually. "I've been the useless one. Okay, so I used my title to get us into the palace, but apart from that, I needed tranquilisers *and* you on the plane, I was rescued by a little old man and a little old lady, I let Clif do all the talking and my assistant saved the day."

"The Bast saved the day."

147

"How?" he said. "Without you, how would this thing you called the Bast have ever come into existence? Why did it take the form of a big cat? Why did you need to find a way into the palace for it? And for that matter, how did you know that was what you had to do? *You're* the scary one."

Stephanie laughed, and then she cried, and then she let Martin wrap his arms around her.

"It wasn't a sexy hug," she said between sobs. "It was an ordinary hug."

"There's no such thing as an ordinary hug."

"But there is such a thing as a not-sexy hug."

They stood in the middle of the rich, once-opulent hall, wrapped together while she wept. She cried out her exhaustion until she was even more exhausted, and he gave her all the time she needed. When she had sobbed out for a minute or two, he whispered in her ear.

"I *can* be scary – sometimes. But not right now."

Stephanie decided that she would accompany Martin on his journey home across land. They all stayed at the palace that night. They actually slept in the palace itself, in big, comfortable beds in air-conditioned rooms. After twelve hours' sleep, Stephanie was woken by breakfast in bed, brought in by Martin and a man from the kitchens. She loved it, and didn't tell anyone that she normally hated the idea of breakfast in bed. Clifton Chase was going to stay in Mbalaya for a couple of weeks to help co-ordinate the aid as it came in from the country's European and Asian allies.

The day was almost over before Martin started on the drive toward Europe in an official car with darkened windows, which Jamal Kenta had given them, telling them it was a gift from the people of Mbalaya. He drove at night, and found hotels for them to stay in by day. They didn't talk much for the first two days. Stephanie didn't think of anything to say to start with, and then in her hotel room she stayed awake thinking of hundreds of questions she should be asking. Then, as they drove towards Europe during the night, she could only think of frivolous things to say on the journey. They stayed in further hotels during the daytime, where she thought of deeper questions before dozing off.

She thought of the cat, and how or why it was a cat. She wondered if it had gone for good. She reminded herself that the cat that had saved her near where Old Rad lived had been a real, physical creature, not the being of energy she had found under Hemmin. So what had happened to create the Bast of Hemmin? But when the night came and Martin was driving them through Spain, having crossed from North Africa near Gibraltar, she couldn't bring the deeper questions to mind. Martin had sedated himself on the short crossing, and had made sure he was fully recovered when he took up the drive again the following night.

"Will I ever meet the werewolves?" she said as they drove northwards towards France.

"Probably. Don't let your imagination run away with you. They are ordinary human beings, just like you. And *me.*"

"You haven't objected to me calling you a vampire."

"I call it Tepes Syndrome – but it's a name that my people used more than a hundred years ago. Nowadays they say... might say... that I have a vampiric condition. But I still prefer to call it Tepes Syndrome. It is a condition. The word 'vampire' is taken to mean something evil, or demonic, certainly inhuman. That's not me."

"I think you could be scary," she said.

"I *am* scary, you said so yourself."

"I think of all these fabulous questions I could ask, but when we drive together, I can't seem to ask them. Why can't we talk about all the deep things I have questions about?"

"Ask me anything."

"Do you have fangs?"

"*What?*"

"When you bite people, your girls, you know."

"I don't kiss and tell."

"Have you ever fallen in love?"

"No. Not properly. Don't get me wrong, I love all the girls I...all the girls I *love*, but I will see them all grow old and die. So no, I can't let myself fall in love. That was a deep question."

"You're making me nocturnal," she said as they stopped at a hotel on the coast of Spain one morning before it was fully light.

"You can sleep at night in the car and go sightseeing in the daytime if you like. The night drive suits me."

"I could drive in the day, and you could drive at night," she replied. "We'd get home quicker."

"Then you would miss the sights of some of the most beautiful countries in the world."

"I'm not on holiday, I'm working."

"I'm glad you feel you still want to work for me."

"Not if the research has me travelling the world. I might get fed up with not being given a bit of peace and quiet to get on with my research, rather than shooting off to darkest Africa..."

"Brightest Africa, if I remember right."

"...to brightest Africa on a... that doesn't sound right. Clif will tell everyone at home you're a... Mr Borland will know it was you who founded the Angel Trust."

"You told Clif."

"Sorry."

Martin laughed. "I think I should have told both of them a long time ago. It got harder, especially when vampires took over the Romanian Embassy. But they're gone now, and I'm freer than I've ever been. The whole reason I started the Angel Trust was in case they came over to Britain, years ago."

"Why Angel? I mean, the name."

"I suppose it was because I saw angels as being the light to combat the vampires' darkness."

Approaching France, Stephanie continued the conversation.

"So what am I researching? Am I still looking at ley lines, or has what happened in Mbalaya finished that?"

"I suppose it's finished with, for the moment at least. Clif will make sure all the loose ends are tied up, particularly any supernatural loose ends. Then he'll hand over to whoever the authorities are and come home."

"Good."

Martin laughed.

"What?" said Stephanie.

"You two."

"There isn't an 'us two'."

"I suppose not. Not yet, anyway. But there could be."

"Will I go to Nieziemski Manor again?"

"Almost certainly."

"I'll compile a list of questions for them."

"They will answer in mysteries and riddles."

"Where does vampirism come from? Is the Bast gone for good? Was it, *she*, a fey creature? Where do werewolves come from? When our energy and dark energy meet, does it produce some kind of reaction that makes people think that they have seen ghosts or UFO's? Is that what we saw in the palace when the Bast pushed that stone giant into the well?"

"These are all worth looking into," said Martin. "Perhaps you'll need to establish a scientific brain base to look into this. The Angel Trust looks at all sorts of mysteries that have happened and are happening over the world. Your job will be to pick up what they find and try to find an explanation for it. And where did those robed creatures come from? What guided and commanded them? What were they really trying to achieve?"

"Like pinpoints on a map that leads to a location? Who put them there?"

"One question of many."

"Did dark energy make vampires? Did it make you?"

"No. But that's a story for another time."

Book 8
Connaîthior

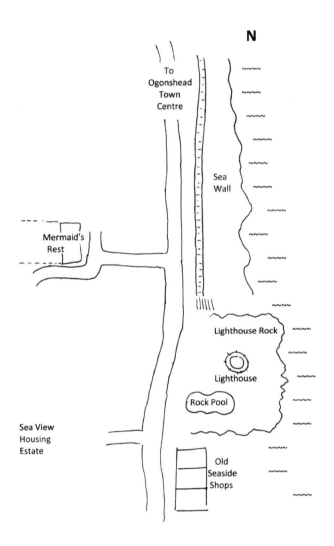

N

To
Ogonshead
Town
Centre

Sea
Wall

Mermaid's
Rest

Lighthouse Rock

Lighthouse

Rock Pool

Sea View
Housing
Estate

Old
Seaside
Shops

One

Helena Grey hated people. She hated rich people and their greed. She hated people who didn't pick up after their dogs. She hated people who were supposed to be in charge of the country to help its residents, but only lined their own pockets – or egos. She hated those bikers that roared up and down along the sea road from the estate to the town.

She didn't really hate her parents, but she felt betrayed by them. They'd split up when she was a child, and her father disappeared a couple of years later, and stopped paying his share towards his daughter's upkeep. As a teenager, she hadn't really fancied boys and couldn't find her way to joining all her girlfriends' giggles and gossip about supposed romances at school. She thought she might be gay, but when she talked to her mother about it she was shut down swiftly.

She'd hated accountants, charging her a load of money to tell her she didn't have any. She used to hate the part of her job that paid, taking photographs of little children by the seaside. On one occasion she'd found a lost child and left her booth on the sea front to find his parents. It took nearly two hours, and the reunion was good to see. She felt good about herself until she returned to her kiosk to find a queue of angry customers all telling her she should've been there.

She really hated Charles Sutener, her predecessor at the Siren's Song, now renamed the Mermaid's Rest. He had used these beautiful, fragile naiads as prostitutes in his expensive brothel. Now Helena was in charge of them and, with no need to earn money because of support from the Nieziemski Manor Estate, she could help them come to terms with what he had forced them to do and she could help them to live free again.

In the last few months, the estate had been quick to procure the house and equally fast to reinforce the old sea front shops on the south side of the Lighthouse Rock. The purchase of the lighthouse and grounds from Ogonshead Council had taken less than six weeks and the house itself had taken a little longer, but by the start of September Helena had been able to move out of her flat to live here.

The shelters on the sea front were sound enough and strong enough to keep at least twenty naiads warm and comfortable in the winter months and the house was now completely refurbished. It was pleasant and roomy now that the unpleasant bits of it were ripped out or decorated over. It no longer felt like a brothel.

There were fey People who needed her, four of them at the moment – Reni, Mara, Rusalka and Virino – all of whom had been harmed at the hands of that creature Sutener, all of whom needed healing. Lady Venner, Queen of the Fey, had started the healing process, but she only visited for a few days at a time. Helena was with them every day. She would hold them in her arms and listen as they talked to her, unburdening themselves. Sometimes they said things she didn't understand, speaking in their own language; sometimes they said things she did understand that made her hate the men who did those things to them even more. She cried with them, and Lady Venner had said that her tears were healing the naiads.

Today, the tears started as fine September rain dribbling down the windows of the Mermaid's Rest. The sky was overcast as if the weather was supporting that the summer season of the seaside town of Ogonshead was well and truly over. Helena looked out of the window of her well-furnished living room, feeling the misery that the weather had brought with it, but pleased, at least, that the motorcyclists would not be out revving up their bikes in this weather.

She was aware of someone at the door, waiting to be allowed in to her lounge. It was Virino. She was the tallest of the naiads, with beautiful soft skin, flowing brown hair and the most captivating eyes Helena had ever seen. Helena turned to her.

"May I sit with you?" the naiad asked falteringly.

"Of course," said Helena gently, knowing that 'sitting with her' meant something different. Virino was really asking to cry with her. Helena moved over to the large sofa and sat down so that there was plenty of space for Virino, who curled up beside her and rested her head on Helena's breast. Then she quietly, gently, *beautifully* wept. Helena held her in what she hoped was the most comfortable position and stroked her hair. It was like caressing silk. After a few minutes, her body stopped shaking and she breathed slowly and deeply as if she was sleeping. But she spoke, almost in a whisper. The words she said were not English – they weren't even a language that had originated on Earth – but they were lovely and full of sadness and they made Helena cry. Virino changed her position on the sofa so that the two of them could rest in each other's arms.

After quite a while Virino stirred.

"Thank you," she said, sitting up straight. Helena knew that she had suffered considerable humiliation at the hands of the Siren's Song's customers in the past few years, but she never spoke of them except in her own language. "Svend is cooking for us tonight," she continued. "I think, if he was human, he would take cookery for a job."

"Why on earth would he want to be human?" said Helena, and Virino laughed and looked at her for a moment.

"Is there something I can do for you?" the naiad asked.

"I am here to serve you," said Helena.

"No, you are here to serve the Contract," said Virino. The Contract was some kind of mystical condition that the fey People had to put in place in order to stay on this world – it meant that there had to be a human living here, and Helena had been chosen to be the one – the connaithior.

"You don't understand," said Helena, "I don't begrudge serving you. This is my heart's desire. I consider myself the most privileged person in the world – because you have allowed me to be your friend. But if there was one thing I would like; it would be to hear you sing."

Virino was quiet for a moment while she considered Helena's request.

"I don't think I'm ready to sing yet," she said. "But I will, one day. I will sing for you."

The downstairs part of the Mermaid's Rest consisted mostly of the lounge, a huge dining room and the kitchens. Helena had a small side room for an office, which she hardly ever went into, and there had been an extension added to the building many years ago to add extra bedrooms to the house. The dining room could hold all of the residents of the big house, but when more came, they might have to make alternative arrangements.

Today, everyone ate together. They made Helena sit at the head of the table as always, although she preferred to play the part of the servant. The Nieziemski Estate had provided a very generous stipend for her, and covered all her expenses, so she was expected to be the Lady of the House, which was probably what the word 'connaithior' meant. They had also provided fey bodyguards, in the form of Lady Haltea Feen of the Sidhe and Svend, an Elven fey warrior of some kind. Feen was happy to talk about anything, but Svend was quiet most of the time. Feen told her he used to chatter all the time, but he had recently lost his two closest friends in a battle (against vampires!), and it had made him quiet and sullen. Perhaps he needed some healing, too, but Helena was less comfortable cuddling a male, even if that male wasn't human.

The only other human at the table was Jason Asher, the son of a rich businessman; he had grown up a bit of a wimp because of his father's bullying. Lady Venner had freed him from his father somehow and he had a remarkable affinity for all things fey. He opted to live in the lighthouse now that the clutter there was cleared out. He was redecorating with the help of Rusalka, with whom he had a special relationship. Helena knew that, many months ago as a wimpy teenager who couldn't get a girlfriend, he had come out from his home in Norwich to spend some time at a brothel.

However, while he was a customer at the Siren's Song he was given an hour with Rusalka. The connection he made with her was more than just physical, and it filled him with guilt that he had used her that way. Rusalka seemed to have forgiven him for that, and now they sat on the rocks, looking out to sea and talking for hours. Jason was building up his muscles a bit, too, since he'd moved a lot of the lighthouse clutter himself, as well as learning new skills as a decorator. He didn't like the cold, though, and was beginning to spend a little more time indoors. He had made the lighthouse into his home, but in the winter months he would probably take a room at the Mermaid's Rest.

Jason's father seemed to be a strange piece of work – he appeared to be pleased with his son for visiting a brothel, and wondered why it had affected him emotionally. He had not cut Jason off from his allowance, which the young man had used to pay his fine. But Jason's own guilt went beyond a fine for using a prostitute against her will. He now needed to help the People he once felt he had hurt. He had cut ties with his family and spent all his time here instead.

Jason sat at the table between Rusalka and Svend and said very little. He didn't seem to enjoy the company of a larger group of people and when he said anything, it was to his one naiad friend.

Rusalka was incredibly beautiful, the most stunning of the naiads. She had slender, toned curves and long blonde hair which, unlike the other naiads, didn't change colour. Her eyes were blue and she always wore clothes when she was in company (the other fey sometimes didn't). She spent some time with the other naiads, who she called her sisters, but didn't spend much time with Helena, Feen or Svend. Helena couldn't work out her relationship with Jason, which was often animated, full of conversation, but with no physical contact.

Reni was considered by her sisters to be the leader, although she rarely acted the part. It was just that it was her contact with Michael Varmeter, the Lord of Nieziemski Manor, which had led to their rescue. She was a calm, quiet woman who seemed to try to be the person everyone wanted her to be. Helena would have liked her to be herself and not worry about everyone else's opinion.

Mara was the smallest of the four naiads, although from the tallest to shortest there was not really much in it. She was quiet except for when she had her own private 'sessions' with Helena, when she was the most vocal about the indignities she had suffered under Charles Sutener. Helena always listened patiently, but afterwards it made her so angry she wanted to hit someone – someone human, that is.

"The local youths were trying to climb the wall again this morning," Feen said as they chatted over their roast chicken meal.

"What did you do to them?" asked Helena cautiously, remembering that the last time they tried it they were suddenly attacked by a swarm of bees.

"Nothing," she said, but quietly so that Helena didn't believe her. Some of the local lads knew that this place was once a brothel, and had heard a rumour that the beautiful women who once worked here still lived here and sun-bathed naked in the walled back garden.

"Really," Helena insisted. "What did you do?"

"The ivy on the wall suddenly became very slippery and they couldn't make it up the side," Svend said with a little smile. "Then the weather changed and they went away. The weather wasn't Feen, though; that was going to happen anyway. Next time they come I'll be there with my griffon."

Helena had seen Svend's griffon before when he practised with it in the back garden. It was a long-handled spear-like weapon similar to the 15th century Ottoman falx. It had a long, scythed blade and he handled it like a master.

"They're only kids," said Helena.

"I wasn't intending to use it on them," he replied.

"They were poking around the lighthouse earlier," said Jason. "The kids. They're not interested in whether it's private property or not."

"When the tourists are here, they just waste their time in the arcades, or watching girls on the beach," said Helena. "But now that the holidays are over and the schools are back, they hang out around nearer their homes. I think they're all from the local estate."

"The arcades are still open," said Jason. "Well, most of them."

"I've walked through the town a couple of times," said Feen. "The places that are open don't want those kids around. They consider them to be trouble-makers."

"So they're *our* problem," said Jason sourly. Svend looked at the unhappy young man as if he was plotting something. Helena hadn't got to know Feen's bodyguard well enough yet, but she felt she should keep an eye on him. That blade of his was too dangerous and Svend's past life was that of a warrior and vampire hunter. She hoped he didn't feel that a few idle kids were in the same category.

"The schools have re-started after the holidays," said Feen, trying to get her head around human culture this time of year. "Surely that should keep them occupied."

"They've left school," said Helena, "and they are idle because they can't get jobs and their friends are still in full-time education."

"There was plenty of work going over the holidays," said Jason, "but *they* didn't do any of it."

The Nieziemski Manor Estate owned the rock and the lighthouse on it, as well as the land on the south side and the derelict shops; a relic from when this end of town was the centre of attraction fifty years ago. The intention was to turn the shops into a shelter for the naiads in the coldest part of the winter, if and when any more naiads came to join them. Structurally, they were sound enough, but all of their windows had been broken, the roof covering all three shops needed some serious repairs, and they needed decent, home-like furnishings inside. Reni had assured Helena that all they really needed was shelter, and basic amenities like these shops provided was enough – they would only be used for the worst two or three months of each year anyway. A high wooden fence had been constructed from the concrete sea barrier on the south side of the shops and along the road to protect the land owned by the Nieziemski Estate from prying eyes or visitors from the town and nearby houses. However, the wall stopped at the sea wall steps on the north side of the Lighthouse Rock, so adventurous youths could still climb from the beach onto the rock where Jason lived in the lighthouse. That meant that, at the moment at least, the naiads couldn't use the large rock pool on the other side of the lighthouse because the local kids could get to it. The intention was to drill holes in the edges of the rock and put up a fence from the sea-wall stairs out to where the rock fell away into the sea. In the meantime, Jason would have to put up with visitors.

The following day was clearer and possibly getting a little warmer. Three young lads, carrying between them two large step ladders, made their way to the wall at the side of the Mermaid's

Rest so that they could climb up and take a peek into the back garden. Helena watched from Reni's room upstairs as Lady Haltea Feen and her bodyguard Svend, both dressed in full Elven armour, walked into the back garden to practice with their weapons.

The youths provided some entertainment for Helena as they struggled with the ladders like something out of a slapstick TV show, eventually constructing them against the part of the back wall that was next to the pavement. Two of them climbed the ladder to take a peek over the wall.

Feen and Svend put on a spectacular show. The grassed area of the back garden was a little overgrown and still damp from the rain but their fey footwork was not hampered by the uneven ground. Both of the combatants had griffons and handled them with expertise and the clash and clatter of the weapons provided a fabulous show for the young lads watching. The two fey warriors danced about each other, parrying each other's strikes and swinging their weapons about as if they were serious enemies. Helena and Reni were mesmerised by the display and forgot to look and see how the youths were reacting.

They finished their exhibition with a bow to each other, and then Feen turned to salute the watchers. At that moment, their step-ladders both collapsed and they fell to the pavement. They ran, leaving their ladders behind them.

Helena went downstairs to ask Svend what that was supposed to have achieved.

"That was stage one," said the Elven.

"And stage two?"

"…Will happen when I go out for a stroll this afternoon to visit Jason in the lighthouse. Would you like to come with me?"

"Very much," said Helena. "Will you be bringing your griffon?"

"Oh, no," said Svend. "I imagine carrying that thing on the streets would be illegal."

There were seven young people and three motorcycles at the rock that afternoon. When Helena saw that two of the youths were girls, she began to worry – boys show off anyway, but with girls around they become much worse. Svend, however, seemed happy with this audience. Since he had arrived at the Mermaid's

Rest he had been quiet and depressed, mourning his friend's death, but this challenge seemed to have brought him back to life a little.

He looked at the bikes for a while, then sat on the biggest, the one at the front.

"D'you know, in all my years, I've never ridden a motorcycle before."

"D'you know, in all the very short time I've known you I've never thought to ask you how old you are," Helena replied with a laugh, and was very pleased to see him smile.

"Hey," came a shout from among the youths who were clambering over the rocks. "That's my bike!" Svend pretended he couldn't make out what the lad was shouting by putting his hand up to the hair that was covering his pointed Elven ear. The youth clambered down off the rocks to approach them.

"I said that's my bike," said the large, chunky lad.

"I'm so sorry," said Svend with a big smile, getting off the bike at once and offering his right hand in apology. "I must have thought, if you can climb on my rock, I must be allowed to sit on your bike."

"It's not your rock."

Svend said nothing, but continued to hold his hand out. Wrong-footed, the lad took it. Svend suddenly gripped it tightly, and Helena saw that some discomfort came to the lad's face.

"I really am sorry, and I meant you no harm," said Svend, projecting his voice so as to be heard by the rest of the gang who were clambering down the rock to see what was happening between their friend and the stranger. He still didn't let go.

"Well, no harm done," said the lad, his voice strained.

"I'm Svend."

The lad didn't give up his name. A little sweat came to his forehead as he tried not to show how uncomfortable Svend's grip was.

"Hey, you were one of those people fighting in the garden," said one boy.

"With that woman," added another.

"She was fit," said the first. "Is she your girlfriend?"

"No, I'm her bodyguard," Svend replied.

"P'raps she's saving herself for Jeff," one lad laughed.

165

"No, Jeff's mine," said the older of the two girls, coming up alongside the lead biker. Svend let go of his hand. Helena tried to work out what the Elven was trying to achieve – he was 'beating' the lad, but not making him lose face in front of his friends. And he'd found out his name.

"I could introduce you to the princess if you like," said Svend, quietly, directly to Jeff, who was rubbing the life back into his hand.

"Princess?"

"She's the daughter of a queen, yes," said Svend.

"She rich?" said Jeff.

"No, sorry," said Svend. "She doesn't own a penny."

"But she'll meet with us?" said Jeff's girlfriend.

"She's a private person, but I think she'd be happy to meet you. If…" then Svend stopped.

"If what?" said Jeff.

"Well, you can't go round trespassing on her land and then expect her to be friends with you."

Bullseye! thought Helena.

Jeff turned to the rest of the gang that hadn't got off the rock yet and instructed them to get down onto the pavement immediately.

"You're a star, Jeff," said Svend, bigging him up in front of his friends. "In a week or two we'll be putting up some proper fencing to stop people getting in at all, but I expect with you keeping the area safe we won't have anything to worry about."

"And we get to meet a princess?"

"Does she wear princess clothes?" said the smaller, quieter of the two girls.

"You want to meet her in all her finery?" said Svend. "Well, I can ask her, but I expect she'll want something in return."

"Like what?"

"Like not being disturbed by motorbikes in the middle of the night," said Svend. Jeff and one of the other lads in biker leathers laughed, so Svend laughed along with them. Helena wondered if Svend could somehow manipulate the young lads, or perhaps his experience in dealing with people across Europe over the last twenty years or so had just given him people skills.

The Elven asked about motorbikes and the lads gathered around, with the older girl whom Helena thought someone said was 'Shir' on Jeff's arm. The boys talked about engine capacity and top speeds and other things that didn't interest Helena. She noticed that the smaller girl wasn't that interested either, and she separated herself from the others and sat on the low sea wall. Helena left the bigger bunch and sat beside her.

"I'm Helena."

"I know," said the girl. "I've seen you in the photo place on the Front."

"I've given that up now. Jamie Decker's taken over from me while I look after the Mermaid's Rest."

"Yeah," said the girl. "He always chats up the pretty girls when he takes their picture. The Mermaid's Rest. It was called something else before."

"It's a different place now. Look, seeing as we're neighbours, can I know your name?"

"Jackie. Jackie Banner."

"Hello Jackie," Helena said, taking a good look at her. She had a fair bit of make-up on that seemed to be covering a bruise on her face. "That looks nasty."

Jackie turned her face away from Helena, twisting her body so she could look out to sea. "I fell," she said. Helena looked at the crowd of lads gathering round Svend, Jeff and the bikes. *Did one of them do that?*

"Does it hurt?"

"It's nothing, really," said Jackie, as if to say, 'Stop talking about it.'

"Look, we've got someone who visits every now and again," said Helena, hoping that Lady Venner would come and see them soon. "She's related to the… princess. She might have some lotion or something that might help." Helena was aware that Lady Venner was a healer.

"It's nothing," said Jackie, and she stopped talking.

Helena hated people, especially people who do that to girls.

Two

Lady Venner, unfortunately, was not due to visit in the next few days. However, Helena received an invitation to Nieziemski Manor. It was a party to celebrate the one-year anniversary of Michael Varmeter becoming the connaithior – the Lord of the Manor – in Buckinghamshire at the end of September. Helena, Feen, Svend and Jason were all invited, and would be picked up by helicopter and returned at the end of the day, so they would only be away from the house for one day. However, Helena didn't really want to go. They needed her here.

"I think I should stay," said Jason when she showed him the invitation. "You go. We'll be fine."

"It will be quite an experience for you," she said.

"But you love Lady Venner and all the others. They say there are hundreds of fey People there."

"They?"

"Rusalka," he admitted.

"Surely you'd love to see how the manor looks after its People," said Helena.

"I…" he hung his head. "I don't deserve to go."

Helena understood, but tried to persuade Jason anyway. "None of us deserve this privilege, Jason. We've been chosen to know about the fey here in our world. But you don't have to feel guilty about… you know… because they've forgiven you. Rusalka has forgiven you."

"Still," he said. "You think one of us should stay here. I think it should be me."

Unfortunately, Helena felt he was right. Not that he didn't deserve the privilege, but that one of them should stay at home, and it probably should be him this time. It was to be a village garden party, and that meant lots of humans and probably not that many fey. Jason struggled when just the household at the Mermaid's Rest was in one room. Helena ought to be there because she was the one that had been chosen to lead this unusual set-up.

Nobody had tried to climb the wall for the last couple of days, and Svend had gone out for walks to meet up with the young people and have a chat. The motorcycles had stopped racing by the house late at night. As far as she knew, Feen hadn't yet joined him. Helena rather wanted to be there when she did.

Clive Matthews also wanted to visit. He'd been the head of the council at Ogonshead and had accepted bribes from Charles Sutener to allow him to continue using the Siren's Song as a brothel. Helena wondered what on earth the old man wanted to come and visit for. The police had charged him for accepting bribes but his sentence was going to be light in return for evidence against Sutener. He probably wouldn't get a prison sentence, although he'd had to resign from the council. Thanks to his son running the local newspaper, the scandal hadn't got out to the general public. She wanted to write back and say something extremely rude to him, but something held her back, and she decided she would meet with him, but not here at the house. She suggested they should meet at the lighthouse.

Jason had been working hard to remake the lighthouse into living quarters. It had taken him the first month just to clear out the rubbish, then he made the first floor into small living quarters for himself. He had made the ground floor into a nice little meeting place.

When Clive Matthews came to visit, the fencing was all constructed except the bit that was going to be built into the rocks. Helena led them both into the building and he looked around appreciatively. He looked a lot older than when he'd worked for the council only a few months ago.

"I see you've got most of your fences up around this place already," the old man said.

"Yes, and work on the old shops is progressing well. Soon, you won't be allowed on the premises at all."

"May I ask why?"

"Yes. We're protecting vulnerable people here," she answered. She didn't have to embellish.

"I wanted to say sorry for my part in the trouble you've been caused. It seemed easy to accept a little money to look the other way, but then I accepted a little more, and then it got out of control. I'm grateful to your organisation's solicitor for going easy on me."

Helena looked at the old man. She wanted to say she had no intention of accepting his apology and could he please go away, but he looked so pathetic now, all his power gone.

"You got lucky," she said. "And it's all come to light at the right time. For you, I mean. I hope you enjoy your retirement."

"Retirement doesn't suit me. I've always been... involved with the town. Doing something in the community. I suppose I still want to do something with my life."

"I can't think of anything I can offer you," said Helena. "Why don't you go and raise money for a charity or something?"

"I was thinking I could do a bit of gardening for you?" he suggested. "At your house?"

"The house is going to be even more private than the Lighthouse Rock," said Helena. "And I'm going to let the garden grow wild, so it's like..." *a fairy garden*, "you know."

"I just wanted to do something to make amends," he said.

"Thank you. I'll live here out of the town and out of your way, and you can go back to your nice home and think of something to make amends. But you don't owe me anything. I don't want to be rude," *actually, I do, but I won't*, "but there's nothing I want from you."

Matthews left, unhappy. Helena felt sorry for him, although she wished she didn't. Perhaps the love and compassion of the People was beginning to rub off on her.

Later that evening, after they had all eaten together, the table was cleared, leaving Helena and Svend to sit there and chat.

"How are your new friends?"

"They are... interesting," said the Elven. "Under normal circumstances, they wouldn't be my friends at all – they seem to have little sense of purpose, and when I suggested they go around the estate and help people, they wanted me to pay them as if I was their employer. This country's system of helping people who can't help themselves has left them feeling they'll get money to live regardless of the effort they make. So they just like to do nothing or cause anxiety for other people. But…"

"But?"

"But there is something there, beneath the surface, that they don't seem to have the courage to display."

"They go around as if they own the place, and you're talking about them not having courage."

"That's all bravado," said Svend. "They don't have any real courage. It's all about what makes them look good to each other. Going round annoying people is a tough image, but it's only an image. I looked up the local demographic on your computer, and what you've got is this – the roads closest to the sea front are full of retired people who have come here to get what they believe to be healthy sea air. Behind them are a load of houses that are empty and derelict because they don't meet the council's safety standards. Back into the Sea View estate itself, it's all community housing with unemployed people with alcohol and drugs problems. A few of the parents make an effort and get jobs, but some haven't worked for generations. And these children come from that background. Why are you laughing?"

Helena had started by smiling at the thought of Svend using a computer, then the smile had turned into a chuckle and eventually she was struggling to hold back a full-on laugh.

"It's the thought of you, the great Elven warrior, slayer of vampires, using words like demographic," she managed to say when she recovered.

"I had to look up what 'demographic' meant," said Svend with a smile that lasted just a few seconds. "But I'm not a great Elven warrior. I'm just the one that survived."

"Sorry," said Helena, wanting to hug him like she did the naiads. She held back.

"You know before…" he took a breath, "before Silvestri died, I was the chatty one. Meeting up with these young people and trying to get my head around their plight has brought some of that back."

"They have a 'plight'?" said Helena. "They aren't just lazy, poorly-parented kids who don't care the slightest bit about the world they live in?"

Svend looked at her long and hard. "You have endless time for us, the People, but you seem to have nothing but contempt for your own kind."

"Perhaps," Helena replied sourly, "if my 'own kind' did something worthy of praise, I might change my mind. But while they are capable of using beautiful People like Mara, Rusalka, Virino and Reni the way that they did, then no, they don't deserve anything else. Not from me."

Svend stood up from his seat and bowed to her. "You honour us. You honour me, for which I thank you. But look to your own people. They aren't all bad."

"You walk the streets?" asked Helena.

"Yes."

"Be careful. You might get mugged."

Svend laughed. "That would be an interesting experience," he said.

"There used to be a youth club near the sea front, I think," said Helena. "It was closed down because the kids were too unruly and wrecked the place."

"I've seen it," said Svend. "It's one of the derelict buildings between the estate and the old people's houses."

"I think I'll try to find out if 'my kind' can be as good as you say they are. I spoke with Clive Matthews earlier, and he said he wanted to do something useful with his retirement. I'll ask him if he can make the renovation of the youth club happen. He still has contacts. That would be a decent retirement project."

The following morning she sent a message to Clive Matthews and wondered if it really would make a difference. She thought it might be a good idea to have a walk around the housing estate herself, and she asked if any of the naiads wanted to walk with her. They all decided to stay at home, and Helena found herself heading for the lighthouse instead.

She found that the biker gang and their hangers-on were there, but staying off the actual rock. Svend had made some progress, then. She made to enter the rock area through the entrance gate they had created in their new wall. One of the young people shouted to her.

"Where's Svend?"

She shrugged her shoulders and made for the lighthouse. Rusalka, whom she had just left at the Mermaid's Rest, was getting out of the water on the south side of the rock, out of sight of the youths. There was an underground waterway between the pool in the back garden of the house and the sea, so she had swum there quicker than Helena could walk. The naked naiad then made for the nearest soon-to-be-renovated shop where she kept a towel and some of her clothes.

Jason, who had seen both Helena and Rusalka arriving, came from his lighthouse to greet them.

"Any trouble from the kids?" Helena asked by way of a greeting.

"Not since Svend had a word with them," Jason answered. "But they still hang around on the road making a nuisance of themselves."

"Doing what?"

"Doing nothing, same as always."

Helena listened and heard herself in his words. She could hardly reprimand him as she agreed with him. Rusalka climbed up on to the Lighthouse Rock, but sat down to the front of the lighthouse, looking out to sea. Jason excused himself and joined her sitting on the rocks. Helena watched as they sat together listening to the wind, the gulls and the waves. They spent hours doing that – it was their way of trying to find healing. Helena decided to leave them to it and go and talk to the gang hanging out by the sea wall steps.

"Anything going on?" she asked them.

"Just hanging around," said one of the lads. Helena looked around for Jackie and caught a glimpse of her sitting on the sea wall, wearing a hoodie and trying to be out of Helena's line of sight.

"Svend about today?" asked Jeff.

"I don't know. He might be out later."

"Do you work for him?"

"No. He works for me."

"I thought he worked for this princess we haven't seen yet."

"It's complicated," Helena replied. She raised her voice to the girl on the sea wall. "Hi, Jackie." Jackie fidgeted a little, but didn't reply.

Having run out of things to say, Helena started meandering towards the town centre. She hadn't spent much time in the town since taking on her new role, so she thought it might be good to see the old place again. One of the bikers followed her, separating himself from the rest. She thought she had heard the others call him 'Goat'. He had the tuft of a beard on his chin.

She turned to face him.

"A word?" he asked, softly and politely. She nodded.

"You don't really want to get involved with Jackie. She's okay, but her dad's a nasty piece of work."

"Thanks," she said, and walked on. Unfortunately, that polite warning was more than likely going to get her more involved with Jackie. *The gang of layabouts cared about her, but her own father didn't?*

Ogonshead sea front was nowhere near as busy as it had been during the school holidays, but there were still customers about. Older couples walked in the quieter streets, trying to take a break while it was still warm, but the crowds were thinner. Half of the amusements were still open, but mostly slot machines for the adults. The children's rides had more-or-less closed for the year. Helena noticed someone fixing wood panels to where a window had been smashed. She recognised the workman from her days on the sea front – Danny something.

"What happened?" she asked.

"Smash and grab yesterday," said Danny, an older man with a considerable tan. He stepped back from his work and looked at her.

"Helena, isn't it?" he said. "You used to be the photo-lady."

"That's right. Jamie Decker's taken over from me now."

"He's not as good as you."

"He's more enthusiastic than I used to be, and just as good a photographer."

"Yeah, but he concentrates on the pretty girls too much. He needs to spend more time chatting to the kiddies, you know. You run the old brothel now, don't you?"

Helena could see the twinkle in his eye, but she bit anyway. "No. I run a... God, was I honestly going to say 'respectable establishment'? Anyway, it's a refuge now," she laughed.

"I know. There's people here think that since you closed that place down, things have started to get better in the town."

Balaur, the Nieziemski Manor lawyer, had said something about the town not being blessed anymore. She hadn't worked out the whole of the story, but she knew that the naiads and their queen were supernatural beings – magical, but they didn't use that word – and now that they had been rescued perhaps the town was getting its blessing back. But not for Danny, it seemed.

"This," she said, indicating the window repair, "doesn't look much like a blessing."

"It's not all going to come back together suddenly," said Danny. "Anyway, this kind of thing happens every autumn. Soon as the main holiday's over, the crooks from the estate come out to have their fun."

"The Sea View estate?" said Helena. Danny looked up at her apologetically, as if just remembering where she lived now.

"'Fraid so."

"They'd make more money if they did it at the height of the season," said Helena.

"Too much attention," said Danny. "They ain't stupid."

"Do they know who did it?"

"Bikers. But they were covered up, so they couldn't see who they were."

"Could they identify the bikes?" asked Helena.

"You'd think," Danny shrugged his shoulders and turned back to his work.

"Well, I'll leave you to it, then," Helena said. He nodded and said goodbye, and she walked on. She always liked the end of the main season, because by then she had less work to do and a little money in the bank. Now, however, she loved her work and didn't really have any money problems and found she could look at the rest of the town with fresh eyes. It wasn't as beautiful and full of fun as she thought it was when she was looking at it through the lens of a camera. The Sea View Housing Estate was old, tired and neglected. The town itself lived for the summer half of the year, and then went bleak. Half of the town council was corrupt, and crime was rife.

And she, Helena Grey, had powerful allies in the form of a sidhe princess, an Elven warrior, and the resources of Nieziemski Manor. There had to be something she could do about it.

"I don't think it was our little group," Svend said when Helena told him about the smash and grab raid later that evening.

"Why not?"

"They're… children."

"They're old enough to ride motorbikes. At least, some of them are," said Helena.

"And some of them aren't. And a couple of them are proper gang leaders, and most of them are followers. But they are all weak, and they know it. They feel as run-down as the estate they live on. They know things are bad, and they stick together, they look after each other. But they aren't burglars."

Helena took a good look at Svend. Svend the Silent, she had called him when they first met, partly because he hardly said a word and partly because Feen had told her that he used to chatter all the time, until he lost his friend in battle. Now, he had something to defend again, a cause, and it was animating him. She really hoped that he wasn't going to be let down by these kids.

"They might not be as saintly as you might like," she said, cautiously.

"Might not?" said Svend. "Of course they aren't. They're lazy, ineffective do-nothings who have no imagination and no future. But I don't think they have the courage or the wit to travel to the town and commit crimes."

"Courage? Wit?" said Helena. "What about honesty?"

Lady Feen was listening in to the conversation, but said nothing. She smiled fondly at her bodyguard – she had, no doubt, been concerned at the way Svend had mourned his friend so bitterly, but seemed pleased that Helena and the estate children had given him something to put his heart into again.

"Honesty?" said Svend, smiling, aware of his Lady's attention. "Of course they don't know anything about honesty. I wonder, though, if we could help them learn."

"How?" said Helena.

"I've no idea," said Svend. "I mean, I'm not even human – how can I do anything for them?"

"It is because we aren't human that we can be the most help," said Lady Feen, joining in the conversation at last. "I think it may be time for me to meet these new friends of yours, Svend."

The following morning Helena, Svend and Feen found the gang hanging round the Lighthouse Rock again. This time, however, a couple of them were climbing on the rocks. Feen waited until they could see her and then, with a nod and a smile to Svend, she turned around and walked home.

"You missed a chance, there," Svend said cheerfully as he joined them. "After all this time, she wanted to meet you, then when she got here you were trespassing again."

Jeff had some sharp things to say to his underlings who had broken the rule, and his girlfriend Shir backed him up with some even stronger words. The young lady *seriously* wanted to meet a real princess. Svend didn't reprimand them for using that kind of language in front of Helena, but he just smiled at the effect he was having on them.

"She's a princess?" said Goat, who had been one of the climbers.

"Yes," confirmed Svend. "I know, she was wearing ordinary clothes. Most princesses do, most of the time. I could ask her to wear the royal kit next time she wants to see you. But..."

"Royal kit?" said Helena, laughing at his choice of words.

"Regalia would be the right word. But they don't get to see her regal ear."

"Wordplay!" Helena said. Although there was a second meaning in his words – Feen would keep her ears covered so that they didn't notice that they weren't completely human-shaped.

"What is she a princess of?" asked Shir.

"You mean what country?" said Svend.

"Yeah."

"Ljosalfheim, in what you call the Netherlands," he replied. "Look it up."

Svend stayed to chat with them, asking them more about motorbikes while Helena checked on Jason. She had a look at the great job he was doing on the inside of the lighthouse. It didn't smell so bad now – it was clean and better furnished on the lower floors at least. Jason asked how soon the last of the fencing would be in place. Helena wondered if she was doing the right thing allowing him to be secluded like this.

After a while, she returned to the Mermaid's Rest with Svend.

"Yos-alf-heim?" Helena repeated as best she could as they walked together.

"Yes," replied Svend. "The nearest translation would be the Last Fey Home. I used Old Norse because they won't know how to spell it so they won't be able to look it up."

"Netherlands?"

"Actually, if we were able to travel there, we would probably use the Caledonian Gate in Scotland. But that was lost to us many years ago."

"So you can't go home?"

"Not yet," replied Svend, and Helena couldn't tell if he was sad about this, or whether he preferred life among the humans.

"We'll be going to visit the manor on Saturday," Helena reminded him.

"Lady Feen will go with you. I'll stay here and support young Jason. He is... lonely, and doesn't feel equipped to deal with Jeff's gang. Hoodlums... is that the right word?"

"If they are responsible for the raid in town, yes, that would be the right word. But you seem to think they aren't actual criminals."

"No. But that's what they might become unless we can help them choose a different direction."

A couple of days later Helena received an e-mail from Clive Matthews. In it, he said he would have been happy to do some fund-raising to renovate that old youth club, but he'd spoken to some of his contacts in the council and had been told that there were no funds available to pay for youth workers, caretakers, or other expenses that would need to be paid before it could reopen.

There was nothing he could do.

'I just wanted to do something to make amends,' she remembered him saying. But he obviously just wanted to say words, and it didn't really mean anything at all.

Three

It was the third Saturday in September, and the village of Mickleton was celebrating its Harvest Festival. They would normally not have done so until later in the autumn, but they had brought it forward this year because they were also celebrating Michael Varmeter's first year as a connaithior at Nieziemski Manor. Although Helena hadn't wanted to leave her charges at the Mermaid's Rest, she really wanted to see Lady Venner's home and the other creatures who were there. As promised, Michael had provided a helicopter so that they could visit the manor and return the same day.

When the helicopter landed on the beach next to the Lighthouse Rock to pick up Helena and Feen, they had a large audience. Svend had told Jeff, Shir and the gang that the princess would be travelling south by helicopter that morning, and most of the young people from the estate had come to watch. There were around twenty of them and, not too far down the road, a few adults had left their houses to see what was going on as well.

Feen wore the regalia that Shir was eager to see, and the sidhe princess looked extremely beautiful in a flowing blue gown with golden bracelets as she walked to the beach. She took the time when she got to the sea wall steps to acknowledge Shir with a nod and a smile. The girl beamed like a child at Christmas. This seemed to be all part of Svend's plan to win over the gang and help them make decisions that might keep them away from crime – if it wasn't already too late. Helena pondered that the fey were more interested in a group of disenfranchised local kids than her own kind were.

Their pilot, John-James Clipper, knew about the fey. Apparently, he was the only pilot in his company that did, and Helena had heard someone say that when he had found out about them he took it in his stride and promised to keep their secret. He bowed low to Lady Feen, which must have impressed the watching teenagers. The back seats of the helicopter were layered with furs for Feen, and Helena was offered a seat next to the pilot.

Helena enjoyed the flight, except that the pilot kept trying to chat her up. In the end, she had to shut him up by telling him she was gay. After the two-hour flight they landed on the wide driveway of the manor house. The enormous front lawn was full of tables, tents, games and general village-fair paraphernalia so John-James landed well out of the way in order to avoid causing a disturbance.

Lucy Waterhouse ran to greet them, giving Helena a hug and bowing to the Lady. Feen acknowledged her and went to the large manor house to seek her mother, Lady Marika.

"Good to see you again, Helena," said Lucy. "Hope you had a good flight. Michael will come and say 'hello' to you at some point, but you're more than welcome to go anywhere in the house and grounds. Well, not anywhere, but it's probably obvious where you shouldn't go. What I mean is, it's really, *really* good to have you here at last. At the manor, I mean."

They laughed and chatted like old friends, although they had only met for a few days back in May. Then Lucy went off to supervise a couple of the older children who were trying to do the face-painting.

Helena walked among the stalls. She actually started to enjoy the fun and games of the village fete and how the residents of the village near the manor accepted the existence of the fey without a problem. The activities were quaint and seemed less, well, *tacky* than the games and activities on the sea front. She saw the dwarf lawyer Mr Balaur, standing by the beer tent. When he noticed her, he raised his enormous flagon of beer up to her in salute. She smiled back at him. She didn't know much about him, but she knew that he was one of the most respected people in the fey community. Perhaps he was more than just a dwarf.

She gradually made her way to the huge lake at the side of the house. It was set a little away from the main event, possibly to give their naiads some privacy. It was also the start of an enormous forest that reached back for many acres behind the main building.

In the lake, some naiads were playing. They disappeared when she walked by, but she thought she saw one of them looking at her, poking her head up from the water behind where the fallen branch of a tree dipped its leaves.

"Hello," she said, but not too loud. "I'm a friend."

There was no reply, but she was aware of someone approaching from the direction of the forest. She turned to see the most beautiful person in the world, the blue-skinned Lady Venner, Queen of the Seelie Court. Helena turned to greet her with the two-handed greeting Lucy had taught her. The touch of the fey queen made her shiver with delight. It was so good to see her again.

"Jada," Venner said towards the lake, and the naiad now poked her head out of the water nearer the bank. "This is Helena Grey, the connaithior to the Mermaid's Rest."

The naiad looked towards the front lawn where people were milling about and, assessing that no other human eyes looked in this direction, she stepped out of the lake. Naiads wore no clothes to swim, but they were shy creatures and didn't like the company of humankind. *I fully understand that*, thought Helena. *Neither do I.*

Dripping wet, the lovely water-nymph stood near to the visitor, being careful not to get her wet.

"You are blessed and a blessing, Helena Grey," Jada said. Helena, unconcerned by how wet she was, gave her a big hug. In spite of having been in a countryside lake, she smelled as beautiful as she looked. Jada tried to respond to the hug, but it wasn't something she was used to. Lady Venner laughed, and the sound was full of magic. Helena almost cried with the feeling of privilege that filled her – she had been chosen to spend her life with these people.

"You don't have to be out here if you'd prefer to be in the water," Helena whispered to Jada.

"Thank you," came the reply and she returned to the lake, bowing to her queen before she left them.

"Your clothes are wet," said Venner.

"Yes," said Helena. "Great, isn't it?"

Lady Venner laughed again, and they walked back to the party together. It was a warm, summer day and she had already begun to dry off. She would have to go back for more later.

When they had arrived, all of the people at the stalls had been human, but now other creatures joined them. Lady Venner's people were there in hooded robes, dryads, most of whom were male, walking among the humans as calmly as their queen. And there were goblins, too – lots of them. Some of them looked like children or very short adult humans; more looked very different, with grey or green tones to their gnarly skin.

When Lady Marika, Queen of the Unseelie Court, arrived via the front main doors of the mansion accompanied by her daughter Feen, Venner parted company from Helena and moved away from the direction in which the sidhe queen was heading. Helena knew that they did not always get on well, although she also knew that Lady Venner had nursed Marika back to health after her horrific injury from a vampire's blade a couple of months ago. Marika had a dressing over her left eye and a livid scar that started above the dressing and marred her cheek all the way to her mouth.

Helena approached the two sidhe People.

"Mother, this is Helena Grey," said Feen. "Helena, this is Lady Marika, queen of the sidhe."

Helena bowed to the sidhe queen, but the Lady did not offer her hands for the fey greeting.

"Lady Venner speaks highly of you. That wouldn't normally impress me, but Lady Feen here speaks even more highly of you."

"That's a compliment," Feen said to Helena in a manner that seemed to be designed to annoy her mother. While the sidhe queen was happy to have Helena with them, she continued the conversation she was having with her daughter.

"In your travels in Europe, you got used to physical contact. More specifically, physical combat. But now that Michael has got rid of the null stones, you can use the tools that come more naturally to us, to our people. Return to the powers; dig into our nature. You may well find that it is more effective than... brawling."

Haltea Feen laughed and, for a moment, Lady Marika looked offended.

"Lady Marika believes I am trying to become human," she said by way of an explanation to Helena. Helena took that as permission to speak.

"I have no idea why such a glorious, beautiful People would want to even *associate* with humans, let alone become one."

Marika stopped walking and stared deeply into Helena's soul. "What has happened to wound you, child?" she said. "I have just counselled my daughter to be fey – to be what she is. Why do you not want to be what you are?"

"I've lived among humans, and I've lived among the fey. I can't see any redeeming qualities about my own people."

"Nobody can see what they are not looking for," Marika replied.

Marika and Feen continued talking about things that Helena didn't fully understand, so she made her way around the stalls again. She bought something to eat and drink, but she was drawn back towards the lake. She wondered if anyone would mind if she just threw her clothes off and jumped in.

However, before she could carry out such a ridiculous plan, Michael Varmeter, the Lord of the Manor, found her.

"Enjoying yourself?" he asked.

"Your place is amazing," she replied.

"I know. It's been a year, and I still feel there is so much to discover. I gather you are getting on well now that all the sales contracts are complete."

"Yes, thank you," she said, feeling formal as if she was talking to 'the boss'. "Jason Asher and Svend send their apologies."

"Thank you. I understand that Svend doesn't want to come back here because the memory of Silvestri would hurt too much. But how is Jason?"

"I'm a bit concerned for him," said Helena. "He's shut himself in the lighthouse – I mean, he's made a good job of tidying it up, but he doesn't like people. His only friend is Rusalka. She's forgiven him, completely, but I'm not so sure he's forgiven himself."

"I'd like Jason to spend a few days here," said Michael, thoughtfully. "It can be a very… healing place. It might help him if he'll come. We'll have to see."

"When you came to Ogonshead, you worked with the police to get rid of Charles Sutener," said Helena. "I wondered if you would give me a local contact."

"Police contact?"

"Yes, please."

"Are you having trouble?"

"No, not really. It's just that the area is so… dilapidated. There's some crime on the estate, and I wondered if we could do anything to help."

"To be a blessing to the area," Michael smiled. "Lady Venner said you would. But today is a party day, so leave your worries at home and come and join in the fun. And I'll ask Lucy to send you any details we have of the best contacts tomorrow."

"Thank you."

Michael went to meet some of the villagers, and Helena found herself alone at the lake. She sat on an old tree-branch almost close enough to dip her feet in. Jada and two or three more naiads popped their heads up to say hello and then carried on playing, occasionally splashing water in her direction. Helena wondered if ever the naiads in her care at the Mermaid's Rest would be able to express the joy that these creatures did.

She remembered her first experience of fey-kind, back in March, although she hadn't been aware at the time that the creature wasn't human. She was out with her camera, trying to take some photos of early spring to put in her art portfolio. Reni was dipping her feet into the rock pool. Helena remembered thinking 'she must be cold'. She said hello, and felt that the shy girl didn't really want company. However, there was something compelling about the lovely creature, dressed in clothes far too light for the end of winter, and she wanted to take a picture. She pointed her camera, finger ready to click the button, and asked the girl's permission. Reni had said no, and that she wanted to return home now. Helena had apologised, and pointed her camera down. Her finger, still on the button, had accidentally taken a picture of her feet.

Later, at home, she realised she had taken the photograph, but, before she deleted it, she took a look and realised that there was something strange about the picture. The girl had webbed feet!

It would be more than two months later before the truth about the people who were enslaved at the Siren's Song massage parlour was to be revealed to her, but something about their short meeting had touched her heart. And now, she had the incredible task of helping the newly-rescued naiads to return to their true nature.

The day was over soon enough and, as the tables and tents were being packed away, the helicopter came to get them. Jada and her friends disappeared deeper into the lake further into the forest when they heard it. Helena heard it and turned to leave the lakeside. Lucy was standing nearby.

"Oh," said Helena. "Have you been there long?"

"Yes," said Lucy with a grin. "But you looked so... I didn't want to disturb you."

"Thank you. I've had a beautiful day."

She said as much to Michael, too, as he and Lucy escorted her to the helicopter for her return journey. John-James didn't disturb them much on the way back, and Helena sat in the back with Feen, snoozing on her shoulder.

Nevertheless, she was glad when she got back home. Yes, it really was home, although she'd only lived there for a few weeks.

Four

On Sunday, late in the afternoon, there was a hammering on the door of the Mermaid's Rest.

"Help! Please, let me in!"

It was Jackie. She was cut and bleeding and her clothes were ripped. When Helena rushed to the door, Svend was immediately at her side. It was almost as if he had teleported there.

"Come in," said Helena, reaching out her hand to guide her in. The teenager didn't want to be touched.

"Don't let him…"

"It's fine. You're safe here."

"I know you're… this place is private, but I couldn't think of anywhere else to go," said Jackie, sobbing.

"It's fine. Come and sit down. We can call a doctor for you…"

"No. Please don't. I mustn't go to the hospital. He'll…" and then she shut up.

"Come and sit down," said Helena, trying not to take her in her arms as she led her to a soft chair. *Bloody humans!*

Svend went to close the door and looked out down the road.

"He's coming," he said softly.

"Oh, God," said Jackie.

"It'll be fine," said Helena. "You *will* be safe here." She looked up at Svend for confirmation of that. Rusalka and Mara stood at an internal door, looking on as the pathetic and tearful Jackie curled up in the chair.

"Get the other two out of the way, please," Helena said to them. They obeyed promptly.

Svend had closed the front door, but not locked it. It was as if he wanted Jackie's father to try to enter the house. Feen came to the inner doorway after the naiads had left, and she glanced at Jackie and looked hard at Svend, who had a grim smile on his face.

"No," breathed the sidhe princess softly as if Svend had said something to her. "We're not going to do it that way." She moved over to stand by Helena who stood between Jackie and the front door.

A big man pushed the door open, and Svend stepped back to let him in. He was less than six feet tall, but he was big, muscly and fat. He had scruffy, black hair, similar in colour to Jackie's. He wore dirty shoes, greasy trousers, a vest and little else. He smelled of alcohol.

"What are you doing with my daughter?" he bellowed.

"Less than what you've done to her," responded Feen, calmly.

"You can't take her from me."

"We can protect her from you," said Helena. In spite of the threat of this man, the Sidhe Lady and her bodyguard were giving her courage.

"Let me get to her. She's mine. What, are you kidnapping her?"

"No," Helena said. "We aren't doing anything against her will, and we aren't going to let you near her."

Jackie, in the meantime, made to get up from her seat, possibly to return to her father.

"Don't," suggested Helena. "We can protect you."

"You can't," the child whimpered.

Her father pointed to the floor in front of him and spoke to Jackie past the two women in front of him. "Here! Now!"

"No!" Helena bellowed in a challenge to him.

Feen touched her arm gently to indicate she would like to take over, and took a short step towards the man, who had remained at the door and not approached them. For all his drunken state, he could still count that they outnumbered him.

"Let me see," said Feen. "Where did you hit Jackie?" She closed her eyes as if searching for something with her mind. "Oh yes, let's start with her face."

There was a hard, harsh slapping sound, although Feen wasn't standing close enough to the man to make contact. His head jerked suddenly. He put his hand up to his face and a trickle of blood stained his yellowed fingers.

"And her ribs," continued Feen. The man doubled up with pain at the invisible punch and Helena was sure she heard a rib cracking.

"And what did you do to her arm?" said Feen. His arm suddenly stretched out in an ugly-looking twist, then he pulled it in and fell to the floor with tears of pain strafing his dirty face.

Feen took a step towards him and crouched near where he writhed.

"Every time you touch your daughter from now on, you'll feel it. Every slap, smack, kick and punch. It will be as if it was being done to you. And we'll keep an eye on her, to make sure she feels properly looked-after. Perhaps you might want to take her to the hospital, to get her checked over. Wait a minute..." Feen suddenly lifted her head up as if she had detected something else. "Is that a cigarette burn?"

"No," he whimpered. "Please..."

"Stop it," said Jackie. She wasn't shouting though, just asking quietly. "I don't want you to hurt him."

"I'm not hurting him," said Feen. "He's hurting himself."

"He's not..." started Jackie. She sobbed and took a breath. "He's not a bad person. It's just that sometimes things get on top of him, that's all." The girl painfully got out of her chair and made her way past the ladies to her father. She winced as she got down on her knees to aid him.

Feen glanced at Svend and he left the room. Only the ladies were left.

"It's alright dad," Jackie was saying, actually trying to comfort her brute of a father. "It's okay. Everything will be okay..."

"Harlequin's bol... eyeballs," said Feen. "How can she do that?"

"She's trapped," said Helena weakly, then to the father, "Mr. Banner. I'm coming to help you up. I'm not going to hurt you."

"Get away from me," he snivelled.

"Jackie's in no fit state to help you stand up. I want to help. Actually, I want Lady Feen to do all that to you again, but she won't do anything your daughter doesn't want." Helena glimpsed up at Feen, who was rolling her eyes in frustration.

"Are you a witch?" said Banner.

"No," said Helena. "I'm just an ordinary person with some exceptional friends. Friends who don't like grown men who beat up children."

"People say funny things about this place," said Banner.

"Well, you can put them right, can't you, Mr Banner?" said Helena. "You can tell them all about us – that would be good. Perhaps they won't take your daughter away from you. Perhaps they won't take you away and lock you in a padded cell somewhere."

Banner finally had the courage to look into her eyes. He was afraid. "I won't tell anyone," he whispered.

"Jackie will, though, won't she?" said Svend from the door. He had returned with two small corked glass flasks with green liquid in them.

"I'll tell everybody," said Jackie quietly. "I'll tell them that, when I needed help, you helped. And I'll tell them that you helped my dad, too."

"Drink these. They don't taste wonderful, but they will help you get better quickly," said Svend, handing the two flasks out to their visitors.

"Trying to poison us now?" said Banner, but his daughter took one of the flasks, uncorked it and swallowed the contents without any fuss.

"Jack!" said Banner. She took the cork from the second flask and offered it to her father.

"It doesn't taste like anything, but it smells like grass," she said. He took it from his daughter, cautiously sniffed it and then drank it.

"Can we help you up and walk you home?"

"So you can find out where we live?" said the man.

"12 Rockery Way," said Svend. Banner glared at him. "You can take a swing at me if you like," the Elven continued. "It's only if you hit Jackie that it'll hurt you."

"Thank you, Svend," said Helena, "but I don't think that was all that helpful." Feen, in the meantime, was trying not to laugh.

"That stuff you just drank," Svend said. "It's only herbs and water, but the way it was made will dull the pain a little and help you heal."

The way it was made, thought Helena, *you mean with fey magic.*

They finally were able to help Banner stand up and Svend let him lean on him for the short walk home to Rockery Way.

"You can stay if you like," said Helena to Jackie.

"No, I can't," said Jackie. "But it'll be alright now, though. Honest."

"Come by after school tomorrow," said Helena. "We can have a chat."

"I don't..." started Jackie. *I don't go to school*; Helena completed the sentence in her thoughts. Svend helped Mr Banner to the point of almost carrying him out of the house and down the road towards Rockery Way. When he came back he reported that everything seemed quiet and peaceful, and that Banner was subdued and Jackie looked like she was in charge – a situation that puzzled Svend.

The following day, Helena walked to the Lighthouse Rock again, hoping to catch Jackie there with the gang. The gang were there, but Jackie wasn't. Neither were any of the younger kids – the ones who might be school age. Perhaps some of them were actually at school.

"Anyone heard how Jackie Banner is?" Helena asked the crowd, but none of them seemed interested in answering. Goat looked like he was going to say something, but he looked up to Jeff first, and didn't have his permission. Helena wished that Svend was with her, or that she knew enough about motorbikes to start a conversation.

Lucy Waterhouse had sent the name of the local police officer that had been involved in arresting Charles Sutener through to Helena's office. When she got back from the Lighthouse Rock, she phoned the police station and asked to speak to him. He wasn't going to be available until Wednesday. It seemed to Helena that nothing was going to happen soon and progress, if there was any at all, would be slow.

Helena wondered where Svend was, and wondered even more where Feen spent all her time. She saw all of the members of her household nearly every day – except Feen, who wasn't around much. Perhaps she visited the lighthouse?

The sky was overcast and threatening to rain when Helena went out for the second time that day. It was afternoon, and the schools would be out soon. The usual mob were at the rock hanging around Jeff and his motorbike. Jackie was still not with them.

Helena meandered southward along the path on the coastal side of the road, looking at the houses that lined the other side. Some seemed to be unoccupied, a few had nice gardens, one or two had big cars in the driveway and a couple had overgrown and unkempt gardens. One of them had an Elven warrior dressed in drab workman's clothes, pulling up weeds.

Helena took a second look. Past the Lighthouse Rock, past the three shops by the beach, past the bit of land owned by the Nieziemski estate, on the other side of the road, *Svend was weeding a garden*!

"Svend!"

"Oh, hello, Helena."

At that moment, an elderly lady came out of the house, dressed in her Sunday best and carrying a little tray with a mug of tea on it and a small plate with chocolate biscuits on. They made a chinking sound as she brought them to him.

"This is Mrs King," said Svend. "Mrs King, this is my... this is Helena Grey."

"Hello, Helena," said Mrs King. "Your Sven, he's been ever so good to me. I haven't been able to do anything with the garden since my Graham died, but he said he'd help me get the weeds down a bit."

Helena's mouth moved a bit but no words came out.

"Mr McLaren, two doors down," said Svend, "has a big tarmacked driveway, and he said now his family have all moved away he's got the space for a skip for garden rubbish if we can tidy up people's gardens."

"We?" said Helena, just about finding her tongue at last.

"Well, me," said Svend.

"Your Sven's an angel," said Mrs King.

"Well, not, not really. Angels are more... oh, yes, I see what you mean," said Svend.

"He's not my Sven...d," said Helena. "Who's paying for the skip?"

"Haven't worked that out yet," said Svend, and he took the mug with a big 'thank-you' smile and gulped it down. He demolished the biscuits almost as fast. Mrs King beamed at him and took her tray back.

"I think *we* can afford to hire a skip," said Helena.

"It might take more than one," said Svend. Helena looked at the pile of weeds, and thought, *only if you are doing more than one garden.*

Two big motorbikes roared past, making the tray with the empty utensils on it shake a bit more.

"Noisy things, aren't they?" the old lady said.

"Kids," said Helena.

"Oh, no, they're not kids," said Mrs King. "Those bikes belong to the grown-ups' bike club. At least, they like to call themselves grown-ups. Boys with toys, that's what I call them. Meeting up like a secret society at the old coppice every Wednesday and Friday. That's why those young people love their motorbikes so much. They want to be like the big boys."

A few drops of rain started to fall.

"Oh dear," said Mrs King. "It's time to stop."

"I can work on in a bit of rain," said Svend with an engaging smile.

"You don't want to be out in the rain," the old lady said. "You'll catch your death."

"I've caught a lot of things in my time," said Svend. "But that's something I've never even tried to hunt."

Mrs King shook her head and went indoors. Helena looked on for a bit while Svend continued his work, but she decided she wasn't dressed for rain, so she returned home to get ready for tea.

Both Svend and Feen were not around for the next couple of days, and Helena spent some time with Mara and Virino. They cuddled up together on the big sofa in the living room and listened to the rain falling outside. The two naiads talked, sometimes in English and sometimes in their own language. Helena loved to listen to their language – it always touched her emotions. Sometimes it made her want to cry, sometimes she just wanted to close her eyes and listen to it, and sometimes she thought it was like a song that was about to be sung, but couldn't quite make it into our world.

On Wednesday, Helena got on the phone again and spoke to the police officer whose name Lucy had given her, David Squire, who was back on duty. They spoke about the trouble on the estate, the robberies in town and how to help the local young people. Squire's answers were all 'there's nothing we can do; domestic issues must be reported by the victim rather than a concerned friend and we have no resources'. Helena finished the conversation as frustrated with the human race as she always was.

Later on in the day, Jackie Banner knocked on the door. This time there was no emergency. Her scars and bruises seemed to be healing well.

"It's good to see you, Jackie. Please come in," said Helena, and the thirteen-year-old came in looking tentatively around for the other residents.

"Lady Feen and Svend aren't here at the moment," Helena told her.

"I know," said Jackie. "They're on the main road, doing gardening."

"Both of them?"

"Both of them and a few more. Jeff and the gang are with them."

"Wow. How did Svend manage that?"

"He didn't really manage anything," said Jackie, shrugging her shoulders. "They are just hanging around with him, leaning on the wall and watching him work."

Reni was in the living room, but she made to leave when she saw Jackie coming in.

"You don't have to go," said Helena to the naiad, who was dressed only in a light cream dress and had bare feet. Bare webbed feet. "Jackie's a friend."

"Are you someone they've saved?" Jackie asked Reni.

"Yes, I suppose so. Are you?"

"I guess. Or they've started to."

Helena guided her young guest to the sofa and then sat next to her. She wanted to put her arms around her like she did the naiads, but she thought better of it. Jackie sat hunched at the edge of the seat, looking down at the floor.

"How's your dad?"

"He's okay. He hasn't... *done* anything since Sunday. I mean, we're okay."

"Tell me about your home."

"It's just me and Dad. Mum died a couple of years ago. Cancer. Dad left his job to look after her, and... well, he started drinking a lot. He'd go all moody. We haven't got much money; the housing people keep sending letters threatening to evict us. He can't get a job now; he gets caught up in it all. Sometimes he takes it out on me. I know he cares about me really; it's just that sometimes it all gets on top of him."

"I don't know what I can do to help, but I'll try."

"Your feet are..." started Jackie, and Helena looked down at her feet. Then she realised that the girl was looking at Reni. The naiad tucked her feet under her legs out of sight. "Sorry," Jackie continued. "That was rude of me."

"Can I tell her?" Reni said to Helena.

"I think so."

"I'm the nearest thing in real life to what you would call a mermaid," said Reni.

Jackie sat open-mouthed for a moment while she processed what she had just been told. "Cool," she said at last.

"Yeah," said Helena. "I'm with you on that one."

Jackie looked at Helena. "Are you...?"

"I'm human," said Helena, guessing what Jackie was trying to ask. "You know if you tell lots of people about this, the... mermaids... will be in danger again."

"I won't tell anyone," said Jackie. "And don't tell Goat. He talks too much. In fact, don't tell anyone. And Svend and the princess, are they mermaids?" Then she coloured up at the thought of Svend being a mermaid.

"No, they are our protectors," said Helena. "As you saw."

"And the princess is a real princess?"

"Yes. The daughter of a queen."

Jackie was quiet for a while, mostly looking at the floor, sometimes looking in Reni's direction. Eventually she asked, "Are they magic? Is that what they used on my dad?"

"They don't call it magic," said Helena. "As I understand it, it's just their nature."

Jackie stayed a bit longer, and Reni got her a drink. When she handed the glass of orange juice over, Jackie took a good look at her feet. This time, Reni stretched them out for her to clearly see the webbing between her toes.

"Cool," she said again.

On Thursday morning, Helena phoned the number she had for Councillor Irene Henderson. She had been on their side over the trouble with the Siren's Song before it became the Mermaid's Rest.

"Hello?" came an abrupt voice.

"Hello. Can I speak to Irene Henderson?"

"Who's calling?"

"Helena Grey." Immediately, the phone went dead. Whoever had answered for Irene had hung up. Well, she wasn't going to leave it there. She would track down and speak to Irene Henderson, somehow. Perhaps the Manor could help again, or that Mic character they used to get them information.

Helena decided she must see Svend and Feen in action, so she took a walk to the main road on the sea front. The fey princess and her bodyguard had just about tidied up Mrs King's garden and the gang were there watching.

"You know, they'd get the job done quicker if you helped them," Helena said to Jeff when she saw him.

"Whatever," he said, and he led his toadies away back toward the Lighthouse Rock.

"I had a bath," she said to Svend as the youths moved away. "Perhaps it was something I said."

"They think you're going to get Jackie's father into trouble," said Feen, bundling the last of the rubbish into a wheelbarrow.

"They don't know what you did to him?" said Helena.

"No. He hasn't spoken about it, and Jackie doesn't seem to have spoken to them either."

"She hasn't been around them much."

"Perhaps they think you've stolen her from them," suggested Svend. "She came to you for help rather than them."

"To us, not just me," said Helena. She felt frustrated that she couldn't make a connection with these young people.

They tidied up and took the last of the garden rubbish to the skip that was in the driveway further down the road. It was already nearly full. Then they went home for some tea and relaxed together in the Mermaid's Rest.

"My muscles ache!" complained Svend with considerable humour. "I once wrestled with a gorgoneth for six hours and my muscles didn't ache like this."

"Have a bath with some powdered mandrake," suggested Feen, who didn't seem to be bothered by such aches in spite of having worked in the same garden.

"I think I might, in spite of the side effects," he said, standing up and stretching.

"Side effects?" asked Helena.

"It makes men…" said Feen, trying to find the right word. "What do you call it?"

"There are lots of human words for its effects," said Svend with a smile.

"You mean…" said Helena, trying to find the politest way of putting it, "It makes you want a woman?"

Svend looked at her and raised an eyebrow.

"Not me," said Helena. "I'm not really your type."

"I think you mean *I'm* not really *your* type," he said, and left them to take his bath.

"The others will be safe from him?" Helena asked, feeling very protective about the naiads in her care.

"He has sworn to protect them. But they might like his company. Particularly Reni. She's very fond of him."

"I thought after what they went through with Sutener, they wouldn't want that kind of contact again."

"It's different if you *want* it," said Feen with a shrug.

"I've been thinking," said Helena, eager to change the subject as she found the image of Svend and Reni together in *that* way a little uncomfortable. "Mrs King said the bikers went to the coppice. Not the kids, the adult biker group. That's further down the south road where the Casterbury Woods go down to the sea. There are some cycle tracks, bridle paths and little clearings. I was thinking that if the bikers met there, that's where they might plan their robberies."

"You think the bikers that meet there are the ones that commit the crimes in the town? What do you call them? Ram-raiders?"

"Ram-raiders use cars, not motorbikes. Where do you get your words from? Do you watch a lot of telly?"

Feen laughed. "The English language has a lot of words."

"Svend thinks it's not the kids and the robberies are being done by bikers, so why don't we look at other bikers as possible culprits? It's a working theory."

"I can go down there and take a look."

"You don't want them catching you spying on them," said Helena, realising as she said it that it wouldn't be Feen who would be in danger if they caught her.

Feen smiled. "I've done this kind of thing before. My People are very good at not being seen. Especially in woods. And for the last twenty or more years I've been travelling Europe, not being seen."

Five

Helena lay in her bed looking up at the ceiling. She was remembering her visit to Nieziemski Manor, particularly the joy of the naiads who swam in the huge lake there. She remembered what Jada had said to her – "You are blessed and a blessing". At first she just thought it was a pretty fey greeting, but she'd pondered the words over the last few days. She was certainly blessed, she knew that. She was blessed to know that there were fey People in our world, she was blessed to be part of the little community here at Ogonshead, she was blessed to be able to help them in her own small way. But how was she a blessing? More to the point, how could she be an actual blessing to the area, to the town, in the way that Svend and Feen were doing their bit to contribute positively to the community?

Feen spent a few days visiting the coppice a couple of miles further south down the road. The bikers weren't there most of the time, but she would be patient. Svend discovered that at least two of Mrs King's friends had troubles with their gardens and would love the help of a big, strong Norwegian man (which is what they thought he was). Helena tracked down Irene Henderson, who she discovered was now a teaching assistant at the local primary school in the town.

She waited outside Ogonshead Primary School after all the children had left. Shortly before 4pm, Irene came out. She looked well, and possibly happier than when she had seen her last. She smiled when she saw Helena.

"Good to see you again. How are things at the Mermaid's Rest?"

"The mermaids are resting," said Helena, and Irene laughed. "You're not on the council anymore?"

"When your Mr Varmeter uncovered the bribery back in, when was it?" said Irene as they walked slowly past the school playing fields. "I was so angry with the council. They were all corrupt, taking bribes and letting all those things happen. Some of them are still on the council now. So I quit. I went back to being a teaching assistant. And I prefer my life now."

"Was it your mother who answered the phone the other day?"

"I didn't know you'd called. So, yes, I expect it was her and she didn't tell me about you. She's still angry at me for siding with you and… she called it wrecking the council. I told her that if you commit a crime, it's your fault, not the person who catches you. And we've hardly spoken to each other since. I'm going to move out as soon as I get the chance – I don't feel that place is my home anymore."

"I'm sorry."

"I'm not. I was always in her shadow. I never really did anything useful on the council. I just followed my mum's lead and let things happen. I feel freer now. Did you want to talk to me about something?"

"Not if you're not on the council anymore."

"I've still got contacts. I might be able to help."

"Well… there's a family on the estate who might get evicted. A single father and his thirteen-year-old daughter. I wondered if there was any way we could help them?"

"Well, I'm pleased to be able to tell you that you don't need the council for that. They can't throw him out of his home because he has a school-aged child still living there. But there are lots of funds and support agencies that can help him. The house would probably be owned by the Ogonshead and District Housing Association. Get in touch with them on his behalf and they'll point him to any housing benefits they have available. He doesn't have to worry, as long as he asks. But he *must* ask – things only get bad if you don't let them know you're struggling."

Helena thanked her for the help and left her to the rest of her walk home. She wasn't sure whether to be pleased for her for quitting the council or sad for the council for losing someone with some integrity. When she got back to the Mermaid's Rest, there was just time to call the housing association, who were very helpful.

The following week was the first full week of October, and the autumn cold was setting in. Most of the town centre attractions were closed down at the moment, but there was still hope for some decent half-term holiday tourist traffic at the end of the month.

On the Wednesday evening, the motorcycle gang had met at the coppice and Feen had listened in on their plans undetected. She reported back to Helena.

"You were right about the bikers being the raider gang. They are planning a raid on the main arcade at midnight on Saturday," she said. "Weekends are best for business, and the arcade makes most of its money late at night, they think, so they believe it will be a big catch."

Helena called PC Squire to inform him of what they found. He was on his day off, so wasn't available. Again. *Did that man ever turn up for work?* She left a message with whoever it was who was answering the phone for him that day. They asked her no questions about how she had obtained the information, and she wondered if they were really that interested. Still, she'd done her duty and it was no longer her problem.

On the Friday morning, while Feen and Svend were out gardening for one of Mrs King's neighbours, there was a knock on the door. Helena had been curled up on the big sofa with Virino, who was just beginning to doze off in her arms. The naiad was disturbed by the knock almost to the point of distress, and left quickly for her room as Helena headed for the door.

It was Mr Banner. He didn't look drunk, and he was dressed reasonably tidily, but he was still a big man.

"Was it you?" he said sharply. Helena was a little nervous. She was alone in the house except for Virino, Mara and Reni. Rusalka was at the lighthouse and they didn't have the protection of the Elven or the princess.

"Was what me?" said Helena, trying to speak as calmly as possible. She had her hand on the door, ready to slam it in his face if she needed to.

"The housing people came round."

"I told them you might need help," she admitted.

"Well, they told me about all the help I could get. They are going to help me pay the rent arrears and reduce my rent from now on. To nearly nothing. They assured me that they wouldn't throw me out of the house and they have made it as easy as they could for me to pay. They did tell me off for not telling them sooner," he added with a shy grin. "I came round to say thank you."

"I really didn't do very much," said Helena, breathing a sigh of relief.

"It might not have been very much to you, but it meant a lot to me. Especially as I was so… you know… when I came round."

"Are you better now?"

"Healing. There's something else I wanted to say." He stopped and thought for a moment, trying to find a way of saying something he found really difficult. He took a deep breath. "I drink too much. I thought I could handle it. Maybe I still think I can. But I'm going to get help. I thought if I said that out loud, it might make it easier, and I thought, as I am keeping your secret, you won't make a fuss about mine."

"That sounds fair. I don't have any contacts, but if you get in touch with…" she was going to say the council, but she had no faith in them. "Actually, I don't know who you should get in touch with. Maybe the local church will know?"

"I'll find someone. And I'm going to try and send Jackie back to school. I was afraid because I thought someone would notice the cuts and get me into trouble. Your kind of trouble was better in the end, though. Anyway, that's what I wanted to say. See you around." And he very quickly turned and walked towards his home, as if what he'd said was embarrassing for him and he didn't want to talk about it anymore.

Helena stood with her arm in the air, fingers hanging over the top of the front door like a monkey for a few minutes, trying to assimilate what had just happened.

Blessed and a blessing.

After calling Virino back in and reassuring her that everything was okay, Helena took a walk to the sea front. She decided to spend some time with Jason and Rusalka. She knew they liked their privacy, so she didn't stay for very long. She didn't understand their relationship. She didn't know why they were friends – why Rusalka had forgiven him, why it was him that she needed for her healing, and why he needed her. They had made some kind of connection, perhaps something fey in nature, but something that affected Jason as much as it did the naiad. He might have some latent ability, rare in ordinary humans, which enabled him to empathise with the fey People in a way that most people wouldn't.

"My dad called," Jason said while she was with them.

"Everything okay?" asked Helena.

"I wasn't rude to him, if that's what you mean. He wants to come and visit to see I'm okay. Actually, I don't know if that's the real reason or not. But he wants to see me again."

"Here at the lighthouse? Or would you prefer we cooked a meal for him at the house?"

"A meal would be good. Sunday lunch? And if you could persuade Svend to cook it that would be... what am I saying? I want to impress my father!" he laughed at himself.

"There's nothing wrong with making it look good," said Helena. "You want to tell him that you're getting on fine without him, and that you're part of a family that actually cares about you."

"That's true. I think he cares about me really," then he thought about it. "No, actually, he probably doesn't. I think he wants to come round to see me fail. To see me living in squalor, helpless without him."

"Then let's show him that you haven't failed."

Jason laughed briefly. "To be honest, I don't really care what he thinks."

Helena once again saw her own disappointment with the human race in his words, so she couldn't try to redirect his heart to think more kindly of his father. She left them to their tidying up the lighthouse, promising that she would ask Svend to cook on Sunday.

She meandered down the southward road until she came to where Feen and Svend were working in another overgrown garden. Jeff, Shir and Goat were watching from the road.

"Hello," Helena said to the young people. Shir nodded back and the others ignored her. Perhaps she could use Jeff's girlfriend to get in with the group. Feen stopped loading the wheelbarrow and came over to the garden wall where the kids were leaning.

"Helena thinks you don't like her, that she's done something to offend you," she said to Jeff.

"No, she's okay," the young gang leader replied. "It's just that she keeps checking on us to see if we're climbing on the rocks."

Helena laughed. "When I go to the lighthouse, it's to check on Jason. I mean, to make sure he's okay and doesn't need anything. I'm not spying on you."

"Oh, right," said Jeff, not sounding like he was bothered one way or the other. "Jason, he's the one that looks after the lighthouse. The one with that gorgeous girlfriend." Shir kicked him in the shins.

"That's right," said Helena. "Except I don't think she's his girlfriend. They're just friends."

"Does that mean she's available?" said Goat. "Would you put a word in for me?"

Helena laughed and said, "No chance."

Someone walked along the sea path from a small side-turning that led to the Sea View estate. It was Mr Banner, dressed in working clothes.

"Hello," the big man said. "I thought I saw you here. Hello, Billy. How's your dad these days?"

"Still off with his mates all the time," said Goat. "I hardly see him, except for meals."

Mr Banner stopped at the entrance to the garden and spoke to Feen.

"Princess," he said. "You don't mind me callin' you that? I wondered if you wanted some help here. I can do a bit of weeding, carry stuff around, that sort of thing. In fact, anything you want me to do."

"You would be most welcome, Mr Banner. And please call me Feen."

He looked at Goat and the others. "So what do you lot do? You stand and watch while the princess does all the work?"

Jeff, Shir and Goat joined Mr Banner and they all set to pulling up weeds. Helena left them to it, deciding not to tell Svend about Mr Asher's visit until later.

Saturday started with a little light rain but in the afternoon Feen and Svend were eager to go out and do some more gardening. Jeff and the others had enjoyed their working session earlier in the week, so they were going to get the whole gang to help them. As all four naiads were going to be in the house, Helena decided to stay with them.

They spent the afternoon doing as little as possible as the house was already tidy and ready for Mr Asher's visit on the following day. Helena told Rusalka what Goat had said about her being available, and she laughed politely, but really, she looked as if she was unhappy that she had been seen by the young people at all. Helena was at her happiest, not worrying about people being thrown out of their homes, or how available local police officers were to solve crimes, or how many local gardens could be tidied up by kids with nothing else to do; she was surrounded by four beautiful naiads, crowding around her on the sofa and at her feet, just... being.

When Svend came back for tea, he was excited to tell Helena that a gang of seventeen kids looked after a total of four front and back gardens, and the various old people who owned the gardens were very appreciative and gave them drinks and snacks. He said he thought it was a first for some of the kids, actually being appreciated, and they enjoyed the experience. Helena would have liked to show their efforts to ex-councillor Clive Matthews or to Irene Henderson's mother, just to rub their noses in it.

As they ate together, they discussed the following day's Sunday lunch with their guest, Jason's father.

"Will you want us all there?" asked Reni.

"I will never ask you to do something you don't want to do," said Helena.

"Be careful making promises like that," said Feen. "Sometimes things come up we don't like."

"Fair enough," said Helena. "I'll amend that to 'I'll *try* not to ask you to do something you don't want to do'. But tomorrow counts as be here if you want to, not if you don't."

"Thank you," nodded Reni. Helena was aware that Jason was looking hopefully at Rusalka, who also noticed.

"There is something I would like to do," Svend said, as if he was asking permission from Helena rather than Feen. "I would like to go to the town tonight. I'll stay hidden, but I want to see the police catching those bikers. I am still convinced that our young friends aren't among them but, well, I want to see for myself. Just to make sure."

"When I listened in the coppice," said Feen, "there were only older men there. None of our young people were among them."

"Let me know how it turns out," said Helena.

The following morning, Svend was in the kitchen getting ready for the meal when Helena came in to see how preparations were going. What she really wanted to do, however, was find out about the previous night's robbery. Svend was not entirely happy with how it had gone.

"After the arcade was closed for the night, the police took over. There were three police cars and a number of officers in full uniform and high-vis jackets, all over the place. Six big motorbikes came into town. They saw the police there and decided to ride on."

"So nothing happened?"

"I got a good look at the bikes. None of them were the ones I've seen with the kids. So that's one good thing. But there was no action. No arrests. Nothing."

"That's a pity," said Helena. *Perhaps they should enlist the People into the police force. Something might get done.*

Virino, Mara and Reni decided they didn't want to meet Jason's guest and so they would eat in their rooms. Rusalka agreed to join the party in the dining room and she and Jason prepared it to look special. The naiads had learned to eat with cutlery, although they normally didn't bother as nobody in the household minded. Rusalka would put on a decent show, even though she'd find it difficult.

Max Asher turned up at midday. The roast lamb meal Svend was making already smelled spectacular as he entered the house. Helena answered the door with Jason standing by her side. Asher senior was a tall, wide man with hair similar in colour and texture to Jason's except for a few traces of grey coming through. He had big arms and looked as if the muscles he had when he was younger were only just beginning to turn to fat. He dressed smartly with a shirt and tie, and looked like he could impress and command any room. Any room full of humans, that is. He gave his son a look of disdain as he walked in.

As he stepped into the living room as if he owned the place, Feen and Rusalka awaited him. Feen was dressed in the gorgeous blue and white robes that Svend had called her 'princess kit', and Rusalka was wearing a pretty dress that Helena had found for her. She wore soft shoes to hide her feet. But whatever she wore, she could not hide that incredible, sweet beauty.

"My friend Rusalka," said Jason, beaming with pride that he could call her 'friend'.

"Rusalka," said Asher. "Russian name?"

"Yes," said Rusalka. "I'm not Russian, but when I chose my name it sounded nice."

Asher did not ask about her choosing her own name or, in fact, what nationality she was, but looked at Feen.

"This is Lady Haltea Feen," Jason introduced her.

"*Lady* Haltea?" said Asher.

"I never know whether to call her 'Lady Feen' or 'Princess Feen'," said Helena.

"My friends call me Feen," said Feen to Max Asher with a wicked smile. "If we ever become friends, you can, too."

Helena's impression of the man was that he was arrogant. He might even have been a little disappointed that Jason didn't show him that he lived in a hovel and had no friends. Jason's theory that he was visiting to gloat over his failure might well have been correct. Feen was out to offer put-downs as much as she could, and Helena decided that she wasn't going to stop her.

"Jason's done wonders with the lighthouse," Helena said as they sat down at the table.

"Directing the workforce?" said Asher.

"Where he needed to. But he's done most of the work himself."

"Menial work."

"English isn't my first language," said Feen, "but I think you mean 'manual' work."

Svend brought out the food. It was, as usual for him, amazing.

"You have your own cook, then," said Asher as Svend served him.

"No, we all take turns," said Helena. "Jason's very good, but we thought we'd let him off the hook today, seeing as you're here. Svend is normally Princess Feen's bodyguard."

"Bodyguard?" said Asher, shocked. "Does she need one?"

"Not really," said Svend. "Not anymore. And she's quite a decent fighter without me. Perhaps we could give you a demonstration afterwards?"

Jason laughed. He was really loving this — Helena hadn't seen him so happy since they'd first met.

"I'm sure that won't be necessary," said Feen. "We wouldn't want to frighten the man on his first visit."

"You mean, we reserve that for his second visit?" said Svend. It was good to see him so animated, too. Helena remembered the quiet man mourning the death of his closest friend... Was it only two months ago?

Max Asher wasn't stupid, and knew that he was being made fun of. So he did what any bully would do — he picked on the person he thought would be weakest.

"What do you do?" he asked Rusalka.

"I swim," said Rusalka, puzzled at the question.

"Professionally?"

"I doubt if she would be allowed to swim professionally," said Feen in a voice that suggested to Helena she was still making fun of the old man. "She'd be too fast for them. You wouldn't want to embarrass the rest of them, would you?"

"Rusalka has been an incredible help at the lighthouse," said Jason. "Perhaps we can take you there after dinner."

"No, I won't stay. I just wanted to see you, talk to you for a moment, privately, and then I will be on my way home."

After dinner, Helena showed Asher and his son into the living room. She stood by the door and listened to the conversation.

"What I really came here for was to tell you I am cutting you off."

"What, do you mean like circumcision?" Jason said with a grin. Feen's cheek had obviously motivated him.

"Don't sass me, boy. You know what I mean."

"Yes, I do. And what I should say is thank you."

"What? Did you hear what I said, boy?"

"How's it going?" said Feen loudly from behind where Helena stood at the door. She was still in attack mode.

"Not very well," Helena said in an exaggeratedly loud voice, going along with the fey princess and making sure that Jason's father knew whose side they were all on. "Mr Asher seems to have forgotten Jason's name. He keeps calling him 'boy'."

Jason turned to talk to Helena. "Boy is like an affectionate nickname, but without the affection."

Max Asher made a harumph sound that was so authentic that Helena felt he must have practised it. His face went red at being ridiculed by his own son.

"I said I was cutting you out of my will."

"Yes, sir, I heard you," said Jason, still struggling to get the smile off of his face and loving the response his unofficial audience was giving him. "And I said 'thank you', sir. It means I don't have to talk to you anymore. I can even pretend you aren't my father. I appreciate your efforts, sir. Just one question, though – without me, who will you bully?"

He harumphed again like a pro, and stormed towards the exit. Unfortunately, he had to go past Helena and Feen to get there and they were laughing among themselves like schoolgirls.

Helena got out of the way, but Feen stood in front of him.

"Sorry that Jason isn't the abject failure you wanted him to be," said Feen. "Nothing without his daddy to look after him. No, I am a princess of the house of Marika, and I am honoured and humbled to know him. I am sure that is what you came here to hear."

Max Asher made to push her out of the way, but she let him go without contact. Helena had made it to the front door by then and opened it for him.

"It was an experience to meet you, Mr Asher. If ever you're in the area again, be sure to remember you should have made an appointment first."

Asher was gone in a second. Helena returned to the living room where she found Jason, arm in arm with Rusalka, laughing until the tears rolled down his cheeks. Rusalka seemed happy, but probably didn't understand Jason's reaction any more than Helena did.

"Sorry that didn't really go the way you wanted," Helena said to him.

"No, it's good. Your job here was always to help the People to be free. Well, I feel free – free from *him* – at last and it's thanks to you all."

Helena looked at Jason and Rusalka together. This was the first time she had seen them in physical contact with each other. "Are you two…"

"Not really," said Jason. "We're just friends. But both of us needed something to free us, and I think today might have been it, at least for me."

"So your dad was good for something."

"Absolutely not. He was the problem, for me, and now he isn't. For Rusalka?"

"I don't really know," said the naiad. "I think being together with someone, together in our minds, is what I was looking for. I don't really know what will happen now. But whatever it is, I'm not afraid of it anymore."

On Monday morning, Helena received a phone call from PC David Squire. "Hello, Miss Grey. PC Squire here. I have to inform you that the information you gave us was incorrect. There was no robbery when you said."

"No, Mr Squire, that's not the case. They called off the robbery because you were stupid. You could have laid in wait for them quietly and secretly and caught them in the act. Then the robberies would stop and you would be a hero. But what you did was make them put off their robbery until another day."

She hung up angrily, wishing she had one of those old phones where you could slam the phone down, and wondered what Michael Varmeter would do to catch these raiders. One thing was certain; he wouldn't do nothing.

Six

Helena meandered into town. She was walking quite a lot these days. She'd passed her driving test before she turned 20, occasionally using her mother's car. However, although the photography business made a bit of money in the summer, it had to carry her through slim winters so she'd never had the funds to buy her own transport. She'd lived at her mother's house, but rented an office in the town a couple of streets away from the sea front.

She had called her business 'Colours' because her surname was Grey and she was amused at the odd humour there. She found herself looking at the old place. The colours on the sign 'Colours' had faded a little, which she also found amusing. She still held the lease on the office, which would expire at the end of this season – which was, in fact, the end of this month. She glanced up at the old, useless CCTV camera, sorted through her keys and went in to where she used to work.

She'd visited the place over the last few months to pick up any post that had arrived for her. There was nothing new there this morning. She'd paid up all her bills and cleared out the pictures and general paperwork, so now there was an empty desk and an empty filing cabinet. Her landlord had said that if she wanted to leave those there for the next client, that would be fine with him. Other than that, her past life was being erased from this place. And she was pleased about that.

She'd been happy to move out of her mother's house. They got on alright, but Mum had been uncomfortable since Helena had said she was gay. Her new household accepted her and loved her for who she was. What a shame only one of them was human.

Thoughts of the CCTV cameras, an empty office, the message from the police earlier that morning, and the motorcycle gang raiders all invaded her mind at once. An idea was forming in her head and she wondered if Feen and Svend would be up for some trouble. She would put it to them later this evening.

On the following day just after noon, Helena found the three 'leaders of the gang' dossing at the Lighthouse Rock. The fencing that they had been waiting for was finally drilled into the rock and the lighthouse area was secure. Only the three who were too old for school were there but Helena only wanted to speak to one – Goat. Except that she didn't want to speak to him directly, as long as he heard what she was going to say.

"Now that you've met the princess," she said to Shir, "what do you think?"

"I think she's cool," said Shir. "She doesn't talk down to you. I mean, we're not royalty, we're not even nice people sometimes, but she'll talk to us."

"And she'll do gardening," said Jeff. "D'you know if she'll be joining us today?"

"Probably not. She's at our other base."

"Other base?" said Jeff. "Where's that?"

"Oh, it's not really a base. It's just my old office in town. From before I came to run the Mermaid's Rest, when I used to run the photography business. I still have my office, but now that I've handed the rest of the business over to Jamie Decker, Princess Feen's using the offices to store her stuff."

"Stuff?" said Shir.

"She's got some of her clothes there, and quite a bit of jewellery. Did I tell you she has no money? I think I did. Anyway, what she has got is lots of jewellery, and she's looking to get it valued. We reckon it could fetch a fair bit, but she probably won't sell it all at once."

"I wouldn't keep it there," said Shir. "There have been some robberies in town lately."

"Yes, I heard," said Helena. "But they've been on the sea front and they've been grabbing cash. We don't have any cash there. We have a CCTV camera outside the building covering the door, and we have one bit of security that is more important."

"What's that?"

"Nobody knows it's there! As far as everyone is concerned, it's just an empty old office. So I think her stuff is safe there – and it will only be there for a few days before we move it on."

Helena was careful not to lay it on too thick, which was why she told the story to Shir and allowed Goat just to listen in. Jackie had told them not to say anything secret to Goat because he would spread it about, which was exactly what she wanted. She'd heard Mr Banner chatting to Goat about his father. She remembered that he'd said something about him hanging around with his mates all the time. She wondered if his mates were bikers, and if they were the ones that met at the coppice down the road. Svend had walked by Goat's house and seen the motorbike in the driveway, so from there it hadn't been too difficult to put the pieces together.

They didn't want the bikers to raid the Mermaid's Rest, so they decided that Helena's old office was the ideal place to set up a raid. All they had to do was plant the story that there was valuable jewellery being secretly stashed there. The police wouldn't be informed this time – at least, not straight away – and Feen and her bodyguard would be the necessary security. The CCTV on the outside of the building was not particularly good, in that it probably wouldn't recognise anyone if they carried a ten-foot banner with their name printed on it, but it was the cameras inside that Helena was most interested in. She still had her contacts from her photographer days, so it was quite easy to get some very decent quality CCTV cameras temporarily installed inside the building.

Feen would return to the woods now and listen out for the bikers' plans. Then they would hide out in the old office, waiting for them. Helena insisted she should be there to operate the cameras, but what she really wanted was to be there to see them in action. Because they were going to be filmed, it was important that they left their griffon weapons behind. Feen seemed happy with this, mentioning something that her mother had said to her about digging in to her own nature rather than physical combat. Svend, although he would have preferred the physical, acquiesced to his lady's wishes.

The bikers met the following day, Wednesday at five in the evening, and arranged to raid the Colours office that night after 10pm, which didn't give Helena and the team a lot of time to get things ready.

However, at 10pm that night, the three of them were there, ready for action. She'd set up the four cameras inside so that they covered every part of the office. Then they turned the lights off so that they were in the dark. A few streetlights outside pushed a little light through the small opaque glass panels at the front of the building.

As she was sitting, waiting in a shadowed corner right at the back of the office, she realised that she could have left this to the two of them. They were more than capable of dealing with the gang, and, to be honest, Helena might even get in the way. It was just that there was something of a child in her – she didn't want to miss the fun.

The sound of motorcycle engines roared nearby, and then turned off. Helena heard someone climbing onto the bit of flat roof at the front, presumably to smash the CCTV camera. Then the gang hit the door hard. It broke open on their second attempt. Torches flashed so that they could see their way around. Helena was in her cubbyhole at the back, and even she couldn't see where Feen and Svend had hidden themselves.

Then, when all six of the heavily-clothed motor-bikers were inside, all the lights came on. Feen and Svend stood between them and escape. The biker closest to Feen fell on the floor unconscious, without being touched. The next two closest bikers immediately attacked the warriors who ducked and dodged them before they, too, fell unconscious. The remaining three stood frozen, perhaps caught between anger and fear. Feen took a step toward them. She was wearing fairly flimsy clothes, trousers and a tee shirt, making sure they could see that she was 'only' a girl.

In spite of her tiny, unthreatening frame, one of the bikers built up enough courage to charge at her but, somehow, he missed and crashed into the door frame behind her, bloodying his nose and falling unconscious. Four down, two to go. Helena was beginning to feel sorry this wasn't lasting longer.

"At this point," said Svend, "I would recommend surrender. Your choice, of course, but you aren't getting out of here before the police arrive."

At the cue ('police'), Helena broke cover and called them on the phone in full view of the two remaining standing raiders. The nearest thug turned to face her, but all of a sudden Feen was in front of him.

"That hurts," she said, and he screamed with pain before collapsing at her feet, for all she hadn't touched him. The four cameras filming the incident would confirm that to the police later.

"I surrender," squealed the last man.

"Where do you stash your winnings?" said Feen.

"Loot," said Svend. "It's not winnings if they steal it."

"Sorry, loot," said Feen.

"Freddie's house," whimpered the last man standing. It still took another eight minutes before the police got there.

The following morning, PC David Squire and an assistant, a young policewoman, visited the Mermaid's Rest. As he came into the building, he looked around the place, perhaps noting how it had changed since he and his colleagues had arrested Charles Sutener here more than four months ago. Helena directed them to the dining room where they took seats around the table. The girls were in the living room and Helena didn't want to disturb them.

"You've done well here," said Squire.

"Yes, it's been good. You're one of the privileged few. We don't let many people in." *Except Jackie and her father and Jason's dad and Clive Matthews at the lighthouse – it's been like Piccadilly Circus in here.* "Are you here to tell us off for catching the raiders?" said Helena.

"Not to tell you off," said Squire, "although we should always tell people to be careful around criminals like them."

"Did you find their stash?"

"Yes," said Squire. "Your information was correct. We raided Freddie Joseph's house and found a lot of the stuff they had stolen from the town. All of the gang are in custody and being questioned. They seem to be co-operating."

Helena smiled. "We were expecting them to put up a fight, but they seemed to back down quite quickly. Perhaps they weren't as tough as they looked."

"From what I've seen so far, they seem to have fainted when they got caught. We're obviously looking at the footage you provided."

"Do you have any questions for me?" said Helena, wondering if she would find an intelligible way to answer them.

"Your staff – they seemed quite competent."

"Lady Feen and Svend. Yes, they are quite competent. I was convinced that they could handle six thugs."

"You knew there would be six."

"Svend went into town last week when we told you they were going to raid the arcade. He counted six motorbikes riding through."

"I should tell you to leave this kind of thing to the police."

"We did leave it to the police," said Helena, barely managing to keep calm. "And you failed to catch them. So we felt you might like a little support. Doing our civic duty and all that."

"What if you had got hurt?"

"There was no chance of us getting hurt. When I said Feen and Svend were competent, I was seriously understating their skills." *They've fought and beaten vampires, for God's sake!*

"Against six heavy men?"

"Yes, well, I suppose we should be grateful it was only six," said Helena. Her anger was beginning to dissipate – now she was desperately trying not to laugh.

"Miss Grey," said Squire, sounding exasperated. "We have a theory that you used some kind of knockout gas on the men."

"I imagine you've given them blood tests and checked out the office. That should tell you, but if you are asking me, I will tell you no, we did not use chemicals of any kind."

"All of them fainted?"

"Two of them fainted. Was it more? I can't remember, it happened so fast. Feen and Svend overcame the others with minimum force. The last one gave in without a fight."

"So that's going to be your story."

"Do I need a story?" said Helena, beginning to lose a little of her calm at last. "I mean, we shut down a brothel that the council turned a blind eye to. We are helping fragile people that nobody else wants to help. We've been engaging young people on the estate when nobody else wants to engage them. We've caught a gang you couldn't be bothered to even *attempt* to catch, and now you're coming here to my home to suggest I've done something wrong?"

"No, no, it's all fine. We just wanted some details to help explain…"

"To help explain how easy it was?" suggested Helena.

"Well, yes."

"We provided you with footage."

"And there is another question," said Squire. "How did you know they would be there?"

"We put a rumour about that there was jewellery being stored there."

"That was very dangerous," said the police officer.

"No it wasn't," said Helena, getting rapidly more and more fed up with this conversation. "Watch the video. It was very safe. For us, anyway."

PC David Squire realised he wasn't going to get anything else out of Helena, so he decided to call it a day. Helena, in the meantime, realised that the gang wasn't going to suggest they had been assaulted by Feen and Svend, so the episode was over.

As she opened the door for the two police officers to leave, she said, "I would prefer not to make a fuss about what happened. If anyone from the newspaper asks, I am happy to say that we co-operated with the police, who caught the gang. Which, to be honest, is more than you deserve. Are you okay with that?"

"Thank you, Miss Grey."

That was not the end of it, however. The newspapers were discreet, at least about Helena's part in the business. Perhaps the police had kept their names out of it, or perhaps the editor of the paper didn't want to pay any compliments to the team who had brought his father, Clive Matthews, down. However, the arrest of six men from the Sea View estate was going to affect the community. One of them was Goat's father. The next time

Helena went to the Lighthouse Rock, the gang was not around. They weren't organising any help for the gardeners, either, although most of the work there had been finished.

Helena found only Jackie and Shir, sitting on the seat by the rocks, looking out to sea.

"They don't like you anymore," said Shir, explaining the absence of Jeff and the rest. "They think you betrayed them."

"How?" asked Helena.

"You lied about having a stash at your office."

"Goat told a gang of crooks that we had a stash of jewels, and somehow *I'm* in the wrong. Someone said to me recently something about not blaming the people who caught you when you've committed a crime."

Jackie laughed. "Shir split up with Jeff for taking Goat's side. Me, I'm with you. And the princess. We think she's..."

"...Cool," Shir finished the sentence for her.

Seven

All four naiads gathered in the living room.

"We've prepared something for you," said Virino as Helena came into the room.

"You've helped us so much since you took over looking after us here at the house," said Mara.

"We wanted to do something for you in return," said Reni.

"Just your company is all I need," said Helena.

"Well, you might like this," said Rusalka as she led Helena to the sofa. As she sat, the four of them knelt together at her feet and started singing. It was a song without words, and the musical instruments were the voices of the four naiads.

All four voices were different, singing in a harmony that created a magic Helena could not have dreamed was possible. Somehow, without words that Helena could understand, they told her a story. They carried her to a land of unbelievable beauty, with animals she had never seen before and plants and flowers of incredible colours. She closed her eyes and was aware only of the mystical music and the tears streaming down her face. She began to understand what Lady Venner meant by her tears being healing – she was even beginning to hate the people she had to deal with a little less.

Much later, she wandered out to the Lighthouse Rock.

She noticed that Feen and Svend were out on the tip of the rock, at its furthest point jutting into the sea. They were wearing jeans and hoodies, looking human. *Why would People who looked as beautiful as they do try to look human*? She joined them.

"We've seen someone swimming in the water out there," said Feen.

"They'll get into trouble with the currents if they aren't careful," said Helena.

"I don't think so. They aren't human."

Helena pulled the mini-binoculars she always carried from her belt and took a look. There were two distinct shapes in the water, playing like the sea was their environment.

"Ours?" she asked.

"No, they're all inside," said Feen. "We were thinking of getting Reni and Virino to go out and say hello to them."

"New People?" said Helena, almost as spellbound as the first time she saw Lady Venner.

"They're naturally shy," said Feen. "We might not be able to persuade them to come in straight away."

"But they're here. Why? They must have heard about us on the wind."

"That's certainly most likely," said Feen, who seemed to appreciate Helena's enthusiasm.

"Yes, please. Ask Reni and Virino."

Feen glanced at Svend, who nodded and obeyed his Lady's command, returning to the Mermaids Rest at a run to get the two naiads. Helena stood with Feen, looking out to sea for another half an hour. She saw the wake of her two naiads as they swam out to meet the newcomers. Her heart swelled with the anticipation of growing her new family.

Perhaps it was time to stop hating everyone and everything. Perhaps she could even learn to forgive people like Clive Matthews. Perhaps she could learn to love again.

Book 9
The Caledonian Gates

One

Ian listened as the first sound of spring came early to his cottage. It was the flickering sound of pixie wings.

"How's tricks, Dix?" he said.

"D'you know, no matter how often I hear that, it never gets… funny," said the small voice of the cottage's first fey visitor of the year.

"If I had known you were coming I would have got some food in – I know how you like your bics, Dix."

"Ha," said Dixie. "I would have said 'Ha *Ha*,' but it didn't deserve two." He flew over to the table and landed on it near to where Ian was sitting. He sat his 8-inch-tall self on Evie's scrapbook – the one Ian was about to open.

"You're sitting on Evie's pics, Dix."

"You know pixie ribs are very small and fragile," said Dixie. "If I laugh too much I could hurt myself. Is that why your jokes are so bad? To protect me?"

"You love it really," said Ian. "So tell me, why are you out of hibernation so early?"

"We don't hibernate. We migrate. Only dragons hibernate – and you should be able to tell the difference between me and a dragon."

"Yes, I remember – dragons are just a tiny bit bigger. But you don't normally visit the cottage until spring."

"I came in here because it's bloody cold out there. Are you here on your own? Where's the brains of your partnership?"

"Evie's gone to Perth for some shopping."

"Perth? D'you think she'll bring some clothes back?"

"I doubt it. She wouldn't normally go to the Dolls' House Shop until the end of March, when she'd be expecting you to turn up. Not the middle of February. But if you want to stay the night, your cupboard's ready."

"It might be a cupboard to you…" Dixie said with a grin. He got off his perch on the scrapbook and took a look at it. "Why has she got this out? Is your daughter coming to visit?"

"She'll be here later today."

"Brilliant. She should visit more often. I haven't seen her for ages."

"She normally visits at Christmas when you're hiber-migrating," said Ian.

"I'll have you know," said Dixie, hands on hips like something out of a pantomime, "that I work very hard in the winter. Especially this winter."

"Santa Claus needed some extra helpers?"

Dixie actually laughed at that one. "I often rest in shops coming up to Christmas. If anyone sees me they think I'm a special effect."

"I bet the children love that."

"I sometimes let children see me, but not the parents."

"You've got a big heart for someone so small. So tell me, what's this 'work' you say you were doing?"

However, at that point, they were interrupted by Evie's arrival in their Dacia Duster filled with supplies. Evie got out of the vehicle as Ian opened the front door to help her unload. Evie was a short, dark-haired, young-looking nearly-fifty-year-old, although Ian, who was two years older than her, would never say 'nearly fifty' to her face. They shared a hug before getting to work.

"Dix is here," Ian said as they lugged in bag after bag of heavy shopping. Ian took stuff for their enormous freezer into the small storeroom while Evie moved the smaller items into their large kitchen. When they met in the middle, Evie said, "He's here a bit early."

Dixie, in the meantime, stayed out of the way. He had no doubt flown to his cosy little cubbyhole shelf behind the central heating boiler and started some housekeeping of his own.

"I think he's on a mission," said Ian when he passed his wife with the next load of shopping. Evie had bought some new bedding. That hadn't been on the original list.

Everything done, Ian moved the SUV to the space behind the cottage so that Mandy could park on the main driveway, while Evie made some tea and said 'hello' to Dixie. It was seriously cold out here, so Ian covered the vehicle with the tarpaulin they kept for that reason. That job done, Ian looked up the glen to the hills where, some way in the distance, he was sure he saw a centaur looking down towards him. That was a rare sight. From the flash of light reflecting off of the weak sun, it looked like he was armed. That was a *really* rare sight. Something was going on.

Ian and Evie were rangers, working unofficially for the Cairngorms National Park, but funded by the Nieziemski Manor Estate. Only a small number of the official staff knew that they were here in Glenshee to protect the more exotic wildlife – fey People who were keeping themselves secret from the world of humanity; People like Dixie and his fellow pixies, and the centaurs, who wouldn't pass as humans in the same way as dryads, naiads and some goblins could.

The Cairngorms National Park was 1,748 square miles of incredible Scottish countryside, but that didn't include what Ian called 'fey space' – folds in the fabric of reality that allowed an entire eminence of centaurs (yes, they had their own collective noun) to live free without being detected. As well as miles of open land, hills, mountains and forests, there were tourist attractions like Aviemore, popular for skiing and mountain walks, and the Glenshee Ski Centre a few miles north of where they were now.

When he returned to sit in the kitchen with Evie and Dixie, the little visitor told them about what he'd been working on.

"There's been some of your people asking some really odd questions about us. Someone has passed around the idea that there are goblins hiding in human society."

"There is always going to be someone who does that."

"Yes, but normally they have what you might call a traditional view of goblins – bright green skin, medieval armour and a poorly-maintained sword and shield. They don't usually equate goblins with technology."

"Which is what real goblins are best at," said Ian.

"Has anyone asked at the manor?" asked Evie.

"No. Nobody's been near the manor," said Dixie.

"So whoever's looking hasn't found what they're looking for," suggested Ian.

"Unless they are deliberately avoiding Nieziemski Manor because they don't want them to know that they know about goblins," said Dixie.

"Which would mean they know about the manor already," said Evie thoughtfully.

"How are they asking?" said Ian.

"What do you mean?"

"I mean, if they are asking other humans, are they saying, 'Do you believe in goblins?' or are they saying, 'I'm looking to develop the best advances on my technology – you don't happen to know where there are any goblins, do you?'. And what kind of responses are they getting?"

"I don't know. Captain Callom had contact with someone we know at Inverness University who normally looks after the Loch Ness studies, and he said someone was describing goblins accurately and asking if they could detect such a creature. Callom sent me and Patulak and a couple of the others across the country because he knows we like to go south for the winter. It's not anywhere near as cold only a couple of hundred miles south of here, although we had a lot of snow last month in Bedfordshire."

"Why is the possibility that people know about goblins a problem for the captain?" asked Evie. Centaurs mostly kept to themselves and existed in that unique place that isn't quite planet Earth – what the ancient Scots called 'mounds' and what Ian knew as fey space. Captain Callom kept in touch with our world mostly to protect his.

"Because the big question they were asking was about how to find the Caledonian Gates."

Neither Ian nor Evie said anything for what seemed quite a while. The Caledonian Gates were the fey's best-kept secret. Not even the People themselves knew of their location. Some thought they were actual gates; some thought they were a complex of caves; others believed that the centaurs themselves were guarding the Gates in their folds in reality, without even really knowing it. It was also possible that they only existed for parts of the year and under certain circumstances. The fey People, the Seelie Court and the Unseelie Court, had been banished from their homes to our world in order to interact with humanity and learn to live in peace with each other because, as far as Ian knew, the magic (or whatever they called it) that would have been unleashed if they continued to fight, possibly thousands of years ago, would have destroyed their world and anyone else's world connected to it. If they could find the Caledonian Gates, they could return home before their purpose here was finished.

"Or their time here is already done," Ian said out loud. Evie gave him an odd look and Dixie said, "What?"

"The People have lived among us for thousands of years, and they've been at peace – or, at least, they haven't been at war, for at least half that time. Perhaps it's time for the Gates to be revealed to them."

"If that was true," said Dixie thoughtfully, "then Lady Marika would know. In fact, they both would. They would be united like they've never been before."

"I gather from studying many human mythologies that things are never as easy to interpret as you think they should be," said Ian. "Whatever supernatural contract is holding them here, part of its resolution might be to rediscover the Gates in a different way."

"And you think that humans asking that question about goblins might be a step on the journey?" said Evie.

"Not necessarily. I'll have to give it some thinking time. We should get in touch with the manor, let them know."

"We already have," said Dixie. "Patulak went there to keep warm from the snow last month and had a long chat with Lady Marika. Do you know she lost an eye in the battle with the vampires last summer?"

"Yes," said Evie solemnly, tapping the scrapbook on the table right next to where Dixie was sitting.

"Ah, of course," said Dixie, who knew that the book was a record of everything that the manor had been involved in – the Romanian Embassy, the Ogonshead project, the London floods and as much as she could find on the new Lord of the Manor, Michael Varmeter.

Dixie took some food to his 'cupboard' and kept to himself, warm against the outside weather. Evie and Ian were ready for their next visitor, who arrived before it got too dark. Mandy, their daughter's Fiat Panda, parked in the driveway in the shelter of the cottage and out stepped Lucy Waterhouse. She hardly had time to stretch after her long journey before Evie ran out to give her a big hug. They brought her and her luggage in from the cold and made her a hot meal.

She flopped into her favourite chair in the living room and didn't stop talking. Ian looked her over. She was eighteen when they'd left to take up this post in the Cairngorms, and she had changed a lot, grown up a lot, in the last five years – only seeing her once a year since then had made Ian notice that – but in one thing she hadn't changed; she wouldn't stop talking.

"You know Jada? No, you probably don't. I don't think she'd given herself a name since you last lived down with us. She's started coming out of the water more. She did it to comfort Michael when he was feeling bad about… and she's come out more since then. When Helena came to visit they spent nearly the whole time together. She doesn't hide in the water anymore."

"Jada's a naiad?" said Evie.

"Yes, sorry, I should have said. Anyway, she just walked straight out of the water and… it's amazing how she doesn't soak everyone every time. Obviously not in the coldest part of winter, and there's been a lot of snow this year. Not as much as up here, but… you know. The lake even freezes up sometimes, and the naiads don't get to swim then."

"They don't wear clothes," said Evie.

"I think Helena's naiads do in Ogonshead – unless they're swimming – but no, ours don't."

"So some of the most beautiful females on the planet come and have a chat to Michael, *your boyfriend* – with no clothes on – and you don't mind?"

"Michael wears clothes," she said with a cheeky grin.

"You know what I mean."

"I think he doesn't see them as human."

"I'd find it hard not to," said Ian, wondering if his cheeky grin looked anything like hers. Evie gave him a *look*. Lucy noticed and giggled. She took a look across at her mother's scrapbook, which they had moved to the living room in order to eat at the kitchen table.

"You got the book out," she said to her mother. Evie always got the book out when Lucy came to visit. It had pleasant reminiscences in it as well as the more severe stories – times when they were a family together in Buckinghamshire, before they had to make the decision to part company. Ian had felt sure it was necessary to move the family to Scotland, but Lucy was keen on studying in Amersham and she had wanted to stay close to the manor. She had been eighteen and considered herself grown up, so they left her in an apartment in the village.

"I'm hoping that you can fill in a few gaps," said Evie, bringing their thoughts back to the book. "And I heard on the news about that incident in Africa, and I wondered if you had anything to do with that?"

"No, we didn't. At least not directly. But we know about it; it was… Look, can we do that tomorrow?" I'm feeling the journey now I'm fed and cosy."

"Of course, and it's getting late," said Evie. Ian had agreed with Evie not to get in too deep about the Caledonian Gates until she'd slept, too. However, there was something they needed to tell her.

"Dixie's here," Ian said in a loud voice so that the pixie, who was listening at the door, heard his cue to turn up.

"Dixie!" Lucy almost shouted for joy. She rested her elbows on her knees and cupped her hands in front of her chin and he flew into them, bent forward and kissed her on the nose.

"They should have told me sooner. Sorry to keep you waiting."

"You're here for a few days?" said the pixie.

"I imagine so."

"Then, if you can manage to pull yourself away from your mother's scrapbook, perhaps I can have a few minutes of your time."

"Would it be about the Caledonian Gates?"

So she already knew about them, thought Ian. Of course, in the last couple of years she'd become Michael Varmeter's PA, so she'd know everything they knew.

"I don't suppose I could speak to the captain while I'm here, too?"

"Are you on holiday or are you working?" said Evie in a warm-hearted chide.

"I'm just living," said Lucy with a huge grin.

Both Evie and Lucy got up late the following day, which wasn't surprising as both of them had worked hard yesterday. Ian went out to check the ground. It was still bitterly cold, but no more snow had fallen since last week. The weather forecast had suggested that the temperature would rise in the next few days, but whether that meant more snow or more rain was uncertain.

By the front gate someone had left an inukshuk, a man-shaped pile of stones, although this one looked very approximately centaurian in shape. The captain wanted to see him.

He told the girls when they got up, and Lucy particularly seemed very excited to see a centaur again. Ian was intrigued that, although for her whole life she had been surrounded by the most beautiful of creatures, she still got excited by the thought of meeting another.

After breakfast they drove out to the high point of the nearest hill. Captain Callom was waiting there, flanked by two unarmed guards. The captain carried a spear held upright in a form of salute.

Centaurs were amazing creatures. They were six-limbed People with the lower body of a horse and a human's torso sprouting from where the horse's neck would begin. Very little was known of their anatomy because they had no interest in letting people study them. The questions of whether they had two stomachs, how they reproduced and just why they looked like they did were none of anyone else's business. Unlike goblins, they were not technologically adept, although it was rumoured that some of them watched a lot of human television. There was also an untested theory that they could run faster than horses.

Callom tried to nurture the human side of himself. He was light brown in colour and the fine horse-hair that covered the equine part of him continued over his chest and neck. His long hair turned into a mane so that you 'couldn't see the join' (a phrase Ian often used to describe him). His face, the same colour as the rest of his body, was gentle-looking, although he tried to put on an expression of deep thinking or 'the burden of command' as much as possible. There was something about him that suggested he did a lot of thinking.

"Mr Waterhouse," he said with a deep, rich, educated English accent.

"Captain Callom," said Ian. "You know Evie, and I think you may have met my daughter Lucy before."

"Hello, Evie," he said in a soft voice. He turned to Lucy and bowed to her with the whole of his human part. "Lucy – blessed of the fey."

"Just Lucy will do," she replied. "It's good to see you again. It's been a while."

"And I see Dixie is here, too," said Callom.

"Really?" said Ian, who was not surprised. "I didn't notice him." Dixie, smiling brightly, flew from near the SUV to join them.

"He's good at that," said Callom. "Anyway, thank you for coming. I wanted to talk to you about these people who are trying to find the Caledonian Gates."

"Dixie tells me he's been in England, looking around for clues," said Ian.

"The Gates are not in England," replied Callom.

"They are possibly not fully on the planet," said Ian. "But I meant that Dixie has been searching for clues about who wants to know."

"Whoever it is isn't connected to the manor," said Lucy. "And they haven't come to us for information, either. If they know about the gates, they must know about us. So we think they might be leaving us out of the loop on purpose."

"We believe they are searching for a group of goblins who may have some information they could use," said Callom. "A particular group."

"Goblins are resourceful," said Evie. "Could it be that the particular group you are referring to is the Oxfordshire family? Krol's old troop?"

Lucy looked at her mother with some emotion. Ian was aware of what had happened a year ago after a human study group discovered, befriended and then slaughtered a unit of goblins. Their leader, Krol, killed the humans responsible rather than going to the fey queen's council at Nieziemski Manor. He was dead now, but the rest of the goblin survivors rejected the offer of a home at the manor and moved away. Nobody knew where they were now. Evie had some extensive details about the incident in her scrapbook.

"Yes," said Callom. "It is, at the least, possible."

"Michael was with Liczik when he died," said Lucy. "It… affected him."

"It must be difficult when you feel the need to take sides with the People against your own kind," said Callom.

"I think Michael finds in a no-brainer," said Lucy. "He's with the People every time. Even Balaur found it hard to punish Krol when he agreed with him."

"What are your plans?" Ian asked the captain.

"We believe that whoever is searching for the Gates will end up here," said Callom. "The region called Glenshee is a clue simply by its name, so they would have to call here at some time. If they find out you have the same surname as the personal assistant of the Lord of Nieziemski Manor, they will also put the pieces together. For that reason we'll put a discreet guard on your house and we would ask you to let us know if anyone contacts you with enquiries."

"Certainly," replied Ian. "Thank you for your consideration." He bowed to the captain. "I have a final question."

"Yes?"

"Do you know where the Caledonian Gates are?"

"Not precisely. I hold with the theory that they rest inside a mound – what you would call a 'fold', so they are here, but not quite here. I believe it is possible that some humans may have discovered them more than a thousand years ago, in 961 A.D. to be precise, when settlers or refugees first founded Glenshee. The most popular theory is that the standing stones, the Four Poster, was the first home of the Gates. But as far as we know, they don't always stay in one place."

Callom was not telling Ian anything he didn't already know, but it was interesting that his information matched other people's input. A trip to the library was called for, but probably after Lucy's visit. He wanted to make the most of the time with his daughter while she was here.

"One of our colleagues, Andrew, is a ranger near here," Ian told the captain. "He knows a bit about the People, but he keeps it to himself. Perhaps we should keep him informed about our investigations."

"I would suggest keeping this to ourselves as much as possible," said Callom. "If the existence of the Caledonian Gates got out, it would be like the legendary pot of gold at the end of a rainbow. The place would be swarming with treasure hunters, and our secrets would be harder to keep."

"Fair point," said Ian. He had always got on well with Andrew, but he kept conversations about the People to a minimum, so he agreed with Callom's thinking.

They made their goodbyes and started making their way back to the SUV. Lucy lingered for a moment, although she looked cold.

"I'd love to spend some with you when there isn't something serious going on," she said to the centaur. "And when it's warmer."

Callom laughed. "The glen in the summer is a glorious sight. We could run side by side in the heather."

"I wish I could run as fast as you."

Callom bent down to say something quietly to Lucy, and Ian just about caught it. "You're still small enough for one of us to give you a ride."

Two

Stephanie Baynes gave her report to her boss, Lord Martin Latham. They were in her office next to his house in Stoke-on-Trent. On her computer screen, the warden of the Angel Trust, John Borland, was listening in from his base in Southampton. This was an occasional habit of the warden, to find out if there was anything he or his agents needed to follow up.

"The alleged curses at Trent College were fakes. It was just some very clever and rather spiteful students playing pranks on their friends. Well, not friends. Not anymore."

"I hope you didn't feel you wasted too much time on that," said Martin.

"Nothing is ever wasted – it was you who told me that," she smiled. "I'd take it as a learning experience."

"And the other thing?"

"My little drive to Telford? I didn't actually find anything, but that doesn't mean there's nothing there."

"What's supposed to be there?" asked John.

"There's a rumour that there's a coffee bar in Telford town centre especially for goblins. But it must be so uniquely for goblins that us mere humans can't even find the place." Stephanie knew about the existence of goblins, but she had never actually seen one. There were supposed to be about fifty of them at Nieziemski Manor, but she hadn't seen any when she'd visited.

"I don't think you'd find the place without an invitation," said John.

"And one other thing," she continued. "There appears to be a coven of witches in Covent Garden. Oh, I just got the joke – 'Coven' Garden!"

"Yes, we already know about them," said Martin. "They're human and they're real. But if you visit them, don't mention my name. They don't like me much."

"What's not to like?" said Stephanie, and Martin replied by making fang shapes over his mouth with his fingers.

Stephanie laughed, but replied, "You should tell me this stuff. There's no point in me investigating something you already know about."

"Sorry," said Martin. He said sorry a lot but never meant it. And yet he managed to charm people anyway. Stephanie always believed it was a vampiric talent.

"Well, that's it," said Stephanie. John Borland thanked her (and *he* meant it) and signed off. Stephanie intended to do a little 'idle research' today, having a look around at anything that might look a bit odd. Martin tapped the letter on her desk – she had some actual mail in the post.

"You've got an interesting one in there today," he said. "It's from France."

Stephanie opened it eagerly in front of Martin. She had been corresponding with Professor Georges Bouvon, so this might be the letter she'd been waiting for. She read it carefully, because it was hand-written and although his English was exceptional, his handwriting wasn't.

"He's coming over," she told Martin at last.

"Brilliant. When?"

"Tomorrow. He'll be flying Air France and landing at Birmingham at 10am."

"I'll pick him up," said Martin.

"I'd like to, if it's alright with you. Sometimes I feel like I spend all my time in front of a computer so a journey out there would be nice."

"...Says the person who's been to Mbalaya, returned via the whole of Europe and has even been to Telford in search of a goblin tea-party. And you've only been working for me for six months."

"A goblin coffee bar," she corrected him.

Later, for a break, she walked out over the field behind Martin's house. Every time she walked there she looked in the distance towards the woods and wonder if she would ever see her totem, the Bast again. Had it died saving them all in Mbalaya?

Do fey legends ever actually die? Was the whole point of her meeting Martin and going out to Africa to take it to its end?

Stephanie had been having dreams again lately – some of them seemed to be very clear and vivid and they wouldn't leave her memory after she woke up. In one, she saw the Bast exactly as she remembered it when it saved her from the murderer in the forest at Dennington. Its eyes shone as it turned to look at her (had that happened in reality, or just the dream?). In another she saw the lynx-like creature that she had seen when she was thirteen. Its eyes shone when it turned and looked at her, reflecting the sunlight in that weird way that cats' eyes do. In another dream it was running alongside a military vehicle in Mbalaya. As it ran, it turned its head towards her and its eyes… there was a pattern emerging here. Could it be that the creature wanted to tell her something?

Most of the oddities/mysteries/mysterious happenings she had investigated had had simple explanations. She suspected that, after the Mbalayan incident, Martin was giving her easy stuff so that she could properly recover from her uncomfortable encounter with the supernatural world. She knew about goblins and other creatures hiding in the world, but she hadn't actually seen that many. In some sense, she didn't want to – the thought of a much wider range of supernatural beings out there frightened her. So she uncovered frauds posing as ghosts or fake curses. Perhaps Martin knew her mind – she had been feeling more and more lately that she wasn't sure that this career she had chosen was for her any more. She wanted a safer life – but how could she stop knowing what she knew?

Stephanie could guess the main reason that Professor Bouvon wanted to visit – he had ruined his career believing in outrageous theories about alien creatures living on Earth and he knew that Stephanie and Martin had been out to Mbalaya where his last archaeological dig was before he retired. He knew that the president of that small African country had been murdered while Stephanie was out there and he would want to know the details, particularly if it had anything to do with his 'talon theory'. She didn't know how much she should tell him. She wanted him to be satisfied that his theories had led to the liberation of

Mbalaya from a serious threat, but should she tell him that the threat was supernatural in nature?

Clifton Chase was a good person to talk to about things like this. However, apart from Christmas with her family in Kent, she'd hardly seen him since they'd parted company in Mbalaya. He had stayed there to assist with leadership transitions; she had returned to England with Martin (via 'the whole of Europe'). Then he'd been off doing some research for the Angel Trust in Leighton Buzzard, then Cambridge University and other scholarly places while Martin had her doing work closer to home.

Christmas had been good, though. Stephanie considered the M25 motorway a great wall separating her from her parents, so she didn't visit them as often as she would have liked, but she always made it for Christmas, and this time Clif came, too. Her parents had a big enough house to accommodate her guest, and having his company was worth the ribbing she took from her sister Paula about the new men in her life.

After Christmas there had been a lot of snow, so she and Clif hadn't met up except for an occasional conference call on their computers. She had mentioned to Martin that, at some stage, she wanted to visit the Angel Trust's headquarters. Martin had simply joked that she wanted to spend some more time with Clif. It may have been a joke to him, but he was right.

The following day, Stephanie's journey to Birmingham Airport was fairly straightforward. She avoided the heavy traffic by taking the M6 toll motorway. Professor Bouvon's plane arrived on time and they were on their way back to Stoke-on-Trent in time for an early afternoon lunch. The professor told Stephanie of his plans to meet friends in Manchester in the evening, where he would stay. They agreed that they would take him to the station in the town centre that evening. It meant that they would have a decent amount of time together to talk about Mbalaya during the afternoon.

Martin was to be the host in his own house, which was bigger and more impressive than Stephanie's place next door. She and Martin had only briefly discussed how much they would reveal to the professor. They would keep the existence of the fey hiding in human society a secret, of course, but apart from that Stephanie wanted to tell him as much as possible. Martin had given Stephanie permission to reveal as much or as little as she felt wise.

Georges Bouvon was a tall, well-built man with well-tanned, weathered skin. As an archaeologist, he had done a great deal of field work, including in hot countries. The cold winter had not reduced the effect of Africa's sun on him. He wore a suit including a waistcoat and plain blue silk tie. When he walked into Martin's lounge, which was richly-decorated with valuable and, more to the point, *old* ornaments, he was suitably impressed. He sat on an old cushioned chair and accepted the food and drink that Martin offered.

"I imagine you'll want to know what happened in Mbalaya," said Stephanie.

"Yes, please, if you would," he nodded.

She told him about how creatures dressed as monks had tried to take control of the president and had used what the authorities called experimental weaponry on the town of Hemmin.

"I have heard everything you've told me so far on the news," he said. "But I want to know what 'experimental weaponry' really means. And monks? The news called them people dressed as monks; you refer to them as creatures. Can you tell me in a bit more detail? I have been holding back from calling them aliens, but the evidence I have suggests that they might be just that."

"You think we might know more than we're saying," suggested Stephanie.

"Think? I'm sure of it," said the professor with an eager smile. "I know the Angel Trust was involved in this business, and if they were there, you can be sure there are no mundane explanations involved. Or are you somehow not allowed to tell me something?"

"Your theory is that aliens planted the 'claw' symbol on artefacts across the world many thousands of years ago," said Stephanie. "Have you ever looked at the idea that aliens don't come from outer space, but something some people call inner space?"

"Yes," said the professor. "Interstellar distances are huge, ridiculous beyond our imaginations. Even with technology far in advance of our own, it would take years to travel the distances

238

between our stars. It's easier to believe that, if there were travellers from another world, they would get here by a different means."

"The other factor here," said Stephanie, "is the theory that dark energy is involved. If this energy contains the ability to power some kind of interstellar, or even inter-dimensional transport, then it's possible intelligent creatures may have crossed over to us to take advantage of its power."

Bouvon nodded, eager that his work might be about to be justified.

"There are some people in this world whose secrecy and privacy I would like to respect," continued Stephanie. "People I have met, personally, and would love to tell you are real. However, what I can say is that you were on the right track. The people who put those claw markers there did so, in my opinion, to help protect us against whoever, or possibly whatever, those robed monks were in Mbalaya."

They chatted on, and Stephanie talked around the subject as much as she could. Bouvon was happy that there was stuff she couldn't tell him, and was more than satisfied that he'd been right. Then Stephanie asked him the question that was on her mind.

"What's the nearest site to here that you know of with the talon symbol on it?"

"Well, I think you can't include the Scottish site, so Iceland would be. Or, let me think…"

"Why can't we count the Scottish site?" asked Martin, who had said very little for the last hour or so.

"Because it is on protected land. The Cairngorms Nature Reserve, or National Park, or whatever it's called. The original dig was in the 1930's, many years before the National Park took control of the area and prevented any further archaeological works there. But I've seen some of the artwork of the original workers, and it is clear that among the things they found there was the claw symbol."

Stephanie leaned forward in her chair. This was something she needed to hear. In trying to recall her dreams, she thought it was possible that Scottish landscapes were involved.

Much later, Stephanie dropped off the professor at the station as planned, and then rushed back to her office to explore the archaeological dig in the Cairngorms. Unfortunately, there was no record of a drawing of a claw in the existing records. The dig had been very small and under-funded, so there wasn't really much to work with at all. There was just one thing that stopped Stephanie from giving up on it. The area where they worked was called 'Glenshee'. That could be interpreted as the glen of the sidhe!

There was a knock on her door – it was, of course, Martin. She let him in, but he only stood at the door.

"It's after midnight," he said.

"Oh," said Stephanie, quite surprised she had lost track of time. She looked at her watch. Yes, it was certainly after midnight – it was, in fact, nearly two in the morning. Martin was a night-time person, and would more than likely sleep all day tomorrow – well, today – but if Stephanie was to speak to Lucy Waterhouse at the manor tomorrow (later today) it wouldn't be a bad idea if she was rested first.

"What do you know about Glenshee?" she asked her boss.

"Not a thing," said Martin. "I mean, I know it's in Scotland, and after what Professor Bouvon said earlier I imagine it might be in the Cairngorms, but nothing else, really."

"I wondered if the manor knew about it?"

"Just because it has the word 'shee' in its name?" said Martin. "I think there are a lot of myths and legends that come from Scotland and I'd guess most of them probably aren't connected with the real People."

"What if the dig at this place was where the claw symbol was found?"

"Now that would be interesting," said Martin. "But not this minute. I mean, what does it take to get you into bed?"

Stephanie had never encouraged Martin's suggestive remarks, but it seemed that, even when he was being serious, he couldn't help it.

Stephanie slept late, and it was afternoon before she finally got to phone Lucy Waterhouse. There was a 'not available, please leave your details' message on the phone. Stephanie left a message and then looked up the landline number for Nieziemski Manor office. She dialled that and got a similar message. Oh, well, she thought, at least she should have some breakfast before she got on with her life. Martin was not around; she thought she remembered that he was going to meet one of his girlfriends today. It was about time she took a break. Perhaps she would find out if Clifton Chase was available and they could meet up somewhere. Then her phone rang.

"Stephanie Baynes," she answered it.

"Hi Stephanie," came Lucy's voice. The reception wasn't as clear as normal. "Just got your message. I've been in a meeting with... well, in a meeting. How can I help you?"

"I wondered if the manor has any connection with Glenshee in Scotland?" Several moments went by in silence. "Hello? Lucy? Are you still there?"

"Yes. Sorry, you caught me on the hop there for a minute. Why do you want to know about Glenshee?"

"There was an archaeological dig there a long time ago, and one of the symbols found there was the same as the one that led us to Mbalaya last year."

There was another pause before Lucy answered. "I'm in Glenshee right now."

"What?"

"I'm here. I'm visiting my parents. They work here. I mean, obviously, they live here and work here. Every Christmas I come and visit, only this year the bad weather turned Christmas into February, if you know what I mean."

"You're in Glenshee?"

"Yes. That's why I stumbled when you asked. Is there anything else you know?"

"About Glenshee? No. Should I?"

"Why are you asking about the place, apart from the symbol?"

"I think the Cat might be there," Stephanie said.

"Your... you called it a 'totem' didn't you? Then you discovered it was an ancient Egyptian goddess."

"Something like that."

"And you believe it died in Africa," Lucy reminded her.

"I've been having dreams lately. I think it's calling to me again," said Stephanie and, strangely, it didn't sound stupid when she said it out loud.

"Wait a minute," said Lucy and she put the phone down for a moment. Stephanie could hear her talking to someone nearby, but couldn't make out what they were saying. Then she came back. "Are you busy?"

"What for?"

"I wonder if you'd like an all-expenses-paid trip to Glenshee? It's not quite as hot as Africa, but it could be just as interesting."

"When?"

"It depends how long it takes to organise some accommodation for you. There is plenty of tourism round here, so we could find a hotel within ten miles quite easily. If it's okay with your vampire boss, we could probably arrange to put you up today or tomorrow."

"Why so soon?"

"Because there are no such things as coincidences. You have dreams about this Bast creature calling to you at the same time that Dixie visits early and the captain puts his troops on alert. Whatever is going to happen seems to be happening soon. Would you like to be a part of it?"

Dixie visiting and the captain and other things Lucy was saying meant nothing to Stephanie and, in the back of her mind, she didn't want another trip like Mbalaya, but she couldn't help herself.

"What if my dreams weren't the Bast calling to me? What if I simply miss it? Her. That my dreams were just me, nostalgic for when she was around?"

"Then stay there and don't worry about anything I've said," said Lucy with a great deal of humour in her voice.

"Stay here?" said Stephanie. "No chance!"

Three

Michael Varmeter stood under the ground in London. Ahead of him was a hi-tech security gate.

"It's me, Michael," he said to the nearest camera.

"What's the password?" came Mic Dracu's voice from a nearby speaker.

"There isn't a password."

"I know, but an intruder wouldn't know that."

"An intruder wouldn't look exactly like me, either," said Michael, although he didn't really know enough about the world of the fey to know for sure that they couldn't do that.

"You never know," came the enigmatic reply. The next set of gates opened for him and he made his way through to see his old friend Mic.

"To what do I owe this pleasure?" said the goblin technician, taking off his spectacles to greet Michael.

"I just thought I'd come and say hello," said Michael.

"Missing Lucy?" said the goblin, putting his glasses back on and returning to his work.

"More like taking advantage of Lucy visiting her parents to get out and visit some of *my*... family."

Mic took off his glasses and looked in Michael's direction. "Family. That's very kind of you."

"I don't have a human family anymore, but I feel you... you all... are like family to me."

"This is an uncharacteristically warm and fuzzy side to you I haven't come across before," said Mic.

"That's the problem – and the real reason I'm here. I am always using you to find out information, or to track down someone or something, or to hack some computers. I didn't want to take you for granted. I just wanted to find out about you – the real Mic Dracu."

Mic did something like laugh and turned in his swivel chair to face Michael. "I think, if I were to tell you all about me, I would say I am my work. This," he tried to do a grand sweeping gesture over all his computers and equipment with his little arm. "This is what gives me the most enjoyment and fulfilment. So you don't have to feel guilty about making me do things for you. I love what I do. Although I do have a guilty pleasure."

"Really?"

"I like a good human party. Show-biz parties are the best. I pass myself off as human and gate crash. I'm quite good at getting invitations, especially since most parties use electronic invitations. Free food and drink and a chance to meet some celebrities. D'you know, Jennifer Lawrence once told me... no, that wouldn't be fair."

"Jennifer Lawrence the actress?"

"Yes, that Jennifer Lawrence."

"And you spoke to her?"

"Yes. And I think she didn't find me unattractive."

"So what did she tell you?"

"I'm sorry, I can't give away her secrets."

"But you've started," said Michael, pushing his luck, "so you'll have to finish."

Mic put his glasses back on and immediately took them off again. "Sorry. I shouldn't have said anything. I'll keep your secrets, but I must also keep hers."

"Then hopefully I can ask you a question you will be able to answer. I have been the Lord of Nieziemski Manor for eighteen months now, and I'm still finding things out. The main reason I exist – as Lord of the Manor, that is – is so that the People can live there. They will, as they put it, *fade* if I'm not there. But there's People like you, and others in places all across the country, that are independent. How is it that *they* don't fade?"

"The existence of Nieziemski Manor, the Mermaid's Rest and the other places ground all of us to this world, even if we don't live there. I mean, I call this place, part of the Underground, my home, but I don't own it, and the computers are paid for by, well, ultimately, you. Without that, I don't have a home, so somewhere needs to exist that I can link to, even if I'm not there. We call ourselves independent, but really, for the People, there's no such thing."

Michael and Mic chatted for a while longer, but in spite of Michael's best efforts, Mic protected Jennifer Lawrence's privacy. At one point, with his glasses on, the goblin looked at one of his screens.

"Well, that's interesting."

"What is it?" asked Michael.

"I just got a message from an independent goblin. From somewhere in Middlesbrough. He's asking 'Have you found the Caledonian Gates?'"

"Who is he asking?"

"Me. I'm not hacking anyone else's conversations at the moment. This is directed at me."

"He would almost certainly know you work with me – so he's not being very discreet, is he?" said Michael.

"How do you want me to answer?"

"Just have the conversation as you normally would."

So Mic typed a reply, while also tracking down the correspondent's exact location at the same time.

I'm not looking. Why do you ask?

I have a clue to its actual whereabouts.

If you think you know where it is, what would you do with the information?

A human has been asking. It might be worth some money.

I would be interested in who this human is.

Why?

Because we are supposed to live among them in secret. I wouldn't want us to be revealed to the world. Perhaps you would let me bring in the People of Nieziemski Manor.

I think the Lady Marika would already know the secret location of the Gates. She knows a lot of things that the rest of us don't.

Are you able to give me the location, or a clue towards that end?

There was no reply. After a reasonable length of time, Mic sent a prompt, but that also received no response. Mic sat back in his chair and took off his glasses to look at Michael.

"I think he is, what's your expression, winding me up," he said. "My kit here is telling me that the Middlesbrough location was a fake. He's hiding his real location. He seems to be working from a laptop and bouncing his signal from several different places."

"Why would he be winding you up?"

"I think he wants me to be suspicious of Lady Marika. I don't know how he knew that we would already be aware that someone's looking for the Caledonian Gates, but the real core of the message is here." He pointed to the line about Marika.

"Can you track down his real location?"

"Apart from much further south than Middlesbrough, no."

"Is it possible," asked Michael, slowly and carefully as he gathered his thoughts, "that they, whoever they are, are deliberately pretending to hide their search for the Gates from us, when really they want us to know about it?"

"I thought the same thing. They didn't make it too difficult to discover that's what they were doing, after all."

"But if that was the case, the goblin who messaged you would be working with a human. How do you know it was even a real goblin?"

"There was a symbol at the beginning of each message," replied Mic, putting his glasses back on to point at the screen where the symbol was on the sender's last post. "It's only used by a few."

"Will you be getting in touch with the few you know?"

"Yes. But there is still the possibility that someone outside our circle has discovered us."

Din Mawr, the manor's giant chauffeur, took Michael home. To replace his favourite car, the Bentley that had been destroyed by a vampire attack, the manor now had two cars, a stretch limo and a fast four by four. Both had been converted to take Din Mawr's enormous frame, and today, Michael had the privilege of being transported in the very comfortable back of the stretch limo. It was smooth and quiet and had a number of little bonuses for the passenger, but he would have preferred to be able to talk to the driver without either shouting or using a radio. It was his first official journey in the vehicle because the other one was so much more practical. They had used this one for a couple of outings for some of the villagers, but apart from that, it was underutilised.

When he got back, he tracked down Lady Marika's goblin sidekick Chochlik quite quickly and asked to speak to the Lady. She would almost certainly have already known that he would want an audience because of her particular foresight.

He met with the Lady at the bottom of the grand staircase as usual and took her through to the office. He opened up a computer and showed her Mic's e-conversation, which the goblin had sent through to him, and explained his theory that somebody might be deliberately trying to sow discontent against her.

"It doesn't offend me that some goblins don't like me," said the Lady. "I would be more concerned that a human might know where the Caledonian Gates are."

"Mic thinks that the messenger, whoever it was, planted the idea that you already know where the Gates are so that it would sow dissent among us. So I hope you will forgive me for asking – but do you know?"

"It is my understanding that the Gates do not stay in one location, but they move. I'm not sure whether they are moved by an individual, but if that was the case they would have to be more powerful than me or my sister. Perhaps both of us working together might be able to move them. But if they can be moved, it would mean that if ever I knew where they were once, that may not be where they are now."

Michael was quiet for a while, trying to work out how to argue with Lady Marika, Queen of the Unseelie Court. While he loved an argument, his respect and fear of this woman was sufficient to hold him back.

"I know what I've done," said Marika.

"It's what you haven't done that concerns me," replied Michael. "You haven't answered my question."

"It is surprisingly difficult to give you a straight answer, for all that the question seemed simple. I could say no, I don't know where the Gates are, and that would be the truth, but I may know how to find them, so it wouldn't be the whole truth."

"I've been thinking since we first heard that someone was making enquiries about them – I may suggest that we find them before somebody else does."

"As far as I am aware," said Marika, "the Caledonian Gates are still Caledonian. They haven't moved away from Scotland. I think I might know if they moved further. Which means that Captain Callom and his People still guard them, even if they don't know for sure what they are guarding or exactly where it is."

"Am I right that the Gates can take you home?"

"We believe that, one day, they will," said Marika.

"I was talking to one of the naiads when they returned to the lake after it thawed out a couple of weeks ago, and she said that a return to your lands would heal your scars."

Marika looked at Michael as if he was being impertinent, but then changed her mind. "These scars are scars of honour," she said, flicking her fingers in front of her wounded face. "Being able to see through only one eye is… inconvenient, but other than that, the rest of my face will heal completely over just a few years. Lady Venner's skills are truly great in this respect."

"What does she know about the location of the Gates?"

Marika laughed. "You are asking me what she knows? You spend more time with her than I do." And she seemed to think that was the end of the conversation. She left the office and returned upstairs. Michael wondered if he had offended her. It was more likely that she wanted to leave the conversation believing that she'd been in charge of it. Michael's mention of Jada's comment to him about Marika's healing had affected her. She may have considered going home to heal, wherever her true 'home' was. But the People, as far as he knew, couldn't just pop back and forward between locations – if she left this world, she probably wouldn't be coming back.

After stopping at his rooms for a few minutes for a bite to eat, he walked around to the lake and from there towards the back-garden woods. At the lake, Jada popped her head out of the water and waved to him. Naiads could cope with all but the very coldest parts of winter. He waved back and continued his search for Lady Venner.

He didn't have to search long before *she* found *him*. It always seemed to work that way. She came to him flanked by two dryads who were just finishing the task of putting her robes on her. They then offered him one of their robes, which he accepted on top of his clothes. He had walked out of the house in fairly light clothing, knowing they would do this. In their robes, he would hardly be aware of the cold at all. That was fey magic, although they would never call it that.

"It is good to see you back with us," the Lady said as he took her hands in the usual greeting.

"It's good to be back," he responded.

"Your conversation with the Lady Marika has left you with questions she wouldn't answer, so you want to ask me."

"As usual, you know everything."

Lady Venner laughed that glorious, life-changing laugh. "If only that were so," she said.

"The Caledonian Gates," he said.

"Yes, they come to bother you anew. Is it because Lucy is in Caledonia right now, or is it because you have new information?"

"Are Lucy's parents guardians of the Gates?"

"No. They are there to be intermediaries between the people of your world and the People of mine. But there are fey People there who guard the Gates, even though they don't know it."

"I think Lucy mentioned the centaurs. And Lady Marika said something about Captain Callom. Is he the leader of the centaurs?"

Venner nodded.

"How do centaurs exist here? Surely humans would notice them? That they aren't just horses?"

"That's why they didn't come south with us to live here," said Venner. "But it is possible, as you know, for us to... help people to see something more mundane when they are really seeing us. There are also folds in space that we use."

"I remember something about folds in space, from when Lucy was helping me learn about the People."

"Walk with me," Lady Venner asked. Even in the cold of this February day, he was always eager to walk with the Lady Venner in the woods. As they walked, he told Venner about the message that Mic had received when he was visiting. He mentioned that he was beginning to suspect that somebody was talking about the Gates knowing that word of it would get back to the manor and that it would, somehow, sow dissent among the People.

"Lady Marika would normally know if someone was trying to trick her," said Venner, "but her own dilemmas stop her from seeing through this one."

"Is something worrying Lady Marika?"

"Yes. A week or two ago somebody visited the witches in Covent Garden. It was a man, but he knew about the fey. He said that Lady Marika could be whole again if she returned to her world. He left before they could quiz him further. They reported it to her, of course, but they haven't had any contact with him since."

"Lady Feen visited here last month because they had a similar visitor at Ogonshead who name-dropped the Caledonian Gates then disappeared. Somebody has been drip-feeding us information just before Lucy was due to go and visit her parents."

"Yes," said Lady Venner, thoughtfully.

They walked a little deeper into the woods than he normally would – he preferred to give the People their privacy. They followed the stream up into the depths of the trees.

"Take a look at the flow of the water," suggested Venner, and he looked carefully at it as it ran towards the house and the lake at its east side. He stepped cautiously so he could walk and watch the water carefully at the same time.

"Did you notice any changes?" she asked after a little while.

"The brook is deeper in some parts, wider in some. The uneven ground changes the speed of the flow. The sounds it makes changes depending on the trees around it and the kind of rock or stone it is flowing over."

"Which way does it flow?" asked the Lady.

"Towards…" Michael started, but she put her hand up to stop him.

"Look," she said. He looked at the water again. He looked carefully. The flow of the water was away from the lake. He looked at the ground around it. It appeared flat, so the water wasn't running uphill.

"When did that start happening? I was watching the whole time."

"Let's walk on a little," she said. "Keep looking at the water."

They stopped a minute or so later, and Michael hadn't noticed any changes – except that the water was running towards the lake again.

"How?" asked Michael.

"The forest here includes a small fold in space. We walked through it, and it changed things. Only a little. You can't notice it at the point that it is happening, but you can notice that it has happened."

"So a human might just be able to notice a fold in space?"

"Normally, no. Unless they knew what to look for. But there are folds within folds. The way to find the Caledonian Gates is to look for the way the water flows *outside* of a fold and then compare it with the flow *inside* one."

It was dark by the time Michael got back to the house, and he was eager to call Lucy with his findings. He got as far as hello, however, when she started telling her part of the story.

"I met with the captain today," she started. "Do you know the captain? No, you probably don't. He's Captain Callom. He leads an eminence of Centaurs. That's what they're called, a group of them. Like a regiment. You never call them a herd. Anyway, he told us they are a bit concerned about this Caledonian Gates business."

"Yes. Something's come up here about that."

"Anyway, d'you know what else happened today? Stephanie called. You know Stephanie Baynes, Paula's sister. The one with the cat. I mean, the one that visited us because she… you know who I mean. She wants to come and visit."

"It'll be great to see her."

"Not there – here! She wants to visit Glenshee."

"Why?"

"Because she thinks her Bast might be calling her here."

"I think she could be right," he said, still trying to put all the pieces together. He didn't know much about Stephanie Baynes's Bast, but he knew it was some kind of protector, and right now if such a powerful protector was on its way towards Lucy, he would feel a lot better.

"Did you say something's come up there?" said Lucy.

The conversation became a little more coherent as they both told their bits of the story. Lucy felt that somebody was ready to go hunting for the Gates, so they should look for them first. Michael agreed, but wanted to add a little additional help first.

"Don't start looking until Stephanie is with you. And I'm going to give her a bit of support, too."

"You're not trying to make me jealous, are you?"

"I most certainly am. I'm going to get John-James to fly her to you. Then you'll both have the pleasure of his company."

"Oh," she said flatly. "Great."

His next phone call was to John-James Clipper, the helicopter pilot. John-James was the only one of the pilots at Clipper's who knew about the fey, and the pilot's quick acceptance that such creatures existed surprised him. However, he now required him to re-arrange his schedule to spend a few days in Scotland.

"Scotland?" he said. "I've never been to Scotland before."

"Seriously?"

"Have helicopter, will travel. But it doesn't always work like that. People don't employ Amersham-based helicopters to fly up north. Mostly we have a short range, so it's all-points south of this country, and a little bit of Europe, mostly France."

"Are you busy at the moment?"

"Right now? Not really – it's too cold for joy riding. I mean, our helicopters are fully heated, but people don't think chopper for a day out in winter."

"This job needs you rather than any other of your pilots."

John-James immediately knew why it had to be him – it was about the fey. He was the only one in his company that knew about them.

"Will I have to take the gorgeous blue lady there? If that's the case, I'm your man."

"Sorry, she's staying here. But you remember Stephanie Baynes? You took her to France last year. I'll be asking her to go with you."

"Beautiful!" he said. "I'm in."

"You'll be staying a few days. We don't know how long. We'll be booking you into a hotel in or near Dalmunzie in the Cairngorms."

"Separate rooms?"

"Of course."

"Ah, well, never mind. I most certainly am still in. Anything I can do to help those People of yours."

"I want you to pick up some cameras as well, and a camera drone. I haven't organised that yet, so I'll let you know when I have a supplier."

"Quality?"

"Best money can buy. Do you know a supplier?"

"Yes, here in Amersham."

"And can you operate a drone?"

"Yes, but not very well."

"Seriously, you're the best helicopter pilot in the world."

"You must have been talking to my father. Anyway, it's fine if I'm right there, sitting in the front seat, as it were, and the world is around me. But remote? That's a different thing altogether."

"Okay. We'll sort something."

After arranging the final details as best they could, Michael called Stephanie.

"Stephanie Baynes."

"Hello, Miss Baynes. Michael Varmeter here."

"Hello, sir."

"Please, just Michael. Lucy's told me you're going to join her in Scotland."

"Yes, si... Michael."

"I wondered if I could help in that respect? I have just asked John-James Clipper if he will pick up some camera equipment for me and take it up to Glenshee for Lucy. May I offer you a helicopter lift up there? It will save you some tiring driving. You know John-James, don't you?"

"The helicopter pilot that flirts a lot?"

"That's his official title, yes," said Michael.

"That's very kind of you. Yes, please. I wasn't really looking forward to the seven-hour drive up there."

"No problem. Lucy will be booking you each hotel rooms and wants to know if you have ever controlled a drone."

"I had a go on a friend's at uni," Stephanie replied. "I wasn't very good at it."

"Ah well. You might get a chance to improve your skills."

"May I ask why?"

"We want to record the flow of a river," said Michael.

"Can't John-James do that? I hear he's a good pilot."

"He's not really into drones, it seems. He prefers the real thing."

Stephanie chuckled, presumably at a private and not very polite thought about the flirty pilot.

"Also," added Michael, "we might want a camera drone and a helicopter at the same time."

"I imagine that you'll be buying or renting a top-of-the-range drone. Nothing but the best. I wouldn't want to crash it."

"Perhaps we should get two," joked Michael, and said his goodbyes.

He sat back in his chair for a few minutes to take a breath. He missed Lucy, who would normally be doing all this for him. Then his phone rang again. This time, it was Helena Grey from the Mermaid's Rest in Ogonshead.

Four

Helena Grey nursed a huge cup of coffee as she sat with her friend Irene Henderson in one of the few coffee houses in the seaside town of Ogonshead that stayed open for the winter. Irene was the one person on the town council who had wanted to see the Siren's Song shut down and its prisoners released. Of course, she hadn't known that they were prisoners, or that they weren't even human, but the point was that she had done the right thing. And she had felt it necessary afterwards to resign from the council as a result.

"My mother tells me bookings are already up for the next season," said Irene. "I seem to remember that when Mr Varmeter and his people were here they said something about the town losing its blessing. Now we've sorted out the problem of the Siren's Song it seems to be getting its blessing back."

"Or it could be the council's investment in the northern amusements," replied Helena. She was amused at how Irene believed in blessings, but didn't know about the fey, while she, Helena, didn't believe in the town council but put its potential success down to them.

"You should go on the council, Helena," said Irene. "You could do a lot of good there."

"I could blacken a lot of eyes there," said Helena with a laugh. "I don't have the patience with hu… with people to put up with what you had to put up with."

"I apologise. What was I thinking? I like you, and I would never put someone I like through that!" They laughed together. But it did give Helena something to think about. Not that she would ever want to go on the town council. Most of them wouldn't speak to her, anyway. But rather that she'd become less hateful of people, human people, since she'd spent more time with fey People.

"I think I'll stick with what I do."

"How did it go with that stranger lurking around last month?" Irene asked, probably in order to change the subject. Towards the end of January, when the worst of the storms that had battered the east coast of England were beginning to abate, they had become aware of a tall, muscular man hanging around outside the lighthouse and occasionally, the Mermaid's Rest. Svend had kept an eye on him, but he didn't cause them any trouble.

"He was here for a few days," said Helena. "He didn't do anything, then left. He hasn't been back."

"Was he a dirty old man trying to get a look at the beautiful women you're protecting?" Irene asked.

"If he was, he didn't try very hard."

"Perhaps he was put off by your bodyguard. That Swedish man you have, he *is* a bodyguard, isn't he?"

"Has your mother asked you to find out?" asked Helena, and Irene laughed again.

What Helena wasn't going to tell her was that Svend had gone out to see what the man had wanted and nothing happened. The stranger, a ginger-haired man in smart clothes, had been hanging around in the roadside near the house, looking up at the great building for a few minutes each day. He nodded 'hello' to the Elven bodyguard and then left.

The same man had later gone to the lighthouse. The Lighthouse Rock was now completely private, with high fences blocking any sight to the rocks, the entrance to the lighthouse and the three recently renovated shops on the south side of the rocks. The stranger had knocked at the gate on the road side of the fence. Jason Asher had answered, and the man had asked if he knew anything about the Caledonian Gates. Jason had answered something like, 'We're a long way from Caledonia, sir,' and the man politely laughed and went on his way. They hadn't seen or heard from him since.

When Jason had reported this incident at the meal table later that evening, Lady Feen and Svend had cast each other a serious look. Since then, Lady Feen had made two journeys to Nieziemski Manor, leaving Svend to be the bodyguard in charge of the house. Irene bringing this up reminded Helena that she needed to ask about the Caledonian Gates.

She got into her new car and drove back to the Mermaid's Rest. She'd never had to walk far before taking on the job as connaithior at the house – her office had been near her photo-booth at the sea front and her mother's house was not too far away. She would borrow her mum's car to go shopping. But now she lived a mile out of town, it seemed better to have transport, so she'd bought herself a car.

Back at the house, she walked in on a heated discussion between Feen and Svend. At least, that was what she would have called it – the two were calmly disagreeing on something.

"Can you tell me about this?" Helena said as she came into the warm living room. Most of the rooms in the house were much cooler because that was how the naiads preferred it; after all, they spent most of their year in the sea. However, Helena kept her own room and the living room cosy if possible. They had seven naiads living there now, but more than twenty in total had sheltered in the converted shops or the house over the coldest part of winter.

"About 'this'?" said Feen.

"About you two. You've both had something on your minds since last month. Feen, you've gone off to the manor, and you, Svend, you've been tight-lipped about something. And now I come home and find you arguing. What's going on?"

"We weren't arguing," said Svend. "Arguing would involve us using our weapons."

"We were discussing whether we should tell you," said Feen.

"About?"

"You recall when that man came and asked Jason about the Caledonian Gates?"

"Yes."

"Well, if it's the same man that Svend met outside here, then he was human. Humans shouldn't know about the Gates."

"Because?"

"Because," Svend said, looking at his Lady for permission to continue, "they are the gateway to our world."

"Nobody knows where they are. Not even the fey queens. That's one of the reasons we're still here in your world."

"But if somebody finds them, you can all go home," said Helena. A little despair crept into her heart. She didn't want them to go home.

"If a human finds them and finds a way to destroy them, none of us can ever go home," said Feen.

"So we must try to find them first."

"Where are they? Caledonia is in Scotland, isn't it?"

"Caledonia *is* Scotland," said Feen. "That was what the Romans called it two thousand years ago. The borders were less well-defined when our People first entered your world three thousand and more years ago."

"It's also a village in America," said Svend. Feen cast him a 'don't complicate the issue' glance.

Helena sat down on the large sofa and tried not to imagine it without beautiful, fragile fey naiads on it. The whole world would be worse off for the People not being part of it. Then she had a thought.

"We don't know where most of the People are," she said. "If you find the Gates, how will you tell them you've found them?"

"Not all of us will return," said Feen.

"What happens to the ones that remain?"

"Most fey are happy here," said Svend. "Most of us were born in this world. All your naiads need is lots of water, and maybe a little shelter in the coldest weather. There are goblins all over the place. As long as there are people like you to care for them, leaving some behind won't be a terrible thing."

"But there are about a hundred People at the manor. If they were to leave, what would happen then?"

"I believe just one person will leave," said Feen. "My mother, the Lady Marika."

"Why her?"

"Because she can be healed. She can get her full sight back."

"She might take a few of her followers with her," said Svend. "But that's what we were arg... talking about when you came in."

"It affects me?" asked Helena.

"Yes."

"How?"

"I would go to Nieziemski Manor to take her place as the Queen of the Sidhe," said Feen.

"She wouldn't come back?"

"Travelling through the Gates is a difficult thing. It's not something any of us would do more than once in a thousand years."

"Does Jason know what's going on?"

"We haven't been speaking English all the time," said Feen. "He's not stupid."

Jason had been living in a room at the house over the winter. As much as he loved his lighthouse, he hated the cold. He went out to the Lighthouse Rock every day, sometimes to check that everything was okay, sometimes to look out to sea with Rusalka. He loved his own company and was happy to be alone, although Helena wasn't sure that 'happy' was the right word. He hadn't completely dealt with his guilt yet, and it bothered her that he might believe that the issue of the Caledonian Gates would be his fault because it was he who'd spoken to the ginger-haired stranger.

She called Michael Varmeter to speak to him. She seemed to remember that Lucy was away with her parents right now, although she didn't keep up with what was going on outside the Mermaid's Rest. She called Michael's personal number and he answered quickly.

"Hello Helena. How's things?"

"I've been talking to Feen and Svend about what happens if you find the Caledonian Gates. Feen thinks her mother will leave us and she'll take her place."

"It's possible. But we don't know anything yet. I've got someone going to Scotland tomorrow to help with the search." He briefly explained that Lady Venner had suggested a way they might find the Gates, although it was probably not going to be straightforward or easy to see. He talked about using drones and a helicopter to scan the rivers for the signs Lady Venner had shown him.

"There can't be that many rivers in Scotland," Helena said, but he knew she was being ironic.

"We only have to look near where we know there are folds in space."

"Now *there's* a sentence I didn't think I'd be hearing when I woke up this morning."

"And do you remember the day someone told you that mermaids were real?" laughed Michael.

"But do we know where the folds are?"

"No. But the centaurs do. And that's another sentence that…"

"Centaurs?" Helena almost whooped with delight.

"There's room in the helicopter, especially if you're good at controlling drones."

"Unfortunately I'm not. And I really would love to see centaurs one day. But I'm needed here, and I won't leave my People."

"Good for you. Anything else you want to talk about?"

"Not over the phone. But we've got to get together soon and have a long chat."

"Agreed. Soon," he said, and hung up.

Helena went to see Jason. She didn't want to make him feel bad over starting the search for the Caledonian Gates, but he needed to know how the manor's investigations were going. He was in the kitchen, helping Mara and Rusalka with the evening meal. She took him into the living room to let him know about the search for the Gates. She explained that finding the Gates didn't mean that most of the People would leave this world – she felt that he would be as bothered by that idea as she was. She told him that Michael was planning to send someone with camera drones to look closely at the rivers there for clues.

"Clues?" he asked.

"Something about rivers that don't flow right. I don't fully understand how it all works."

"So they're going to use drones to look for evidence of folds in space that can be seen by the human eye, but not easily?" he summarised.

"Yes."

"They'd need to be steady with the drone control, then. I mean, their controller would have to be pretty expert. The pictures would be transferred to a computer, and everyone else would have to know what they were looking for. They shouldn't have a shaky camera picture for that. Although, the best cameras have anti-shake devices."

"Tell me what's on your mind," said Helena. Jason hardly strung a full sentence together normally, but now he seemed animated by the idea of drones hunting for fey magic.

"We had a Remote-Control Club at school," he said. "It was mostly cars, races, stuff like that, then a few of us had mini helicopters. But then drones came in – serious, expensive ones. I was one of the best UAV operators in the school. I won awards for it."

"Would you like a trip to Scotland?"

"To be honest, no, I'd much rather stay here. But if they need me there, then I'll go."

Helena took out her phone and dialled Michael's number again.

Five

James Chaney stood up tall. He was tall anyway, but he always wanted to make himself look taller whenever he walked into *that* coffee-bar, if only to annoy the other customers. He stood on the wide walkway of the shopping centre in Telford with the fountain some way behind him, looking carefully for something other people couldn't see. There was a wall that was not quite real.

Or perhaps it was real in a different sense. But he spotted what he was looking for, whatever it really was, and took a step through it.

Inside, the ceiling was high enough to accommodate a tall man like himself, but everything was really going on at a lower level. This was, after all, a goblin coffee bar, and he hadn't yet met a goblin as tall as a human adult. There were only about six goblins in there at the moment, which was good as the smell got worse exponentially as the number of goblins increased. He got a couple of severe looks as he walked up to the bar, then one or two recognised him and went back to their drinks, chats and games of Yu-Gi-Oh.

The barista looked at him as he approached and gave a look of 'Oh, no, not again' as James put some money on the counter.

"Hello Herdie. Follet in?" he asked.

"I imagine he's expecting you out the back," said Herdie, scooping up the money. James went around to the back room, which he hoped was as well-ventilated as the last time he was here. Goblins stank.

Luckily, there was only Follet and one bodyguard there. The bodyguard was fat, or possibly muscly, for a goblin, although not any taller than the other goblins, and he stood in a pseudo-threatening pose with his arms crossed. He looked like the playground bully in a primary school. Follet, meanwhile, was seated at a card table with a small shoulder bag resting at his feet. He offered James a seat opposite.

"I'll stand if it's alright with you," James smirked, knowing that it would most certainly not be alright.

"I'm not talking to your crotch," said Follet. "If you don't want this conversation, kiss off."

"I think the word you're looking for is…"

"I don't care what the word is. I believe *you* wanted this chat. Personally I don't care whether you want to be in here or not. The whole point of this establishment is that humans don't come in here. So the sooner you're gone, the better."

For the sake of the integrity of his nose, James sat down on the not-quite-big-enough chair opposite the goblin boss. His knees nearly came up to his face, and he wondered if Follet knew how silly he felt. Perhaps that was the point. He waited for the boss to speak next. Follet, in the meantime, was waiting for him to speak. There was something culturally different between the way the goblins and humans did business.

"I have your payment," James said eventually.

"I have your… product," said Follet.

"May I see it?"

"You first."

James shrugged his shoulders and pulled a small parcel out of his pocket. He opened it carefully and put it on the table. There were six diamonds inside.

"Industrial grade. Cut for lasers, or whatever else you'd want to use them for."

"It's none of your business what we'd want to use them for."

"Just saying." He sat back, at least as best he could in this awful chair, leaving the diamonds on the table.

"We could kill you and take them."

"You could try. After you and two or three of your friends are dead, you might succeed. Then my associates would come and rip this place apart."

"Ah, yes, your associates. Your boss, you mean. Whoever's *really* in charge of this operation. Is he human or fey?"

"No," said James with a smile. "Now it's your turn."

Follet reached down into the bag on the floor by his feet. He pulled out a large clear plastic test-tube, corked and filled with a grainy powder that looked like the scrapings left over after children have been playing with different-coloured glitter.

"Extra strength," said Follet. "That'll kill anything. Take a taste, make sure it's genuine."

"I trust your honesty," said James with a smile, putting it into a plastic bag, rolling it up, putting it into a second bag and putting it into his pocket. He didn't trust Follet's honesty, but he did trust the goblin's fear of reprisals.

"You're going to do it," said Follet.

"Oh, yes."

"Soon?"

"Soon. You want your revenge; well, you can have it without even lifting a finger."

"Without lifting a finger? You have no idea how hard it is to get that stuff. But we have something else that can help you."

"Go on."

"Well you know Krol, when he was around, he had some nasty little allies. A harpy, a succubus..."

"Yes, I heard."

"Well we can get the last of them. Oddly enough, exactly the right one for Scotland. He's already up there."

"Tell me."

"A Bain-Sidhe."

"A banshee?"

"Yes. The bane of the sidhe."

"How do I control it?"

"You don't. We do."

"And how much will it cost me?"

"Let's make it free. We want to show you and your boss... associates... that we are on the same side and we want the same thing. Even if they do make us deal with humans."

"You wouldn't want to deal directly, believe me. But free? That's not your style."

"We'd rather like to be on the winning side. It's free for a number of reasons. One is that Bains-Sidhe are notoriously hard to control, and if it fails we don't want you to ask for a refund. Another is that we will have done you a favour, and in future, if we need a favour in return, we won't feel bad about asking."

"So it's not really free at all."

"I suppose not. But it's not expensive."

"It can find its... prey?"

"Without a doubt."

"And the contact with that goblin in London? It's done?"

"Yes, of course," said Follet as if he was offended by James questioning his competence. "And I'm sure the next question is whether he can track down where the messages came from. No, he can't. We're in the clear."

"Then just sit back and enjoy the show," said James as he stood up carefully, not wanting to knock over his chair and ruin his exit. He saluted the goblin with a nod of his head and left the café as quickly as he could without looking like he was rushing. Dealing with goblins had taught him how precious fresh air was.

The next bit of James' day was the bit he'd been looking forward to. He had booked a hotel room not far from the town centre, but far enough away so that the goblins didn't know where it was. He locked himself in his room and took a shower. When he had lathered and rinsed himself thoroughly, he did it again. The smell of goblins took some shifting. By the time he was done, he had used a lot of the hotel's water and actually felt clean and ready. Ready? He'd been ready for days.

Over the last months he had run around the country setting little traps and manipulating people. He'd been to Ogonshead – what a dreadful town that was; he imagined not even a sunny summer could make that place appealing. He'd hung around long enough to know which person there would be the best person to drop the words 'Caledonian Gates' to – the young lad at the lighthouse. That would get the word back to the manor quick enough. He'd got in touch with a few other people and dropped the 'Gates' idea as much as possible. There was a witches' group in Covent Garden; they were an easy mark. But he wanted to be subtle enough that they weren't suspicious of how easily they were getting the information. The manor had to believe he really did know how to find the Gates. Then they would go about finding them for him.

He dried his ginger hair, wrapped the huge towelling robe around himself and made his way to the bedroom where his clean clothes were.

"You won't need your clothes, *bibic*," came a heavily accented, seriously sexy voice from the lounge room. She was here already! He hadn't heard her come in, but that was no surprise, really. He went to his bedroom door and leaned against the doorframe.

"Hello Christina."

Christina Redevec stood by the table in the lounge, her fingers stroking the packaging around the goblins' poison. She was dressed in a long, dark red, zip-fronted dress. It was loose enough to be relaxed, but tight enough to show off her amazing figure, and the silky texture of the dress make it catch the light differently whenever she moved. Her heavy outdoor coat was draped over the dining chair, and a small, sharp-bladed knife was on the table.

She had other men, he knew, but when they were together she was whole-hearted in the attention she paid him. She was tall, but not quite as tall as him. She had red hair that was probably her natural colour, a body to make any woman jealous, and her eyes... James could feel his heart beat faster in anticipation. As they spoke, his eyes wandered over her body, lingering on the best bits... which was most of her. She seemed to enjoy his attention.

"I see you have completed the transaction," she said unnecessarily, glancing at the test tube on the table. But then her eyes returned to look at him in that way that made his blood roar.

"The goblins sent the messages to that London goblin. And they've offered us a little extra. They want to send a banshee to Scotland to hamper things."

"They have a banshee? Of course they do. You said yes?"

"I did. They aren't charging. They just want to ingratiate themselves to us."

"Hope it doesn't kill anyone up there. Actually, I don't care whether it kills anyone or not – I just hope it doesn't kill all of them."

"I don't know much about banshees."

"I do. They hate the sidhe. If I had a swarm of them I'd gift-wrap them and send them to Lady Marika in her little house in Buckinghamshire. But even one will cause Lucy Waterhouse and her group of misfits a bit of trouble. As far as you know Michael Varmeter hasn't sent any fey up to help them?"

"Not as far as I know."

"Good," she said. "Now, enough talk about business. I'm... hungry."

She walked languidly towards him; her eyes were focussed wholeheartedly on him. He led her into the bedroom by a hand. When they stood and faced each other, he played with the zip on the front of her dress. She took his hand and held it up so that she could see his wrist. Using the tiny blade, she snicked his wrist sufficiently expertly so that he hardly felt it. As the blood welled up, she drew it up to her lips and drank.

It was going to be a good night.

Six

John-James Clipper sat still. That was a rare thing for him, unless he was at the cockpit of a helicopter. He was a fidget, and he struggled to fully relax unless he was flying. He hadn't taken his first helicopter ride until he was seven years old, in spite of his father owning a helicopter company. But, as far as he remembered it, all he wanted to do from that moment onwards was fly.

This morning, he was going to be flying to Scotland via Stoke-on-Trent to pick up a beautiful woman. His perfect day – or it would have been, if Michael Varmeter hadn't changed his plans to include a detour to Ogonshead to pick up a young man on the way. As he sat looking at the route planner on his phone, he knew that there was no way he could justify picking up the lady first.

It was under two hours to Ogonshead, and then an hour and a half to Stoke. He would refuel there, then pick up Stephanie from her back garden (apparently her boss had a big back garden) and then fly on to Glenshee. By then, it would be dark and they would stay at a hotel for the night before starting whatever it was that they were supposed to be doing tomorrow morning. Whatever it was included plotting the course of a river, but apart from that, John-James knew nothing.

'Apart from that, he knew nothing' would be the sentence that best described John-James' relationship with Michael Varmeter and his strange menagerie. Apart from flying mermaids to London to save people from the floods, apart from flying Stephanie Baynes to France before she went off to Africa to save the world, apart from being allowed to attend the funeral of two noble, non-human warriors who had fought to keep the country safe (from vampires, possibly), he knew nothing. On one occasion they even had one of his pilots *pretend* to fly someone around.

But, thinking about it, he loved it that way. He tried to ignore whatever was special about Michael Varmeter's house guests. They were fey beings, incredibly beautiful people who were hiding in this world. He'd been sworn to secrecy about their existence, and he considered that a privilege. But he normally kept people's secrets anyway – he'd flown businessmen and their secretaries to weekend 'business meetings' in hotels where they seemed to inadvertently have only booked one bedroom; he'd flown politicians to secret locations to meet with leaders of other countries who shouldn't really be there. He normally just switched off his imagination and flew his helicopter. But the manor's fey creatures, they were something else. He began to enjoy when they asked him to fly them somewhere even more than he normally enjoyed flying. There was something unique and special about 'the People', as they were called; something that made him feel special about being involved. And now he was going to do something more than just fly for them – he was going to be joining them on some kind of search.

One of his team had picked up two hi-tech Unmanned Aerial Vehicles, each with integral cameras, and an additional camera and clamps to attach to his Eurocopter AS350. The equipment filled his two luggage holds, so any other luggage his two passengers had would have to be carried with them. Luckily, he could carry six people, so there would be enough space.

He landed on the beach next to Lighthouse Rock in Ogonshead in the middle of the morning, having checked in advance that the tide would be out. He met briefly with Helena Grey who saw his passenger off, but the other People were not around. His passenger was Jason, and he had only a couple of soft bags for luggage.

A young woman stood on the balcony of the lighthouse to wave Jason off. John-James took a look at her. She was unbelievably beautiful.

"Your girlfriend?" he said to the new passenger. "She's gorgeous."

"I'll be sure and tell her when we get back."

"You could introduce us."

"No."

"Sorry?"

"She's quite shy."

"Is she...?" John-James wasn't too sure how to put it. 'One of *them*?' didn't seem appropriate.

"Fey? Yes," said Jason. "She's a naiad."

"You're a lucky man."

"I didn't say she was my girlfriend," said Jason. He looked like he wanted to say something else, but had decided not to. In fact, he gave the impression he didn't really want to talk at all. It was going to be a boring ninety minutes.

Despite his first passenger's recalcitrance, beautiful scenery and the sheer joy of flying made the time go quickly and they soon arrived to refuel at a Stoke-on-Trent airfield, and then travelled on to Stephanie's house. The house in the countryside belonged to Lord Martin Latham, and Stephanie's rooms were in a converted barn on the other side of the driveway. Behind the houses there was a large field leading, eventually, to woods. John-James was able to land the helicopter in the field and he and Jason got out to have something to eat, provided by Lord Martin in a large hall that might have been a dining hall in a previous life.

Lord Martin had a lot of antiques in his house, including a rich mahogany table that they sat around to eat. John-James was nervous of marking the table or even spilling crumbs on it, although Lord Martin was a relaxed, genial man who probably wouldn't mind a bit of mess.

"You've worked with the manor before," Martin said to him.

"Yes. Well, I've flown people about before, like the lovely Stephanie here; this will be the first time I've done anything other than fly with them."

"What about you?" Martin asked Jason, who shrugged his shoulders. John-James and Stephanie shared a glance that said 'We've got a three-hour flight to Scotland with this young man'. Still, they could sit him in the back while they enjoyed each other's company.

After a break, they were on their way again. Stephanie sat in the front with John-James while Jason sat with his eyes closed for most of the way in the back seats with all the luggage.

Stephanie took an interest in everything on the journey, pointing at landmarks and asking about things. She even bantered back when John-James flirted with her. He was only having a bit of fun, of course, but he did wonder if she had a boyfriend...

It was cold, dark and snowing a little when they got to Dalmunzie. Lucy was waiting for them at their hotel.

"Lucy Waterhouse!" said John-James by way of greeting. "I would travel the length and breadth of the country just to see you. Actually, I think that's what I just did."

Lucy ignored him and looked at Stephanie. "You had to put up with that for the whole flight."

"Don't be mean to him," said Stephanie. "He was brilliant."

John-James leaned in towards Lucy and said, "She's right. I really was brilliant."

Flying never seemed to make John-James tired – at least, not for the duration of the flight. However, when a long haul like this came to an end, it seemed to catch up with him quickly. And after a meal near a cosy, open log fire, he was ready for bed. Jason had gone as early as he could leave the company and still be considered polite, and Lucy had gone to her home a few miles south of the hotel, so if he left now, that would leave Stephanie on her own.

"Are you okay?" he asked her. "I mean, can you put up with my company a little longer? It's not often I get to share a hotel with a beautiful woman."

"Thank you for your kind consideration," Stephanie played with him. "But I'll be settling down soon. I'm excited for tomorrow, but I really need to sleep."

In the morning after breakfast, John-James flew the other two a few miles south to meet at the Waterhouses' cottage. Seven of them crowded into their living room for a briefing – Ian and Evie Waterhouse, Lucy, Stephanie, Jason and John-James were the humans, but there was also a small fairy creature, a pixie, perched on Lucy's shoulders, who added his voice to the team.

"Captain Callom will meet us at this ridge," said Ian Waterhouse, pointing at a map. "From there we'll try to find an entrance to fey space."

"What's fey space?" asked John-James.

"It's a fold in space that the fey People sometimes use to hide themselves."

"Is it a danger to the helicopter?"

"No. Normally it can't be found at all by us humans. You could fly right through one and wouldn't know it was there. I know where one or two folds converge with what you might call 'real' space, but I doubt if I just could walk into fey space without a guide."

"That's what I'm here for," said the pixie. "But the captain and his People are better at it than I am."

"Lady Venner at the manor has told us how to find anomalies outside the folds. If we find an impression of the water running the wrong way while we are outside fey space, then it's possible we are near the Caledonian Gates themselves. What we then do is go inside the fold and follow the changes in the flow of the river until we find what we're looking for."

John-James went outside for moment. Jason followed him and practised with one of the drones. Stephanie also came out and idly took a look at the other one, but without much real interest.

"I know why Jason's here," said John-James. "But you're not here for the same reason as everyone else, are you?"

"No. I'm here to find a particular type of fey creature. In Scotland they call it a cait-sidhe. Mine is called the Bast."

"Is that its name, title or species?"

Stephanie laughed. "It could be all three. Bast was originally the name of the Egyptian goddess of cats."

"So what's it doing in Scotland?"

"I don't know," said Stephanie. "There seem to be waypoints across the world that the Bast uses to travel. But it... *she* might not even be here.

"You don't seem..." started John-James. "I'm not sure how to put it, or even if it's my place to say anything, but you're not settled here."

"I'm not even sure I'm in the right place," said Stephanie, looking forlorn. "But now that I've joined this team, I'll help in any way I can." But that wasn't what John-James meant. He thought she wasn't settled anywhere in the manor's strange area of speciality.

Ian Waterhouse drove some of them to what he called the ridge, while John-James flew his two original passengers there. Ian had helped him fix the camera to his helicopter, but they both felt that the drones would do the best work.

The ridge wasn't really much of a ridge. The glen was a wide expanse of land with plenty of flat ground, trees, occasional hills, and plant life that John-James hadn't seen before. From there Jason got his drone ready, and the spare one was left in Ian's SUV.

Although the landscape was such that John-James could land his helicopter quite easily, he didn't see where the centaurs came from. But they were there, quite suddenly, where they hadn't been before. Was this the effect of folded space, or whatever Ian had called it?

The centaurs were truly magnificent creatures, each as big as a horse, but looking bigger because of the human-like form that grew out of their bodies instead of a horse's head. As well as their four legs, they had two well-muscled arms. They didn't wear clothes, and it was hard to see where the horse part ended and the human part began as their skin texture seemed consistent regardless of whether it was equine or humanoid. They wore equipment belts with water bottles and some of them had weapons. They walked, or possibly trotted, in a formation, with the leader at front and centre and the other four flanking two on either side.

John-James was aware that his mouth was open so he shut it and put on his 'I'm okay with this' attitude. He was aware that Stephanie was covering her mouth in shock, but Lucy stood by her side for support. Jason looked up from his controls for a few minutes but, strangely, didn't show much reaction. Either he had seen these creatures before or he didn't care.

Introductions were made – the leader of the centaurs was Captain Callom. Once they found the folded space with the strange effect they were looking for, he would lead them into it.

The drone flew off northwards at the captain's suggestion, followed by two of his centaurs. Ian and Evie watched the camera feed on their laptops; apparently Evie had the sharpest eyes of all of them so she was the most likely to find the water-flow effect. The UAV had a range of several miles so they could stay put and look carefully. Jason expertly steered the vehicle up the Shee Water, and they found nothing after an hour's work.

Stephanie sat with him in the helicopter while everyone else was finding something to do.

"I think…" she said.

"What?" said John-James, once again noticing that she didn't seem to be part of this project.

"I'm not really sure. On the way here, just before we landed, I thought I saw something."

Suddenly a bone-rattling screeching noise filled the air. Captain Callom and his team pulled their weapons from wherever they were hiding them and stood alert. Lucy huddled down as if she was in pain and Dixie vanished from sight. They looked around to try to find the source of the howl.

"What was that?" demanded John-James. "Some kind of guardian?"

"It's a Bain-Sidhe," said the captain. "They don't normally *guard* anything. Someone's trying to stop us from finding the Gates."

"Or driving us to try harder," said Lucy, beginning to recover. Ian gave his daughter an odd look.

One of the centaurs pointed southwards to the sky. John-James tried to follow where he was pointing and saw a creature flying towards them at some speed. Or was it flying? It looked like it was leaping from tree to tree. There was plenty of open ground between them and the creature, and it looked like the centaurs were planning to use that to their advantage. However, its leaps were huge and it seemed to use that disturbing screech to ride in the air.

It was a large creature, probably bigger than a man, but it had misshapen head consisted mostly of a mouth full of long, bent, sharp teeth and its huge hands held long, sharp, clawed fingers. It was on the group in a matter of seconds, attacking the nearest centaur, raking its side leaving long, bloody gashes before and leaping away into the trees.

The remaining centaurs readied their weapons for the next attack. The two centaurs that had followed the drone returned at a gallop. Jason continued to control the machine, his face straining with concentration as he fought back against his fear.

The thing screamed again; the sound was worse because it was closer. It leaped from a tree near to where it had hidden and tried to plough into where the humans were. Ian dived to protect his wife, but too late. It bounced off her, sending her flying, and then flew away to the trees. Its target, however, was her laptop, which crashed to the ground and smashed. Ian rushed to her aid as the Bain-Sidhe targeted John-James.

Before it hit, however, it came into contact with the returning drone, whose sharp, spinning blades cut into the fragile arms of the attacking creature, sending it off course and rolling on the ground. John-James was aware that, although it screamed when it attacked, it stopped screaming when it was hurt.

"Yes!" hissed Jason as he continued to attack the Bain-Sidhe with the now-damaged drone. The creature flailed and struck out with its spindly arms, striking the UAV several times and sending it crashing to the ground. However, by then, it was too late for the thing, as Captain Callom and two of his soldiers were on top of it, driving their spears into its chest

Its body started decomposing immediately, turning into some kind of goo in front of their eyes. John-James found his voice.

"Thank you, Captain Callom," he said. The centaur chief nodded acknowledgement and made to check on his wounded soldier. John-James looked at Jason, who had stood up and was walking towards the wreckage of the drone. "You're a hero, Jason," he said. Jason grinned.

"I'm afraid I've wrecked your drone," the young man said to nobody in particular.

Lucy and Ian were crouched over Evie, who sat up slowly, looking dazed but otherwise unhurt. Lucy, though, looked shaky and her nose was bleeding, although John-James wasn't sure how that happened. He seemed to remember that she was 'blessed' in a special way when she was a baby, by that winged creature who had been killed in the battle of the embassy, a sidhe creature. Perhaps the scream of a Bain-Sidhe would harm a sidhe-blessed human more than the rest of them.

Lucy stood up on shaky legs and stood by Jason's side. She put a hand on Jason's shoulder.

"Good thing we brought a spare," he said.

Ian had checked his wife for wounds and she was fine apart from a gash in her heavy coat. The other laptop was undamaged and Ian instructed John-James to get the second drone out.

"I think we should keep going if you're up for it," he said to Jason.

"I'm good," the young man said. "I just sat there and did the controls. You're the ones that seemed to be in trouble."

"And if there is another attack?" said John-James.

"We will stay near this young man," said Captain Callom. We'll protect him from any other incursions."

"Are these things rare? Banshees, I mean," asked Stephanie in a wavering voice.

"Very rare," said the captain. "That's the first I've seen in more than twenty years."

"And it turns up right now," said Lucy. "Odd, that, wouldn't you say?"

"You've spoken to Michael," said Ian to her daughter. "Has he got some suspicions?"

"Same as yours, I think, dad," said Lucy. "That someone has engineered all this. It's possible that they're trying to get us to try harder."

Everyone seemed to be pulling themselves back together quickly, thought John-James. Then he noticed Stephanie still sitting quiet and alone in the helicopter. She was very pale, close to melting down. He went over to speak to her, to try and pull her out of herself.

"What did you say before that... thing attacked?" he asked.

"I think we should take to the air again," she said. "I wonder if you could fly us around a bit?"

"Let's take a breather," replied John-James. "I don't think we should be doing anything until you've got yourself together."

"No," she replied, eyes shining with tears. "I think I saw something on the way in. It might have been just my imagination, but it's been playing on my mind. I'd like another look."

John-James felt that if, perhaps, he gave her something to do, to focus on, it might be what she needed. He looked to Ian, who nodded that they could go ahead. Lucy, Jason and Ian moved away from the helicopter as they got in. Ian asked his daughter something about what she had said earlier about driving them to try harder and Michael's suspicions, but John-James missed her answer, whatever it was. As soon as everyone on the ground was clear, he started up the helicopter.

He flew it above the ridge and tried to retrace his flight path as best he could from here back toward the Waterhouses' cottage. He hovered the vehicle carefully and slowly so that it would cause as little disruption to the people on the ground as possible whilst still enabling Stephanie to see what she wanted to see. He was only up there for a few minutes when Stephanie pointed.

"There!"

"What am I looking at?" asked John-James.

"The rocks, the trees, the formation of the bushes. They make the shape of a claw, a talon. Where it comes to a point, that's where we'll find what we're looking for."

John-James looked, but the image of the foliage making a shape was unclear. There was something there, but surely bushes and trees couldn't be a trustworthy map reference?

Seven

Lucy Waterhouse looked at her father after the helicopter had lifted off.

"What did you mean about the Bain-Sidhe sent to drive us to try harder?" her father asked.

"In a battle between a flank of centaurs and a single, solitary Bain-Sidhe, who would win?"

"The centaurs, without a doubt."

"Do Bains-Sidhe ever flock? Go around in groups?" said Lucy.

"I don't know for sure, but we don't have a record of it."

"So whoever sent that one knew it wouldn't survive," said Lucy. "I've been talking to Michael about all this. He has an alternative theory."

"About the Caledonian Gates?"

"No, about the person who has been travelling the country letting people know that he knows about the Gates."

"Michael wonders if this person has been planting ideas just to get us to find them for him," said her father, putting the pieces together.

"He spoke to the witches of Covent Garden. To Jason here. He's done everything he could to avoid speaking directly to Michael or anyone connected to the manor, while at the same time making sure that it gets back to us."

"So are you saying we should abandon our search because we're playing into his hands?"

"Or Michael's theory could be wrong. He thinks we should continue our search and see what happens."

"And the Ladies? Do they agree?"

"Lady Marika can't see this one as she had an emotional connection to it – people are trying to persuade her to go home so she can be healed. Lady Venner gave us the information we needed to find the place."

The helicopter landed a little further south of them. As soon as its noise had died down, Lucy's telephone rang. It was Stephanie.

"We think we've found the doorway to the Gates," she said. Lucy passed this on to the others and they packed everything into the car. Lucy's father drove it and her mother to where the helicopter was now stationed and the others walked. It was a little more than half a mile from them.

Shee Water widened a little at that point, but when Lucy got there she looked carefully and she could see the way the river seemed to run in two opposite directions at once.

"How did you find it?" she asked Stephanie.

"When I got involved in the Mbalaya situation last year, I met an archaeologist who found that there was a simple symbol that appeared in digs all across the world. It was like a simple drawing of a talon, a cat's claw, if you like. If you drew a line between all of the sites on the planet where this symbol was found, they also make a talon, and the tip of the claw was in Mbalaya where we found… well, you know what we found there. I'm here because one of those digs was around here. However, when we were up there, the rocks, trees and foliage all made a talon symbol pointing to that bend in the river." She pointed at that part of Shee Water.

"Foliage is transitory. In a few months it will make a different shape," said Ian, but he didn't sound as if he was completely missing the idea.

"How many times have you been in the right place at the right time?" asked Stephanie. Lucy cast her mind back to the year before last when she was on one of her very few trips to London when someone had called up a demon there that only she could deal with.

"It doesn't have to be there in a few months. It only has to make that shape right now," she said.

There is a fold in space here," said the captain after looking around for a while. "It's very strong. It is strange that we haven't found it here before."

"Can you take us in?" said Lucy's father.

All of them followed the centaur. He now had two of his group with him – the one that the Bain-Sidhe had injured had gone to have his wounds seen to in the company of his companion. Dixie was around again, but flying high and out of the way, on the lookout for more attackers. Lucy was aware that pixies used the folds in space in their travels around the country, so assumed he had disappeared into a smaller fold when the creature attacked them and remained safe.

The landscape hardly changed, but now there appeared to be a strange bridge made of stones over a narrower part of the river. The bridge hadn't been there before, or at least, it hadn't been visible. The party crossed it carefully, although the heavier centaurs jumped over the water instead. Lucy looked at her mother. She had always been strong, but she had never, at least as far as Lucy knew, been attacked by a fey creature before. Evie caught her eye and must have read her worry in her expression, because she smiled and mouthed, *I'm fine.* Lucy wasn't sure, thinking she still looked pale and shaken. She took her hand and gave it a squeeze.

The land dipped down inside the fold so it looked like they were going down into a valley. It would have been below the level of Shee Water, if the water was still anywhere near them. Ahead was a rocky outcrop and inside the rocks was a cave.

The cave mouth was large and wide. Even knowing what she knew about the fey and about her father's theories about folded space, she was surprised that nobody had found a place this big and this… obvious before now. The group stood and took it in for a moment. Her father took a step forward, but Stephanie stopped him.

"Don't," she whispered. She was staring towards the cave mouth.

"What?" said Lucy. She tried to follow Stephanie's line of sight.

"There's…" said Jason, pointing. Then it moved, whatever it was, back and forward like a tiger pacing his ground at the zoo. It was a big cat, made of shadows. Stephanie took a couple of steps towards it, but even she was tentative.

"I don't think it wants us to go in," said Stephanie.

"But this is what we've come here for," said Lucy's father.

Stephanie kept walking slowly towards the cat. It was as big as a tiger, but looked more like a puma. Lucy was sure that this was the Bast, the thing that Stephanie had come here looking for. However, even if Stephanie wasn't actually afraid of it, she was still approaching with caution. Lucy finally made out eyes in the creature's head as they looked towards the young woman.

Stephanie was now right next to the thing.

"We can't go in," said Stephanie. She only just refrained from touching the cait-sidhe. Lucy wasn't completely sure what had happened out in Africa, but she'd heard that Stephanie had got hurt when she tried to touch it.

"So what do we do now?" said Jason.

"I think we can't come this far and turn back," said Lucy's father. "If somebody wanted us to lead them here, we just have. They know it's here now. We must go in there… to protect it, somehow, if we can."

"Can you get it away from the cave mouth?" said Lucy.

Stephanie looked like she wasn't sure what to do or how to do it but, somehow, she led it away from the rocks and towards her. It looked up at Lucy's parents as if they were old friends as it walked past.

"Something for the scrapbook," Lucy whispered to her mother as it paced by.

"If we get back," came the reply.

"I'm going in," said Lucy's father.

"I'll stay out here with Stephanie," said Jason.

"Do you mean some of us are staying here and some are going in?" asked Lucy.

"It doesn't want us to go in," said Stephanie, "but it won't harm anyone who does. It will protect the ones who stay out here."

"Protect us?" said Jason. "Surely, it's the ones that go in who need protecting?" Stephanie shrugged her shoulders.

"I think I should stay out too," John-James said, "and look after these two."

Lucy understood John-James' desire to be by Stephanie's side, but he probably felt that young Jason needed his support, too. The poor kid was out of his depth among this party.

"Me, too," said Dixie. "Pixies aren't known for their courage. Or, for that matter, their abilities in a fight. But the protector knows we should stay out here, so that's where I'm going to be."

Lucy's family and the three centaurs walked slowly and carefully into the cave.

Inside it wasn't dark. A few metres in, the cave turned a corner and the daylight disappeared. But, although there seemed to be no source of light, the six travellers were able to see clearly. The cave opened out into a huge cathedral of granite-grey rock, glistening and shining, a tall roof over a flat bed.

And on the bed, something slept.

It was the biggest creature Lucy had ever seen. It was grey like the rest of the cave, with shimmers of silver that might have been the source of light that enabled them to see. It was big and long with rippling muscles that moved when it breathed in its slow, deep breaths. Its rear legs were as thick as old tree trunks; no, thicker. The legs at the front seemed a little thinner, but were long and wiry with curled-up claws on finger-like limbs. Its enormous silver-grey wings covered most of its body like a blanket, and one front limb covered its long, thin head.

Lucy was transfixed for a moment, although she knew that she should turn and run with all her might. She stared at the dragon's claw, Stephanie's 'talon' that had been drawn deep inside archaeological digs, and on the face of the planet, and on the surface of the glen outside. This was the creature that had provided what Stephanie had needed to find the Bast.

"We've got to get out of here," she heard her father whisper past the pounding of her own blood in her ears. "Now!"

A hand grabbed hers and dragged her away. She found her strength and ran for the cave mouth as fast as she could. When she got outside she saw the people who had wisely stayed out were some way away from the cave mouth, and one person she had not expected to see was standing right in front of them.

"I hope you left him sleeping," said Christina Redevec, standing at the cave mouth dressed in a black, figure-hugging jumpsuit, her red hair as flowing and lustrous as ever. She held in her hand a long-bladed knife which seemed to shimmer in the weak daylight.

Lucy's slow mind started to put the pieces together. She couldn't quite work out how Redevec knew something that even the Ladies of the manor did not – that the Caledonian Gates were not just a doorway to the fey worlds, but a hiding place for a hibernating dragon.

"Well," came an echoey voice from the semi-darkness behind them. "That's the second time in two years I've been woken up early."

The centaurs bowed, and Lucy's parents stood aside to welcome an elderly-looking dwarf in an ill-fitting suit as he came to the cave mouth. Balaur acknowledged the Waterhouse family and their centaur guard of honour, and looked past them to see the flame-haired vampire standing ready for battle, poisoned dagger in hand.

"Christina Havelock Redevec," he said with great humour. "The efforts you must have gone to, to make this happen!" He seemed to sniff the air. "Whoa, that is a potent little trinket, isn't it? It's a good thing my friends here woke me up, or that might have been the end of me."

He held out his hand and the dagger was no longer in Christina's possession. He held it himself. He sniffed it and pulled his head back as if smelling something exceedingly unpleasant. Then, the dagger seemed to dissolve into dust and disappeared into a mist in the air.

Suddenly, out of nowhere, a very solid-looking Bast leapt onto Christina Redevec and threw her to the ground, vicious teeth inches from her face. Stephanie, Jason and John-James ran forward to find out what was going on, but still kept their distance from the giant cat-creature and its prey.

"Miss Stephanie Baynes, I presume?" the dwarf said. "I don't believe we've met. I read a bit about you at the end of the summer last year. I intended to track you down and say hello when I woke up."

"Woke up?" said Stephanie.

Lucy finally found her voice again. "This is Balaur. He's a dragon."

Stephanie nodded, but Lucy got the distinct impression she was humouring her.

"I surrender," said Christina.

"You spoilsport," said Balaur. "Why don't you *not* surrender? Just this once. For me."

"No," said Christina, quite calm in spite of an ancient Egyptian goddess's teeth inches from her face. "I definitely surrender."

"You have broken the terms of your last surrender," said Balaur.

"I met your conditions. I left the country."

"But you came back."

"Oh," said Christina with some sarcasm in her voice. Lucy wondered how she could do that with a bloody great cat-goddess on her face, "I don't remember you ever saying I couldn't come back."

Balaur waddled up to the vampire, stretching as he did so to regain the strength in his limbs.

"I would like you to meet Stephanie Baynes," he said. "No, please, don't get up." He chuckled at his own joke. "She's the reason you're still alive. You see, the Bast here was my guardian while I slept. When Stephanie arrived, her priorities changed. Otherwise she might have ripped you limb from limb the moment you got here. Maybe your enchanted dagger might have done it some harm, but then it wouldn't have been able to hurt me – there's only so much goblin poison can do. It was goblin poison, wasn't it? I imagine Krol's old gang would have prepared it for you. But Stephanie here formed a very strong link with the Bast many years ago, and when she turned up here... well, it now serves her as well as me. Now, let me see, did I tell you that Stephanie also works for someone you know?"

"Martin," Christina spat his name as if it was dirt.

"And you're sure you want to surrender? I could end it easily – no pain. Well, not much pain."

"Sorry to disappoint you, but I will live on today, thanks to your chivalrous nature."

"Damn!" said the dwarf. "I can't kill you when you're powerless." He held out a short arm and his fingers briefly brushed the cait-sidhe, who backed away from its vampire prisoner. Christina slowly, carefully and, Lucy was pleased to note, painfully stood up.

"Go," whispered Balaur, and Christina ran past Stephanie and the men towards what Lucy assumed must be the way out of fey space.

"I'm sorry we woke you," Lucy said.

"I might be dead if you didn't."

"She wouldn't have found you if it wasn't for us."

"Fair point. In that case, I forgive you."

"Will you go back to sleep now?" Lucy's father asked.

"No, it's too late. I probably sleep more than I need to, to be fair. Although, I think next year I'll choose a place a bit further away and sleep until May," Balaur chuckled. He sniffed the air. "It's cold. Can we go in the warm somewhere?"

"The hotel has a big dining lounge," suggested John-James, who, until this point, seemed dumb-struck by everything that was going on. "It's probably a bit closer than the Waterhouses' cottage."

"Sounds good to me. I expect you're all quite hungry by now. I'll treat you all. Although," Balaur passed a wink to Lucy, "I'll be using your boss's money."

Lucy decided she would travel to the hotel in the helicopter rather than with her parents. The reason was simply that neither Stephanie nor Jason had met Balaur before and John-James hadn't done more than fly him about and must, before today, have assumed he was human. Stephanie kept saying, "He's a dragon?" and Lucy couldn't find a way of explaining things to her. Jason was a little bewildered by the whole thing and would probably have been more at home if he'd had the chance to use that second drone. He must have known that the fey world was bigger than his experience of it, but he seemed to prefer *not* knowing.

John-James came up with an idea to explain it to Stephanie.

"I'm a pilot," he said. "I'm called a pilot. I'm also called a flyboy; pilots of conventional aircraft say helicopter pilots aren't *real* pilots. I expect Lucy has one or two names for me that aren't that kind, either, but in the end, they're all just names. It doesn't matter whether Mr Balaur is a called dwarf, a lawyer or a dragon. He's just him."

"I don't entirely agree with John-James' idea, but it's a decent starting place. And maybe later, I'll tell you some of the things I've called *him* in the past," Lucy told Stephanie, but she felt much more kindly towards the pilot now, so she probably wouldn't. Probably.

The meal was wonderful, and they all relaxed together in the large dining room. Dixie managed to sneak in and Lucy passed him a bit of their food.

Balaur explained what the Caledonian Gates really were.

"For the most part, you're right. We will, eventually, use the Gates to go home. What happens at the moment is that I use their general location to hibernate. I will change their location later in the year for when I settle down in November. It will probably be within a couple of hundred miles of here. Did you know for a few years I hibernated near Loch Ness?"

"So you're…" started Stephanie.

"Oh, no," said Balaur. "I'm not *him*. But I'm sure I added a bit to the legend."

"And you're a dragon," said Stephanie (again).

"Yes."

"Why didn't the Ladies at the manor know that was where you hibernated?"

"Nobody was supposed to know. But when you think about it, the vampires of Transylvania still have the greatest collection of research about the fey in this world. Christina Redevec, when I banished her from the Romanian Embassy last summer, would have gone home and researched until she came across that snippet of information, then she came here and tried to find a way of finding out exactly where I was. I have an idea I know where she got the goblin poison from."

"A coffee bar in Telford?" suggested Stephanie.

"Very good. Have you been there?"

"I wasn't even sure it existed. I went to Telford Shopping Centre, but didn't find it."

"They are quite good at hiding. Last year, I was woken up to deal with their boss, Krol, but it seems some of them bear a grudge. I will pass that over to Lady Marika to deal with. I can't act out of revenge for their part in an attempt on my life. Revenge and justice aren't the same thing."

"Am I right that Miss Redevec has tried to kill you before?" asked Evie. Lucy wondered if that was a gap she wanted to fill in her scrap-book.

"Yes. About seventy years ago. They tried to use what you call 'magic' against me. That was a silly idea – using what I'm best at against me. A few vampires died that year, as did a few fey. But Christina survived, as usual."

"You let her live this time," said Jason. Balaur took a long look at him.

"We've not met before today, Jason, but I've been aware of you. You did something bad, and you were given a chance to change things – to make amends. You've befriended the Person you harmed, and, from what I've heard in the last few minutes, you attacked a Bain-Sidhe to save your friends. You have been saved, as it were, but I doubt if Christina will ever be as noble a saved being as you. You never know. Still, letting her live wasn't about her, it was about me. I will kill in self-defence. I have been appointed a judge of the People, which means sometimes, I regretfully have to take a fey life; but if someone who is helpless surrenders, I won't execute them. Christina knew that, which is why she surrendered so easily."

"Where is she now?" asked Lucy.

"She would have had help escaping. I think the manor will ask the Angel Trust to track her down, her and whoever helped her. They'll want to find out if she has any more nefarious plans for us to foil." He chuckled to himself in that way that Lucy always found so peculiar. It was good to have him back – the world was a safer place when he was awake. Even the thought of Christina being alive and well and probably not too far away didn't frighten her while Balaur was here.

Stephanie stood up and left the table. Lucy looked at her as she leaned on the window-sill, a little away from the others. She looked lost. Lucy followed her and saw tears tracking down her face.

"Are you okay?"

"Yes," said Stephanie. "I suppose. I mean, I found what I was looking for."

"The Bast."

"It's… *she's* alive. It's what I wanted."

"But?"

"But the world – *your* world – is bigger than I thought, and I'm struggling to cope with it."

"I know what you need," said Lucy, putting her arm around her to comfort her.

"What?"

"A week at the manor with Lady Venner. You can ask her anything. She won't answer, not so you'll understand, but at the end you'll feel satisfied. You might even begin to find your place in our world."

Stephanie looked at Lucy as if she was about to ask her another question, but decided not to.

Eight

Clifton Chase looked across the coffee table at Lord Martin Latham. They'd decided to meet here in the coffee bar rather than at Lord Latham's home because Stephanie was there, and they wanted to talk about her.

"I think Stephanie will quit," said Martin with some disappointment in his voice. "We've piled it on her a bit. I think she would have quit the moment she found out I was a v..." he looked around the other people in the coffee shop, "I have Tepes Syndrome, if it wasn't for you."

"If it wasn't for me?" said Chase.

"You were trapped in Mbalaya, and she stuck with me to help you."

"We'll be sorry to lose her," said Clif. *I'll be sorry to lose her,* he thought. *We might have gone somewhere in our friendship.*

"I was hoping..." started Martin.

"That I would persuade her to stay?" Clif finished for him. "No, I won't even try. She's got to make her own mind up about that."

"She keeps going on about dragons and dwarfs."

"I'm not supposed to know that Mr Balaur is really a dragon in disguise," Clif said.

"So how did you find out?" asked the vampire.

"Stephanie told me when she got back from Scotland. She couldn't stop talking about it. There were centaurs, pixies, a banshee; she still hasn't actually seen a goblin, but she knows there are more of them in the world than all the others put together. Lucy Waterhouse is trying to persuade her to go to the manor to spend some time with Lady Venner there, but she doesn't want to."

"It would probably help."

"It would probably help her come to terms with all of the fey creatures she has become aware of. But she doesn't want to come to terms with them; she wants them all to go away. She wants not to have found out about them in the first place."

"And that's something Lady Venner can't make happen," said Martin.

Clif thought back over his relationship with Stephanie. Martin had encouraged him to be a listening ear for her in September when that Bast creature saved her from the murderer Jack Hardington. Then she had travelled to Africa to save *him*. Then Martin had, quite wisely, tried to give her less full-on jobs, investigating things she might find a logical, reasonable explanation for.

Their friendship had been strong enough for her to invite him to spend Christmas as a guest of her family in Kent, which he had really enjoyed. It had been a long time since he'd had a taste of 'ordinary' life, and he found it really refreshing. He was treated like one of the family, and he had met Paula, Stephanie's sister.

Stephanie had always told him that Paula was 'the good-looking one' of the two sisters, but Clifton didn't agree. They were similar in looks and stature and Paula was more confident in her demeanour and in the way she put on her make-up. But Stephanie was just as beautiful, although she made less fuss about it, which, to Clif, made her even more appealing. One morning after Christmas Day at their house, he had been looking at her with some admiration as she moved about her home when he was aware of someone looking at him. He glanced around to see Paula watching him looking at her sister. She was smiling. Was that an 'I caught you' smile or a smile of approval? Or a little bit of both.

He wondered if it was possible for him to get an ordinary job and live an ordinary life somewhere, with someone like Stephanie as a companion. Then his text alarm rang, interrupting his reverie. He looked at his phone, and read that Christina Redevec's agent, James Chaney, had been tracked down. Mic Dracu, a mysterious computer hacker in London whom Clif suspected might be a goblin, had been following his movements through his hotel bookings and taxi journeys. He'd spent some time in London and Dover, possibly to try to reach Christina Redevec before she left for Romania. According to Mr Balaur, he would have failed to get to her before she left. Then he returned to his home in Manchester, but didn't stay there long. Now, it seemed he had booked into a hotel near Telford he had used before. Telford wasn't far from here.

"Something interesting?" said Martin, watching him read his text.

"They've found where Chaney is."

"Where? Still in the country?"

"Yes. He hasn't got a passport. He's booked a room in a hotel in Telford. He's slipping – he's been there before and Mic's been keeping an eye on it. I'm going to… *meet* him now."

"Can I come along?"

"Definitely," said Clif in a loud clear voice so that everyone in the café could hear. "A vampire is always good to have on your side in a fight." Nobody in the room paid him any attention.

On the way to Telford, which was a short, 50-minute drive, they continued to talk about Stephanie.

"She's made some kind of psychic connection to this cat thing," Martin said. "It will probably be with her forever. How can she leave that behind?"

"I think it's quite, well, *interesting* that she's connected to a cait-sidhe, and you hate cats."

"I don't hate cats; they hate me."

"They're such discerning creatures, aren't they?" suggested Clif. Martin gave him a look, but Clif was concentrating on driving so he only just caught it.

"I just had a thought," said Clif as they approached Telford.

"Take a little break, you'll get over it."

"When we find James Chaney, what do we do about him? We can't arrest him for the attempted murder of a dragon, or dealing in the illegal substance of goblin poison."

"We could beat him up?" suggested Martin.

"He'd probably enjoy that. After all, he seems to like having his blood sucked."

"Don't knock it 'til you've tried it," said Martin. Then Clif's phone, which was perched in a cradle next to the car dashboard, sounded its text alert. Martin picked it up.

"It's from Mic Dracu. He says he tuned in to Telford Shopping Centre's cameras, and Chaney's there."

Telford was a modern, pleasant place, and there was plenty of parking around the shopping centre. They made their way to the fountain in the centre of the shopping area, and looked around for their prey. It was Martin's sharp eyes that found him, standing on his own, looking at a wall.

"Covering your tracks, Mr Chaney?" said Clif, walking up to him. Chaney turned to look at them.

"Do I know you?"

"No. But this gentleman here knows your red-haired friend."

"She might have mentioned me," said Martin. "Martin Latham."

Chaney's face showed that he recognised the name, and probably the reputation, of the renegade vampire. Clif wondered why the tall, ginger-haired man was looking at a wall. Perhaps this was where the goblin coffee shop was hiding itself, and they were about to be swarmed by the little bu... creatures. Then he had a thought.

"Passport!" he said. "You haven't got a passport, so you've come to Telford to see if your goblin suppliers can help you get one to get you out of the country and into the arms of your beloved Christina."

"Could be," said Chaney with a shrug. "Except they're dead."

"Dead?"

"The goblins. At least, the dealer, Follet, and his barman Herdie are dead. I've just come from their place in there." He nodded at the wall. "The others have all done a runner."

"That means Lady Marika got there first," said Martin. "I think we should leave."

"Now?" said Clif, confused.

"When Lady Marika targets someone, believe me, they are in trouble," said Martin. "The goblins are gone, so that leaves you, Mr Chaney. I'd run if I were you. Don't go back to your home in Manchester, don't try to leave the country; you already know she'll have someone watching all of the airports and Dover. She's probably got Mic searching for you – the goblin from London you sent that message to that was meant to sow distrust of the Lady. She really won't like that. And don't hang around us. I don't want to be there when she finds you."

Martin's threat seemed to work. The blood seemed to drain from his face (yes, Christina had left him some), and he backed away from Martin and Clif, then he turned and ran.

"I'm not sure that was exactly what the manor wanted when they asked me to find him, but I think that went quite well," said Clif when he was long out of earshot.

"I think if Lady Marika wants anything else she'll have to do it herself."

"Do you think it was her? That *she* killed the goblins?"

"Yes," said Martin.

Clif met with Stephanie a few days later. She had taken some time off and visited her parents, but she went out for a meal with Clif in London before returning to work.

"Martin thinks you'll quit because you've seen more than you really wanted to," Clif broached the subject after a fabulous meal.

"I wanted to," said Stephanie. "But I got into this business in order to find out the truth. I can hardly back away just because I don't like the truth I've found."

"And you can't unsee what you've seen."

"No. I see it all every night in my dreams."

"Martin tells me you didn't take up Lucy's offer to visit Lady Venner at the manor."

"I wanted to, but there's so much going on there. I thought I might visit the woman, what's her name, Helena Grey, in Ogonshead instead. After Easter when it's a bit warmer. I was going to ask Martin for a month off."

"I'm sure he'll say yes. He wants to keep you. As a researcher, I mean. But, Ogonshead? Why?"

"Because, from what I heard, they're not inundated with fey, just a few naiads. She's obviously done wonders for Jason Asher. Ms Grey is a healer, and more to the point, she's human. And I think that's the sort of company I need right now."